THE CURSE OF
KIM'S DAUGHTERS

Modern Fiction from Korea
published by Homa & Sekey Books

Father and Son: A Novel by Han Sung-won

Reflections on a Mask: Two Novellas by Ch'oe In-hun

Unspoken Voices: Selected Short Stories by Korean Women Writers by Park Kyong-ni et al

The General's Beard: Two Novellas by Lee Oyoung

Farmers: A Novel by Lee Mu-young

The Curse of Kim's Daughters by Park Kyong-ni

THE CURSE OF KIM'S DAUGHTERS

A NOVEL

Park Kyong-ni

Translated from the Korean by

Choonwon Kang
Myung-hee Lee
Kay Ho Lee
S. Keyron McDermott

Homa & Sekey Books
Paramus, New Jersey

FIRST AMERICAN EDITION

The publication of this book was supported by a grant from
Korea Literature Translation Institute.

Library of Congress Cataloging-in-Publication Data
Pak, Kyæong-ni, 1926-
[Kim yakkuk æui ttaldæul. English]
The curse of Kim's daughters: a novel / Park Kyong-ni ;
translated from the Korean by Choonwon Kang...[et al.].—
1st American ed.   p. cm.
ISBN 1-931907-10-2 (pbk.)
I. Kang, Choonwon. II. Title.
PL992.62.K9K513 2004
895.7'34—dc22   2003028254

Homa & Sekey Books
3rd Floor, North Tower
Mack-Cali Center III
140 E. Ridgewood Avenue
Paramus, NJ 07652

Tel: 201-261-8810; 800-870-HOMA
Fax: 201-261-8890; 201-384-6055
Email: info@homabooks.com
Website: www.homabooks.com

Editor-in-Chief: Shawn X. Ye
Executive editor: Judy Campbell

Printed in U.S.A.
1 3 5 7 9 10 8 6 4 2

Contents

Translators' Note

Our choice of *The Curse of Kim's Daughters*, essentially the story of the fortunes of five women, is for us at least fairly transparent. Women, except for their ancillary roles as wives and lovers, have seldom been the primary focus of literature in Oriental societies. Essentially egalitarian in conception, Park Kyong-ni's book is concerned not only with the problems of Kim, the patriarch of the family, but those of his wife and five daughters, who are as intriguingly different from one another as total strangers. It was a natural, even inevitable choice for us.

The writing career of Park Kyong-ni (b. 1926) spans fifty years. Park is best known for her voluminous novel *Land,* which is considered her masterpiece and was voted number one on a 2003 Internet survey of Korean reader's favorite books. The book follows the fortunes of a Korean family through the dark, first half of the 20th century. She is currently at work on a new novel called *Butterfly* after a ten-year break following *Land.*

Widely read and well-respected not only for her superb storytelling, Ms. Park also serves as publisher of a literary magazine called *Breathing Sounds* and is also well-known as an environmentalist. While her novels are dominated by the tragedies that have befallen the residents of the Korean peninsula in modern history, her creative genius consists in transforming both her characters and readers with the catharsis that is the essence of literary art. Her work has been translated into German and English.

Ms. Park lives in the small town of Wonju and the Toji Cultural Center is an extension of her personal residence, expanded to preserve the historical basis as well as the ambiance of her fiction. The Toji Center has become an attraction for writers and visitors.

The Curse of Kim's Daughters was published in 1962 and treats her favorite theme, the personal struggles of Koreans living their lives against the backdrop of "the Hermit Kingdom" entering the modern era. Her work has successfully put the town of Tongyong and the surrounding areas not only on the Korean national map, but also on the map of world literature.

This translation was made possible through a grant from the Korean Literature Translation Institute (LTI Korea) – to whom we are deeply grateful. Ours was an unusual group both in number and composition, consisting of three Koreans and one American. When Keyron McDermott began teaching at Kyungnam University, a conversation about the paucity and quality of existing translations spurred the decision to form the consortium and apply for the LTI grant.

The three Korean speakers rotated through the scenes in each chapter translating each in succession and then turned it over to Keyron. She then rewrote the first drafts in an effort to neutralize personal stylistic differences and provide a unified prose style replicating Park's terse one insofar as possible in English.

We met weekly to discuss the details of romanizing names, how to describe uniquely Korean customs, whether or not to explain unfamiliar words, and hash over the best way to express the subtle differences between Korean and English terms. Making our way through the Keyron's rewritten text sentence by sentence, we discussed, haggled, argued the predominance of one connotation of a word over another and eventually came to a consensus.

We tailored the spellings of the names of people and places to make them as simple and "user friendly" as possible. Nonetheless, we found it necessary to travel early on to Tongyong to have a first-hand look, especially for Keyron to have a look at the countryside to have concrete images of the 19th and 20th century Korean construction.

This weekly four-way tête-à-tête, for which we became increasingly grateful as we worked, gave us a fund of resources to draw on to bridge the chasm between the two languages and cultures. Each of us brought her strength – Choonwon, an academic understanding, always consulting the dictionary; Kay Ho with a wider perspective analyzing situations; Myunghee looking beyond the words to the emotional reality being conveyed; and Keyron concerned with the final literary affect upon the reader. As we fell into the rhythm of the work it began to feel like the joy of playing in a quartet must, and each of us began anticipating the delight of these sessions.

With the translation nearly finished, personal decisions made our weekly meetings impossible, as Choonwon and Keyron were in the U.S., while Kay Ho and Myunghee remained in Korea. E-mail revisions became a fact of life. We wore out colored markers in multiple proofreadings, wishing mightily for the personal contact, which had not only been charming but productive.

We hope that the translation will provide a glimpse into Korean literature and culture for those who might not have had a chance to experience them, and as always remain deeply grateful to the people who made it possible – Park Kyong-ni and LTI Korea.

Choonwon Kang
Myung-hee Lee
Kay Ho Lee
S. Keyron McDermott

THE CURSE OF
KIM'S DAUGHTERS

Chapter One

ॐ

Tongyong

Then Tongyong was a tidy little fishing village near Tadohae Seashore National Park. It sat on the bay half way between Pusan and Yosu. The town's younger generation called it the Napoli of Korea for the crystal blue waters offshore. Since the islands of Namhae and Koje protected the area from the rough seas of the Korea Strait, the waves were gentle, the climate mild, and the town was a pleasant place to live. Small islands circled Tongyong like orbiting moons. In fact, one might easily have mistaken it for an island — sea surrounded it on all sides except for a narrow crane's neck of land along which ran the road to the north. The slopes above the town were a patchwork of terraced fields. Houses on the hillsides seemed to have sprouted there — like mushrooms.

Naturally, the primary industry was fishing. Tongyong was the distribution point for the superb, abundant seafood caught off shores, which commanded a premium in out-of-town markets. Thanks to this and to an adventurous spirit, the town prospered. Of course, there were many more fishermen than farmers. Most of the property around Hadong and Sachon stayed in the same families, passed down from father to son for generations.

Tongyong fishermen practiced a kind of primitive capitalism spurred by a get-rich-quick greed one finds among gamblers and the upper class where the economy is in a constant state of flux. The sea was the jackpot and fortunes were made and lost in it. They say that in the old days when people down on their luck came to Tongyong, they left their broad-brimmed

1

aristocrat hats on a tree outside of town. No point putting on airs there. So it is not surprising that feudalism disappeared here before it did in the rest of the country and that a "money-is-the-be-all-end-all" attitude replaced it.

In addition to fishing, a small-scale traditional handicraft industry flourished in the town. One rarely, if ever, sees the old fashioned broad-brimmed hats now, even out in the country. However, it was widely acknowledged that until the end of the Choson dynasty the best hats of the horsehair imported from Cheju Island were made in Tongyong. A cheap imitation of the fine Tongyong dining table is still being sold as "the real thing." Both hats and tables fetched a pretty penny for their excellent and intricate handwork.

The town was also famous for its black lacquer and abalone furniture. This industry developed early here because turban and abalone shells were plentiful. Shells collected from the sea around Tongyong were luminously beautiful as pearls but far more colorful. Workmen cut designs from the shells and glued them onto pre-cut pieces of wood; then they began the time-consuming process of applying endless coats of lacquer. Everything from huge wardrobes, dressers, dining tables, and vanities to school rulers was made from abalone and lacquer.

It might seem strange that such artistic crafts developed in a vulgar atmosphere where most men made a living slicing fish open and hacking their heads and fins off, but the sea was beautiful, the weather good, the citrus ripened bright yellow and the camellias bloomed fire red.

In 1864, as King Kojong ascended to the throne, his father, Taewongun, seized power. An economic crisis following the 1866 French invasion of Kangwha Island – prompted by Taewongun's massacre and persecution of Catholics — put Taewongun's daughter-in-law, Queen Min, in power. But even with the Min clan on the throne, there was still turmoil. Extremists struggled for control — the pro-Japan group against the pro-China, liberals against conservatives against progressives, the Mins against Taewonguns. Predictably, the country suffered.

But Tongyong thrived. The town grew, fanning out from the middle of the Kosong Peninsula where it overlooked the sea and the endless coming and going of fishing boats. At the foot of Mount Andwi stood the military and municipal offices like twin symbols of the sword and pen. The streets of the town reached up as if to grasp the mountain. It had a total of five gates — one in each direction, north, south, east and west — plus the Sugu Gate, the fifth, between the East and South gates.

From the municipal office through the South Gate the bay curved like the two arms of a giant goddess. Tongchung and Mount Nambang embraced and protected ships as they came and went. Ferryboats shuttled between them regularly. From Tongyong one can also see Kongji Island, with its two lone pine trees. No one can figure out how the pine cones ever got there. You can see Hansan Island in the distance, though Koje Island is pretty far.

West from the municipal office at the foot of Mount Andwi was a village called Kanchanggol. Across from it was an archery range for military officers and the levee where the ceremony to the Wind God was held each February. Tongyong's West Gate can be seen from the top of a steep hill, so it was called West Gate Hill.

Beyond the West Gate is Mt. Twiddang, actually one of the slopes of Mount Andwi. Chungnyolsa was a memorial to Admiral Lee located in front of the bamboo forest that people considered a sacred place. Large camellia trees lined the road leading to the shrine and the blood red flowers bloomed on hazy spring days. Nearby, the two Myongjonggol wells had been dug side-by-side like husband and wife. In February, before the ceremony to the Wind God, young women swarmed there to draw pure water to offer to the God. The air was perfumed with the scent of their face powder. Across from

Mount Twiddang is Mount Ahn, beyond which were three inlets where red anchovies spawned in spring.

A village called Taebat (Bamboo Garden) sat across from West Gate Hill and the wells. Walking away from them, the road led to Pande, a place known for its excavations. At the end of the 16th century, the Japanese invaded and dug a canal, but the Korean navy retaliated and defeated them. Later during the Japanese occupation, this canal was named after a Japanese general who never even visited it. Miruk Island directly across from Pande was once connected to Tongyong, but since the Japanese diggings, they have been separated.

On Mount Yonghwa, torches were lit to signal other villages. Below Yonghwa was Pongsuggol, and farther on, the ferry terminal from which you could see Tongyong. Here, according to local legend, a woman drowned herself to be with her husband who died at sea. Beyond Mount Yonghwa and many other small fishing villages there is a scenic overlook from which one can see a panorama of Sarang, Chu, Tumi, Yokji and Younghwa, a few of the bigger islands.

To the east stood Tangsan, which, because of its proximity to the municipal office, used to be where people appealed to the governor. Complainants climbed up and shouted down at him. The East Gate was just around the bend from Tangsan, and not far from it was Sugu Gate. The open area before it served as a marketplace.

Up the seashore was a poor fishing village called Mende meaning "a far-away place." People had always lived hand-to-mouth there. Fishermen fixed their small boats and patched their nets, while their wives dried fish and seaweed along the sandy beach. They listened to the wind and waves and watched the clouds. From Mende one could see Chi Island.

The North Gate behind the municipal office was closest to the town's one and only road to the mainland. Just past Tosonggol was the muddy red hill of Changdae, over which each fall landowners hauled the farmers' harvest on donkeys from Kosong and Sachon to Tongyong. In spring, poor fishing village women carried sacks of dry fish and seaweed over to sell to keep from starving in early spring time before the gardens produced.

Nearby was a cemetery where a colony of lepers lived. Every spring and fall, they held a group wedding ceremony. They had a novel way of assigning marriage partners. Bachelors put their water bowls down in a row; each girl chose a bowl and married the man whose bowl she chose. The lepers grew yams, potatoes, squash, and Oriental cabbage and sold them to merchants on the sly. Their vegetables were so big that people whispered they must have been using water from the cemetery or their own feces as fertilizer. As a result, the biggest produce never sold well in markets.

In the village of Kanchanggol lived the two Kim brothers. Pongjay, the elder, in the old tile-roofed house his ancestors built; Pongnyong, the younger, in a blue-tiled house at the foot of the mountain. Pongnyong's house, constructed when their parents were still living, was newer and far more elegant than his brother's.

Pongjay was nearly forty and held a government pharmacy license. A low-ranking bureaucrat with a regular salary, he was a middle-class man. However, since his ancestors had been rich, powerful and well-respected, he was content with his uninspired practice of Oriental medicine.

Pongnyong was twenty-three, but the two brothers could easily have been mistaken for father and son. They had one sister, Ponghee, but all their other siblings died young. Unlike his older brother, who was a fine scholar, Pongnyong was a young man of good health, but his intense eyes reflected instability. He was so proud of his ancestors that he considered himself holy and behaved rudely to anyone who disagreed with him. Most likely because he was the spoiled, youngest son, and became violent. As he was good-looking, his appearance alone could have made him a leader, but he had one peculiarity — light brown hair. A friend once asked him jokingly if he had any Western blood and Pongnyong almost beat him to death.

Pongnyong had a beautiful wife, his second, who had given him a son the previous fall. His first wife had died two years after their marriage — it was rumored in the town — of the effects of his repeated beatings.

ॐ

Death Visit

Next to the stone step, a dog, legs stretched out, lay dozing in the sun. The wind was blowing through the pine trees on Mt. Andwi. Pongnyong's house looked deserted, apart from the village. He had gone with his servant, Sogwon Chi, to the archery range at the levee.

A strange young man seemed to be trying to conceal himself behind the trunk of the old zelkova tree in front of the house. Thin and vulnerable-looking, his face was pale and his lips moved as if talking to himself. He wiped the sweat from his forehead on his sleeve.

A hawk with outstretched wings circled slowly in the cloudless sky. From time to time, you could hear a serpent hissing in the ivy on the stone wall.

The stranger moved toward the gate and peeked in. The dog slept silently. The young man, still mumbling to himself, turned around and staggered along the stone wall. His face was a ghostly white against the dark green of the tree and ivy. He looked down at his shoes, which had been specially made for this trip, now wet with mud. The upper part of his socks was so worn that he could see his bare feet through the seams.

He murmured to himself, "Should I give up and go back to Hamyang?" forcing the laughter that followed the question back inside his mouth so that it sounded more like a cry. He had run away from his new bride on their wedding night.

"I must be crazy," he said, "Why have I come here?"

Since he had arrived in Tongyong, he kept mumbling this question to himself. Sitting down, he clasped his arms around his knees and laced his fingers together. He stared at the toes of his shoes for a while and then lifted his head. In the distance, he could see people walking about near the pier; perhaps a fishing boat had just docked. Soldiers drilled on the parade grounds of the military building below to his left. Turning his head back to Pongnyong's house, he saw a woman come out with a baby tied to her back and covered with a light pink shawl. He could hear the drumming of wooden clubs from inside; someone was ironing.

The stranger stood up abruptly and skidded down the hill from where he had been sitting, startling the dog awake. It began barking. The sound of the ironing clubs ceased. A woman looked out from the main hall. Trembling, he stepped inside the gate and said, "Sukjong!"

Instantly, the woman's eyes became wide with fear. The dog began barking furiously.

"Nanny," she commanded in a sharp voice, putting the clubs down and standing up.

"Nanny!" she shrilled again and ran into the room, kicking her long, dark blue skirt before her, and sliding the door with a bang behind her.

"Sukjong!" he called, desperately reaching forward as if to try to touch her. There was no response to his entreaty.

"Who are you?" asked an old woman who emerged from the back of the house drying her hands on her apron. He froze and said nothing.

She quieted the dog, which had begun barking as if it would attack. She then stepped closer to him and said, "God in heaven, you're the gentleman from Kamaggol, aren't you?"

The nanny shuddered and said, "You *know* what is going to happen! Go away! *Please!* Mr. Kim will be here any second. What if he finds out?"

Pongnyong's wife, Sukjong, was from Hamyang. Her mother had died when she was born and this nanny had raised her — she knew very well that Wuk, the son of Song from Kamaggol, was secretly in love with Sukjong. He had not been allowed to marry her because an astrologer had said whomever she married would have bad luck. Sukjong's family married her to widowed Pongnyong, and Wuk's sent him to his mother's home in Seoul.

"Are you crazy coming here? You must leave immediately. When Mr. Kim gets home he'll. . . *please.* " The nanny tried to usher him out the gate. The thought of Pongnyong's violence and his unwarranted suspicions made her sweat.

"Nanny, I'm a married man now," said Wuk as if he were talking in his sleep. "I have come on my wedding night because I want to see her just one more time...." Tears rolled down his cheeks as he spoke.

"What a stupid thing to do! — When did you get here?" It made her feel helpless to see him cry. He held her bony hands in his without responding to her question.

"Please let me see her one last time. I will not come here again until I die. I don't care if you laugh at my foolishness. Just please let me see her."

"It's not possible. You two are not meant to be together. You better forget her, sir. She is a Kim now, and you yourself have a bright future before you. You must forget her," she said, trying to persuade and comfort him at the same time.

Just then, Pongnyong flung the gate open and marched into the yard. The nanny's face turned white.

"Who is this?" Pongnyong screamed, approaching Wuk. His eyes wide, Wuk turned and ran for the gate. "Catch that bastard!"

Standing nearby but unsure what to do, Sogwon took off after Wuk, bow and arrow case still in hand.

"Who is he? I want to know who that bastard is!" he demanded of the nanny. Her body recoiled in horror and her face began to sweat. "Who is he? Where did he come from?"

"Ah, ah, gentleman from Kamaggol...." she stammered, with no time to make up a lie.

"Ek-k," he howled, running into the front hall with his shoes still on. "You slut, Sukjong. You whore! Where did you meet him?" Lowering his head like an angry bull about to charge, he kicked the doors and roared. Sukjong looked up at him. Pongnyong fixed his blazing eyes on her smooth forehead shining like a piece of polished jade.

"What you are saying is harsh and untrue," she said calmly.

"Hah!...you whore! I saw him with my own two eyes. Do you think I am blind?"

Pongnyong laughed loudly and his eyes turned murderously red again. "I'll cut your goddamn head off. You better tell me the truth. Tell me the truth, I said!"

"I am willing to die, but I don't want to be falsely accused." She spoke quietly without emotion or gesture. Suddenly, Pongnyong slapped her, and the jade hairpiece she was wearing fell to the floor. He crushed it under his shoe and began beating her mercilessly. She did not even moan.

"Oh my, what can I do?" The trembling nanny ran into the room, grabbed Pongnyong's arm, but he kicked her and knocked her off balance.

Just then, Sogwon, who had lost Wuk, came back into the house panting, his face red, the bow case still in hand. "Sir, ah...." said Sogwon with the voice of a dying man.

Pongnyong, red-faced with rage, emerged from the room. "Didn't you get him?" he demanded.

"H-he hid in the forest."

"SHIT!" Pongnyong screamed and pommeled the servant with his fists. Howling in pain, Sogwon fell to the ground pretending that his back was broken.

"I'll get the bastard. He can't have gotten very far with those weak legs. I'll get him and kill them both. *Then* I'll be able to sleep," raged Pongnyong as he pulled out a knife, ran through the front yard, and out the gate after Wuk.

While Pongnyong was running around the forest with his knife drawn, foaming at the mouth like a rabid dog looking for

Wuk, inside the house the nanny was trying to revive Sukjong, who had collapsed. Despairing of a life of constant abuse, Sukjong had taken poison. When Pongjay arrived trying to save her, it was already too late; the poison had spread throughout her body.

"He has disgraced the whole family," said Pongjay bitterly.

"Sir, I beg you, *do* something," cried her nanny, but Pongjay didn't say a word.

Pongnyong returned at dawn, breathing heavily as if he had been drinking blood. He tossed the blood-stained knife into an open shed and went to his room. The entire household was in an uproar but soon they heard him snoring.

The next morning when the rays of sunlight hit the windows of Pongnyong Kim's home, Sukjong died.

The funeral was held three days later without notifying her parents and family because Pongjay didn't want it to become known that she had taken her own life. However, the news reached them anyway. Sukjong's brothers and their servants came from Hamyang. Pongnyong knew they would kill him and hid in the forest. Figuring Pongjay knew where his younger brother was, Sukjong's brothers dug up her body and brought it to him, demanding to see Pongnyong.

That night, Pongjay gave Pongnyong the money that allowed him to escape Tongyong.

Sogwon Chi

It was drizzling as Sogwon Chi in a rain slicker strolled past the haunted house and noticed a young man standing in front.

"Hello, Songsu, what are you doing here? You will catch cold walking around in this rain," he said. Pulling his voluminous raincoat around Songsu to protect him, he asked, "What are you looking for?"

Again, the young man didn't respond. Sogwon walked slowly tugging on the edges of the raincoat to protect them. "This young man has a beautiful face, looks just like Sukjong," thought Sogwon. His father, Pongnyong, had been gone for sixteen years now. He pulled the boy close to keep him from getting wet and spoke warily, "Young man, you shouldn't be here. Your blood will dry up — you even look pale."

Songsu finally responded bluntly, "And why not? It is my house, isn't it?"

"If your aunt finds out, you know she'll be furious."

With his mouth closed and his jaw set, the boy looked at Sogwon stubbornly.

People say Pongnyong's house is haunted. They say that on rainy nights the ghost of Sukjong and her lover come back here to meet. Some people are afraid to come by here even before the sun sets.

Well away from the rest of the village, the Pongnyong house looked abandoned. Holes and missing bricks in the crumbling wall around the house served as entrances for toads and snakes. The garden itself was overgrown with weeds. At the front, the century-old tree stood and at the back, the forest from which the wind whispered eerily through the pine trees. The place seemed haunted even if you didn't know its bloody history. All the more on cloudy days.

Some villagers said they had even seen Sukjong in fine *hanbok* ironing with wooden clubs in the hall, and others said they had seen her walking with the man Pongnyong killed. Women with unruly children threatened to leave them at the haunted house to make them stop whining. Nevertheless, the apricot, cherry and pomegranate trees flowered profusely in spring, and in fall they sagged, heavy with fruit. Allured both by luscious taste and the delicious excitement of stealing, children slithered through the garden walls to pick the fruit, but adults believed the ghosts of Sukjong and the stranger had picked it.

When Sogwon reached Pongjay's house in the village, he entered by the rear gate and pushed Songsu in, saying, "Go on, please. But promise me this first," he frowned deeply, "Promise you'll stay away from that house. If you don't, your blood will freeze and you will die."

Songsu only stared at the smiling Sogwon, soaking wet and his black moustache outlining discolored teeth.

Sogwon then headed off toward a tavern near the tidewater. He was a cheerful, good-natured man. Since he was not indentured to any one master or owner after Pongnyong disappeared, he worked as a servant for anybody who would hire him, and could leave their service if he so chose. Effectively then, though he was from the lowest class, he was free. Not knowing who his parents were or even where he was born, he had grown up and spent his childhood doing errands around a fishery. When he was twenty, he had come to Tongyong and worked for Pongnyong.

The world had changed a great deal during the sixteen years since Pongnyong's disappearance. There had been two major national news events: the 1882 military revolt (*Imo Kullan*) and the 1884 coup d'etat (*Kapshin Chongbyon*). By turns, Japan, China, Russia and England had each tried to snatch Korea like a fresh piece of meat off a cutting board. The country had problems from within and without. Reacting to government policies, corruption and mismanagement, farmers rebelled in 1894, which began the *Tonghak* Revolution.

During this chaos, Sogwon became a soldier. He didn't know, or even feel it was his business, whether his side was right or wrong. The government changed hands so many times he couldn't keep track of it anyway. He didn't care who recognized him, but he liked wearing a uniform and carrying the heavy gun around the streets. Most of all, he was honored to have the status of a soldier.

Sogwon frequented taverns and gambling houses to drink; flaunted his status. Whenever he drank, the world seemed manageable to Sogwon; he could be innocent and playful. The problem was, he often drank too much. Of course, it was chiefly the waitresses in his favorite haunts who had to put up with his nonsense, but they didn't really hate him. They regarded him as just another duffer, content as long as he had the money for drink.

"Thirty-five years old, no home, no family, no nothing," they said.

"Some soldier you are, Sogwon," they teased, "you aren't even brave enough to get a woman for yourself." He only laughed and ignored them.

"Hey, did you hear that Puturi, the hat maker, got himself a girl over in Mende? And Kiyon, the smithy, found one in Pande? What about you, Sogwon? Gonna spend your whole life doin' nothin' but drinkin' and peein'?"

Among the lower class in those days, for a man who didn't have money to get married or a family, it was acceptable to kidnap a girl and live with her in a kind of common law marriage. Of course, such marriages were not acceptable in a family with a good reputation, but were for someone like Sogwon.

"Hey, did you hear about the girl Kiyon, the smithy, got?" somebody asked. "One night he was walking along the road to Pande and she was carrying a pail of water on her head. Well, she must have had a great ass, because he fell in love with her on the spot and carried her home on his back. Only in the morning when he got a look at her, he almost died — she was ugly as a mud fence in a rainstorm."

Sogwon laughed, shrugged and said, "Well, what can you do? You bring her home; you're stuck with her!"

"Aw listen, Sogwon, even a cross-eyed, butt-ugly broad would be too good for you," one of the women said.

The women at the tavern teased Sogwon, but he ignored them. He liked women, but once rejected, he did not persist, perhaps because all the times he had been rebuffed. However, Sogwon was the soul and spirit of persistence when it came to drinking. If they cut him off for running up his tab and not paying, he created scenes and tipped over other customers' tables, insisting they serve him. Unfazed, he would show up the next day smiling as if nothing had happened — and always managed to borrow the money to pay the bill. When they got sick of the scenes and wanted to teach him a lesson, bar managers reported him to military police, so he was often beaten.

The policeman would holler, "Get over here, Sogwon! You got drunk and raised Cain again last night. Take off your pants!"

Dutifully, Sogwon lowered his pants and lay down on the ground as the guard rolled his eyes with rod in his hand. He began counting the strokes even before the guard did, "One!"

As the rod went up the second time, "Two!"

Likewise, the third time, "Three!"

But as the guard smiled bitterly and raised the rod for the fourth time, Sogwon got up and began putting his pants back on saying, "Shit, I owe you only two strokes. I have already taken three — that is payment plus interest!"

"You fool," the guard said, dropping the rod.

Whether or not the punishment fit the crime, it never prevented its recurrence.

Having left Songsu, Sogwon followed the road from Kanchanggol through the South Gate of Tongyong to the pier. It had just stopped raining and dusk was settling onto Tongyong, when Sogwon walked into Okhwa's bar.

"Oh Chri-ist no, would you look at what the cat drug in," Okhwa groaned, shaking her head irritatingly. Her hair was shiny with camellia oil.

"Hey, don't look at me like that. I've got money — real money, cash," said Sogwon as he took off his raincoat, tossed it in a corner and joined a crowd of other drinkers.

An old fishing boat captain named Chon chewing on a mouthful of raw fish and red pepper paste, grimaced and said, "Sogwon must be crazy about Okhwa. He's always in here."

"Hey, knock it off, would you? Besides, you might spoil what I have in mind, heh, heh, heh," Sogwon giggled.

But Chon continued goading Sogwon, "Let's see ya kiss Okhwa. Drinks are on me if you get the job done!" He widened his eyes, focusing Sogwon in his bleary gaze.

"Cut the crap," Okhwa said winking at Chon, "I don't give a shit how much money he brings in here, Sogwon ain't my type."

"I want you to know, Okhwa, when I wear my uniform and carry a gun, girls all over this town sit up and take notice," Sogwon said.

"OH-h, I bet they do-doo!"

"Ho-ho-ho." The room was filled with laughter.

Sogwon drained a bowl of rice liquor in a single gulp, stuck out his tongue and placed a piece of squid on it. Chewing it thoughtfully, he grabbed Okhwa's hand.

"Give us a break and let go of my hand. Do ya think they look at you because you're handsome?"

"Well, it's a fact."

"Hardy-har-har-hardly. They are blind if they do," someone said, and the group erupted in laughter again.

"Women are a bunch of goddamn fools. They go crazy over some gorgeous guy because they are too dumb to know that a decent ordinary guy like me is generous, open-minded, and a fine soldier on top of it." Sogwon's nostrils quivered as he spoke. Okhwa laughed raucously.

The stuffy odor of cigarette smoke that mingled with the smells of food cooking and sweat filled the room. The tavern patrons danced, drank, sang; they told stories and jokes and gossiped, unwinding from their daily labors.

"Man, you are so funny you even make my toes laugh. You call yourself a soldier? I'd bet any money you don't know a single army song. Anyway, you ain't singing for your supper in here. Pay your tab before I kick your butt black and blue too!"

"You women are so fickle. Last time I come in here you say you like me, now all you care about is money."

"Aw, get out a here! That's a giant lie. When did I ever say I liked you?"

"Last night. You hugged me like this and said, 'Let's be lovers.'" He stretched his arms wide as if to embrace someone, imitating the tone of Okhwa's voice. "And then you said, 'I like you, hairy Sogwon.' Yeh, you did."

The crowd, oohing and ah-ing, commented as they listened. Some of the other men, secretly in love with her, observed the proceedings with rapt attention, not really believing what Sogwon was saying but monitoring the goings-on carefully nonetheless. They were all having such a grand time ribbing him they kept asking ...and then...and then...and then, hitting the tables with their chopsticks.

For her part, Okhwa didn't try to disabuse them of suspicions they might have or discourage Sogwon. Suddenly, Sogwon opened his mouth wide enough for everyone to see his tonsils and began singing an *arirang* loudly and off key.

Old Chon couldn't resist needling him a bit more, "Oh my achin' ears! Goddamn, stop that yowling. You sound like a pig bein' clipped. Damn! I thought you knew a soldier's song."

Okhwa and Old Chon liked to tease Sogwon about being a soldier as much as he liked being one. He was often seen in the local division military parades, marching smartly, gun stiffly at attention, winking and smiling at the girls. Of course, he risked a beating for this too, for if he were caught, that was the punishment. But as with other things, the idea of it didn't deter him. He was just careful not to get caught, taking care to flirt while no one important was looking.

However, when it came to military songs, he really didn't know any and was forced to make up his own words to tunes he did know. He bobbled his head in time with the music he was making, destroying the rhyme and rhythm as he went, amusing the company all the more for this uniquely Sogwonesque rendition. Occasionally, he stood up and marched around in time to his tune. The sight of him marching stiffly, head bobbling, paralyzed some of them with laughter. Eventually, however, the drinkers tired of their amusement, drained their bowls and headed home. Old Chon was the last to leave. He could hear that the wind was up, so he went by the pier to secure his boat.

When he had gone, Okhwa, without warning, pinched Sogwon on the arm. The skin of her blanched face was bumpy but shiny.

"Ouch!" he said, raising his arm to study it, his long eyelashes raised.

"Sogwon," she smiled coquettishly.

"Stop making eyes at me. We'll see the sun rise from the west tomorrow morning. You're too sexy." Red-eyed now and frantic, he looked about in all directions as if he really were afraid, but the bar had been empty for some time.

Okhwa stopped laughing, sucked in a long deep sigh and said, "Here, drink as much as you want." With that she filled his bowl again.

"Hey, what are you up to? You know I don't have any money."

He pushed the bowl back to refuse it, totally uncharacteristic of Sogwon. He felt awkward and uneasy at her advances.

"You don't have to say nothing. Just drink up. You're a good man for a drunk," Okhwa said, sprinkling tobacco on a cigarette paper and after rolling it deftly between her fingers, licked it and lit up.

"I think it's my lucky day, but there weren't any lucky dragons in my dreams last night, heh...heh...heh." Sogwon continued. "Both of us are bitter from life in this endless vale of tears...." He was embarrassed and smiled awkwardly to keep it from showing.

"I keep wondering," she went on, "will I die unmarried? How can I go on with all this bitterness and failure? What good is a woman who can't even meet a man and get married?" Her eyes brimmed full of tears.

"My, ah don't cry," though embarrassed, he tried to be serious. "Do you want to talk about it? You'll probably feel better if you do."

She took a long drag on her cigarette and released the smoke slowly in Sogwon's face. She narrowed her eyes as if gazing off into the distance and then said, "Did you hear Pongjay's daughter, Yonsoon, is getting married? Is that true?"

Sogwon blinked his eyes, surprised.

"Why are you asking me?"

"Figured you might know. Is it?"

"I heard it is."

"God Almighty, I can't believe those people! Are they out of their minds or what — marrying off a girl on her deathbed?"

Sogwon raged back at Okhwa with surprising vehemence, "Shut up and mind your own damn business!"

"Hey bullshit. It stinks, and you know it. Just because you were Pongnyong's servant you don't have to defend it," she said pouting. "You think they are going to put up a memorial for your loyalty? Hah, they could give a care!"

"Well, if she wasn't sick, she wouldn't have to marry a bum. Someone from a good family shouldn't have to marry a loser like that. It is none of my business, but it just ain't fair. It just *ain't*, and she's their only daughter. Imagine! Marrying her to a bum like that. I just can't understand it." The more he thought about Yonsoon's marriage, the madder he got about it — as if he were the victim himself, though admitting she was very ill.

From the look on her face, you'd think Okhwa was trying to read his mind. "Come on, fess up, you don't think it's any better than I do, do you?"

"It's none of my business, and it ain't a question of fairness."

"Well, then you ought to tell her so."

"Tell her what?"

Her eyes narrowed and burned with jealousy, "Tell her not to marry him."

"I don't have the right to say that! No way. No way in hell I am going to say anything like that."

18

"Well, then, tell her this: that bum, Tackjin, is the father of my baby. He is already as good as married to me! Tell her *that!*"

Sogwon looked wide-eyed and alert as if he hadn't had a thing to drink all night long.

"WHAT?!"

"Yah, tell her that, don't tell her who told you, but tell her that!" Okhwa stared at him angrily, feeling helpless and frustrated as a dog that had cornered a hen and then let her get away.

Mrs. Kim's Concern

Each day as the sun set in the west, Pongjay Kim's only daughter, Yonsoon, was flushed and feverish. Crystal tears sparkled in her brown eyes as she was clearly suffering from tuberculosis. The nineteen-year-old girl had light brown hair and a complexion white and flawless as milk. Pongjay cherished his daughter, calling her "golden treasure."

"Oh, she's just delicate," Pongjay told people, but in his heart he knew that if she had been born to a poor family, she would already be dead.

He tried every preparation, potion, health food, and medicine he knew of to try to recover her health. He concocted extracts made from the vitals of young goats, fetal pigs and puppies. He even tried one made of yellow-spotted snakes, but nothing worked — it only seemed to maintain her tenuous grip on life.

"Might marrying help?" Pongjay wondered the night he decided on Tackjin. It broke his heart to see her chances for a good match destroyed by illness. God knows Tackjin was anything but a suitable prospect. He had the look of an aristocrat: precise features and white skin. Having lost his parents and fortune, Tackjin had become nothing but a lowlife. He squandered his time becoming the gigolo of sluts and whores in the bars along the pier. But this was not the main reason Pongjay was reluctant. He could honestly forgive Tackjin's womanizing; it was understandable after all, considering his situation. If he had shown the slightest inclination to be a responsible, mature adult in other ways, Pongjay would have been willing to give him anything.

That, however, was not the case. Tackjin was small-minded, mean-spirited and petty. Though he had been educated, one could hardly tell; he was a second rate scholar at best. Along with being an ignoramus, he had the reputation of a con artist. The prospect of Tackjin for a son-in-law infuriated him, but Pongjay Kim had no other choice.

"Maybe he'll change when he has a wife to take care of," he rationalized, but still felt he was deserting his long-suffering daughter.

Spring was now in full swing. Showy displays of bright yellow plums had already bloomed and begun to lose their intensity. The wedding day approached. Her mother and Aunt Ponghee sat cross-legged on the floor sewing Yonsoon's dress and trousseau. Ponghee was a tallish slim woman; Mrs. Kim was short and rather stout. Ponghee wore a white ribbon, the sign of a widow in mourning, her hair in a chignon. Ponghee's scholar-husband had died eighteen months ago, leaving her only a son and no inheritance.

Ponghee took a hot iron off the fire pot, began pressing the bodice of the *hanbok* on which they were working and observed idly to her sister-in-law, "Well, you can stop worrying about Yonsoon now that she is getting married."

"I seriously doubt this marriage will relieve the concerns I have about her...." Mrs. Kim responded, knowing fully well she wouldn't feel any better after her daughter was married.

Ponghee closely examined the collar of the bodice on which she was working and asked, "I don't know why this won't lay right. What do you think? Is it passable?"

Mrs. Kim inspected it, "I think it's all right."

"Some people say that if a girl is disagreeable, her collar won't lay flat," Ponghee said.

Mrs. Kim sighed, "Everybody knows Yonsoon is a sweetheart." When Yonsoon was little, Mrs. Kim had such high hopes for her daughter's marriage prospects that she delighted in dwelling on them. "It's her fate," she said, "but in return for this marriage, I can only hope she is rewarded with a long life."

"Me too."

"It's senseless to feel sad on this happy occasion, but we could not stand watching her become a spinster. Who knows, she might have a son...." Choked with emotion, Mrs. Kim could not finish the sentence. Knowing what she knew, she dared not wish that her daughter would live long enough to have a son and watch him grow to manhood.

In a vain attempt to change the subject Ponghee said, "The older she gets, the more Yonsoon looks like Pongnyong, especially that light hair...."

"Ah yes, she looks a lot like her uncle," Mrs. Kim agreed.

"Nobody could deny he was one handsome man. Handsome is as handsome does — his good looks may have shortened his life."

"I have to admit at a time like this I miss him. He would certainly be at the wedding if he were still around."

Ponghee squinted bringing the needle she was threading close to her face. "We certainly can't hope he will show up for Yonsoon's wedding when he hasn't shown his face or come to see his own son for sixteen years. With that bad temper of his, I seriously doubt that he is still alive, though."

Rumors of Pongnyong's fate were plentiful. It was said he was killed by robbers. Someone else claimed that he was beaten to death when someone from the Park clan, Sukjong's family, caught up with him. Others believed he died of malaria, but nobody had actually ever seen him alive.

"Poor Songsu, he's as good as an orphan."

Ponghee's sympathy for Songsu irritated Mrs. Kim — especially the word *poor.* "Aren't you wasting your sympathy, Ponghee? I mean, doesn't he have good clothes? More than enough food? An uncle who doesn't let him do without a single thing he needs? Honestly, my husband treats that boy as if he were a piece of ice that might melt in his hand," Mrs. Kim said, indignantly.

Ponghee hesitated and then reproached her sister-in-law with calm understatement, "But he needs his parents!"

"Mrs. Kim! Mrs. Kim!" A servant, Togi, called from the courtyard.

"What's the matter?" she responded, without either opening the door or missing a stitch.

"I saw Songsu at the haunted house again."

"What?" said Mrs. Kim, flinging the door open. Togi realized Ponghee was glaring at her.

Mrs. Kim wailed, "Songsu was at that haunted house again!"

"Yes." The girl avoided Ponghee's intense glare.

"Does he want to ruin our reputation completely? Why does he keep going there?" said Mrs. Kim, hitting the floor with her hand.

Ponghee grabbed a hot iron fuming, "And what were *you* doing there yourself? Have you nothing better to do?"

"It's on the way — I was going to get pine needles to steam rice for the wedding. I only happened to see him."

"Well, get back to work."

Mrs. Kim thought angrily that her sister-in-law had no business getting involved, but refrained from saying so. There was no point in fighting with Ponghee while trying to get ready for Yonsoon's wedding. She knew she ought to shut up altogether, but emotion got the best of her and she said, "You know what they say — there won't be any children in a family where somebody takes arsenic. He has been told not to go there and he knows he is not supposed to. I can't understand why he does it."

"Songsu has a life and the right to live it. The fact that his mother committed suicide is not his fault," Ponghee argued, exasperated.

Though Mrs. Kim had raised Songsu, she never loved him. That she was not his biological mother couldn't really explain her discomfort around him. Actually, she feared him. Perhaps because he reminded her so much of Sukjong. Seeing Songsu, who looked uncannily like his mother, was for Mrs. Kim like seeing the ghost of her dead sister-in-law.

For this reason she tormented the boy, repeatedly telling him the story of how the house became haunted. She did her very best to set him against his mother by describing her as a sly fox. Mrs. Kim continuously disparaged her memory in the most pejorative terms: "How," she would ask Songsu incriminatingly, "could a mother with an infant son commit suicide? If she is not in hell, she's in purgatory for half of eternity. So, now do you understand why her ghost wanders around haunting that house?"

However, Mrs. Kim's deprecations did not have the desired effect. They only made him more distrustful of her. The more she tried to turn him against his mother, the more he resisted; the more he resisted, the more frightened she became of him.

In fact, Mrs. Kim had a number of other reasons to resent the boy: Sukjong had been far more beautiful than she herself and had never showed Mrs. Kim what she considered to be the proper respect, due an older brother's wife. But what bothered her most was her own husband's attitude toward Songsu. Yes, of course, he had a familial duty to the boy, but he had done his duty and more. Her husband sympathized with his nephew, she felt, unnecessarily. Furthermore, it angered her deeply that Songsu, instead of their own daughter, would inherit their money. That's the way things were; women couldn't inherit. Still, it galled her. In the end, fear was the chief cause of the animosity she felt for the boy. She was convinced something ominous was going to happen whenever she looked at

Songsu. She could feel it in her bones. Sukjong's ghost seemed to hover about the house. The shamans were called to perform their rites many times, but they never dispelled her fears.

Songsu's limpid eyes unnerved her, and when he looked at Yonsoon with them, she felt an ominous sense of death. "That boy is going to destroy my daughter," she thought, and Ponghee said, "What are you cutting them for?"

"Oh no! What have I done?"

"You cut the bodice ties in half; it's a bad omen."

Ponghee laid them back together. Though they were on the inside and wouldn't show, now they had to be pieced.

Outside in the yard, a servant was shooing the geese, "Shoo, git outta here, shoo, shoo!"

The Haunted House

Overhearing her mother and aunt in the next room, Yonsoon snuck out of the house and tiptoed along in the new spring grass to the haunted house. The sun reflecting on the pine trees on Mount Andwi tinged them with white highlights. In the distance, a woman was seen coming back from the well.

Yonsoon peered through the opening in the wall. Just as Togi had told her mother, she could see Songsu sitting on a willow tree that had fallen in a windstorm several years before. The villagers, however, believed the tree had been struck by lightning. Deep in thought, Songsu sat, chin in his palms staring up at the sky.

Mischievously, Yonsoon flipped her long braid over her left shoulder and tiptoed into the yard, but Songsu was so engrossed in his thoughts he didn't notice her.

"Boo, Songsu!"

He turned his head abruptly, red-faced and frightened as if he'd seen a ghost. After a moment he smiled at her, looking puzzled. "How did you know I was here?"

"You have lost weight lately," she said, sitting down next to him and tucking her skirt under her legs, and she surveyed his gaunt face with its large eyes.

"I guess the ghost is haunting me," he said, turning away from her.

Dismayed, she replied, "You talk nonsense."

"What are you doing here? Yonsoon, you know your mother will be furious."

"What am I doing here? What are *you* doing here?"

"It's different for me."

"What do you mean, different for you?"

"I mean I'm haunted by the ghost of this house. Everyone — including your own mother — says so."

"Stop that nonsense!"

A magpie flew into the zelkova tree just outside the wall and began to scold noisily. "Caw, caw, caw." Apricot and cherry blossoms were fading.

"Come on, Songsu," she began, but he closed his mouth, setting his jaw so rigidly that the muscles in his cheeks twitched, "Why do you come here?"

"I am hoping to see my mother," he told her defiantly.

"But why?" she whispered, as if trying to pacify him. Songsu turned his face to her and they stared at each another for a long moment.

"Oh, I just want to leave," he said in the flippant tone they used with each other when they were younger.

"Where would you go? Some place far?"

"I want to look for my father. If he is already dead, at least I will know where he's buried."

Yonsoon listened as they watched a ship leaving the harbor. She realized he had come here not only to commune with his dead mother's ghost but to watch the ships leaving. "Why is he suddenly so interested in his father? He never seemed concerned before," she wondered. Sunlight glinted brightly off the waves, as Songsu stared at the ship slowly sailing away from them, and finally said, "I hear my father looked like you."

Yonsoon contemplated Songsu's face, watching the large vessel running from beneath his chin to above his collar. "Of course, I don't know, but that's what people say."

"Do you suppose he had light brown hair like yours? I wonder if it was silky as yours." He mumbled, as if he were talking to himself.

Her face became a shade whiter with fright. "You'd better stop believing he's still alive. Besides, how will you support yourself if you leave? You'll be a beggar. Plus, there are robbers and thieves everywhere. It really scares me to hear you say that, Songsu."

"Why are you getting married, Yonsoon?"

"I don't want to be an old maid and humiliate my family. You know I am not well. They worry incessantly about me wandering lonely for eternity, as people do when they are not married."

"Don't marry," Songsu begged her.

Mulling over his plea, she leaned across and pulled a piece of lichen from the rotting tree, then looked up at him, and said, "Both of us must get married soon. You are going to marry a pretty girl, aren't you?"

"No, I'm not," he said forcefully, breathing the scent of camellia oil from Yonsoon's hair.

"Oh, come on! You will, too."

While Songsu and Yonsoon were deep in conversation, Sogwon, on his way back from the military office, happened to glance through the hole in the garden wall and spied them sitting on the downed tree. Sogwon was astonished.

"Oh, God!" he thought, "She is here with Songsu — this place must really be haunted just like everybody says."

He craned his neck, stuck his head in the hole and hollered, "Miss Kim!"

Startled at hearing her name, Yonsoon stood up and saw Sogwon, "Get out of there, hurry up about it and bring Master Songsu." Together, they hustled out of the yard.

"What are you two doing here? Your mother would wring both your necks if she knew, and you know it," he reproached them angrily, blowing his nose by pressing his thumb against one nostril.

"Let's get out of here," he said, walking them to the cross-road and bidding them goodbye there. He continued on his way thinking, "Yonsoon should marry Tackjin even if Okhwa doesn't like it. That poor skinny girl can't live long. Nobody should have to remain single and have their ghost wandering around for eternity, attached to no one, no family. Of course, I don't need to worry; I still have plenty of time to get married."

Walking along the road to Okhwa's tavern, Sogwon felt optimistic about his future. With the prospect of free drinks before him, he was convinced he'd live to be a hundred. "Poor Okhwa. She is nothing but a weed on the side of the road for Tackjin; he will walk all over her. She was good enough not to babble the truth — that Tackjin is the baby's father — but *he* won't appreciate it. Still, no reason why I shouldn't get a few free drinks out of the deal though."

The prospect of free drinks also made him forget he had been attracted to Okhwa himself. He found the tavern crowded as it was market day. Okhwa winked at him and came running with drinks and food, which both pleased and unnerved him.

"How do you rate the best service in the place?" one of the other men grumbled.

"Hey Okhwa, how come all of a sudden Sogwon gets the de-luxe treatment? Did he give you a bunch of money?"

"Exactly, I appreciate the fact that he has paid off his tab."

"Would you listen to her! 'I appreciate the fact....' How sweet! Whoa, Sogwon, I bet you'll be dreaming of Okhwa tonight, ho, ho, ho!" jeered Mr. Park, a carpenter. But Sogwon kept on drinking.

"Slow down, man, you're going to choke, drinking so fast," he said, but Sogwon ignored him.

He was drunk by the time he was ready to leave, but not so drunk to realize that Okhwa would question him about Yonsoon's wedding, and demand to know if he had told her the truth about Tackjin. He couldn't face it.

Okhwa grabbed him by the collar. "Hey, where are you going so early?

"I'll be back again, don't worry," he said wiggling loose.

A salt sea breeze blew, lights from fishing boats flickered in the harbor and Sogwon could hear waves breaking against the sea wall. "I'm drunk," he thought; nevertheless, he counted the money in his pocket and staggered into another tavern. After a few more drinks, he fell asleep, snoring loudly, so drunk he couldn't hear the barmaid yelling at him.

The news that Songsu and Yonsoon were at the haunted house together spread immediately. Children all over the village began singing this rhyme:

Oo-oo, Oo-oo, when do the plums ripen?
Ee-ee, Ee-ee, when do the cherries ripen?
Oo-oo, Oo-oo, whose ghost will get them when they do?
Ee-ee, Ee-ee, Songsu, Yonsoon, me or you?
Oo-oo, Oo-oo, when do the plums ripen?
Ee-ee, Ee-ee, when do the cherries ripen?
Oo-oo, Oo-oo, Oo-oo, Oo-oo.
Ee-ee, Ee-ee, Songsu, Yonsoon, you or ME!

Togi reported the children's song to Mrs. Kim, who was naturally furious, more irate than ever with Songsu.

The Wedding Day

It was a fine spring day. During the night there had been showers, but when the sun rose into a cloudless sky behind

Kongji Island, day broke clear and beautiful. Mrs. Kim's wish for a perfect wedding day had been granted.

The servant woman from Hadong came out of the kitchen, trying to ingratiate herself to Mrs. Kim, "You've certainly got a grand day for a wedding." She worked part-time for the Kims, but lived in the village.

Dark circles under Mrs. Kim's eyes revealed she had not slept soundly, worrying about the weather. Only a stroke of luck could give them a sunny day in such a wet spring.

"Heaven couldn't have refused me as fervently as I prayed," said the heavy-set Mrs. Kim going to the front yard.

Just past lunch time the bridegroom arrived, and everyone came running to greet him. The happy children created a festive atmosphere, squealing, running around, greeting everyone and filling the air with anticipation. "Here comes the bride, skinny as a broom. Here comes the groom, big fat and wide," they sang.

Finally, a man from the village announced the wedding in a booming, dignified voice. Guests and servants gathered around the wedding table, with the bride and groom standing on either side.

At the fringes of the group, the guests and servants gossiped in hushed tones: "What a beautiful couple," someone said, "they are lucky, it is late for both of them to be getting married."

"I see a ghost hovering above that couple, myself," said the woman from Hadong. Ill-tempered as usual, she could never stand to see anybody else happy, cursed the pair, and when the rest of the servants left the kitchen to watch the wedding, she stole a set of silver flatware and hid it in the front of her dress. Then she went to the front yard with the rest of the guests and began shoving.

A young woman with a sleeping child tied to her back said, "Please stop pushing; you're going to hurt my baby."

The Hadong woman then began whispering to an old woman next to her, "Everybody in the whole place knows what Tackjin is up to — he's only interested in Pongjay's money. Besides, seriously, how long is Yonsoon going to live anyway? Ha! As if that skinny girl could satisfy a man!" She sneered, screwing up her face, which made lines around her eyes distinctly visible.

"Can you read the future? Nobody knows how long she will live," an old lady countered.

"Look how beautiful she is — one night might be worth it."

"And what's the use of a beautiful face with one foot in the grave?" asked the mean-spirited Hadong woman grimacing uncomfortably and pushing up the silverware she had stolen, which was now sliding down the front of her dress.

"Yonsoon Kim looks like an angel from heaven," declared the old woman who sympathized with the beautiful but vulnerable-looking little bride.

"Tackjin is a lucky stiff even if this marriage lasts only a year or so. How else would *he* have married somebody decent?"

"Right, but the Kangs were once nobles; Kims were dirt by comparison."

"Some noble blood! He ought to be ashamed — no job, no house, no money, consorting with lowlife, barmaids, and gamblers," a man grumbled as if he knew Tackjin from personal experience. "Anyway, he's lucky to be the son-in-law of Pongjay Kim."

"Well, at least he looks handsome in his wedding clothes," commented another.

After the ceremony had finished and the food was served, fights erupted on the straw mat outside the gate among the beggars and lepers who came in hopes of leftovers. Mrs. Kim sat looking and feeling relieved, watching her guests be served. Children looking like little squirrels were running around with their hands and cheeks full of rice cakes. In the men's quarters, Pongjay was busy serving the guests drinks and receiving their congratulations. Inside the house, helping Yonsoon change her dress, Ponghee tried to revive the exhausted bride with chicken noodle soup.

Songsu was nowhere to be seen; in fact, he had not been seen since early morning. The day wore on. Outside, the lepers became drunk and began dancing The Leper's Jig. Sogwon, who also drank freely, shouted from the gate, "I don't think it is fair, but I wish you a long life, Mistress Yonsoon."

He then headed for the tavern at the pier. No matter what the weather, he went every evening. It was his second home. On the way, he saw a crowd. "Oh good, another wedding!" he said, wiping his nose on his sleeve and joined the crowd.

He craned his neck to get a better look and asked, "What's going on?"

"See for yourself," said Bau's mother, a boisterous woman who had been deserted by her husband, shoving him.

"Ouch," Sogwon complained, blinking, "Wow, look at that; there's smoke coming out of it. It must be a whale."

"You moron," she said. "Birth God's mistake. An afterbirth became a person."

"It's moving — f-fast," said Sogwon, "It must be a ship then."

"It *is* a ship, cretin. A ship full of Westerners, coming to rape and kill us all."

"Don't worry," he said full of drunken bravado, "I'll shoot them dead. Bam-bam. Bam-bam." Swaying drunkenly, he pantomimed shooting a gun.

Bau's mother laughed heartily as a man. "You are really full of shit and snot, Sogwon. Now that you are over forty, could you even please a woman?"

"Well, I'll come to your house tonight and show you."

"Awh, get out of here," she said, pushing him away and then flouncing off swaying her hips. In the distance, the steamship disappeared over the horizon, leaving only a trace of black smoke. The crowd on the pier began dissolving.

"What is going to happen to us?" a worried voice asked, "When Taewongun was in power, foreign ships didn't sail into our harbor whenever they damn well pleased. No sir."

Someone else criticized Queen Min, who was killed the previous year by Japanese assassins, "Petticoat governments never last long. Only Japan appreciates them — easy to take advantage of."

"You mark my words," began another man, "there'll be another revolt. There's no fish in the sea and no grain in the fields. People are hungry; that's the recipe for revolution."

"Maybe the government will release some more grain."

"Don't hold your breath. Even if they did, we wouldn't get any. Even if they had more grain than sand on a beach, *we* wouldn't get any. Not one *sok*, by God. We were born to live helpless and hungry."

A shriek was heard over the muttering and mumbling crowd. "Sogwon! You bastard!"

It was Okhwa, and the minute he realized it, he took off running.

"You goddamn bastard con-artist," she hollered after him. She knew he was not to blame, but there was no one else to vent her anger on. She sobbed long after she closed the tavern and far into the night. "Fate is cruel. I have tried and tried to live like other women. Sweet-talking Tackjin has made a fool of me. Oh, my poor baby. He will never have a father."

The Death of Pongjay Kim

Two donkeys trotted along a road winding through the rice fields. A servant led one of them with Pongjay Kim riding on its back. Songsu followed his uncle riding the other. The setting sun glowed warmly in the fields of yellow fall stubble.

Gesturing to encompass the checkerboard of recently-harvested rice fields before him, Pongjay said, "We own all the land you see before you, and these fields produce even in droughts." There were small reservoirs dotting the landscape here and there. Songsu followed, listening in silence. A flow of startled crows scolded and flew off.

Each fall Pongjay went to Kosong and Sachon to survey his fields. Formerly Pongjay had one hundred and fifty *soks* of rice from his own field and another thirty from the government field, as an annual allowance. As they walked along, a hamlet of tenant-farmhouses huddled in the valley became visible.

"Now that Yonsoon is married," began Pongjay, "since Tackjin is not a blood relative, you must manage the estate, Songsu. And — you must get married next year." He advised his nephew to prepare himself. Because tradition did not permit two marriages in a family in a single year, Songsu's was planned for the following year.

Songsu listened in resigned silence.

Pongjay Kim was wary of his new son-in-law. Tackjin seemed to be always hanging around the pharmacy, complimenting his gullible mother-in-law.

"I am so very proud of my son-in-law," Mrs. Kim praised him to her husband, "He is polite and kind as a true blue blood." However, Pongjay kept his distance from Tackjin. Secretly, he never regarded his son-in-law as a member of the family, and when he went to survey his lands after the fall crop was in that year, he took Songsu, not Tackjin, with him.

As they arrived in the village, the farmers came running to greet them. Someone led their donkeys to the stable. Others spread straw mats on the wide porch. One old farmer rubbed his hands and bowed repeatedly, asking, "Was it a long journey? Would you like something to drink?"

Songsu noticed a young girl, who had come into the yard carrying an armful of sesame stalks. She reminded him of Yonsoon, though he couldn't figure out exactly why. He found it difficult to take his eyes off her.

Pongjay and Songsu seated themselves on the porch mats. This family was one of the most well-to-do in the village, but they lived like animals. However, they served their masters chicken, rice and beans, and homemade wine. When they'd finished eating, the girl who had come into the yard with the sesame stalks, brought rice tea. Her sun-tanned face was quite different from Yonsoon's; it was her eyes that reminded Songsu of Yonsoon.

They heard a voice from the kitchen, "Kapsoon, take this chicken to Tongdol's house."

"They are sharing the leftovers with relatives," Songsu thought, "Kapsoon. Yonsoon."

The crickets were chirping loudly in the grasses nearby. When a dim kerosene lamp was brought in, Songsu realized the days were getting shorter.

The old farmer stood before them bowing, "Please accept my apologies for this poor meal," he said, exaggerating his bows.

"About the crops," Pongjay, puffing on a pipe, asked the farmer, "I understand the barley was not successful, but the rice was fair. We certainly had enough sun this year."

"In spite of the good weather, the crop was not good. So I hope you will be generous with us."

"How can I be generous again this year? How can you say you haven't had a good harvest when others admit they have?"

"I have a son who is sick in bed," the old man continued, bowing to Pongjay, his landlord, searching for a sign that he might yield, trying to say the right thing to sway him, "The problem this year was insects."

"You *never* have a good crop. I have never come here and heard you admit that you had a good crop. *Never!*" Pongjay said, turning his face away, refusing to listen to the old farmer any more.

Hearing Pongjay's words, the rest of the farmers no longer had the courage to plead their cases. Nevertheless, the old man continued, "... what's more, I have a daughter who must be married this fall...."

Late that night Songsu questioned his uncle about his lack of compassion. "Don't take them too seriously," he explained.

"Every year they say the same thing. Naturally, they try to pay less. I know how much they sweat in the fields, but generosity is not the best policy. The more generous we are, the more selfish they become. Remember this when I am dead and gone."

Pongjay was very concerned about the estate once he was no longer able to manage it. He worried that lenient, soft-hearted Songsu would give the peasants everything. Normally, he himself was much more sympathetic to their pleas, but this time, he wanted to show Songsu how to be resistant to them. If Tackjin were sincere, Pongjay could have relied on him to help Songsu. But who could trust that scum? Nor could he depend on his wife; Yonsoon was her whole world. As for Yonsoon, how could he rely on her?

"I am fifty-seven years old now," he thought, "If Songsu doesn't take the reins, this family doesn't have a single descendent left to run things." Thinking about it kept him from falling asleep.

The following spring, Pongjay went deer hunting and took Songsu with him. Every spring they shot deer, marinated the meat in nursing mother's milk, and dried the strips of meat in the shade. Then, this delicacy was sent to Seoul and presented to the king as a tribute from the Tongyong area.

A servant cut the antlers from the deer they'd shot. Songsu felt dizzy at the sight of the poor bleeding deer with its big eyes and fragile long legs. Pongjay pushed his nephew toward the deer, saying, "Suck up the blood. Be a man."

Songsu knelt and sucked the blood from the antlers of the dead deer. As he felt the warm liquid going down his throat, the blue sky seemed to glow red. He thought of the red sunset glowing across the fields he had surveyed with his uncle on the donkey last fall.

Young girls who had been picking herbs were sitting on the sea wall, chatting and taking a break. Songsu thought of Kapsoon, "I would rather have her for my wife...." He thought of her eyes, which suddenly appeared before him — hers or

Yonsoon's, he couldn't be sure which. At any rate, he must marry the girl Pongjay chose.

Hunting continued the following day. Late in the day, the hunting party stopped to rest by a stream after tramping the mountain all day long. The whole party was smoking, talking and telling stories. Pongjay's feet ached. Maybe his hunting boots were too tight, he had walked too much. He took off his shoes and socks, put his feet in the cool stream and lit his pipe.

In the back of his mind, he could hear his wife haranguing, as she did often: "Think about it! Our own daughter doesn't have a pittance, and you give everything to Songsu? Must he perform the memorial service for us? Let me tell you I wouldn't take so much as a sip of a drink offered by him. How could I, when Yonsoon is nothing but a beggar? And why is she a beggar? You! Giving everything to Songsu. After we die, she will have absolutely no one. Oh, my poor little girl!"

Mrs. Kim nagged Pongjay relentlessly because Tackjin constantly complained and urging her to appeal to him.

"Would you please stop?" Pongjay shouted at his wife, "Yonsoon is married; she has a husband." At the same time he pitied his daughter, knowing fully well she could not rely on her husband.

"I hope she outlives us," Pongjay thought, standing up, starting down the hill with his socks and shoes in his hands.

"A snake!!!" Pongjay stopped and held Songsu back with one hand, but when he looked down, there was blood on his instep. With its head in the striking position, the serpent sat coiled on the edge of the path. Songsu grabbed a large stone and crushed it. It shook its tail for a few moments. Back in the village, a servant sucked the venom out of the wound and put antidote on it.

However, Pongjay Kim died that night — not of the venom of a poisonous snake, but of tetanus.

Home Again

"What on earth have you done? Have you really passed over your perfectly healthy son in favor of your son-in-law? How could you do such a thing?" cried Ponghee, pointing an indicting finger at Mrs. Kim.

Saying that Songsu was too young to inherit property, when her husband died, Mrs. Kim allowed her son-in-law's name to be entered on the government rolls as heir to the pharmacy.

Mrs. Kim mumbled, trying to minimize the offense to her sister-in-law, "I can't believe that you are making such a fuss over this. Songsu is only a kid; he can't deal with a pharmacy business. When he is older, perhaps."

"An eighteen-year-old is a kid? How old does he have to be to be considered a man? Besides, everybody in the whole place knows your son-in-law's intention — to get his hands on the Kim estate. I just can't let that happen." Ponghee's angry eyes looked foreboding.

"What are you saying? That a son-in-law isn't a son?" Mrs. Kim asked obstinately.

"Well, let me ask you this...Is this the Kang or the Kim family?"

Loud voices in small villages attract attention and people had already gathered, whispering. Sogwon Chi was among them, grinding his teeth and clenching his fists in anger.

"Didn't you at least expect your disinherited son to have a few defenders while you and your son-in-law squander the family fortune?"

"Look, who do you think you are anyway? Mind your own business. This is my family. Songsu is a distracted, haunted kid; if I let him try to manage the pharmacy, he'll lose it for sure," Mrs. Kim was now red-faced with anger.

"Do as you please. But if you think that I can't affect the situation just because I'm a married woman, you are dead wrong, sister." Ponghee stood up, folded the hem of her skirt and pushed through the crowd that had gathered. Then she turned around and shouted in a threatening tone, "I'm going to Tangsan!" where she believed the deity lived. Hearing this, Mrs. Kim turned white.

"Let's go with her," said Sogwon, agitating and goading the people around him. Ponghee's son and several others followed. They passed the municipal office where a wooden statue stood guard and marched on to Tangsan. The morning sunlight began to burn away the mist and shone brightly. The crowd shouted across from Tangsan, appealing to the governor in the case.

"Ridiculous! A son-in-law received the property of the family instead of a son!" they shouted in unison three times. Then they went home.

The next day the magistrate heard the case and decided in favor of the son.

As he was unmarried, Songsu put on a mourning hat and hurried to the office to receive the letter of appointment from the governor. But even after Songsu was made the official heir, Tackjin Kang hung on like a leech.

Mrs. Kim sent him to the herb market in Taegu to purchase their stock for the year. She herself kept all the keys to storage rooms in a large inside pocket of her long skirt. Thus, control of the pharmacy and other Kim properties gradually came into Kang's hands.

At that time, there was a custom prohibiting joyful celebrations during the three-year period of mourning accorded parents. Therefore, Songsu's wedding — though no bride had been chosen — was postponed. Songsu wasn't disappointed.

Meanwhile, a year passed. Chungku, Ponghee's son, married one of the Yoon girls from Waygol. The father and brother of the bride objected to the marriage because the groom was the only son of the poor widow, Ponghee. But the bride's mother was thrilled to have a scholar in the family. "Plus, his mother's people are known for their good looks. So it's not surprising he is both handsome and smart," she said, singing his praises.

But the bride's father wasn't impressed, "Beauty is as beauty does," he said.

"Our daughter, Chongim, is a beauty herself. They are a perfect pair," the mother of the bride insisted.

"You can't live on love or good looks," the father objected strenuously, but his wife was determined and the marriage went forward as planned.

It was publicly acknowledged and agreed that she was the most beautiful of the out-of-town brides in Myongjonggol. Her pink lips and features were lovely and light hair curled down her forehead. However, only Songsu went to the wedding. Mrs. Kim, who had grown distant with the groom's mother over the estate management, stayed home.

There he met Yonsoon, whom he had not seen since her own wedding. At first, she seemed to have gained weight and looked healthier than before. But the fever soon tired her, so she lay down to rest.

Two months later, Songsu again unexpectedly showed up at Yonsoon's door.

"What a wonderful surprise! What brings you here?" She rushed out to him, grabbing his hands and holding them tight. This was his first visit since she was married. A hint of a smile flickered across his lips. She invited him in but he didn't move. She ordered the maid to bring a cool drink, and she fanned him as they talked. She was wearing an Andong linen dress and had a white ribbon braided into her hair, but she looked puffy, and the light brown hair on her white forehead was wet with perspiration.

The whiff of camellia from her hair wafted to him, "Mom is totally unrealistic, it upsets me." Her eyes, bright and clear as he remembered them, stared at him, but now they were filled with sadness, loneliness, and agony.

"So how are you doing?" he asked in a low whisper.

"I am always sick."

He paused a moment lowering his head, "I have decided to leave...."

The look on her face became despair, "What are you talking about?" she asked.

"I want to go someplace else and live."

"Oh, please don't. You know I have so few people to rely on. How long do you think I will live?" Tears welled up in her eyes. "Please don't go, Songsu." He began crying too. He blew his nose and wiped the tears from his eyes.

"Next year, the mourning period for our father is over. You'll be free to marry and manage the pharmacy yourself. Mom is so naive...oh, poor Mom, when I'm gone...." she continued. "She doesn't believe my husband is taking advantage of her. To begin with, he married me because he knew I was going to die. Of course, I married him so I wouldn't die a spinster. Not surprising we don't have much affection for one another. Perhaps I am being punished for the sins of my past life. I hope, though, that when I die...." she couldn't go on.

Even Songsu, not terribly attuned to local gossip, had heard that Okhwa was Tackjin's mistress and had his child. Using the pretext of ill-health, Yonsoon kept her husband at a distance, and even encouraged him to go to Okhwa. As for him, he cared very little for Okhwa and felt no responsibility for the child. In fact, instead of helping Okhwa, he tried to wheedle money out of her. He loved easy money, and it was available from Mrs. Kim. He had sex from Okhwa and money through Yonsoon.

Songsu rose, leaving his drink untouched, and left. He stopped at the gate, glanced back at Yonsoon and said, "Do you think we will meet in the next life, Big Sis?" When they were kids, he had always called her "Big Sis."

"Of course, we will," she assured him. "If not, it would be just too sad."

He departed with sure, firm steps, leaving Yonsoon at the gate unable to hear his response, "Bye, Sis."

As the setting midsummer sun waned, the leaves began to revive from the midday heat. Songsu walked past the hill near the North Gate. Suddenly, he felt tears welling up in his eyes. Heading for the top of the hill, when he couldn't see the road, he sat down. The familiar sight of dusk gathering around the back of Mt. Andwi made him even sadder.

"I'm twenty years old," he said, and then asked himself, "What is the point of leaving Tongyong? Have I really anywhere to go?"

He could hear the sound of a bugle from the military compound in the distance. He recalled Sogwon passing the haunted house, his bushy whiskers, and his silliness. He contemplated saying goodbye to Chungku and his pretty wife, and his mother. Yonsoon's last words weighed heavily on him: "Please, don't go. How long do you think I will live? I have so few people to rely on." He mulled them over until his head ached. Finally, he staggered to his feet.

Just then, Mrs. Kim and her son-in-law came running to him, but he regarded them without emotion. Tackjin was flapping along in a fine linen overcoat. Mrs. Kim carried Songsu's bamboo mourning hat.

She sank to the ground wailing, "You ungrateful whelp, leaving your mother and going off — to god-only-knows where!" He didn't bother to look at her, but she continued, "My god, I have raised a barbarian." She pounded the ground.

"Here — you came for these things, not to take me home. Take them and go." Songsu handed her a bundle, but Kang grabbed it. In it were the antlers of a buck and some gold nuggets, which Songsu had stolen from a secret cabinet in the house.

"Come on," said Tackjin, "he's already made up his mind to leave. Let him go!" For his part he was only too pleased to have the valuables, but Mrs. Kim naturally felt the affection a mother would, having raised the child. Besides, if Songsu left, the Kim family line would end.

"Kill me, you might as well just kill me," Mrs. Kim hollered hysterically as she untied her belt and looped it around her neck as if to hang herself.

Tackjin was mystified. "What are you doing?" he asked her, shocked.

She only intended to threaten him, but they were surprised she became so emotional. Yonsoon's words echoed in his brain, "How long can I live....? Poor Mom, without me Tackjin will always take advantage of her."

Casting a scornful look at Tackjin, whose fishy eyes reflected his disappointment at having his get-rich-quick dreams dashed, silently Songsu rose and walked down the hill toward home.

The Flower-covered Coffin

In the autumn that ended Pongjay's three-year mourning period, Songsu married. Yonsoon appeared far more eager than Mrs. Kim to have Songsu married, as she thought it the best way to keep him there. His bride, Punshi, was the daughter of Mr. Tak, a generous, affluent farmer from Hanshil. She wasn't terribly pretty, but sweet and very kind.

On the wedding day, Sogwon got sloppy drunk, and began lamenting: "Oh, woe is me! I know my poor master, if he were alive, he would never fail to be here even if he had to travel a thousand miles. Oh Master Kim, you left so young...have you gone so far you can't come to your own son's wedding?" Then, he began in a loud, off-key sing-song moan, "and my poor young master Songsu, so full of regret, full of remorse."

When she heard it, Mrs. Kim angrily berated him, "You sot, how dare you come here whining and making a scene. Get out!" Sogwon unnerved her, so she had a servant throw him out.

"Cranky old bag," sighed Sogwon drunkenly, leaning against the wall for support. Then he went back to the gate, stuck his head in and hollered, "Hey, I'm a human being too! Don't treat me like a dog!" But he ran off when Mrs. Kim sicced the servant on him again.

After Songsu's wedding, Tackjin opened another pharmacy with his mother-in-law's support outside the East Gate. Operating the original Kim pharmacy had taught him the business. A master manipulator, he played cunningly on patients' gullibility. He was a quack, not a healer.

Kang's home was attached to the new pharmacy. The window of Yonsoon's room at the back of the house was open and the sparrows were chattering in the bamboo boughs.

"Child, eat this; it will give you strength." Believing that it would help, Mrs. Kim was trying to feed her daughter gruel of ground sesame and rice.

However, Yonsoon, lying on the bed, knew better, "It's not going to make me any better, Mom."

Nowadays, she frequently coughed up blood, but she still looked well.

"Mom? How are Songsu and his wife?" She asked her mother about them every time she came to visit.

"How can I say? I never see him; he spends all his time in the guest room. To me, Punshi seems like a wonderful girl. I have absolutely no idea why he has no interest in her."

"You know that's how he is, Mom."

"Well, none of us know him, and I have a feeling he doesn't like me. If Songsu tries to honor me when I am dead, I won't be happy. Please ask the monks at the temple to do it. Mrs. Kim's hair was now gray. Once quite plump, she had lost a lot of weight. Yonsoon studied her mother's wrinkled face, and smiled sadly, knowing she would never outlive her mother.

Mrs. Kim lowered her voice and said, "Songsu avoids me because he hates me, but surprise of surprises — he brought his wife some medicine because she is showing signs of pregnancy."

"Signs of pregnancy?"

"I believe so," said Mrs. Kim.

Yonsoon sat up all night with the back window open. It rained steadily in the bamboo forest. She suddenly took a turn for the worse. When Songsu and his wife came to visit, she didn't open her eyes. Her weeping mother wandered aimlessly in and out of the house. The next day Songsu came by himself, but since Yonsoon was still sleeping, he went back home in the drizzling rain.

While Mrs. Kim, exhausted from sitting up day and night throughout her daughter's illness, was taking a nap, Yonsoon died in her sleep. When her mother awoke and discovered this, she began writhing, sobbing and hugging the dead body of her daughter. Then she fainted. Songsu rushed to the house and began wailing, hitting his head against the doorpost.

When Ponghee, her son and daughter-in-law, and Punshi arrived, they cried, not for Yonsoon, but for her mother, who was deranged with grief. They tried to console her, but none of them were even aware of Songsu's grief.

Tackjin held the wake at home; he seemed unmoved. The neighborhood women came and whispered, "That poor fool, Mrs. Kim, she trusted her rotten son-in-law too much."

"And Songsu will never forgive her either, will he?"

"How could anybody be so stupid as to presume that a sick daughter would outlive her?"

Instead of sympathizing with Mrs. Kim over the death of her daughter, they pitied her for her unwise decisions.

Yonsoon's funeral was held five days later. Despite the large crowd of mourners, it was heart breaking. The pallbearers carrying the flower bedecked casket stopped for a few minutes just past the North Gate. The dirge sounded all the more depressing because it was for someone so young:

> Auh Ha Nam, Auh Ha Nam
> It's a long way to Hades
> I leave you now
> Never to return.

Good bye to my parents
Good bye to my siblings
A tender age,
Now I leave you,
Never to return.

Auh Ha Nam, Auh Ha Nam
The winding road to Hades
Curves like a bow and
I fly like an arrow.

Serving as one of the pallbearers, Sogwon hoisted the coffin to his shoulders, blinked his big eyes and blew his nose. Only with the help of Punshi and other women was Mrs. Kim, overcome by grief, able to follow the funeral procession. Tackjin walked, his bowed head covered with a hemp hood.

Cousins Songsu and Chungku, staring straight ahead, walked side by side. Along the route, some spectators cried when they heard the dirge sung for the dead Yonsoon. But others whispered: "Songsu paid for the carriage. That skinflint Tackjin spent as little as possible on her. Whose money is it anyway? Her family's, of course. How dare he? He doesn't remember when he was penniless. And how will her poor mother carry on?"

Auh Ha Nam, Auh Ha Nam
Now I leave
Never to return
I'll sleep in the underground
I'll sleep under a sheet of grass
Friends with the flies
When it drizzles
Who will come to mourn me?
Auh Ha Nam, Auh Ha Nam.

The pallbearers and the coffin covered with white flowers struggled down a muddy hill. Faintly, the drone echoed across the hills and funeral flags fluttered in the wind.

Mrs. Kim

Summer twilight lingered long after dinner. Mrs. Kim was sitting by the kitchen door rocking a baby to sleep.

"Baby mine, Baby mine, a little flower in my kitchen garden...."

Though her hair was white and dry, wrinkles and liver spots revealed her age, her eyes shone with peace and contentment, as she sang to the child.

"Aunt Ponghee has come to visit," said Punshi, entering and taking the baby from her mother-in-law.

"Feed him some more," she said, "He can't go to sleep...." Mrs. Kim directed her daughter-in-law, and then went to the hall to meet with her sister-in-law.

Fanning herself, Ponghee asked, "What have you been up to?"

"Trying to put the baby to sleep."

"Where is his father?"

"Out, I think," said Mrs. Kim.

Punshi had peeled and served melons and the two women sat in the living room, chatting and eating. "Has Tackjin shown his face since he's remarried?" Ponghee asked.

"Haven't seen anything of him," replied Mrs. Kim, sounding discouraged and a bit embarrassed.

Tackjin had remarried the previous month to the daughter of a rich widow. Okhwa again tried to stop the marriage, having no more success than she did his first one.

"I poked my finger in my own eye," Mrs. Kim often said after her daughter died. The minute she was gone, Tackjin became a different person altogether.

"I did not see the man for what he was," she said, "it's all my fault. I would love to see him dead. He deceived me." Whenever Tackjin's name was mentioned, Mrs. Kim became visibly agitated and began to rant, "So much for his honor! All he cares about is money! How could he marry into such a family?" She was referring to his new mother-in-law, who had a reputation as a loose woman.

"Forget it!" said Ponghee. "He is no longer a member of this family. What he does is none of our business."

"You're right," Mrs. Kim conceded, but continued to belittle herself.

"Sons-in-law are all thieves, they say," Ponghee told her.

"Not all sons-in-law are the same. Mine was sadly the worst of the lot, and you know how well I treated him — gave him everything," Mrs. Kim said, exasperated.

"Well, it is your own fault. The biggest mistake you made has been not how you treated Tackjin, but your own son. You should have treated him better; he's the one who will honor your ancestors!"

On the subject of her son, Mrs. Kim had nothing to say. Her daughter-in-law was a kind, sweet girl who made her feel comfortable, but she still felt estranged from Songsu. Observing that this dispirited her, Ponghee changed the subject to her favorite grandson, "I heard Yonghwan was sick."

"Yes, and I was scared to death, but he's all right now." Mrs. Kim's face softened as she talked about her grandson.

"Punshi is blessed to have a healthy son in this family of few children. My daughter-in-law still has not conceived, and I am worried sick," Ponghee confided.

"Stop worrying," said Mrs. Kim, "she's still pretty young."

In her loneliness, Mrs. Kim doted on Yongwhan and indulged his every whim. When he was six years old, and would wake up from his nap, he would go immediately to his grandmother and say "Come on, Granny, let's go 'yeng-yeng." They communicated in baby talk, "Yes, sweet boy, if you'd like yeng-

yeng, we'll go." She would tie a silk scarf on him to protect his ears, and carry the kite and spool to where they flew it. On rainy days, when he begged her to go fishing, she always took him to the stream. Summer nights, they caught fireflies together in the forest. Through Yonghwan, Mrs. Kim gradually began to feel closer to Songsu, but her precious grandson died suddenly of smallpox. Mrs. Kim tried to overcome the pain by bashing her head on the threshold. After burying the child, she staggered around the garden, deranged, singing and sobbing, "Baby, little flower by my kitchen garden...."

The warm-hearted Punshi tried to console her mother-in-law, saying, "Don't do this to yourself, mother! Please stop crying. I can have another baby."

But two months later, Mrs. Kim died saying, "I shouldn't have tried to raise a child whose mother died of poison...."

On August 29, 1910, the year Songsu Kim was thirty-two years old, the dishonorable treaty uniting Korea and Japan was signed. Korea as a country officially disappeared. However, when his cousin, Chungku, visited, with his eyes bleary, Songsu stared at him in stoic silence, as if he hadn't even heard.

In the chaos, Sogwon, who had joined the loyalist troops, showed up unannounced at Kim's. It was an autumn evening. The branches of the persimmon trees drooped, heavy with fruit.

"What brings you here, Sogwon?" said Punshi Kim opening the door. Sogwon was fidgeting awkwardly, straightening the quilt he was holding.

"Oh my God, what is that? A baby, isn't it?" she asked.

Bashfully, Sogwon sniffled.

"Well, come on, where did you get it? Whose child is this?" she came out and asked him to have a seat. He hesitated momentarily and then laid the baby wrapped in its quilt on the floor. "This is a newborn; where did it come from?"

He mumbled vaguely, "I didn't mean to."

"You mean this is your child?"

"Birth God is crazy to have made it, and me such an old man. The poor child!" he answered. Punshi glanced back and forth between him and the baby, amazed. The baby was making faces and moving its tongue. "A sad fate, the poor little thing. . . I can't think of any other place to go," he said.

"Who's the mother?"

Sogwon sighed deeply. Fifty years of futile life was apparent on Sogwon's stained dirty sleeves. "Dead. She's gone."

"Oh, I'm so sorry."

"He would have been better off to have been born a dog in a rich house."

"That's in God's hands. A boy, is it?"

"Boy. Boy or girl, it was born in the wrong place."

The baby sucked his fist and began to cry feebly, wrinkling his face like an old man.

"Aw, he must be hungry," she said.

"Yes, he is. He has had nothing since last night, except a few spoons of honey soup." Tears welled up in Sogwon's eyes.

"How sad," she said, picking up the baby. Sogwon knelt and began crying.

"I'll nurse him inside, you wait here," she said and went in to nurse the child. After she had lost her first son, she had given birth to two daughters.

"M-Madame...." Sogwon called from the hall.

"Yes?"

"Ah...."

"What is it? Speak up, Sogwon! I can't hear you."

"Well, I don't know how to ask you this, but... could you take care of him for a few months? Please, I'll come and get him later, as soon as possible...."

"I figured that's why you came here...I must ask my husband first."

The hungry baby sucked madly at her breast. Looking down at him, she was overwhelmed with tenderness. When she returned, Sogwon was gone. At first she thought he'd gone to the bathroom, but he never returned.

"Unyon!" she called the maid.

"Yes, Ma'am."

"Did you see Sogwon here?"

"Yes, he left."

"He's gone!?"

"Yes, I saw him leave."

In the end she had no choice but to take the baby.

"I feel sorry for him," Punshi Kim said.

The maid giggled. "Tee-hee-hee, is this Sogwon's baby?"

Three months after Sogwon disappeared, a neighbor said she heard he had died fishing at Yokji Island. Some villagers eating venison in a nearby field had seen Sogwon wandering around the seashore late at night. Next morning they found him dead between the rocks.

"What a pity! Poor old Sogwon...." Punshi really felt sorry for him, but she also worried about the unexpected burden of his child.

One day, Ponghee came to visit, hobbling on a cane. "Oh come in, Aunt!" said Punshi as she ushered her into the hall.

"Terrible. Did you hear that Sogwon died?" she mumbled, as she was now also toothless.

"Yes, I just heard it."

"What are you going to do with his baby?"

"Well, what can I do? Raise him myself."

"They say his mother was a shaman."

Punshi Kim frowned. "A shaman?"

"Yes, from Miwu Hill. I heard she died in childbirth and Sogwon took the baby."

"Poor old Sogwon. It's one thing to raise his child, but people say shaman's children are a bad omen...." the old woman said, looking worried. "What does your husband think?"

"He said nothing."

"Sogwon's life was so sad. I suppose, knowing he would die soon, he must have fathered the child...."

Chapter Two

ॐ

Homecoming

Twenty years passed since the Japanese had occupied Korea in 1910. At night the lighthouse beacon shone as it always had. Steamboats came and went from Tongyong blowing their horns, and the sound made travelers homesick.

On a rainy night, as the blue kerosene lamps flickered in the roadside stands by the pier, a man got off a ship. From his clothing — worn boots and cotton overalls — he was obviously a laborer. He looked about thirty-five years old. He strangled a woman as she was passing Minul Hill with a loaded shopping basket on her head. He went to the police station a few days later and turned himself in for the murder. He was Okhwa's son, who had been in Japan looking for work much of the time.

For a year he wrote and sent money, but then for three, they had no news of him. Another man said he had seen him collecting garbage in Osaka. That was all Okhwa heard.

When the news and money stopped, his wife opened a tavern on Coqe past Minul Hill. Then she took in a bum for a lover and kicked her six-year-old son and mother-in-law, Okhwa, out in the street. Cane in hand, Okhwa, led by her grandson, went from door to door begging for food.

"I used to eat good food, drink fine wine, why, even had facials," said Okhwa, squatting on the floor of a restaurant kitchen, slurping leftover soup. "The good ole days are gone forever, and now I'm nothing but old and broke. She then handed the soup bowl to her grandson, waiting his turn anxiously, and lit up a cigarette butt she'd found in the street.

The waitress, having come to the kitchen to escape a drunk in the dining room, looked at Okhwa, her eyes puffy and red from crying. Seeing this wretched old woman, she realized that she herself could end up just like her.

"Don't you have any children?" asked the waitress in a dialect that indicated that she was from out of town.

"Yes, I had a son."

"And he abandoned you like this?"

"My son...he's dead...." she said. Hearing this, the waitress took a wallet from between her breasts and gave a small bill to Okhwa....

"Thank you, gal. God bless you."

The laughter of men and women, Japanese songs and conversation came from the tavern. One group was trying to part a boat captain from his money. Okhwa tucked the bill between the layers of her skirt and tied it tightly, then said, "Better save your money, gal. Children and husband ain't much good when you get to be my age. What old women like me need is money. When you are young and healthy, save for old age and illness. You know what they say, 'Travel with your son and you get hungry; travel with money, you never go hungry.'"

Okhwa kept mumbling to herself, "Ah youth passes so-so quickly. Oh, so quickly," until the cook, tired of listening to it, threw her out.

When Tackjin Kang died, Okhwa and her grandson were begging in front of his gate. His daughters, mourning their father, wailed, "How dare she come here?! She knows whose house this is!" But Okhwa guzzled the liquor the servant gave her and her grandson took the basket of rice, and they stepped aside.

Okhwa disappeared from the streets of Tongyong shortly thereafter, and only her grandson was left to beg with a basket on his arm.

Returning from Japan, her son found the boy begging and placed him in the care of some store owners he knew and headed for his wife's tavern in Coqe. He begged her to take care of the boy for only a year, promising to get a job and send money. She refused. He entreated and pleaded, but she refused. The next night he hid under a tree on Minul Hill, and when she passed by on her way back from the market, he strangled her.

A ship horn blasted from behind Mt. Nambang. It was windy and the sea was choppy. In the dark, whitecaps broke against the rocks of Kongji Island.

"I think it's here," said Mrs. Songsu Kim with a sigh of relief, patting Yongok, her fourth daughter.

When the horn sounded, porters, smoking next to the stands and stalls fronting the pier, stood up, adjusted the carrying frames on their backs and hustled out to the pier. Wary vendors selling rice cakes and rice rolls ran past the boats, secured at the pier. They watched out for steamship line employees.

"Look at the size of those waves! Poor Yongbin, I bet she was really seasick," said Yongok as the hull of the ship appeared around the Kongji bend.

"Not if she's chewing the ginseng I gave her!" said Punshi, on her tiptoes craning her neck to see.

Punshi's second daughter, Yongbin, had finished high school in Seoul and was in her second year at a Junior College. For the past six years, her mother had packed ginseng in her suitcase and instructed her to chew it to prevent seasickness.

As the ship entered the harbor, the horn sounded again, with an animal-like roar. Then, as it approached the pier, it slowed. One of the crew threw a rope and hopped off. The pier was suddenly a madhouse, horns blowing, people shouting and milling about.

"Need a porter?" a man hollered at them, trying to get ahead of others.

"Mom, I see her! I see her! She's right there."

"Where? Where is she?"

Yongbin, in a white linen bodice and black skirt, spotted her mother from the gangplank of the ship and smiled. Her teeth were white and even.

"My baby! Yongbin!" Mrs. Kim hollered, waving to her, but it was so noisy that Yongbin couldn't hear her mother. As she got off the ship, Yongok grabbed her sister's suitcase.

"Mom, you've lost weight," Yongbin said in a low voice hugging her mother. Her baby was now a head taller than Mrs. Kim.

"Why, no. The one who is away is the one who gets home-sick. Were you seasick?"

"A little."

"I told you to chew ginseng."

"I forgot."

"That's a fine note. I pack it, and you don't even use it!"

"That suitcase is quite heavy. Let me help you."

"It's okay; I can manage."

Yongok, 17 years old, had fair skin, while Yongbin, 21, was darker. Yongok was not pretty; she had full lips, a long nose and dark eyebrows that grew close together over the bridge of her nose. This feature caused some older people to predict a hard life ahead for her. Yongok, who talked very little, had great respect for her older sister.

"Let's go," Mrs. Kim said to her daughters, but the two sisters were already on their way. Yongbin stopped at a road-side stand lit by a kerosene lamp, which seemed quaint as a fairy tale. They were selling a variety of goods: cheap cosmetics, soap boxes, and belts, which mainly appealed to the island-ers.

"I know I am home in Tongyong when I see kerosene lamps; they're so sweet and sad," she said, but she didn't look espe-cially unhappy.

"You must love them. You said the same thing the last time you came home."

"Did I really?"

"Don't you have kerosene lamps in Seoul?" asked Mrs. Kim, studying her tall, attractive second daughter.

"Oh, of course, but in Seoul they don't give me the same feeling as here in Tongyong. It's like there are people everywhere, but there are special ones here," Yongbin said, explaining her longing for home with the simple smile of a nursery school teacher.

"Where's Hongsop? Didn't he come with you?"

"He's coming in a couple of days."

Walking up to Ganchanggol, they gossiped about a murder the day before.

A Sailor Boy

Ten years before, Songsu Kim had closed the pharmacy, quit practicing Oriental medicine, and invested in a small fishing fleet. After his aunt had died, he remodeled the haunted house and moved there. He had five daughters now. Having lost their first son, Mrs. Kim then had five girls.

The first, Yongsook, married at seventeen and now, at twenty-four, was a widow. Yongbin was the second and Yongnan, the third, was nineteen. Yongok was number four, and Yonghay, the youngest, was twelve. When Ponghee was still alive, she used to say that Yonghay looked a lot like her grandfather Pongnyong. Nobody ever knew when he died, so they selected July fifteenth for his memorial service. Seeing Yonghay, on the day of the annual ceremony for her brother, Ponghee would feel especially bad because she reminded her so much of him. However, she reminded Songsu of his mother. Naturally, he didn't say so, but she sometimes gave him the illusion of seeing Yonsoon. He called Yonghay his "golden treasure," just as

57

Pongjay had called Yonsoon that for light brown hair. All his other daughters had dark hair.

Mrs. Kim was embarrassed that she had not produced a son, an heir. In fact, she was so ashamed she even asked her husband to take a mistress so that they might have a son, but he ignored her.

Mrs. Kim thought highly of her daughters. She believed Yongsook was such a good housekeeper and so competitive she would make an excellent first daughter-in-law for a wealthy family. The second, Yongbin, was intelligent and handsome enough to pass for a son. The third, Yongnan, didn't even know how to sew ribbons to her bodice, but she was so beautiful that everyone wanted to wait on her, and she would be dearly loved by her husband. The fourth, Yongok was the least attractive of the lot, but she was a good homemaker, kind and frugal, so she could manage even the poorest household gracefully. The youngest, Yonghay, couldn't even sleep without her mother by her side, but she was cheerful and cute, soft as a ripe pear and would be well suited to be the youngest daughter-in-law in a wealthy household.

But when Yongsook was widowed, Mrs. Kim's illusions were shattered. "How the first daughter turns out will affect the futures of the rest," said Chongim who had two sons. This was a blow to Punshi.

"Is Mr. Kim in?" asked a man with a deep voice. Yongbin, reading on the floor, raised her eyes from the book.

"Oh! When did you get home?" asked the dark-skinned man in overalls, who looked rather stubborn. Wiping the sweat from his brow on the towel tucked into his waistband, he walked up to Yongbin.

"Day before yesterday," she said, closing her book.

"My father's in his study."

"And your mother?"

"Shopping. . ."

"Yomoon!" he called the girl who ran household errands.

"She went with Mom. Can I get you something?"

"Just some water, thank you."

"I'll get it."

"No, no. I can do it myself."

Keydo Soh, who was in charge of Songsu Kim's fishing fleet, was already lowering the bucket into the well when Yongbin got up. Formerly, his father had worked for Mr. Kim, but he was not tough enough to handle the fishermen, so he resigned, and his son was put in charge. Mr. Kim trusted Keydo, regarding him as a sincere, brave man and a good leader, and let him manage the whole Kim fleet. Songsu was the money behind the operation, but he didn't know how to run it. Keydo, a graduate of Tongyong Fishing School, had the knowledge and ambition to become a fleet captain. He gulped from the bucket and began washing his face.

"Look who's here, sailor boy!" said Yongnan, coming from the backyard. He stopped washing and glared at her, his eyebrows arched. Without responding, he dried his face with the towel, tucked it back into his belt, and went to Mr. Kim's office.

"You have a nasty mouth," Yongbin scolded her sister.

"Well, he *is* just a sailor boy, isn't he?" said Yongnan, hoisting her skirt and sitting on the floor.

"Who might just smack you in the face."

"Oh, come on, he wouldn't dare."

"If he does, it'll be your tough luck. Do you think he'll treat you decently because you're the boss's daughter, when you talk to him like that?"

"If he does, I'll break his neck. Besides, he's too arrogant."

"Yah, you will! Who's going to marry a girl with a mouth on her like yours?"

"Don't you worry about it, okay? Just get yourself married," Yongnan advised cynically, as if she were talking to a younger sister, not an older one.

"I don't know what to say to you...."

"Well, Keydo shouldn't order Handol around," Yongnan said. Yongbin returned to her book. Handol was Sogwon's son, and Yongnan and Handol were very close, being the same age.

"It's cool in here. I can feel a breeze," said Yongnan, lying down. Her small feet looked pretty.

The two sisters were strikingly different. Yongbin had a wide forehead and large, cool, thoughtful eyes. Her high cheekbones gave her a look of both pride and intelligence. Yongnan, on the other hand, was simply beautiful. She had a perfectly sculpted nose and fair, flawless skin. While Yongbin's cheekbones were large, Yongnan's were soft and pretty. Yongnan's eyes changed constantly — first innocent as an angel, then again fiercely instinctive as a wild animal.

When she was a child, Yongbin began attending Sunday school, and was dearly loved by the British missionaries Reverend Hiller and Miss Kate, who lived in a red brick house not far from Kim's. They regarded Yongbin as a child whom God had blessed with the gift of intelligence. Every morning and evening they went past Kim's to the church or their missions. Thin Reverend Hiller, perpetually in a meditative mood, walked slowly. Heavy-set Miss Kate strolled in a *hanbok* on nice spring days.

Acting on their advice and counsel, Mr. Kim sent Yongbin to a junior college after she graduated from the missionary school. Yongsook learned Chinese at home, but before she mastered the language, she got married. Since Yongnan didn't care to study, even her knowledge of her own language was shaky. When Yongok finished elementary school, she didn't want any more education, so she stayed home and did housework. Yongbin was determined to take responsibility for Yonghay's education.

Yongbin was the *de facto* son of the Kim family. Songsu consulted her on family matters and took her advice seriously, although he did not discuss them with his wife. Yongbin had become a Christian, and therefore, was familiar with Christian culture and thought. However, of late, she had begun to have doubts — though not serious enough to affect her basic beliefs. When it came to Christianity, Yongok was more sincere than Yongbin. Mrs. Kim and Yongsook preferred going to the Buddhist temple, but they were, strictly speaking, not believers; they were simply superstitious. When they were concerned about the future, they went to the temple or saw a shaman. Mr. Kim and Yongnan didn't believe in anything. They weren't interested in going to the church or temple; they simply didn't care.

Presently, Keydo came out of Mr. Kim's office. Yongnan glanced at him and got up slowly.

"Is your mother home yet?" he asked Yongbin.

"Not yet."

"Well, then, I'll go."

"Why don't you stay for dinner?" Yongbin asked, but Keydo stepped out without responding to her invitation.

With a mocking laugh, Yongnan said, "Well, then, I'll go," imitating the sound of his voice.

"Oh! You are so-o nasty," shouted Yongbin, whacking her sister with the book.

A Lone Tree

When Yongbin and Yongok returned from the Sunday church services, they saw that their eldest sister, Yongsook, was visiting. They found her chatting with their mother, eating melons.

"Hi Yongsook, you're here!"

"Well, since you don't come to see me, I guess I have no choice but to come to see you," she said in a snide voice, though she hadn't seen her sisters for months. Yongsook, wearing a sky blue fine-combed skirt and bodice, looked fresh as a fruit tree in full bloom. Her almond eyes had boldness and daring about them, but in contrast, she whined when she spoke.

"I was going to visit Aunt Chongim and then stop by your house tomorrow," Yongbin answered sweetly.

61

Mrs. Kim chose a sweet yellow melon from the plate. "Tayoon came by a while ago."

"Oh, he did. When did he get back?"

"I think he said. . .the day before yesterday. . .Come and have some melons, you two."

Tayoon was the girls' cousin, Chungku Kim's second son, a student at Aoyama Institute in Japan, and home on vacation. Yongbin and Yongok sat down and helped themselves to the melons Mrs. Kim was peeling and slicing.

"Did you bring these melons?" Yongbin asked.

"I wouldn't bother. You have never even brought me so much as a needle from Seoul," Yongsook said pointedly. Yongbin didn't mind.

"Tayoon brought them," Mrs. Kim said, as she continued peeling, glancing back and forth between Yongsook and Yongbin. Yongsook was rude to Yongbin. However, she usually ignored her elder sister.

Punshi seemed like a mother bird feeding her brood.

Yongsook pulled a white linen handkerchief out of her sleeve and dried her hands. She wore a green jade ring on one of her long, slim fingers, matching earpick, and jade hairpin through the shiny bun at the nape of her neck. Having finished the three-year mourning for her husband the previous year, she was very much the merry widow now, a zest for life clearly seen on the set of her thin, pursed lips.

"Tayoon brought melons? Come on, that's not a man's gift," Yongsook said finding fault with him, dabbing her lips and re-placing her handkerchief.

Yongok, who had said nothing so far, stopped chewing and frowned, "You are always criticizing somebody or something."

"Oh, shut up."

"Mother, where's Yongnan?" Yongbin changed the subject to quiet Yongsook. Yongbin did not like Yongsook, whom she felt was bossy, even though she was her eldest sister.

"She said she needed some powder. I think that's where she went."

"Today, girls are growing up too fast. When I was your age, there was no such thing even as face cream. We were lucky to get soap to wash our faces. Now," Yongsook said, "women even go to college when some guys can't afford to," aiming the comment directly at Yongbin, who was studying.

"When did you ever wash your precious face with soap?" Yongbin remarked.

This effectively silenced Yongsook, who had done everything to be as beautiful as she could herself, though she was perfectly willing to criticize her sisters for doing the same. In fact, she insisted on ground mung beans wrapped in cotton for her face washing. Perhaps the reason her skin still looked silky and soft.

"Yongbin, father wants to see you," said Yonghay, who had stopped in his study when she returned from school.

"Did you want me, Dad?" Yongbin asked as she entered.

"Yes, please come in."

Yongbin raised the bamboo blind and went in. Her father was playing checkers alone.

"Have a seat," he said, putting the checkers into a bowl, setting the checkerboard aside and looking at Yongbin. Her father was fifty-two, but looked a good deal younger, in a linen summer suit, vest and gray socks tied with silk foot bands. He seemed dignified and serious to his daughter.

Mr. Kim took out a cigarette, lit up slowly, and drew deeply on it. Uncomfortable with the subject he was about to bring up, he smoked half of it, pulled the ashtray toward him, stubbed it out nervously, and looked at his daughter.

"Are you seeing Hongsop in Seoul?"

"Sometimes...." Yongbin answered, blushing. Hongsop was a law student in junior college and was Yongbin's boyfriend.

"Uhm ...."

"What do you think of him?" Mr. Kim asked after a long pause, looking away from his daughter.

"...."

"Have you thought about marrying him?"

"I think he's nice," she said. Mr. Kim stared at her. It was not easy to read his face; she couldn't tell whether he approved him or not.

"Mr. Chong has proposed marriage between the two of you. I have no objection to Hongsop, but I don't like his father, so I didn't agree."

Cookju Chong was Hongsop's father and Mr. Kim's business partner. Though they were partners, Songsu Kim did not consider him a friend.

Cookju was the son of the woman from Hadong who worked in the Kim household when he was very little. He grew up poor and began working as a potter. He managed a fishery, but no one knew how he got enough money to invest in one. However, the business prospered. When he sold the fishery at a handsome profit, he started a brewery and began making high-interest loans, becoming one of Tongyong's millionaires. Being pro-Japan, he was quite influential.

"Obviously, the reason I bring up your marriage is Yongnan."

"Of course."

"Since you are in college, it's all right if you marry late, but Yongnan is due to be getting married, and you, being the older, must marry first."

"But I have to finish school."

"Are you saying she must wait till you graduate?"

"Just let her get married."

"I thought about that...but could you get married and continue to study?" Mr. Kim asked her, gauging her reaction to the idea. Cicadas screamed in the tree outside the gate.

"I can't...."

"...."

"I can only consider marriage when I graduate."

"Well, I'll leave it up to you. Now, about Yongnan...."

"...."

"I've decided to marry her to Keydo."

"What?!" Yongbin was obviously surprised. "That's why Mr. Soh was here."

"I wanted to talk to him about it."

Yongbin could barely restrain her laughter when she thought of Yongnan's disrespect to him earlier.

"Now that his mother has passed away, leaving him younger brothers to take care of, he needs a wife."

"I seriously doubt Yongnan can manage that poor household."

"Keydo will be a perfect husband for her. She needs a strong, tough man."

Regardless of whether he was good for her or she for him, Yongbin thought they would be an odd couple in any case. Her mother said there was no man in town who would make a good husband for the beautiful Yongnan. She was not lacking for proposals, but Mrs. Kim was not happy with any of them.

"Does Mom know this?"

"It is not important whether your mother knows or not...."

Mrs. Kim's status would not allow her to interfere with her husband's plans, which made Yongbin feel sorry for her mother. She liked and respected her father, but she was not pleased with the way her father ignored her mother as if she were a stranger — or didn't exist.

"Mother will be very disappointed," she said, trying to imply this. However, Mr. Kim didn't respond and Yongbin didn't persist.

"As long as Keydo works for me, Yongnan won't starve. And even if he quits and goes to work for somebody else, he won't make her life difficult."

"But what about Yongnan? How does she feel?" Yongbin was not against the marriage. She simply felt that her sister's feelings should be taken into consideration in the matter.

"In your case, you can decide who you will marry. Yongnan is not capable of making such a decision herself. She will marry the man I choose."

Yongbin could not argue with his dictum. She rose and returned to the courtyard. A gust of wind shook the leaves of the lone banana tree growing there. She watched a bug making its way slowly up one of the leaves.

"Just like my parents," she thought. "My father, a lone tree and mom like a beetle hiding under one of its leaves, always on the verge of slipping off."

"Yongbin's been in there too long. Father sees her every day and still thinks he needs to talk to her. Why today?" Yongsook said when she saw her sister come out of her father's study. "I come all the way over here to visit, and he doesn't even look at me when I greet him!"

From childhood on, Mr. Kim hadn't liked his first daughter; she'd always been a thorn in his side. He scolded none of his other daughters, only Yongsook. He either called her "coquette" or ignored her. Oddly enough, he didn't have such strongly negative feelings about Yongnan, who was rude as a tomboy.

"A personality clash. They just aren't going to get along," said Chongim, when Mrs. Kim complained about her husband treating Yongsook like she wasn't even his.

Predictably, the more Mr. Kim disregarded Yongsook, the more protective Mrs. Kim became of her. For her wedding, her mother bought her so many things for her trousseau without Songsu's knowledge that she couldn't even get it all in one chest of drawers. She made one hundred and fifty pairs of fine cotton socks, several comforters — one hand-made quilt, one plain light cotton, one queen-size brocade, one damask silk, one twin-size brocade, and two of ramie for summer. Clothes filled a zelkova wood chest the groom's family had sent, two persimmon wood chests her mother had bought, and the rest of her things had to be packed separately.

"We're lucky not to have to buy presents for the groom's parents, since they are dead," said Mrs. Kim repeatedly, for her husband's benefit.

"A big beautiful trousseau doesn't make a happy marriage," said a jealous woman who attended the wedding. But what surprised the sewing women, who had made most of it, was that Yongsook took everything of her own from her parents' house, even spools of thread with very little left on them.

"The grass will grow in her yard," the wags said, implying she would have no friends because she thought of no one but herself.

For his part, Songsu Kim couldn't find a single good quality in his eldest daughter.

"You should be relieved now that I'm out of here," Yongsook told her mother on the day of her wedding.

Yongsook asked Yongbin when she sat down again, "So what did father have to say?"

"What?" Yongbin replied, deep in thought.

"Stop acting like you're deaf. I asked you why father wanted to see you."

Because she had decided not to say anything — even to her mother — regarding Yongnan, Yongbin lied, "Ah...he asked me to quit school...."

"Well, he may be planning for you to marry." Yongbin didn't respond and Mrs. Kim gave her a worried look. "You look ready to get married, yourself, but I wonder what man would stand your skyrocketing pride." Yongbin didn't respond. "Well, Yongbin, didn't you say you were going to Uncle Chungku's house?" Yongsook asked.

"Yes."

"I'll go with you. I have a favor to ask him."

"All right."

Yongsook explained, "Mom, I'm going to ask him to make me a chest."

"You have so many already! What have you done with them?"

"Not enough."

"I am not sure your uncle will be willing to do it."

"I intend to pay him."

"Perhaps if he were younger. But even then he turned down jobs if he didn't like the work, the person...."

"No harm in asking, though. I know he's retired, but I hope he will consider doing just one more piece for me."

Mrs. Kim prepared a present of her best cherry liquor and the finest shrimp and mackerel in her pantry for her daughters to take to their uncle's home.

An Artisan

Chungku Lee, Ponghee's son, lived with his wife in a small, tile-roofed house outside the East Gate of Tongyong. Their elder son, Chongyoon, graduated from Taegu Medical School the previous spring. He was now working at the provincial hospital in Chinju.

Though Chungku and his wife were lonely and sad at never having had a daughter, they got along very well, loving and respecting one another. While she cooked, her husband chopped firewood. They always took their simple meals together. This made Punshi Kim, who had never eaten at the same table with her husband, jealous and embarrassed.

"A marriage made in heaven," Punshi often remarked, "I would give anything to have that kind of relationship with my husband. For even a single day."

Chungku had learned woodworking because his family was poor. Even before the Japanese annexed Korea in 1910, public officials sold government posts. Realizing this, and unwilling to compromise, the stubborn Chungku stopped studying. In those days, it was common for the sons of impecunious scholars like Chungku to learn woodworking in their spare time.

It was true that he received financial support from his mother's family. It was likewise true that the straightforward, independent Chungku hated taking it, but he simply could not have educated his own two sons without Songsu's help. He could not earn enough to pay college tuition, no matter how many hours he worked.

Chungku was an extremely talented craftsman. People said that he was far more than a simple furniture-maker — he was an artist. His black lacquer and abalone, and zelkova wood chests combined beauty and utility and became well-loved heirlooms. He was so particular about every detail of the process that he worked alone, even without an apprentice. It took him forever to finish a piece. This, of course, made his work so expensive that only the rich could afford it. In addition, he never took orders from people with bad manners. Sometimes customers told him how they wanted the work done, but he always did it his own way.

That wealthy, powerful men and women did not like Chungku should come as no surprise to anyone. They considered it very pretentious for a mere furniture-maker to be so arrogant. The wife of Cookju Chong, one of the wealthiest in town, once came to order a dining table. As he thought her insolent and disrespectful, he refused to acknowledge her presence by saying a single word.

He developed elegant expression in clothing and in personal belongings as well. When he made a fan or an ashtray for himself, it was artistic and practical. Even when he split firewood he made a neat pile. Though coal was hard to come by, he used it to save wood. He developed a novel way of making charcoal briquettes: mixing a little water with coal dust, pressed the paste into hollow lengths of bamboo. Then he dried and cut them open, ending up with neat cylindrical bars.

Chungku's taste in clothing was as refined as the objects of art he created. When his widowed mother died, he wore mourning clothes for three years. His long ramie coat was always neat. He made a cone-shaped hat to wear over his cloth one. Everyone admired him striding along the street in that coat and hat, covering his face with a fan. He was quite handsome, but in those days it was rare for men to pay much attention to fashion, so he automatically attracted a lot of attention. Before he went out, Chungku spent a lot of time in front of the mirror. He twisted his hat string until it was shiny and replaced the paper of his mourning shoes whenever it became soiled.

"How come an old man like you is paying so much attention to his appearance?" his wife teased him, "Going to meet your girlfriend?"

"Don't make fun of me," he said, amused.

Yongsook and Yongbin passed the police station and had just reached the East Gate.

"Wait a minute, would you? My skirt is slipping," Yongsook said, handing the bundle to Yongbin, who held the wine bottle in one hand and a bowl-shaped bundle in the other. When she arranged her skirt, Yongsook asked for it back.

"What's this?" Yongbin inquired.

"This — a rice bowl."

"A rice bowl?"

"I asked mother if I could have it. Isn't it beautiful?"

Yongbin was flabbergasted. She knew that Yongsook was greedy and asked for whatever she wanted when she came home, but Yongbin found it difficult to believe she'd asked for a rice bowl.

"Yongbin."

"...."

"Have you heard the rumor?"

"What rumor?"

Yongsook hesitated. "It's so unbelievably strange, I can hardly bear to speak the words with my own mouth. I tried to tell mother, but I just couldn't do it."

"Regarding Yongnan. They say she is haunted by a virgin-phantom."

"Oh, come on. A virgin-phantom?" Yongbin laughed dismissively. "There's no such thing as a virgin-phantom."

"Wrong. There *is* such a thing."

"What does it have to do with Yongnan?"

"They say she jumps the garden wall and goes up the hill behind the house every night."

"Oh stop repeating nonsense, please!" Yongbin tried to ignore her, but Yongsook went on.

"Look, that man is staring at you. He thinks you are very beautiful. Come on, let's hurry up." Yongbin knew the comment would distract Yongsook and get her to stop talking about Yongnan. Yongbin smiled bitterly at her little ruse.

Chungku's house could be seen in the distance. Beanstalks with bright purple flowers covered the garden wall. Beans covered it every year from spring to fall.

Yongbin called for Chungku's wife as she pushed the gate open. "Aunt Chongim."

"Who's there?" Chongim dropped the pestle in the mortar and stood up to greet her nieces. "Oh, it's you, Yongbin!" With her fair eyes and curly hair, she looked beautiful in spite of her age.

"Yongsook, you came along too. What brings you here?"

"Is uncle home?"

"Yes, he's in the shop."

"He's working these days then?"

"Of course. You know how he is. Once he gets going on something, there is no stopping him."

Yongsook looked into the mortar and pestle as Yongbin and Chongim spoke.

"Aunt, what are you making?"

"I'm grinding pine needles and raw beans."

"What for?"

"A special food your uncle likes."

"Health food?"

"Well, he says it helps him maintain energy and stamina. Why don't you go to the shop?"

"I'll go see him." Yongbin went to the workshop next to the barn.

"Hello, Uncle."

"Hi, Yongbin."

He raised his head from his work. His hair was cut like a Buddhist monk now, and his thick beard had begun to turn gray.

"You are certainly hard at it, Uncle Chungku," Yongsook observed, peering over Yongbin's shoulder.

"Yes," he answered, without stopping. Wood glue was melting on the hot plate.

"Why don't you take it easy on a hot day like this?"

"I work for my pleasure. When did you come down from Seoul?"

"A week ago."

"Really?" He applied glue to a piece of neatly planed wood.

"Why don't you go have a seat to the living room? I'll come as soon as I finish here."

When they sat down, Chongim brought them cool drinks, saying, "The water from our well is very cool. Try it."

"Is Tayoon out? I missed him when he dropped by this morning."

"He was at your house? I don't know where he is now. He's not home either."

"Aunt," said Yongsook, "I think you are going to have a fine bean crop this year."

"I figure about a hundred pounds."

"That much!" Yongsook marveled, her eyes wide.

"What do you do with all those beans?"

"Boil them till they shed their skins, then pound them to use for rice cake topping on New Year's Day. It has a softer color and a sweeter taste than mung bean topping. I also use them in soup and porridge, especially in the summer when we have no appetites."

"May I have some in the fall?"

"Sure. I'll give you some."

"How do you manage to keep the house this clean, Aunt?" Yongsook said glancing around.

"Well, the children are all gone now. That's how."

"Just look at the shine on this floor."

Yongbin was not interested in discussing the specifics of keeping a house, and Chongim was kind enough to ask her how she had been getting on in Seoul — what kind of food they ate and about life there.

"Yongsook, I hear you have become a Buddhist," she said to bring Yongsook back into the conversation.

"No, I just go to the temple and pray. I don't understand it."

"I think I should become a Buddhist and prepare myself for the next world...." said Chongim.

"Yes, Aunt, it is high time for you to get some religion, now that Chongyoon is out of college."

"You're right."

"Isn't he going to get married?"

"It's up to him. These days sons don't do what their parents say. I hear he has a girlfriend in Taegu."

"I bet he makes lots of money."

"Not yet. He pays Tayoon's tuition."

"But he will, though. Doctors are always rich."

"And how is Tonghoon?"

"A weakling is a difficult child to raise."

"I know what you mean, but an only child is always that way. Now, you two sit here and chat while I fix dinner."

"No, Aunt. We really have to leave now," said Yongbin standing up and heading for the door.

"I won't hear of it. Sit right down there and I'll be back in a minute."

Fanning herself vigorously Yongsook said, "If she had a maid to help her, I would feel much more comfortable."

Chongim served the dinner and though she hadn't had time to shop, there was an array of side dishes, pickled vegetables, salted and dried fish. Her kimchi looked fresh and delicious.

"Honey, dinner is ready," Chongim shouted to her husband.

"Okay, I'm coming!"

Having washed his hands, Chungku arrived, stretching his aching back.

"Yongbin brought us this," she said as she poured the cherry wine for her husband.

"Uncle, I see you are about finished with the project you are working on — are you going to start another soon?" Yongsook began sounding her uncle out after dinner.

"Who is it for?"

"It's for me."

"No, I am far too busy to start anything new now."

"I am not in a hurry; I can wait."

"Is your father at home most of the time these days?" Chungku responded with a question as he did not want to argue with his niece.

"Yes. He rarely goes out," Yongsook replied, spitefully, becoming red-faced with anger.

Chungku smoked an after-dinner cigarette, and left without saying another word. Yongsook, quite angry at being spurned by her Uncle, suggested they leave.

Outside, unable to contain her anger, Yongsook railed at her sister, "He acted as if I asked him to do it free. He ought to remember that his precious sons would never have gotten near a university campus if it weren't for father."

But Yongbin was brooding over the rumor about Yongnan. It was not uncommon to hear that this or that one was "haunted," so that was easy enough to laugh off, but had someone actually seen her go over the wall? On her way up the hill? Walking there? That was quite a different matter.

"I'll ask Yongok," she thought.

After Yongbin parted from her sister, she walked along the road, passed the police station and Pongnae Cinema. There, Yongbin saw Tayoon coming toward her.

"Tayoon!" she hollered. Surprised, he didn't notice her until they were almost face-to-face in the street.

"Yongbin?"

"You have your glasses on and you still didn't recognize me?!"

"Oh, I was thinking about something else...."

"I am coming from your house."

"Is that so? I was over there, but you weren't home."

Tayoon removed his glasses, wiped them and put them back on. He squinted at her across his sharp nose. He had a bush of hair, now it was neatly combed back.

"I was at church. And where have you been?"

"I got a haircut, bought a book, and met a friend," he smiled shyly.

"Why don't you come with me?" she asked.

"I'll stop by tomorrow. I have to meet a friend this evening."

"That friend?"

"No, no," said Tayoon, flustered and avoiding her eyes. Yongbin smiled as if she were reading Tayoon like a large-print primer. "Well then, I'll see you tomorrow," he said, rushing off abruptly.

"Tayoon," she called after him, "don't do anything I wouldn't do!"

He didn't answer her.

When Yongbin arrived home, it was already dusk. She asked Yongok to take a walk with her, a pretense for her real intention, to discuss Yongnan. Yongok was reluctant initially, but finally confided in Yongbin.

A Love Affair

Crickets chirped loudly in the tall grass. Blue moonlight shone on the kimchi jars in the kitchen garden.

"Mom, tell me a story, please," Yonghay begged as she lolled against her mother's arm.

"I don't know any good stories."

"It doesn't have to be a good one, Mom. Any old story will do. I can't fall asleep."

"Stop bothering Mom, Yonghay," Yongbin told her youngest sister, "you're acting like a baby."

"I bet you wanted to hear stories when you were my age!"

"Okay, okay. I'll tell you one," said Mrs. Kim, "Once upon a time, a man with a squigamarig goes to the whirligig jig."

"No, no, not that one!"

"All right, then how about this one, and if you don't like it, I'm finished. I don't want to hear any more of your whining." She began singing:

> In a forest of young pines,
> Behind the curtain of her skirt
> A young lady was lying, lying
> With a baby on her belly, belly.
> Is she fast asleep?
> Is she weeping or is she dying?
> Doesn't know her husband has come
> In the light of the bright moon
> Above the mountain.
> My mother won't show me the way
> To my love, but the light of the bright moon does.

"What is that song, Mom?"

"Well, once upon a time, a young man went up to Seoul to take the state examination. His wife was pregnant; her belly was round and swollen as the baby was almost due. Just as she went into labor, her foul mother-in-law ordered her to bring a pail of water from the well on the hill. The mother-in-law insisted that the baby was not ready to come, so the girl had no choice but to go after the water. Half way up the mountain, she draped her skirt between two pine trees and gave birth to the baby there. When he came back from Seoul, the young man asked where his wife was. His mother answered she went to fetch a pail of water. By the light of the moon, the young man set out in search of his wife. He found the white skirt fluttering between the trees, and behind it, his dead wife and the frozen baby on her stomach . . . In the old days, there were couples who loved one another very much."

Yonghay was already snoring.

"Mom, is that the *only* story you know," Yongbin said, smiling. Mrs. Kim used to tell it to her when she was a little girl.

"It isn't a story, it is a song. In the old days, people were so simple and sincere."

"But weren't you, Mom?"

"I never had the chance to be."

They were interrupted by the sound of Songsu coughing in his room.

"Well, I'd better get to bed. Good night, mother."

"G'night, dear."

Yongbin went to her room across the backyard. Yongnan was already in bed, and Yongok was embroidering.

"Yongok, turn off the light and go to bed. I can't fall asleep with the light on," Yongnan complained, but Yongok threaded the needle, ignoring her sister.

"Do you have cotton in your ears, or what?" Yongnan jumped up and switched off the light. Shafts of blue moonlight shone through the shade over the door frame.

Yongok put away her embroidery hoop, pulled on her nightgown, lay down, and fell asleep quickly. Yongbin, with her day clothes on, lay down next to Yongok and listened for her breathing to become regular. Yongnan and Yongbin both closed their eyes and feigned sleep.

The clock in Mrs. Kim's room chimed eleven.

Yongnan raised her upper body silently and stared at Yongbin and Yongok, listening for their breathing. Coughing was heard from Songsu's room. Yongnan snuggled into the pillow and sighed deeply.

Again, the coughing came from Songsu's room.

"Why is he still up in the middle of the night — hunting phantoms?" Yongnan sighed. Yongbin pressed her eyes closed and smiled.

The coughing stopped. Yongnan put a white linen blouse over her slip, raised the shade at the door and tiptoed out of the room. Yongbin got up stealthily and followed her sister. She stopped next to the back gate.

"Yongnan!" Yongnan spun around and the moonlight shone in her face with an almost audible gasp.

"Where are you going?"

"None of your damn business," she hissed, spitting like a cornered cat.

"Stop it, ple-ase," Yongnan couldn't tell if Yongbin was teasing her or trying to persuade her not to go.

Yongnan addressed Yongbin as if she had forgotten the respect she owed an older sister. "You sly little fox! Why are you following me at this hour of the night? It's time you were in bed. What are you — a virgin-phantom or something?" Nevertheless, Yongbin couldn't help smiling at being called a virgin-phantom.

"Please, let's go back to bed. What would neighbors say if they knew about you and Handol?"

"What do I care?" In the shadow of her eyebrows, Yongnan's eyes were dark; her breasts rose and fell as she panted.

"Do you intend to marry Handol, a servant?"

"I didn't say I wanted to *marry* him, for god's sake."

"Then why are you meeting him all the time?"

"None of your damn business. You're not your sister's keeper!"

"What do you think father will say if he finds out?"

"...."

"Aren't you ashamed?"

"Hey, who are you to point the fingers at me? You go out with Hongsop."

"Oh God, I might as well talk to a deaf-mute."

Yongbin was in a quandary. Yongnan refused to listen. All she could think about was escaping Yongbin and meeting Handol. Still facing her sister, she sidled toward the gate as she spoke and fiddled with the latch, trying to open it without looking.

"I have no choice but to tell father, you know. And he will kill Handol. Don't you even feel sorry for him?"

"If you tell father, I will pull your tongue right out of your mouth, do you hear me?" Yongnan snarled, then opened the gate and fled.

"Yongnan!"

Her white skirt fluttered in the moonlight, exposing her white legs as she ran.

Yongbin collapsed on the stone step and stared at the sky. If she tried to stop Yongnan, she would wake the rest of the family. Try as she might, she could not control her sister. Suddenly she heard someone coughing. Surprised, Yongbin bolted up and found herself face to face with her father, a walking stick in his hand.

"Oh, Father!"

"What are you doing here?"

"It's too hot, and I just wanted some fresh air."

Without a word, Songsu stared at the half-open gate.

"He knows," she thought, studying his eyes shining with fury.

"Go back to your room and go to sleep," he ordered, his voice calm as still water.

"Good night, Father," she said, but he didn't answer. Instead, he pushed the gate open with the stick.

"Oh, dear God," Yongbin thought, hiding herself and watching him head out in the direction Yongnan had gone, brandishing the stick.

Yongbin followed him, as he stomped off through the pine grove using the stick to keep branches from hitting him in the face.

Songsu stopped within sight of grassy knoll between a grave mound and a boulder. Mottled moonlight shone through the trees. Yongbin hid herself among the trees and watched. Her father covered his eyes with one hand, staggered back and sat down on the ground. Yongbin snuck forward, and strained to see, but then covered her eyes with both hands.

"Oh, no!" She felt so dizzy she almost fainted.

In the bright moonlight, Yongnan and Handol grappled on the ground like a pair of wild animals, without shame or fear.

"How horrible!" Yongbin wanted to run, but she couldn't move, as if her feet had taken root where she stood. The blood rushed to her head.

Exhausted from the exertion, Handol and Yongnan looked at one another for a long time. Then they began pulling on their clothes, discarded with abandon and strewn by the rock. Sweating heavily, Songsu sprang on them.

"You bastard!" he hollered as he raised the stick and began hitting Handol.

"Ai-ee!" he screamed in pain, protecting his head with his arms and hands. Yongnan ran down the hill barefoot, mad as a tiger, her white slip slapping at her calves.

Songsu's stick broke in half after a few blows. Handol, barely able to endure the pain, finally raised his bloody head and said,

"Spare me, Master. I deeply regret what I have done," and then began to cry.

Songsu glared down at him. An owl hooted in the distance. "Leave this village and never come back again."

Yongbin got home before Songsu to find Yongnan, whom she figured had run away, sitting in the bedroom scowling.

"You bitch! I am going to kill you with my own hands."

"You are just disgraceful." Yongbin said, pulling out of her sister's grasp, but Yongnan only attacked with new ferocity.

"You two-faced rat-fink bitch, Yongbin! I *know* you sleep with Hongsop. Why do you fault me?"

Yongbin slapped her sister's face. Yongnan screamed and attacked, biting Yongbin on the arm.

"What on earth are you two doing?" asked Mrs. Kim as she rushed into their room. This racket has awakened the sewing woman and Yomoon. Yongok rose, knelt by her bed and began praying and crying.

"You are going to wake your father, carrying on in the middle of the night like this. Yongbin, what is the matter?"

She did not answer, only got the iodine bottle and painted the bite on her arm. Yongnan still hadn't calmed down, but sat cursing breathlessly.

Other Lovers

Handol disappeared. Yongnan was insanely and savagely angry. Songsu beat her. Mrs. Kim lamented and said she wanted to die with Yongnan, but nothing affected the situation. Whenever Songsu was out of the house, Yongnan attacked Yongbin, scratching and biting her like a wildcat.

Yongnan seemed to harbor no regrets over the incident. She never missed a meal, and vented her fury on Yongbin every chance she got as she remained convinced Yongbin had reported her to their father.

"I can't kill her, and I can't change her," Punshi Kim sobbed. "I am certainly being punished for what I have done in a previous life...."

The Kim family had to ignore the shame they felt in front of the neighbors, but the hardest part was Yongnan herself. She was so completely remorseless and unapologetic and there was no point in saying anything.

Yongbin decided to return to Seoul even though summer vacation was not yet over. After packing, she visited Reverend Hiller and Miss Kate. She greeted the Reverend and found Miss Kate reading in a rattan chair in the garden. Sunset glowed in the western sky.

"Well hello, Yongbin," said Miss Kate warmly and closed the book. Her blue dress emphasized the blue of her eyes. Her skin was rosy and her hair pale. She was past thirty and still single.

Yongbin seated herself across from Miss Kate and informed her, "Miss Kate, I'm going back to Seoul tomorrow."

"But why, Yongbin? Vacation isn't over for...."

"...."

"What happened to your face? You are full of scratches."

Yongbin smiled bitterly and tried to cover her face with her hands.

"Yongbin, what is happening?"

"...."

Miss Kate knew something serious had happened, but decided not to pressure her.

"Miss Kate," Yongbin asked in English, "may I ask you something?"

"Why, yes, of course."

"I am certain you have heard about my sister, Yongnan." Miss Kate said nothing, only listened. "What do you think of her?"

"...."

"Will God ever forgive her?"

Considering Yongbin for a long moment, Miss Kate said, "Sure he will. I know many such women who are sorry for their sins, have reformed their lives and become good Christians. Let's pray that Yongnan will." She closed her eyes as if thinking deeply.

The maid brought two cold drinks. Yongbin was thirsty, but she only took a little sip.

"Miss Kate, only those with consciences can repent, but Yongnan doesn't seem to have one. She doesn't feel guilty or sad. She doesn't even seem distressed. Never cries."

"You mean she's not ashamed or sad?" said Miss Kate, frowning.

"No, she seems to live in her own little world. She doesn't appear to have any emotion but anger, rather acts like an animal, furious that a meal has been snatched out of its mouth. I suppose all human beings were like that in the beginning," said Yongbin with great difficulty. "She doesn't seem to know shame...or even love, only instinct. Like a child, she wants what she wants." Yongbin, as a young single woman, found it painful to express these ideas, and furthermore, she was not a good speaker to begin with.

"This is difficult to discuss, isn't it....?" Miss Kate could see Yongbin was embarrassed, but had thought she was open enough to talk about sex.

"Yongnan would have done the same thing with any man. She just happened to pick Handol. That's just the way she is."

"When God created us, He gave us a body and soul. But she seems lacking one; honestly, she doesn't seem to understand vice or shame. She doesn't think about love, Miss Kate, but you know, what's odd, at the same time she's pure as an angel," she said, trembling with emotion that grew as she spoke. "I wonder why. I have never thought of her as evil in spite of her indecency. Maybe it's because God has endowed her with great beauty. One should be able to tell the difference between good and evil, but with her I hardly can. She has become a sinner in God's eyes, yet it doesn't even faze her. She is totally unaware of it, like lilies of the field, the grass or the weeds. I suspect she has no sense of awe or the power of God." Yongbin was overcome as she spoke. "But how could God possibly punish her if He gave her a body and instinct rather than a body and soul like the rest of us? Everybody upbraids her, father beats her, but she doesn't suffer because she doesn't see what she has done as evil. Only father, mother, and we — her sisters — suffer." Too uneasy to look at Miss Kate, Yongbin stared at the ground.

"Yongbin, your faith in God is wavering."

"You're right, Miss Kate. I am so confused," Yongbin said, but could not look at her.

"Your faith is being tested. God often tests us this way. In the end, I believe your faith will be even stronger." Yongbin still could not look at her.

The sun had set. Yongbin said good-bye and left Miss Kate. As she walked from the garden, she could feel Miss Kate staring at her back. She hadn't intended to talk about Yongnan to Miss Kate. "I was too upset," she thought.

Her conversation with Miss Kate did not clear her dense fog of doubt she felt, but it did help her to calm down. She walked down the path through the woods. Though fall had not yet arrived, it was very dark and the wind was cool.

"Ah!" she exclaimed, covering her eyes. Someone shone a flashlight in her face.

"Hey, Yongbin!"

"Oh goodness, you frightened me!"

"Ha, ha, ha...I'm sorry, really sorry...." Hongsop laughed.

"I stopped at your house. They said you went to visit Miss Kate, so I came to meet you." Hongsop said, turning off the flashlight.

"Why are you turning it off? The path is rocky here."

"Let's sit down for a while," he said and picked a spot under a tree.

"No, let's go home and talk."

"Why?"

"You don't need to know why."

"Oo-oo, I'm scared of you."

"I'm scared, too. Scared people will say the elder sister is haunted by a virgin-phantom as well."

"Come on, sit down. There is no moon tonight, nobody will see." Yongbin sat down.

"Are you really going back to Seoul tomorrow?"

"Yes."

"Why? Summer vacation isn't over yet."

"I want the chaos at home to stop. When I am gone, Yongnan will return to her senses."

"What? Brave girl, have you given up on your sister?" Yongbin and Hongsop had been friends for so long that they no longer used honorific language when they spoke.

When he was younger, Hongsop had loved literature. In middle school he once wrote Yongbin a poem. In it, he described her as a brave and spirited woman warrior. Yongbin liked it, though she had to admit it sounded a little childish. Still, he occasionally called her "brave girl" as he had in the poem.

"I ran into Tayoon today."

"What did he have to say for himself?"

"Nothing."

"You know he hates me."

It was not true that Tayoon simply hated Hongsop; he actively loathed and despised him. Yongbin knew it. Tayoon called him an ambitious coward and felt the combination would lead him to betray what few ideals he had.

Yongbin had once protested to her cousin. "Tayoon, you are unfairly prejudiced against Hongsop because of his father. He himself is quite innocent,"

"It's true he is naive, but not in the sweet, positive sense of the word. Furthermore, he pretends to be a Christian, loyal to the word of the Bible, but he is not. He is sly and shifty."

Yongbin disagreed, but she did not argue with him; she loved Hongsop.

"After I got back from Seoul, my father asked me if we plan to get married," said Hongsop, toying with the flashlight.

"Mine did, too."

"When do you think we should get married?"

"We have to graduate from college first."

"That's the year after next!"

"I'll be twenty-three and you'll be twenty-four. That's not too old."

"I know, but what worries me is Yongnan. She could prevent us."

"Did your father ask you about her?"

"Yes, he did."

"She embarrasses you, doesn't she?"

"No, I just don't want to be bothered."

"It will bother you just the same whether we are married or not."

"You are always so rational. Does this mean you don't really love me?"

"It's because you don't have a strong will, sir," Yongbin laughed, addressing Hongsop formally.

"Don't make fun of me, Yongbin."

Yongbin stood up, and Hongsop followed her. "I have to go. See you in Seoul." They walked together for a few paces and then Hongsop embraced her.

"No, no." Yongbin shouted, but Hongsop kissed her anyway. She pushed him away and stared angrily in the darkness. She turned and ran down the path without saying anything. Hongsop chased after her.

"I'm sorry, Yongbin, I apologize."

Yongbin slowed down.

"Are you angry at me?" She didn't answer, but walked on. "Please tell me, Yongbin, are you mad?" Again, she refused to answer.

When they were almost to the front gate, she looked back at him and said, "No, I am not angry with you. But I will really be furious if you ever do that again!"

Hongsop turned away sadly.

A Marriage Proposal

Life returned to normal at the Kim residence after Yongbin went back to Seoul, and Yongnan's hostility disappeared. She became her old self again, wandering around the garden singing love songs to herself. When she took a notion to do a little housework, however, she dropped the dishes and broke them to pieces.

One fall afternoon she accidentally stepped in a dog pile in the yard and yelled at the dog, "You damn mutt! Why do you have to shit all over the place?"

Overhearing her daughter, Mrs. Kim, as she sewed, mumbled, "This girl has the mouth of a Cheju Island diver on her."

Now that Yongnan calmed down, Mrs. Kim was embarrassed that the neighbors gossiped about her family. They said she was too lenient and spoiled her daughters, so she ended up with her eldest a widow and the third, a slut; thus the remaining girls would never marry into decent families.

"What should I do?" she wondered. "Children have minds of their own; they do as they please. However, my daughter's misbehavior is likely the result of my past sins. . ." Punshi Kim attributed all her misfortunes to the sins of her past life.

Fall came and went; winter was suddenly upon them. The news that Yongbin and Hongsop had been arrested in Seoul reached Tongyong. On October 25, 1929, students in Kwangju began a resistance movement opposing the Japanese colonial policy. Hongsop and Yongbin were among those arrested on November 3.

Their fathers, Songsu Kim and Cookju Chong, went to Seoul. Songsu sat smoking silently at the police station. Irritated, Cookju said, "Damn it all anyway. I sent that boy of mine to Seoul to study, not to march in demonstrations and get himself thrown in jail. What a waste of money!"

Songsu Kim, wearing a conservative gray coat with gray hat and black shoes, looked refined, but the fat Chong in a thick coat resembled a snowman carrying a cane. His heavy face with its cow eyes, shapeless nose and scarred lips was a curious contrast to his son's aristocratic one.

Yongbin and Hongsop were released from police detention shortly afterward.

"God damn you, Hongsop," the father raged at his son. "Marching around in demonstrations isn't what I sent you up here for. You can sit on the sidelines and watch if you want, but have the good sense to leave when the police arrive."

Songsu looked his daughter up and down quietly and asked, "You haven't been hurt, have you?"

"No, Dad, I'm all right."

She looked fine, in fact, her eyes shone brightly, but Hongsop looked pale and intimidated.

"Well, Mr. Kim, these two don't study. They go to demonstrations. She doesn't set a good example for him. What is to become of our families?" asked Chong. The two men agreed to the betrothal of their children, though Chong complained about his future daughter-in-law.

"They are young and vigorous; useless if they don't resist," said Mr. Kim, regarding Hongsop coldly. In contrast to the resolute Yongbin, Hongsop wavered. Later, Songsu glanced at the leafless winter trees from the window of the inn where they were staying.

In Tongyong, Mrs. Kim, suffering the anguish of not knowing what had happened to her daughter, had a regular visitor.

"Well, hello there, Mrs. Kim. How are you doing?" The matronly woman stole in like a cat. She was a local matchmaker, who now visited frequently.

Punshi didn't want visitors. "Oh, you . . . I wasn't expecting. . ." But the woman didn't wait to be invited.

"What brings you here?"

"I came to talk about your daughter's marriage."

"My daughter's marriage? I have no time to worry about such thing. . ."

"Ah, I heard that your second daughter was arrested by the Japanese police. True?"

"This year is really the worst. Absolutely the worst year of my life."

"Many students demonstrated for independence, but your daughter will be all right. Don't worry."

"I don't know what to do. I couldn't go to Seoul; it's so far. Poor Yongbin, in jail in the dead of winter."

"Exactly ten years ago, the same sort of thing happened. One day my husband went to the market and came back spattered with ink and trembling. The Jap cops arrested many people that day too." The old woman went on whispering the names of people who died or were crippled. She rolled her bug eyes as she spoke, making Punshi feel as if a millstone had been hung around her neck.

Suddenly, she dropped the topic and said, "Oh, I practically forgot why I came here. What will you do for your daughter? If an acceptable suitor makes you a proposal, will you allow her to marry him?"

"My second daughter living in Seoul has been engaged and the fourth is too young," she said, obviously omitting any mention of Yongnan.

"What about your third daughter?"

"You mean Yongnan?" asked Punshi Kim, genuinely surprised.

"Yes, the prettiest of the lot."

"Who on earth wants her?"

"The Sangho Che family."

"What? The miller Che?" asked Punshi.

"Yes."

"That old man wants to marry my daughter?" Punshi said, blushing with anger. She'd rather Yongnan marry Handol than see her married to an old man.

"Don't jump to conclusions, Madame Kim, Old Che has a wife. He wants Yongnan for his son."

"But I don't understand. There are lots of virgins in Tongyong that a family like Che may choose from. Why would they want Yongnan?"

Punshi couldn't believe what the matchmaker had said. Old Mr. Che, who ran the rice mill, was exceedingly rich. Rumor had it that he was a little stingy, but still, in all, he had a good reputation. She was frankly surprised that the Che family would even consider Yongnan, who of course, had the reputation of being a loose woman.

"You're absolutely right, Madame. There are scads of girls who would like to marry his son, but the son wants your daughter. Fascinated by her. You know, good looks are a great blessing."

The devious matchmaker alluded to the fact that in spite of her reputation, Yongnan had managed to attract a man from a good family.

"I can't say yes or no. My husband will decide."

"Certainly, but your husband won't be foolish enough to turn down such a good offer. You should do everything you can to speed it up."

But Punshi Kim was at sixes and sevens — should she enthuse over her third daughter's good fortune or cry over her second daughter's misfortune?

90

Ill Winds

Day by day it grew colder. A thin layer of ice covered the well. The sea was quiet and the warm sun shone at noon.

"Too damn warm yet for a decent catch!"

"No shit! We are in a world 'a hurt if we get as few cod as last year."

"Boat owners'll lose their asses."

Porters gassed among themselves as the steam from the hot soup rose and wet their scraggly mustaches. The quay began to emerge from the morning mist. A motor boat put-put along the shore. Small boats gathered through the fog at the mouth of the river.

"A good year would make the boat owners happy, bar owners happy and us happy!"

"That's something none of us — only old Neptune — can do!"

Porters with carrying racks on their backs hauled firewood to homes in the fall and peddled fish in the winter. To combat hangovers they stood drinking steaming broth, for which they paid from stained pockets, then wiped their mouths on their sleeves and headed off toward the market.

Meanwhile, Kim's residence was hectic, cooking for the cod workers and getting ready for Yongnan's wedding. Yongbin was back home, having returned with Songsu on her release from police custody. Fortunately, it was her winter vacation. Thanks to cooperation from both families, preparations for Yongnan's wedding proceeded with unanticipated haste. The groom's family wanted it within the year, so the date was set for December 23, and the bride's was only too happy to get her out of their house. Compared with the average — a year from the time of a proposal — Yongnan's happened in a flash.

A gift box from the groom's family arrived for the bride. In it were a gold hairpin engraved with a phoenix, a gold ring, and some expensive fabric. Punshi was delighted, and observed, "Yongnan's mother-in-law must be a prudent manager."

"Yes, indeed," said Chongim, "such a perfectionist. No water spots on her glasses! Yongnan will have a very hard time pleasing *that* mother-in-law."

"I'm worried sick," Punshi admitted. "That girl can't sew a stitch. How will she survive in her new family?"

"She'll learn. Anyway, they picked her for her beauty; undoubtedly they know what they are getting! It's up to fate!"

"Br-r-r, it is absolutely freezing out," Yongsook said, as she entered. "Oh, Aunt, how are you?"

"I'm fine, but you're a little late," said Chongim.

"Well, I have been busy with a lot of little errands. It is so cold, I'm afraid the wet rice for the cakes will freeze. What are we going to do if that happens?" she asked shivering as she took off her gloves and warmed her hands.

"Half done rice cake is quite auspicious," said Chongim.

"Really? If that's true, then I should have married in the winter, ha, ha, ha." Yongsook giggled, her shoulders shaking under her purple coat. The white silk scarf at the neckline set off her lovely face.

"Are you going to remain a widow?" Chongim asked.

"Aunt, don't tease. Yongnan scandalizing everybody is enough for one family."

"Stop!" Punshi rebuked her. "Why are you always berating your sister?"

"Mom, you can't hide it; the whole town knows," said Yongsook, sulking.

"Yongsook, don't bad-mouth your sister. You know she can't help it; it's her fate. No person can resist what fate has in store for them. But if you, her eldest sister, treat her like the neighbors, who will protect her?" Chongim asked. Secretly, she believed Punshi had spoiled her daughters, but watching Yongsook being so insensitive to her mother agonizing over Yongnan, she found her niece simply rude, and she took it upon herself to lecture the girl.

"Yongsook, if you spit in the sky, it will land on your face. You're her sister — how can you talk about her like one of the neighbors? Good god. . ." Punshi said, tears welling up in her eyes. The embarrassment she felt around Chongim, who had two educated sons, one a doctor, was unbearable.

"Thank you very much. You're like the man who goes home and kicks the dog. Taking it out on me." Yongsook left the room in a huff.

"Inconsiderate little . . .!" Chongim was irritated at Yongsook's impertinence to her mother, and finally blurted out to Punshi, "You have spoiled your daughters...."

"I know. I am suffering for my sins in the past life. To give me a chance to repent, all this misfortune lands on me."

Yongsook slipped out into the backyard and went across to the girls' room, leaving the work of the wedding preparation behind. When she entered, Yongnan was lolling on the bed singing to herself.

"Well dear sister, I hope you're having a good time," she said.

"And if I'm not, what do you care?" replied Yongnan, in her usual impudent fashion.

"What is with you, lying around all day singing cheap love songs?"

"Why are *you* so jealous of me?" said Yongnan, trotting out of the room, humming and clicking her heels as she went.

"What a snot! No shame at all, absolutely none. I am so ashamed of her carrying on," Yongsook said to Yongok, who was sewing on Yongnan's trousseau. Yongsook took off her coat, hung it up, sat down, tucked her hands beneath her legs, and continued, "But what's really amazing is he proposed to her. Everybody knows about her...."

"Yongsook, do you really want Yongnan not to marry and end up a spinster?"

"No, I just think it's odd."

"But why? They say he is wonderful."

"He may be out of his mind!"

"Well, if I were a man, I would marry Yongnan — she's beautiful."

"Pish. If being beautiful is all it takes, why aren't the *kisaengs* all married then?"

"Are you saying Yongnan is a *kisaeng*?" asked Yongok, looking up from her sewing.

"Might as well be. Any woman who makes love — even once — to a man is not a virgin. Chastity is more precious than beauty, little sister," Yongsook advised Yongok.

"You are our eldest sister, how dare you talk about her like that?"

"Like what?"

"You call your own sister a *kisaeng*, and I am supposed to respect you? Hardly," Yongok argued in an unusually forceful tone of voice.

Actually, Yongsook didn't want to find fault with her sister, but the family's protective attitude toward Yongnan galled her. "I'm saying this because we're sisters, but I don't understand this family. It seems everybody is proud of Yongnan's behavior — they praise her and condemn me."

A fierce wind howled on Yongnan's wedding day. Between preparations for the ceremony and securing the fishing fleet, everybody was bustling about busily. Songsu disappeared without saying anything to anyone. The family tried to find him, but gave up, finally realizing he had decided not to attend the wedding. Chungku took his place and gave Yongnan away.

The groom looked grim. The matchmaker said he had fallen in love with Yongnan, but he was pale and certainly didn't look very enthusiastic about his bride or his wedding.

"Why he isn't even walking straight," Chongim said to herself, shaking her head.

The Fishery

"We can't fish with this fucking wind." Keydo shouted directions to his crew as he ran up and down. "Get those last boats in the cove behind the rocks!" The wind howled and high white caps pounded the shore. Tugging and shoving, the men dropped masts, until they struggled two boats past the rocks. It was grueling work, but they finally managed to anchor and lash the boats to the rocks.

"Batten the hatches!" Keydo, in an old peacoat and mariner's boots with the wind whipping his hair, hollered himself hoarse. When they finished securing the boats, they tied the dinghy down. Low tide usually carried them far out to good fishing grounds, but that day the high wind prevented them from leaving the bay and even made being on the shore difficult and dangerous.

"Shit, what a bitch of a goddamn day! Might as well get drunk!" said old Yom, his teeth chattering with cold, "Won't catch a single cod on a day like this."

"What the hell difference does it make to us if the fuckin' wind blows? Only the boss gets rich when there's a good catch," said a man named Kim, as if he were sneering in Songsu's face.

Suddenly enraged, Keydo screamed, "You dumb son of a bitch! No catch, and we all starve!" and punched the man.

"What are you hitting me for? Can't say what's ragging you?" said Kim, rubbing his jaw and glaring at Keydo.

Keydo hit him again, "You stupid fucking bastard. Respect your boss."

"Hey, cool it, would you? He's just joking." The other men said, trying to calm Keydo, who had been in a foul mood since morning. "He don't mean nothing by it!"

"Look, if you don't want to work here, get the hell out. There's lots of guys who would give their eyeteeth for a reg'lar paycheck!" Keydo stomped off, his rain boots squeaking in the sand.

"Goddamn Keydo, venting his anger over losing that bitch, Yongnan, on us! The young bastard will be sorry, that's all I can say. Myself, I've been eating the Grim Reaper's rice for five years." Kim pulled up his sleeves and assumed a fighting stance. Five life-threatening years of grinding out a living as a fisherman had left him unintimidated by a little fist-fight.

"Hey shit-face, I'll see you eating boss Kim's rice for a long time to come," he said, spitting a large green wad of phlegm.

"Oh, shut the fuck up! He was furious at Yongnan. A girl who gets married on a day like this will have many hardships." Old Yom pushed Kim aside and began singing as if nothing had happened:

> You looked like such a beauty
> But now I see it's only me —
> I'm blind! Oo-ee, Oo-ee, Oo-ee
> Ah, yes, you looked like such a beauty
> You looked like such a beauty to me....

Old Yom stopped singing and asked Kim to buy him a drink. "Hey man, buy me a drink for helping you let off steam. This weather's fucking with my head too."

"You ain't helping; you're only adding fuel to the fire," Kim answered blandly.

Pits, now wearing a towel over his head, ridiculed Kim, "I never seen this fuckin' tightwad buy nobody nothing!"

"I dare you to say that again, asshole," said Kim yanking his sleeves above his elbows.

The wind picked up. Sand and dirt pelted the workers as they struggled toward the fishery huts. "God Almighty, it's raining sand," someone shouted, rubbing his eyes as he went. They might have been taken for beggars in ragged and patched quilt pants and long coats, tied shut like Judo suits.

"Jesus save us! My house will never stand against this wind."

"Mine either!"

Suddenly, a woman's shriek split the air, and when they swung around, they were surprised to see it had come not from a woman, but from old Yom.

My home is gone
My children are orphans
Scattered like bowls of rice
Where are you, my darlings?
My poor darlings, driven by
Ill winds deep into the abyss
Prey of shark and octopus?

"This weather is a widow maker," old Yom sighed, as they huddled over a camp fire eating chowder. Dusk fell early as it does on such days. Far from Tongyong, in the blackness around Chi Island Fishery, the crashing waves and howling wind sounded like the roaring and running of beasts.

Keydo drank his supper. Later, lying in his bunk smoking, he cursed Yongnan, "Fucking bitch. I'd like to kill her."

When he heard about Yongnan and Handol, he wanted to kill her. He knew someone like himself could never hope to marry the boss's beautiful daughter. But when Songsu proposed they marry, he was secretly elated.

"You'll be ruined by your beauty," he thought.

He bolted up and stomped out his cigarette, but he could not find a way to release his anger. He couldn't tell Songsu he would marry her in spite of the scandal. Only a man without pride would accept damaged goods. But still he felt his boss had betrayed him — not telling him about her marriage.

"It's my own damn fault," he thought, "why didn't I tell him I wanted her. Why?" Now that she was being married, he regretted he hadn't.

A boy rushed in shouting, "Keydo, come quickly. They're fighting!"

Keydo answered bluntly, "Let 'em. I could give a good goddamn!"

"But they're using fire logs!" said the freckled boy, his nostrils flaring.

"If they run out of logs, give them oars," Keydo didn't move from his bunk.

"But they'll *kill* one another if nobody stops them," the boy said frantically.

"Who's fighting?"

"Pits and Hobo. They were playing cards; Pits cheated."

"They deserve it. Let 'em fight." Keydo said, standing up, flexing the muscles in his powerful shoulders.

Sailors seem to need fighting, even if it's over something inconsequential.

Keydo attacked the two of them with vengeance, kicking Hobo in the butt and socking Pits in the face. He beat them as if there were no bottom to his furor. "You fucking bastards."

"You Cocksucker Pits! I know you spent a year in jail for stealing."

"Son-of-a-bitch! You don't get your bitch, 'n you take it out on us," said Hobo, wiping the blood from his nose. He peppered Keydo with insults, but Keydo kicked sand in his face and gave it back, "Shut your mouth, cunt!" Then he hollered at the crowd that had gathered, "Where do you think you are, the fights?"

"No, this is better; this is the real thing!" someone replied.

In the midst of the brawl, the old woman who had sold them the liquor howled for her pot and cups.

In the end, Keydo left the men and headed out along the sand. The force of the wind tried to lift him off his feet. The sound of the wind and waves filled his ears. He licked his finger, and the taste of salty blood filled his mouth. His knuckles were bleeding. He spat on the dike, saying, "God damn bitch!"

Chapter Three

ॐ

The Disabled

Yongsook hadn't seen her parents for a long time. She arrived with her son, Tonghoon, on a maid's back. Everyone was surprised as Yongsook almost never took him anywhere.

"There he is, our little boy," said Mrs. Kim, happy to see her grandson, but when she held him, he whined discontentedly. She tried to divert him with dried persimmons and apples, but he rewarded her with a disinterested frown. He was a pasty-faced, strangely fragile-looking boy. Blue veins were clearly visible in his forehead, and he appeared to have spent no time in the sun.

Yongsook loosened the scarf around her neck, laid it in her lap and said, "I'm coming from the doctor's office. I'm absolutely sick of it, but he's forever whining."

"That's because he's an only child. What did the doctor say?"

"Feed him! Well, I was mortified. What does he think? That we're poor?"

"He's finicky, and doesn't have a good appetite. You have to feed him more often. You're not taking good care of him."

"I can't be dancing attendance on this child all the time. Shit, I wish he'd never been born."

"Lower your voice, girl. Somebody will hear you! Do you really think you'll be better off without Tonghoon?" said Mrs. Kim, embarrassed and astonished.

"A nun with no children has no problems, no troubles." replied Yongsook.

"Don't say such a thing around your child. Parents' words are like legal documents. And you'd be lonely if you didn't have him." Looking at his mother, the boy grimaced.

"How is the cod harvest going this year, Mom?"

"Truthfully, I can't say whether they are having a good year or not."

"You always say you don't know."

"Well, how could I? It's your father's business."

"Father doesn't know anything about it either. So who knows? He leaves everything to the manager. I don't see how he can make *any* profit."

"You always come here complaining. Since last year was the worst anybody can remember, this year can hardly be as bad."

"You're going to just sit and wait? In any case, I need about a hundred and fifty fish."

"How many?! What for?"

"I'll pay for them; I'm not asking for a hand-out."

"It's not a question of the money. Twenty should be more than enough for you. You have plenty of roe and fish paste. That much cod will go bad before you are even able to eat them."

"I'm not going to eat all that fish, for god's sake!"

"Well, what are you going to do with it?"

"Store it till spring and then sell it."

"You will not! What will people say? Do you need money? You have enough to wear and eat. You have only one child. They'll say you're crazy with greed. You have more than you can spend."

"Mom, you don't know anything about it. Do you have any idea how tough it is for a widow? I have to raise Tonghoon, provide his education, his wedding...I don't know how I'll manage."

"Nonsense. You're afraid you won't have enough to raise one child?"

"It's easier said than done. Do I have any income — even a penny's worth? If I keep spending the principal, it will be gone. Then what? Everyone is trying to take my money."

"Who?"

"Mom, there are some things you don't know. Tonghoon's uncle is ready to take advantage of me and grab everything."

"I don't believe it. He should be embarrassed to see you having to make a living for your child."

"All he thinks about is ways to take advantage of me. His wife is no better. She is running around the neighborhood, saying I am going to get married again. I think she's jealous of my money."

"I don't. It is because you are young and pretty. And if you don't marry, you'll prove her wrong. You are older; be generous with her."

"She's so rude to me. I just don't deserve it," said Yongsook angrily, as if she were in the act of confronting her sister-in-law. Tonghoon stopped whining and began to fall asleep. Mrs. Kim laid the baby on the warm floor and slid a pillow under his head.

"Grow up, Yongsook. Granted, it is not easy to act like an adult, but since your brother-in-law doesn't, there is no point in blaming him. Ignore him. Now that his parents are dead, you should take their place as the head of the family."

"I am not some sort of monk, able to endure endless humiliation. We're all alike; we all feel the same." Yongsook had become so enraged she could barely speak, but after she calmed down, she resumed making her original request.

"Well, Mom, are you going to let me have those fish or not? Because if not, I'll have to look elsewhere."

"Giving them to you is no big deal. But for the life of me, I can't understand why you want to do this when you don't have to."

"You know Mrs. Cookju Chong? Her husband is a millionaire, but she's selling all sorts of stuff. If she can, why can't I? After all, I am not going to sit out in the open market and sell them. Merchants will discreetly come to my home and buy from me."

The two women continued to argue for some time.

Tongyong women weren't simply housewives. Diligent and independent, many made good money on the side in small businesses. Middle class women grew bean sprouts and they sold to street vendors, or pressed sesame and camellia oil and sold to friends and relatives for pin money. Then they pooled their savings in a "*kye*" without their husbands' knowledge.

However, wealthy women were in business on a far grander scale. During cod season they bought hundreds of fish and hired workers to harvest the roe and gills. They dried the fillets and fermented the gills and roe. They salted and sun-dried whole for sale during the summer. These women averaged a two hundred percent profit on their operations. Some even diversified beyond cod, purchasing wheat, malting and selling it. Others bought rice, sesame and red peppers. They stored them in barns until the supplies became tighter and prices went up. This way, they profited without turning a hand; their money made money. Women without it were locked out. But naturally, not all women with money went into business — only those with the requisite ambition and avarice.

While Mrs. Kim and Yongsook were arguing, they were interrupted by a man's cough, a polite entry warning from the courtyard.

"Is Mr. Kim in?"

Sliding the door open, Punshi saw Keydo standing just outside.

"He's out, but come on in. It's cold," she said affectionately. Without a word, Keydo stepped into the hall and entered the room, but when he saw Yongsook, he fidgeted awkwardly, as if suddenly facing a young woman made him uncomfortable.

"Have a seat," Mrs. Kim said. Keydo sat down smelling of the sea.

"Yomoon! Bring us hot *shikhay* to drink," Mrs. Kim shouted.

"No, thanks."

"Oh, try it. It'll warm you up on a cold day like this."

"Don't like sweets."

"How is the cod catch going?" Yongsook asked impatiently. It seemed that was all she could focus on at that moment.

Bluntly, he replied, "Better this year."

"It's hard work in this cold weather, isn't it?" Mrs. Kim asked, as if she were talking with her own son.

"No work, no money," he said.

Much later, long after Yongnan was married, Mrs. Kim learned of her husband's initial decision to marry Yongnan to Keydo. She didn't find out from him or Yongbin, but from Yongsook, who reported that Keydo's father had told someone. By then, Yongnan was already married. Punshi was not only sorry to have been left out of the decision, but that her daughter had missed such a good match. She believed Keydo was a good man, would have made a fine son-in-law, and she felt close to him. It seemed to Mrs. Kim that Yongnan would have been better off with someone like Keydo because she had so many faults and was now so miserable.

"Mr. Soh," Yongsook said, addressing Keydo formally and politely. He stared at her, as if he already didn't like what she might ask.

"From your next good catch, send me one hundred and fifty fish. I just cleared it with mother." Keydo said nothing.

"You're so stubborn...." Mrs. Kim said, giving up.

"Only the good ones, you hear?" Yongsook commanded when Keydo didn't answer.

Keydo had known the Kims for so long that he knew most of what there was to know about the family, especially Yongsook's meanness. He was sick of her arrogance and domineering tone. He didn't like her for trying to take whatever she could get from her parents.

"Mom, by the way, have you seen Yongnan lately?" Yongsook asked, deliberately trying to hurt Keydo. When he heard Yongnan's name, he became angry and felt the blood rising to his head.

"It's been almost a month now," Mrs. Kim replied, pretending to be unconcerned at discussing the topic in front of Keydo, but she was secretly incensed.

As a matter of fact, Yongnan had been home every three days or so, carrying a small bundle of her possessions, but Mrs. Kim persuaded her to go back. Mrs. Kim was so sorry for her daughter that she was often in tears. Her son-in-law was impotent and an opium addict. The uninhibited Yongnan came home and told her mother everything.

"Rumor has it that you sent as many as twelve spice jars to save her marriage, but what if it doesn't last?" Yongsook continued in her sarcastic tone of voice.

Since Songsu despised Yongsook, Mrs. Kim had given her far more clothes than necessary for her wedding to try to make up for the love she missed. Likewise, since Yongnan had her own flaws, Mrs. Kim had sent a dozen spice jars, just as the rumor said. Mrs. Kim's efforts to make things right for her daughters had not, however, succeeded.

"Enough. Her fate is hers; yours is yours," said Mrs. Kim angrily, as she did every time Yongnan was mentioned.

"I've got to go. I'll be back when Mr. Kim is here," Keydo said and left without acknowledging Yongsook.

"He's a wicked little serpent."

"By you, nobody else is any good," said Mrs. Kim, wide-eyed and upset.

Calculations

"My good Mr. Kim, please hand me your glass." Mr. Chong filled his partner's glass.

It was early January and warm sunlight had already begun thawing the frozen earth. From the window, they could see children flying kites on the opposite bank. Gentle winds blew and the sea was calm. Wearing their holiday *hanboks,* Songsu Kim and Cookju Chong toasted one another. Kim's silk jacket had silver buttons. Chong's sienna skin looked even darker against the brown *hanbok* with its amber buttons. On one wall of the study hung a scroll drawing of some fish and on a low chest were documents and books arranged tidily. The brass and wood of the chest had been carefully polished. The room matched the clean, conscientious grooming of its owner, Songsu Kim.

"Mr. Kim."

"Yes." Songsu's eyes were red, and he was getting quite drunk.

"You know Sochong, don't you?" Chong's shiny face brightened as he spoke.

"Sochong, who?"

"Come on, don't tell me you don't."

Songsu sipped from his glass. Certainly he knew the *kisaeng* Sochong — everybody knew her. She was pretty, a good dancer and had a beautiful body. Many men were in love with her. Songsu had first seen her close at Chong's birthday party the previous spring. Sochong and several other *kisaengs* were there, along with most of the VIPs of Tongyong. However, afterward, whenever he met her on the street, Sochong bowed politely to him.

"I heard Sochong is in love with you. You ought to go see her some time."

"That's rubbish. Stop it."

"Rubbish? You think I'm making it up?"

"We're too old for this nonsense."

"Old? Man, you look young. And men our age need young mistresses."

"I have daughters to marry, so let's not get into it."

"What are you afraid of? Kids will fall in love and get married. We don't need to worry about that; we have to worry about ourselves."

"...."

"Songsu, what kind of life do you have — sitting home day in, day out?"

"It's what I like, sir," he said with a lonely smile.

"My friend, what is this? There are aphrodisiacs for this. Didn't you have them in your pharmacy?"

In response, Songsu only sipped his drink.

"She flirts with you; she's crazy about you. If you're not impotent, how can you ignore her?" Kim laughed heartily as Chong continued, "Sochong has a fortune; you don't have to spend a *won* on her. She's different from a wife; she's delicious, waits on you hand and foot."

Mr. Kim pulled out a cigarette and lit up.

There were, in fact, many women infatuated with him. In the days when he was practicing Oriental medicine, women often came to be examined without any recognizable symptoms. They were all women who liked him, one was even married. However, Songsu never allowed himself to stray. It bothered him that he thought about Sochong occasionally.

"Enough! I have a favor to ask," Songsu was eager to change the subject.

"What?" Chong's loose eyes seemed to focus suddenly.

"I need a loan."

"What for?"

"I want to buy two fishing boats."

"What are you going to do with the ones you've got?"

"They're old sailboats."

"Yes?"

"I want to buy steam-powered ones."

"For deep-sea fishing? That's a big project."

The larger fish of open waters required steam boats over one hundred tons, which could cruise to the open sea and lower their nets to far greater depths. However, the boats were costly and required a large amount of capital.

"Not deep-sea, but *underwater* fishing," he said.

Submarine fishing also required steam boats, but smaller ones. Kim had two permanent functioning fisheries. The one in Chi Island was so large it took five thousand bags of gravel to create. From there, with forty employees, he operated three sail boats, and caught cod, Spanish mackerel and tuna. The other was in Hansan Island. It was smaller and mostly dealt in anchovies. Though it was smaller, it employed more people because processing anchovies required more hands.

"Why underwater fishing?"

"Surface fishing is doomed because the Japanese have grabbed up all the good fishing grounds."

"Then you are going to close down existing operations?"

"I'll wait and see. When they no longer turn a profit, I'll get rid of them. For the time being though, I'd like to send the underwater boat to Cheju for clams."

Chong sat deep in thought for a long time. His head was spinning to calculate the pluses and minuses of Kim's request. When it came to money, he was sharp and highly organized.

"How much do you need?" asked Chong, in a businesslike fashion.

"Five thousand."

"Five thousand!" His startled surprise was clearly visible on Chong's face. That was a lot of money.

"I can give you the land deed as security, if you want."

"...."

"...."

Having finished his calculations satisfactorily, Chong agreed without reservation. "We're friends, Kim. No need for the deed. I'll lend you the money."

"I do appreciate it," he said, and they filled their glasses again.

"Whose idea was this?"

"Mine."

"Ah-hah. I thought you weren't interested in business, but I was wrong."

"Every man is good at something."

"You're right. By the way, it is my turn to ask a favor."

"What is this — tit for tat favors from the New Year — I do you one, you do me one?" Kim smiled gently.

"Your cousin Chungku's son, the doctor."

"You mean Chongyoon?"

"I hear he's in Chinju. Is that right?"

"Yah, working at the provincial hospital."

Chong licked his scarred upper lip and drew closer to Kim. "I've been thinking... I believe he'd be a perfect match for my eldest daughter." Caught off guard by the proposal, Songsu Kim looked surprised. "What do you think?"

"What do I think? What I think doesn't count. My cousin will decide. You know he's notoriously stubborn."

"Runs in the family — what about *your* stubbornness?"

"You think he would listen to me? Anyway, what's the point of marrying her to the son of a down-and-out artisan?" he asked, as he wanted very much to avoid proposing it to his cousin.

"As long as he's capable, I don't care if he has money. It's what he is that matters."

"You realize what you are doing, don't you? You'll be twice related to the family of a stubborn man," Songsu tried to make light of the whole idea.

"So much the better. You'll be my son's father-in-law and I'll be your nephew's."

"I don't know if Chongyoon is thinking about getting married...."

"I'm a fool to say it, but she's a nice girl, and we get so many proposals. Hard to choose."

"Well, if she's your daughter, she should be good...."

"Absolutely! Who could refuse Chong's daughter?"

Songsu suddenly lost his appetite for liquor. Chong's arrogance and the marriage proposal — which he knew would never be given a moment's serious consideration — disgusted him. When it came to sneering at Chong, his cousin never quit. In fact, Songsu himself was not pleased with the engagement of Yongbin and Hongsop. However, eager to discuss his daughter's future, Chong went on about it for a long time. At last, he changed the subject.

"My son and your daughter will graduate from school in Seoul this spring, so we'd better have the wedding in the fall."

Songsu knew it was going to happen, but he was reluctant to admit it.

As the sun set behind West Gate Hill, Chong rose to leave, quite drunk. Songsu accompanied him out to the front gate. He could see that Chong was pretending to be drunker than he actually was. When he saw a skirt and white hands holding a bundle slip behind the zelkova tree, he quickly said goodbye to Chong and retreated to his study.

A Secret

Yongbin spent New Year's Day and the January full moon of the fifteenth at home. As she would be returning to Seoul in a few days, she went to see Tayoon. She looked slim and elegant in a black wool coat and matching shoes, as she slipped into the post office to mail a letter.

"Ah, Soonja!"

A woman with her hair in a bun spun around.

"Yongbin!" the woman appeared happy to see her. "Mailing letters?"

"Yes, you too?"

"Soonho had an argument with Dad and went back to school early, so I'm sending him long underwear." Soonho was her brother, attending middle school in Pusan.

"Haven't seen you for a long time. How have you been?" Yongbin asked, trying to read Soonja's curious expression. She was smiling, though her eyes were wary and scared.

"You graduate this year, don't you?"

"Yes."

"You must be thrilled."

"I'll be glad to get out."

"I hear you're getting married right afterward, true?"

"We'll see...."

They walked out of the post office together. As it was market day, the street was crowded with vendors and shoppers. Yongbin grasped Soonja's hand firmly, as they made their way through the crowd. "Soonja...." but she tried to pull her hand away as if she were afraid. Yongbin let go and swallowed what she was going to say for fear of hurting Soonja's feelings.

"Which way are you going?" asked Soonja, looking down at her shoes.

"To my uncle's...."

Soonja shrugged, "I-I...." She forced a smile, but the effort gave her away. She looked more like she was crying than smiling. Yongbin found it difficult to watch, said goodbye and turned toward her uncle's.

"Poor Soonja, I wonder what Tayoon is going to do about her," she thought.

When Yongbin arrived at her uncle's house, she was greeted by Tayoon. "Well, what prompts an evangelist to pay us a visit?"

"You're mean. Where's my aunt?"

"Gone to market."

"I had forgotten today is market day. Is your father working?"

"Yes," Tayoon told her.

"I'll talk to him when he takes a break; I know how he hates to be bothered when he is working."

"Whenever I went to your house, you were always at church. Do you go to church every single day?" Yongbin just smiled. "You're very devoted."

"You've lost weight," Yongbin said, changing the topic, "you must be worried."

"I just got a haircut," he said, feeling his own face.

"Ah, you've got a date tonight?"

"A date doesn't require a haircut."

"Hum...."

"Don't you worry."

"Didn't they put a little hair cream on it?"

"I didn't let them; I hate that grease the barbers use."

"Like father, like son. You're so picky."

"*That* makes me picky?"

"Yes. I don't like fussy men. Men shouldn't be nit-pickers."

"Preaching to me again, Miss Evangelist?"

"No."

"Don't badmouth my dad. He is a fine gentleman, not picky but discriminating, also strict and brave at the same time."

"Are you claiming these characteristics for yourself too?"

"Yes, I am. Ha...ha...I know this is your favorite soapbox."

"Of course. A hot-headed man who doesn't think isn't in tune with modern times. He was a hero in the old bow-and-arrow days. But those *heroes* often end up either disgraced or fleeing."

"Ho...ho...ho."

"By the way, Hongsop hasn't come down from Seoul yet, has he?"

"He said he would, but apparently he hasn't."

"Yongbin?"

"What?"

"Do you really like Hongsop?"

"Yes, I do."

"I suppose it's only natural," he reflected.

"Why do you say that?"

"Well, strong women like you are attracted to weak men...."

"Hongsop is not weak," she insisted.

"Well, you know the old saying: Love is blind. Pockmarks look like dimples, even a limp becomes a dance step when you are in love."

"You ought to talk!"

"Our situations are very different. For you it's a matter of personality. Hongsop stinks," said Tayoon, smiling bitterly.

"Of what?"

"Religion, ah Christianity, but you don't."

"You're making allowances for me because I'm your cousin!" she laughed.

He didn't respond, but added, "When it smells natural, then it is. When it begins to stink, the person has gotten too full of himself."

"You're wrong about Hongsop; he's a devout Christian."

"No, he's so holy he stinks," Tayoon insisted.

"That's a contradiction."

"I've been thinking that devotion is just an external." Tayoon argued, "It's not what you believe, but a form, the outward appearance of it, especially for Christians."

"I'm confused. The more insistent you are, the more I feel I must argue against you."

"Ah-ha, so you don't believe a word of what you just said!? At least you're honest."

Yongbin grinned. "You know, I really don't know. My faith is not as strong as it was when I was younger." She sighed.

"That's the truth. God! I sound as bad as an extremist myself. What I am trying to say is the process of doubting is where you begin to discover the real truth. Anyway, I heard someone say that, and it sounds logical."

"So you are attacking people who believe in Christ without knowing what you believe."

"Yes. There is nothing we can know for sure."

"Then there is no truth."

"It's an illusion. We can only move toward what seems to be truth. Reality is closer to us than God, therefore, closer to the truth."

"You think you can explain everything. There are so many things in life that can't be explained or expressed."

"Mysteries?"

"Yes. Do you ever think about dying?"

"Yes, but it scares me terribly. I know I can't depend on God. Everyone dies — do you know anyone who hasn't? Even your Jesus Christ *died* on the cross."

"That's blasphemous."

"Only if you glorify Christ as God; I respect him as a person. He was a great and wise man when he walked this earth. That he lived on earth is a historical fact, but he's gone now."

"No, he's not. I'm sitting here and He lives in me as I live and breathe," Yongbin said firmly.

"That's absurd. When you listen to weak people, you end up being taken advantage of by people who use Christ's moral authority to control."

"So what's the point?"

"What's important is a good life in this world."

"Ah yes, make a lot of money, be successful at work, marry a pretty girl," Yongbin said, trying to dismiss the topic. However, Tayoon was not ready to.

"Korean men were helpless," he asserted. "Those who had accepted Christianity were especially passive. Worse, like Westerners, they were selfish, interested only in their own well-being. Hongsop was typical of the type."

"Stop knocking Hongsop. You don't know about love. Feeling is what it's about. You berate Christians but you are prejudiced and discount their love. They are the ones who have fought against Japanese imperialism," Yongbin said, now becoming angry herself, "I met Soonja on my way here."

Tayoon's face turned red and he fell suddenly silent.

"Are you surprised? I'm not judging her, but I don't understand you...."

"I...."

"You are only hurting her feelings, seeing her when you can't marry her."

"What makes you think I won't?" he asked in an edgy unpleasant voice.

"And makes you think you can?"

"Marriage? I don't need a wedding to be married. We will just live together, but for now it's our secret because I have not yet figured out how." Tayoon's eyes seemed to sink deep into their sockets.

Soonja had married a grade school friend of Tayoon's, but shortly after the wedding her husband had disappeared. It was rumored he had gone to Manchuria or Japan or died.

ॐ

Homage to the Wind God

A rowboat approached the Tongyong pier. Dark islands against the shining water made the scene seem like a monochrome watercolor. The sea shone with colonies of nightlights.

The young boy rowing the boat pushed a jellyfish away with an oar. It expelled phosphorescence that outshone the nightlights.

"Youngsam."

"Yes?"

Removing the cigarette from his lips, Keydo addressed to the boy, but said nothing else. He spat the tobacco flakes that stuck to his lips and asked him, "They say you saw Handol. Did you?"

"Yeah, in Yosu."

"What's he up to?"

"Going to sea, I think."

"What did he have to say for himself?"

"Only asked me if I seen Yongnan."

"Uhm...." He asked no more. The boy had confirmed the rumor around the fishery. Youngsam had been to Yosu to see his mother.

Keydo got out of the boat, told the boy not to wait for him and headed for Myongjonggol.

"Just coming home?" Keydo's sister, Keysoon welcomed him as she emerged from the house carrying a water jar.

"Going to fetch water?"

"Yes, sacred water."

He knew it was time for the ceremony to the Wind God. Keysoon disappeared.

"Father, are you home?" Keydo called, standing in the court-yard.

Mr. Soh slid the door open and said, "I need to talk... to you."

Soh was an old man with a big face, but his body was healthy as man half his age. However, he looked a little sly. Keydo removed his shoes and stepped into the room.

"Keysoon has received a marriage proposal. But what are we going to do about you?" Keydo said nothing. "She's getting older, and we'd better not miss this chance while she's young and courted."

"...."

"You are already twenty-seven, and it's time for you to have your own family. If you wait too long, you may not get a good woman."

Keydo sighed deeply and said, "Let her marry first."

"You know we can't do that. You're older and single; it's not right. Besides, when she's gone, who's going to do the housework?" Keydo had no idea. "My suggestion is...you know Kim's fourth daughter."

"You mean Yongok?"

"She's not pretty, but she'll make a good wife."

"...."

"Of course, we are not good enough for them, but Kim himself suggested this to me."

"...."

"I know him. He won't bring it up again, so if it's all right with you, I'll pursue it."

"...."

"Look, her family's rich, and she knows how to manage a house. You won't find anybody that good if you go around looking yourself."

"Let's wait and see," Keydo said getting up, "I've got a lot to do."

"It's dark already. Why don't you spend the night?"

"I can't. I told the boatman to wait." Keydo lied, not because he didn't want to discuss his marriage, but because he didn't like his father and didn't want to stay with him. He left the house, went to a bar and had a few drinks, and then headed for Kanchanggol.

"What a surprise! What are you doing out this hour of the night?" asked Punshi Kim when Keydo entered the courtyard. Punshi was embarrassed because Yongnan was sitting in the

116

living room. He had been drinking, and seeing Yongnan, whom he still loved, made him feel brave and angry.

"I had a couple drinks," he admitted, breathing heavily, and sat down on the floor opposite Yongnan.

"I figured you came for the goodies," she said, actually trying to say the right thing, but it came out in her usual flirtatious fashion. Keydo had come to vent his anger, but seeing her defused it. For her part, Punshi didn't know what to do about her daughter's behavior. Servants hustled and bustled around as if it were the day of the memorial service. The lamps in the courtyard shone brightly.

"Did you pay homage to the Wind God?" asked Keydo.

"Yes, today in fact," replied Punshi.

People believed the Wind God came to earth at dawn on February 1 and remained until February 20. Each household picked a day to honor him – 9, 14, or 19. So the day of the ceremony varied from household to household.

"Want something to eat?"

"No, thanks, I already ate."

"Don't be uptight. Come on, have something, okay?" said Yongnan, smiling and trying to keep the conversation going. Keydo squinted at her, looking bleak in a white bodice and green skirt. Only the thick gold ring on her finger shone and her eyes looked like a cat's.

"Yongnan, go to your room! Quickly, please." Mrs. Kim said, rolling her eyes as if she couldn't tolerate her daughter's presence another second.

"Don't worry. We're old friends." Feeling helpless, Mrs. Kim said no more. Keydo smiled bitterly. Yongnan continued, "When we were kids, I played at the river with Handol. You knew where to find the rocks with the best oysters on them. You already knew then how to sail a boat, ho...ho...."

Yongnan was stretching the truth. When she was six or seven, he was a young man of thirteen or fourteen. Since she was the boss's daughter, he took her wherever she wanted to go — down to the sea, up the mountains. At night, he gave her piggy-back rides when she wanted them. Whenever she went out, Handol followed her.

"Remember the time you found me that clam — big as a baby's head?" Yongnan asked. He stared blankly at her. He didn't remember any of it, and didn't understand how she could refer to Handol in front of him. It pained him.

"We brought the clam home. Yongsook opened it up, and we found a tiny clam inside. Handol and I felt so sorry we took it to the pier and put it back in the water. We were so innocent then."

"Same old story...." Mrs. Kim mumbled, not knowing how to stop her daughter. "By the way, I hear you didn't send the cod to Yongsook."

"No."

"Why not? She is very serious about this."

"We distribute directly from the fishery, and I don't have the time to run to Tongyong with special orders."

"Well, she's angry with me."

"How come she is so greedy?"

"You simply don't understand how tough it is for a single mom with a child," said Mrs. Kim, covering for Yongsook, though she agreed with Keydo. "I understand we're going to start underwater fishing, is that so?"

"According to your husband, we are."

"I don't understand what he's doing. He has to borrow money on top of everything."

"...."

"He should not expand now, but just keep things on an even keel."

"To fish underwater, do you have to go very far?" asked Yongnan, barging in again.

"Probably to Cheju Island," he answered, looking straight ahead.

"Will you be going?"

"I don't know."

The squeak of the gate was heard. "Is that you, Yongok?" Mrs. Kim hollered stretching her neck.

"Yes, Mother." Yongok, Yonghay, and Yomoon with a large wooden dipper on her head entered. When Yongok saw Keydo, she hesitated a moment and went to the kitchen with Yomoon.

"Mom," Yonghay called, smiling at Keydo.

"Was Yongsook home?"

"Yes." They had taken some food to Yongsook. "She said the vegetables were a little bland, not enough salt."

"She's wrong, but she never fails to find fault with something. Yonghay, get ready for bed. It's late."

Keydo stood up. "Well, I'd better get going. Is Mr. Kim in yet?"

"No, he's still out," said Mrs. Kim, seeing no light in his study.

"Are you leaving? But you haven't eaten anything," said Yongnan, glancing at him and then wiping her nose on her bodice tie.

Keydo turned his powerful glance on her and left.

A Chaste Lady

As Keydo left, Mrs. Kim was gazing at Yongnan, furious. She would have liked to punch her daughter for being so forward in front of him, but it was more imperative that she persuade her daughter to go back home.

"Yongnan, I am going to walk you back home. Let's get going before your father returns," said Mrs. Kim, rising.

"I am not going back there."

"Now you know you can't stay here, don't you?"

"I'm not going home. Yonhak is always hitting me."

"Why, oh why? I have never done anything bad in my life; why, oh why am I plagued like this?" cried Mrs. Kim. Yongnan looked vacantly up at the sky. "Come on. Either he'll beat you to death or he won't, but you have to go," Mrs. Kim said blowing her nose, but continuing to sniffle.

She came down the courtyard and took her daughter's hand. They had played out the same scene now several times since Yongnan's marriage. Punshi would cry and implore her to go back home, and eventually take her by the hand and walk her back to Yonhak's house. Yongnan went out the gate with the bundle at her side. After passing the dark alley, they entered West Gate Hill. It was crowded with women fetching water from the well. Yongnan, looking as docile as a goat, followed her mother. Mrs. Kim herself felt like a shepherd returning a lost animal whenever she passed this hill, crying and escorting Yongnan home. As they passed Taebatgol, fewer people were about. Night was falling and the place was deserted and silent. They crossed the bridge to the west. The tide was coming in and waves were splashing against the dike. Their shadows reflected on the water seemed to be playing, leapfrogging one another.

"Mother?"

"Why?"

"The other night Yonhak beat me so badly I ran to Yongsook's."

"...."

"When I got there, she was with the doctor. She said Tonghoon was sick."

"She didn't say he was sick again."

"But he was sleeping, and the doctor was having a drink."

"A drink?"

"Yes."

"Maybe Yongsook gave him a drink because she was embarrassed at having called him out at that hour of the night." Though she spoke in a natural tone of voice, she had her doubts.

She wondered why a doctor would be having a drink at a widow's house that late at night.

"I can't live with Yonhak any more. Even his parents don't have any respect for him, and his younger brother beat him up too."

"Oh, how dare they? He's their older brother; they owe him respect whether he is a decent person or not."

"He's stealing, Mom! I really can't stand him any more."

"You just have to adapt yourself to what he is. There should be a way. . . " But Mrs. Kim knew very well her daughter was stuck in a hopeless situation. The extent of the tragedy, which the girl did not know, broke her heart. The mother and daughter paused in front of the gate of the big house in Torogol.

"Yongnan, my dear baby," Mrs. Kim continued sweeping the hair up off the girl's forehead, "send the servant girl to me with any sewing you have. Laundry too. I'll take care of everything and send it back to you."

Mrs. Kim took a handkerchief from inside her sleeve and blew her nose.

"Now, go on." She pushed Yongnan through the gate, standing ajar, and stood listening.

Then she could hear his voice. "Where is that bitch? Jesus Christ, coming back at this hour?" Yonhak screamed.

"Yongnan, hurry and get in there," her mother-in-law's voice was heard.

Mrs. Kim backed up, mincing as if someone were watching her from the house.

When she got to Taebatgol on the way back, she recalled what Yongnan had told her about Yongsook. So she went around and knocked on the gate at Yongsook's.

"Yongsook!" she hollered, but nobody answered.

"I suppose they're in bed," she thought. It was quiet all around.

"Yongsook!" She knocked on the gate one last time before deciding to return home.

"Who's there this time of night? Don't you know what time it is?" an old servant woman, with instructions from Yongsook, grumbled as she came out.

"Oh, Mrs. Kim. Mrs. Kim from Kanchanggol?" She opened the gate and seemed frightened to see Punshi.

"Has Yongsook gone to bed already?"

"Ah....Well ....Um...." She was obviously lost for an answer and stood stuttering. Punshi entered.

"What's going on here?" Punshi stared at the servant woman suspiciously for a while and then said, "Look, I have been to Torogol, and I just stopped off to see my daughter on the way home."

She removed her shoes to enter the room and called out, "Are you sleeping, Yongsook?"

The door then opened abruptly. Yongsook appeared and stood blocking doorway. "What brings you here at this hour, Mother?" she asked. She wasn't wearing a hairpiece and the long, loose hair cascaded over her shoulders.

"I am on my way from Torogol. It's quite cold, true to form for February, time of the Wind God ceremony. They say that water will freeze in gourds now." Mrs. Kim blathered and was about to step into Yongsook's room, when she heard something moving, then the door to the backyard.

"Is someone in there?" she asked, turning pale.

"Who could be here?" Yongsook asked, so embarrassed that she couldn't hide the anger or panic in her voice or on her face.

"Somebody...went out...I just heard...."

"You're hearing things, Mother. That's nonsense," Yongsook said, her voice still trembling. Then there was a dull thud from the backyard, as if someone jumped from the wall around the house.

"Now, what is that?"

"Burglars maybe," said Yongsook boldly in a calm tone of voice, as she had now recovered her composure.

"Oh my god!" said Mrs. Kim, covering her face with both hands.

"You'd better keep quiet, or the neighbors will hear."

At the mention of the neighbors, Mrs. Kim left.

"Lock the gate," Yongsook ordered the servant. The woman complied quickly.

"Why did you open the gate and mess everything up?" said Yongsook, spitting angrily toward the bottom step.

"Oh, don't worry about it. Please — your own mother will understand! Heh, heh, heh." Her vulgar smile puckered her already wrinkled face.

Yongsook stepped into the room and sunk down beside the tousled bed.

"Nobody can blame me. 'Chaste lady?' If my husband were alive, I would be," she mumbled. She picked up the belt the man had left behind, coiled it and placed it in a chest drawer.

Mrs. Kim headed to Shaman Rock. She sat down with her legs stretched out before her and began sobbing. Soft winds dissipated the sounds of her sobs and carried them away.

Intoxicated

Songsu Kim was drinking in a room filled with the fragrance of face perfume. His eyes were becoming red. Through the window the sky glowed as the sun set. The lamp with its shade of beads lit the room with soft, seductive light. Sochong, hands on her knees, all in white, contemplated Songsu. Her cheeks flushed pink; she was young and beautiful. They sat in silence for a long time — an uneasy silence, not the quiet calm in which they could communicate the secrets of their hearts to one another. Sochong tried to begin a conversation, but she was put off by the cool look of his eyes.

"Sir, why don't you talk to me? Say something — anything."

He only stared at her face.

"I feel bad when you just sit here and say nothing to me."

"I don't know what to say."

He took a cigarette out and placed it between his lips. Quickly, Sochong lit a match. But he ignored her and lit the cigarette himself. This made her blush with embarrassment, but she endured the shame she felt and put the match in the ashtray, saying nothing.

"Because I am always alone...."

She realized he was trying to apologize for the rebuff. Her eyes watered, and she lowered her head. Songsu was at a loss. His loneliness had made him decide to visit Sochong in the first place, but when he got there, he wasn't sociable enough to express his affection for her, so he just sat. It was embarrassing for both of them. Though he occasionally fantasized about the girl, when he was in the same room with her, he felt little different.

Her place seemed feminine and warm to him, as he had long since become accustomed to the cold solitude of his Spartan study. Naturally too, as a man who knew no women but his plain, dowdy wife, Sochong looked fresh and pretty to him. Still, this was not enough to make him fall in love with her. It was strange; he didn't want to leave her either. He felt unsteady, suspended as if floating in a hot bath.

"You are so cool, always so aloof," Sochong said, deciding she must bite the bullet, but she showed her dissatisfaction indirectly and regarded him discreetly. Songsu only smiled sadly.

"Well," she said, "what were you thinking about when you came over here?"

"I wasn't thinking about it. My feet brought me here before I even decided." He laughed. Sochong's eyes shone brightly.

"Can't you just say, 'I wanted to come and see you'?"

"It doesn't make any difference."

"You seem as tense as a new bridegroom on his wedding night...sitting there silent....Do you want me to play something on the *komunko* for you?"

"Oh no, no. I don't have a good ear for music."

"Ho-ho-ho. Then what do you want? Just to sit there and play dumb?"

Handing her the wine, he said, "Here, have another drink." She emptied her first glass, then another. Sochong was a woman who could hold her liquor.

"Sir?"

"...."

"If you think a woman like me knows neither love nor chastity, you're wrong."

"...."

"I have ended up in the profession of pleasing men because I was born with bad luck, but that doesn't mean I give my heart to every man who comes along. Do you think only the decent women are the chaste ones? We who live catch-as-catch-can like weeds on the roadside have chaste hearts. Men violate our bodies, but we have hearts pure as white jade."

Sochong focused her alcohol-sharpened gaze on Songsu. "Do you know the story of Hongnang in Ongnumong? Yes, she was only a humble *kisaeng*, but nobody has been chaster, more modest than Hongnang. If you regard me as a prostitute, I would rather you didn't come here."

Songsu paused, fumbling for a response.

"Well, I'm not as heroic as Changcook Yang in the story," he said, trying to be witty, but it didn't come out that way.

"And I'm not as beautiful as Hongnang either. Look, what I am trying to say is that I want to consider everything, as I change the way I think. I can have the luxuries I want, though my life isn't like that of upper class women. I'm not looking for money from you. I really like you, but you despise me. You think it's unseemly for a respectable man like yourself to consort with a *kisaeng* like me. I know that very well." Sochong began to sob. The liquor had made her feel passionate and free. Songsu didn't try to comfort her, but only pour himself another drink.

"When did I treat you badly?" he asked after a long silence.

"Badly? When did you treat me anyway? You don't know how much I think about you every day, night and day."

"Please, don't cry. Fill my glass."

She filled the glass, continuing to sniffle.

It was very late. It was quiet around the house; probably Sochong's errand girl had already gone to bed.

"Sochong?"

"Yes, sir."

"How old are you?"

"What do you care how old I am? You don't care about me. I'm twenty-nine."

"Do you have any family?"

"Nobody here in Tongyong...brothers and sisters up in Masan."

"Is that so?" Songsu pushed the low wine table away saying, "My, I think I'm quite drunk."

"It's late, please stay with me."

He took out his pocket watch and saw it was well past eleven, noting he had been drinking since dinner.

"Are you leaving?" Sochong asked, her eyes anxious.

"Do you want me to stay?" He stood up, and Sochong supported him, saying, "I'm afraid you'll fall." When he tried to walk, he toppled over bringing Sochong down with him.

He pushed her aside, and stood up shaking his head and saying, "I'm drunk. I'm drunk."

"Stay here tonight, please." Sochong said, as she wiped the floor and removed the liquor table. Then she went to the pine-and-crane-lacquer armoire and took out silk blankets and coverlets. She looked up at him after she spread them out.

He stood stock-still as if he were stuck to the floor. After a moment, Sochong stood up, and began opening the buttons on his vest.

"I'll do it myself," he said, shaking off Sochong's hands.

"How cold you are...."

The next morning when he awoke, he found that Sochong was not next to him. She had already awoken.

"I am hung over," he said, groaning.

He rose, put on his clothes and hat. Without washing his face or saying goodbye to Sochong, he left.

The Christening

A christening ceremony for the new ships bought by Kim Fisheries was set before they departed on their maiden voyages.

"Ceremony aside, I wish he would go out and see...." Punshi Kim was not the one to complain about her husband. Furthermore, she was anxious about the preparation of the food for the ceremony, which absorbed all of her time and attention.

Songsu had borrowed a considerable sum of money from Cookju Chong and invested it in two large steam-powered fishing vessels without saying a word to her, and then delegated the management of them to Keydo Soh, which made her frustrated and uneasy, in spite of the fact that she was normally the kind of woman who deferred to her husband in all things. Typically, Songsu didn't even come out of his room on a busy day like this. Old Soh, Keydo's father, would preside at the christening ceremony offering a sacrifice to the spirits, but Punshi Kim thought it was her husband's responsibility. *He* should preside. Several pigs would be killed at the seashore where the ceremony was to be held and Keydo was busy arranging everything, but there was as much to be done at home. Every dish had to be prepared in advance and sent there.

"Yongok, your Aunt Chongim hasn't shown up yet. What is the matter with her?"

"I was wondering about her myself. She can't have forgotten. Oh, she'll probably be here any minute," Yongok answered without stopping what she was doing.

Nobody mentioned Yongsook. Since the night of Mrs. Kim's late-hour visit, she had not visited her parents. She didn't want to confront her mother.

Cookju Chong sent two kegs of rice wine and Yongnan's in-laws at Torogol sent a side of beef. But neither Yongnan nor her husband came, which made Mrs. Kim very relieved.

"I just feel so lonely whenever this family gets together..." Punshi grumbled.

She had reasons to complain. Certainly she had enough servant-help, but when it came to family, she could only rely on Yongok. "I always thought I wouldn't be so lonely when my daughters were married and I had sons-in-law. Nothing has turned out as I anticipated."

"Now that Yongbin has graduated, everything will be all right," Yongok said to her mother, who seemed to have gotten older lately.

"They are not going to live here," said Punshi.

Yongbin had graduated and visited her mother for a few days in the spring. She didn't stay long because she had gotten a job in Seoul, and she didn't say anything about marrying Hongsop, which she was supposed to do in the fall. Hongsop, who had also graduated, didn't come down either. Mrs. Kim was worried by Yongbin's disinterest. Songsu, naturally, didn't say anything.

"Mother, somebody's here from Yongsook in Taebatgol...." Yongok said.

Yomoon, the servant, returned.

"Is Yongsook coming?" Mrs. Kim asked, looking tense.

"No, she's not." Yongok replied, when the servant woman from Yongsook's house entered carrying a basket of fresh fruit on her head.

"You must be frantic getting ready," the woman said, and Punshi Kim was embarrassed to look her in the face.

"Yongsook sent me because she is so busy herself."

"...."

"She had me bring you these beautiful fruits."

"Why didn't she send Togi instead of you, an old woman?" said Mrs. Kim in a soft, ingratiating tone.

"Togi is not with us any more."

"What!? Where is she?"

"Oh, been gone — ah, dismissed — for quite a while. There isn't much work in a small household, ya know."

"You're both made of the same stuff — getting rid of that girl and...." she thought.

The old woman disgusted Punshi, but she put aside her anger and said, "Well, sit over here and have some rice cake."

"Thanks, anyway, Mrs. Kim, but I must run; lots of chores, ya know." She was hungry but pretended she wasn't.

Nevertheless, there was something arrogant in her refusal. Punshi, on the other hand, spoke contritely as a sinner though she despised the servant woman secretly.

"Oh, please, I insist. Do have some," she said, and had Yomoon bring in a tray.

Yomoon regarded the old servant suspiciously as she set the dishes before her. Mrs. Kim then excused herself, pleading the need to oversee the progress of everything in the kitchen, but when she got there, she couldn't concentrate.

"If that old biddy opens her mouth and blabs about Yongsook...." she thought, watching the servants scurrying around.

The old servant ate her fill, left the table wiping her mouth with her bony hands and went to the kitchen. "Well, thanks so much for the nice snack, Mrs. Kim. I had plenty and I must go."

Punshi hopped toward her like a scared rabbit. "Oh no, have some more."

"Honest to God, Mrs. Kim, I had more than enough."

"One moment then, please," Mrs. Kim said as she hurried into her room. She returned with a five-won bill that she took from one of her drawers clasped tightly in her hand. As she pressed the bill discreetly into the old woman's hand, she whispered, "Now, you just might need this."

"Look, you don't need to...."

"Ple-ease don't say anything," Punshi pleaded, her eyes and voice betraying the combination of fear and loathing she felt for the old woman.

At sunset, Keydo arrived in his work clothes, and Mrs. Kim quizzed him, "Keydo, is the offering ceremony finished?"

"Yes," he replied, entering the room with a forlorn look on his face. Yongok, who was with her mother, fled the room the second she saw him.

"We really appreciate all the trouble you took with the ceremony today. Where's your father?"

"He went directly home."

"But why? Why didn't he drop by on the way?"

Keydo replied with a silent scowl.

"What's wrong?" she demanded.

"One of them probably took it. We can't help what the sailors do."

"...."

"Before the ceremony began, somebody...."

"...."

"Somebody stole the *Sandai* cake!"

"God in heaven," Punshi said, her face hardening to fear.

The large, round cake made with sweet rice flour the Japanese used for the offering ceremony was called "*Sandai*." In those days, they had no choice but to accept Japanese customs.

"Maybe we weren't sincere enough in our offering."

They sat face to face, pondering the problem. It was impossible to ignore such an inauspicious sign. That the main offering, the *Sandai* cake, had disappeared was no small matter. Fishermen, wherever they are found, are deeply religious folks.

"We can't control the actions of every person," Keydo said, trying to overcome his discomfort and view the occurrence in a positive light.

"Oh dear, something always happens," Mrs. Kim fretted. "And my husband is to blame. He should have gone out there and taken care of things...."

"We know we can't change him."

"But how dare he thumb his nose at the God of the sea when he owns a *fishing* business?"

Again, they sat together silently, contemplating the question.

"Well," Punshi finally asked, "when do you think you will be back?"

"Around *Chusok.*"

"Your father said you might be interested in Yongok."

He did not respond, only stared at the floor. Mrs. Kim studied him intently, trying to read his mind, but to no avail.

"There's no hurry...I'll talk with Mr. Kim," he said, and went to Songsu's study to report that the offering ceremony had been completed. However, he did not mention the missing cake.

"The divers are a constant problem...."

Mr. Kim squinted and lit up, as if to give Keydo the signal to continue. "We were scheduled to leave the day after tomorrow and now they say they have better offers from other ship owners...."

"And?"

"Well, it's obvious — they want more money."

Of the two ships Kim Fisheries had acquired bound for Cheju, one was brand new, and the other was rebuilt. Each had four divers and a large crew including an engineer, a cook and a back-up. Divers had to be treated differently from other workers. By nature, they were danger-loving daredevils or they wouldn't have become divers to begin with. They risked their lives every time they went down. As a group, they had many more accidents than other fishermen and a cramp meant certain death. In fact, several of them died each year. Divers were avaricious and adventurous sons of fishermen who learned diving to support their families. They were paid in advance higher wages than the rest of the crew for their high-risk profession. Once they earned the living expenses for their families for a year, many of them took off for Cheju or Japan. Some of them blew a year's wages on wine and women.

"You take care of it," said Songsu Kim, once again leaving the task to Keydo.

ॐ

The Voyage

In Keydo's absence, Old Mr. Soh could oversee the fishing operation in Tongyong.

Keydo left for Cheju, in command of the two ships. The new Namhae and rebuilt Choonil slipped out of the harbor side by side keeping an even distance between them as they went. Their flags fluttered on the breeze. Keydo listened carefully to the sound of the engine coming from below the deck of the Choonil. It sounded fine. The engineer in greasy overalls craned his neck and smiled to Keydo from the engine room. His teeth glowed white, perhaps in contrast to his dark face. The sailors could see Youngsam on the deck of the Namhae looking for something.

"Hey, man, fix plenty. I'm starving!" shouted the chief engineer, who had skipped lunch, making last minute engine checks.

"Don't worry!" Youngsam shouted and waved to the Choonil.

"Would you like something to eat?" Keydo asked the engineer.

"Yeh, I'm hungry as a horse."

He crawled up out of the engine room, covered with grease. Keydo brought from the cabin some of the rice cakes and steamed fish Mrs. Kim had prepared. The engineer sat down on the deck and stuffed his mouth full.

One of the divers, a man named Kim came strolling out onto the deck and said, "Great weather we've got!"

"The sea is so clear; I think I can see the bottom."

"You divers only look down, but the sky is blue and clear too," the engineer replied.

"That fish looks delicious. I'm going to get us a drink," the diver said, heading off to his cabin. He returned with a bottle of *soju*. Sitting down across from the engineer, he said, "Keydo, my man, want a swig?"

Keydo shook his head. "I'd rather not. Don't offer too many drinks to the engineer."

"Oh, don't worry."

Keydo stared back at Tongyong disappearing into the distance.

"As a matter of fact, I'd like to catch me a nice big red snapper and have *sashimi*," the engineer said, chewing a mouthful of dried fish behind a gulp of liquor.

"You're nuts, man. We'll all have our fill of fish by this time tomorrow — and we ain't gonna see nothing but fish till we get back."

Divers dug abalones and giant clams from the sea, but they sometimes speared a fish for *sashimi* if one got close enough.

"Fish from Cheju ain't very good though," the engineer complained and Kim agreed, "You're right."

"The abalones are bigger, but they can't hold a candle to the ones caught around Tongyong when it comes to taste. Just not as chewy. Not bad, but not great. Just big."

"You know, I heard of this abalone that swallowed a girl. Swallowed her whole," said the diver, rubbing the nape of his veined neck.

"Aw, bullshit. Now an octopus can swallow a man, but no goddamn abalone can."

Keydo, smoking quietly by the ship rail, ignored them.

The ships skimmed along the waves at top speed. Youngsam smiled and waved at a passenger ship from the Namhae. He was happy. He liked long voyages and was pleased with the pay. The spring sun warmed the deck.

"The abalone got this girl in Cheju. A looker she was too, goddamn good lookin'!" He licked his chops. "An' a hell of a good diver too. Made a boodle o' money, this one. Was engaged to a man, with a big ole dowry."

"Lucky stiff. That's the kind 'a woman I need. Then I wouldn't have to work. Man, you want the good life, get yourself one a them gals."

"Stop interrupting. See, she had this place she had to go to fish by herself, nobody — even her friends — knew about. And she was smart enough to keep it to herself. That's why she collected more than all the rest and made, like I said, a boodle 'a money. One day they all came out of the water and noticed she wasn't there by the fire."

"Ya s'pose she died?"

"Hell yes. That was the end. And her parents did everything they could to find her body, but it never came up. Why they even had a shaman in and all."

"How could a body float if an abalone ate it?"

"Listen and stop interrupting. She told her fiancé all about the secret place she used to fish, so I'll be damned, he goes down there, though he don't know the exact spot. He finds this enormous cave. Thousand-of-years old abalones, mussels, and oysters — big mothers — stuck on the walls inside the cave like scorched rice on the bottom of a pot." The diver's eyes grew wide and his voice melodramatic as if he'd seen it himself.

"Listen to this: he found her hair stuck to a big rock."

"She didn't float to the surface because she drowned inside the cave."

"No sir. You know what — it was a giant abalone, the guy mistook for a rock. That big sucker just sucked that girl right up."

"Oh, give us a break. Abalones don't grow that big."

"And why not?"

"You said it swallowed her whole?"

"Yes! Big as a boulder, and ver-ry possible."

"Did you see it with your own eyes — the dead girl in the abalone?"

"No, but I know it's true."

"Well, did it suck up the guy too?"

"No, he the hell out of there!"

"You better be careful. A man with a wife and kids. Could happen to you!"

"Must have been her destiny. That's what I think," the diver said.

"All-ee up," the engineer said, and stood up stretching his arms.

"If I could get enough money ahead, I should live on land like normal people. Shit...."

"Myself, I can't live on land. It's too boring. Maybe I'm haunted too, a sea creature...."

"You're destined to die in the sea."

The engineer stretched legs on the deck a bit and then climbed back down into the engine room.

"Keydo." The smiling diver, his face flushed with the liquor, walked toward Keydo, standing alone, and said, "You better make a haul this time."

"Why do you say that?"

"What do you mean, asking me 'Why'? Aren't you going to be married?"

"Be married....?" Keydo Soh smiled bitterly, ignoring what he had heard. "Hey man, I heard you are going to marry the boss's daughter."

"Who's talking that trash?"

"Your father!"

Keydo scowled without looking at him. The diver was eager to discuss the topic, but noticing the depressed look on Keydo's face, dropped it. "Ah, it's none of my business. I am better off to find a card game."

He touched the rubber diving suits hanging next to the cabin, and went below.

They were far from land now. The ship had traveled many miles. The sun was setting. Keydo had agreed with his father that Yongok was a good marriage prospect. But it was impossible for him to forget Yongnan.

People without a Country

The night the ships had left, Chungku arrived at the Kim's, looking worried.

"Hello there Chungku!" Punshi said, welcoming him.

"Is Songsu in?"

"Yes, in his study."

"Punshi, you've done a lot of work to get these ships off."

"I try to be helpful. By the way, is Chongim sick?" she asked.

"No," he replied gravely, heading toward Songsu's study.

"Chungku, come in!" Songsu said.

"Well, I heard your boats finally sailed."

"Yes, they did."

"I am sure you were frantic with the details before their departure."

"Keydo made all the arrangements. I didn't do much actually."

"For a young man, he is quite reliable."

"Indeed he is, so I trust him to make most of the business decisions," Songsu admitted.

Chungku fidgeted nervously. "Well, I intended to be there, but because of something unfortunate at my own house, I was unable to, but I am relieved to know that all went well."

"Something unfortunate? What?"

"The police showed up and searched the place."

"What for? Why?"

"They told me Tayoon was under arrest in Japan."

"Tayoon!" Songsu blurted out.

"I'm confused because they didn't tell me exactly what the charges were."

"Young people often become tangled up in their own ideology," Songsu said.

"I am sure he didn't violate the law, but I am worried nevertheless," Chungku said.

The two men exchanged rueful glances.

"Did you send a message to Chongyoon?"

"I sent him a telegram, and I'm going to Japan with him."

"Certainly. I understand."

"These days the world has become so evil nobody can live an honorable life. We don't have our own country, we die when these imperialists say we must. What a wretched world we have. Even the old folks who don't care about anything else despise Japanese policies here, and of course, it is the nature of a young man to rebel against authority." Though he was worried, Chungku defended his son's actions.

"Nothing can last forever, and that includes the Japanese," Songsu said, trying to placate his cousin.

Chungku shook his head shaved smooth as an egg, and waggled his beard, "Give me a date. I don't think you and I will see our country free again." Together, they fell into silent contemplation.

"Sir, may I get you something to drink?" Yomoon asked from the doorway.

Neither man responded. The room now glowed with a warm red light.

"Ah... shall I bring something to drink?" Yomoon asked again.

Songsu finally noticed her and said, "Oh yes, please do."

"My son...he will suffer much because of his rebellious attitude," Chungku said, and went on to reveal his worst fear, "I am afraid the Japanese will torture...cripple him."

"Surely not," said Songsu, not wanting to worry Chungku any further.

"I am afraid the Japanese police will treat him more harshly because of the student revolt a couple of years ago," Chungku said.

"Maybe....."

"There are folks who say children are more of a curse than a blessing, and I see what they mean. Children, even grown ones, are a lifelong heartache. My poor wife is sick in bed over this...." Chungku rattled on, smoking and fidgeting as he spoke.

The servant brought drinks and dried fish and together they sipped indifferently.

"I heard Yongbin is teaching in Seoul," Chungku said.

"Yes."

"She is getting married this fall and will have to quit. Why did she get a job?"

"She knows her own mind."

"That she does. She's the type who will manage wherever she goes, whatever she tries to do, but...." Chungku said disapprovingly, as he still disagreed with Yongbin's decision to marry Hongsop.

"Cookju Chong proposed the other day...." Songsu interrupted him.

"Again? Come on, he's not so stupid that he doesn't know they are already engaged."

"Not Yongbin, Chongyoon."

"*My* son, Chongyoon?"

"Yes."

"Never. Never in a thousand years. Never in a million years. Even if my son were a perfect louse — which he is not, thank God — I wouldn't let him marry Cookju's daughter." Chungku became more furious. Songsu smiled silently. Any other Tongyong father receiving such a proposal from Cookju Chong would be flattered and accept with copious thanks, but Chungku flat-out and sternly refused even to consider it. Songsu regretted having consented to the marriage between Yongbin and Cookju's son.

"I don't like him, but I'm not in a position to prevent Yongbin's marriage...rich or poor, people should be honest and upright. Have you ever seen a child who didn't revert to type and imitate his parents?" Chungku demanded.

"Not all of them," Songsu said.

"Maybe you're right. We can't change their fate, but if the parents are good people their children are more likely to be."

Then he realized he was hurting Songsu's feelings by implying that Yongnan was evil, not ill-fated, so Chungku took another gulp of his drink and changed the subject. "The wind has picked up," he said, listening to the sound in the trees outside.

"It's not a strong wind."

"I pray all goes well with your ships. They should be close to Cheju by now."

"I think so."

After Chungku left, Songsu asked to see his wife.

"Did you call for me?" Punshi asked, as she entered looking ill-at-ease. She'd heard the rumor that her husband often visited the *kisaeng*, Sochong. She presumed he was going to inform her that he wanted to make Sochong his concubine.

"I want you to go to Chungku's at the East Gate...." Songsu said, as if talking to himself, avoiding his wife's eyes.

"But—he was just here!"

"Yes, that's why you need to go there."

"I do?"

Absorbed in his own thoughts, Songsu opened the safe beside his stationery chest, counted out ten ten-won bills and put them into an envelope. He said, "Take this to...."

"What's wrong?" Punshi asked cautiously, studying his expression.

"Tayoon was arrested in Japan."

"Oh my goodness! Tayoon!" She was shocked and upset, as it reminded her of Yongbin's arrest earlier in the year. "Is this really true?"

"Chungku said so. Chongyoon will certainly give his brother bail money, but this kind of thing requires big money. And they are traveling to Japan...." Songsu handed her the envelope.

"Dear God, what will become of him?" Punshi wrung her hands.

"Chongim is heartbroken. You should go and try to console her."

"How could this have happened?"

"And you'd better hurry," Songsu said, frowning irritatingly. He lit a cigarette staring at the back of his wife, who hurried off.

Since he had begun visiting Sochong, Songsu Kim felt awkward around his wife. He didn't know whether Punshi knew about her or not, but the fact that she never mentioned it made him more uncomfortable. She would agree to his having a concubine, because she had already suggested he take one in order to conceive a son, but he didn't want her to know about his affair. And he didn't want to take Sochong as a mistress and live with her.

ॐ

Missing Ships

A week after the ships left for Cheju Island, Songsu received an urgent telegram from Nagasaki, Japan. It said that the Namhae was missing in a storm and the disabled Choonil had drifted to a Japanese port.

"Ooh, no-o-o," Songsu groaned. Disaster was the farthest thing on his mind. The day the ships departed, the wind had picked up, but it was calm enough to sail. Two days later Songsu received a detailed explanation of what happened by mail from Keydo:

Dear Sir,

I think I should write and inform you as much as I know, though at this time we are concerned about the Namhae. All was well with both ships until the evening of the first day. The Namhaehwan was leaking a little and the men had a hard time bailing, but land was within sight and we continued. However, the Choonil's engine broke down in heavy seas. High winds of the storm separated the two ships. The Choonil drifted three days before meeting a Japanese trading vessel and currently it is being repaired in Nagasaki.

My deepest regrets —

Contemplating his loss, Songsu couldn't finish reading the letter. He was convinced the Namhae was wrecked. The family was totally distraught. Songsu had instructed them not to tell anybody, but the crew's families had gotten wind of it and were collecting in the courtyard creating pandemonium.

"Oh, my God, what am I going to do? We are all dead, too."

An old woman with unruly gray hair like onion roots pounded on the ground. A young wife with a baby tied on her back paced, sweating profusely. Children cried, whined, scrapped and fought.

"Please. Please everybody. Let's remain calm. We cannot even say what's happened until Keydo comes." Though exhausted himself, Songsu tried to soothe the relatives.

No news of the Namhae arrived before Keydo.

"You poor man," Punshi said, welcoming the haggard Keydo. When their eyes met, each instantly recalled the missing *Sandai* cake.

When Keydo entered Songsu's room, Songsu looked up as if he had given up all hope. Keydo sat and lowered his head as if prostrating himself and said, "Sir, I am so very sorry."

"Let's not worry about the ship. What will we do for the families of the men?" Songsu spoke in a monotone.

"The wind wasn't that high...it was as if we were haunted...I should have ordered the men to abandon the Namhae," Keydo said.

"Yes. That way, we could have saved their lives even though the ship went down," Songsu agreed.

"It may be drifting in the open sea...." Keydo was unwilling to abandon his hope that the crew survived.

"We can't do anything but wait."

They looked at one another wretchedly, as neither had a better plan than to wait and hope. From the garden they heard hollering. The missing crew's families had gathered to hear what Keydo had to say.

He went out to the courtyard. Though his cheeks were hollow and his eyes blood-shot with fatigue, he walked straight to them. The crowd quieted. All eyes were on Keydo. He pressed his hand to his forehead. Punshi and Yongok stood dejected, like chicks in the rain.

"YOU are alive!" the old onion-haired woman shouted, pounding the ground as she demanded, "Where is my son, Mansu?"

Keydo made no response.

"I want my son back! You're here, but where is my son? I'm an old woman alone, o-o-h-h, Mansu, Mansu!" she wailed and her keening ignited the rest of the crowd, which began weeping bitterly.

"Ahy-go, ahy-go! My poor unlucky son! While other sons slumber in warm rooms, you sleep at the bottom of the deep salt sea this snowy, windy winter night. Poverty drove you to your death. Oh, woe is me; how am I going to live without you Mansu?" the old woman moaned. The young woman perspiring heavily around her face and neck gave her breast to the fretful child. The infant sucked hungrily, but she had no milk to give him and he began crying over the dry breast. Looking down at him through her tears, she asked, "Why, oh why were you born?"

Keydo stood frozen like a statue of himself. Yongok and Yomoon made sesame soup in the kitchen and invited the mourning women in the courtyard to have some. But the old woman ignored them and continued wailing.

Keydo studied Youngsam's mother, who had once been to the fishing hut. Smoking her cigarette, she got a bowl of soup from Yomoon, and without pausing, stubbed out the cigarette with one hand, gripped a spoon and dug in. She had come from Yosu, and camped out in Kim's courtyard awaiting news of her stepson.

"Poor Youngsam!" Keydo said, feeling a stab of horror. Freckled-faced Youngsam was a sailor at heart, who preferred being at sea to working on the island, and his only ambition was to be a captain.

"Please stop, this won't solve the problem," Old Mr. Soh complained. "We do what we can to stay alive. A person is not always in control of a situation. You know, the Kim family will be reduced to poverty like many of you. It's throwing oil on the fire for you to wail here at this house. What will they do?" He had been harassed by them before Keydo came back and his voice reflected his irritation.

"What are you talking about, you damned old bastard! You're just relieved your son is back safe and sound. Yeah, you're happy. Sure, you're feeling fine." The old woman stood up abruptly and walked toward him pointing an accusing finger. He disappeared without responding to her.

"I don't care if the Kims get rich or poor! I have lost my treasure, my child, my precious son! Hayh-u-h," she sobbed, falling to the ground and tearing at it with her hands.

"Look, who knows? The ship may have drifted south to an island. Stop crying and hope," Keydo said, putting his arm around her shoulders, but suddenly he was despairing of seeing it again himself.

As the sun set, red clouds gathered over Kongji Island. The seagulls spread their pink wings diving for fish, crying like infants.

Two Brothers

Tayoon was lying on his stomach with a pillow under his chest, reading. Freshly shaved and looking dispassionate, Chongyoon sat propped up against the wall, trimming his nails. Both of them wore glasses.

Chongim, sitting next to them, put her sewing things into the box saying to herself, "Both our families are doomed to misfortune this year. Poor Punshi! That Songsu is totally ignorant of reality...." Then she went off to the kitchen to fix dinner.

Tayoon had spent a month in prison. He had been arrested simply because he spoke out about independence from Japan, not because he had been involved in a demonstration. Tayoon didn't mention it because he realized it was stupid to have gotten arrested.

"Uncle Songsu is going to have big problems." Chongyoon said, clipping as he spoke. A sunbeam from the window fell on his wide forehead.

"He is wealthy enough; he will not lose everything...." Tayoon closed the book and reached for a cigarette. He looked pale, but not depressed.

"Well, losing one ship is certainly not enough to wipe him out, but the crew's families are there day and night demanding compensation."

"That's to be expected. He has to support those widows and orphans," Tayoon said.

Chongyoon looked up at his brother and said, "That's nonsense. Even a multi-millionaire couldn't do it."

"You mean, you don't mind whether widows, orphans and aging parents starve," Tayoon said, in a critical tone of voice.

"They are going to have to find their own way through this. If the owners have to be responsible for the family of every victim, the fishing industry will fold overnight," Chongyoon said, resuming the pink-pink of trimming his nails.

"When did you get so bourgeois, brother?" Tayoon asked.

"The day I was born. An individual is responsible for himself. More's the pity; I'm flat broke."

"Oh, yeah. Well, you'll be raking it in soon enough," Tayoon exhaled slowly through his nose.

"Ah yes. I will live as well and flashy as I can. Parade everything I own in front of the poor." Chongyoon smiled enigmatically.

"You've changed — you've gone from a coward to a mean-spirited egoist." Tayoon extinguished his cigarette and stretched out.

"Well, I'm certainly not a big-mouth idealist or revolutionary like you. Or a hypocrite either. You are inconsistent, talking trash that is nothing but self-deception. You don't make sense." Chongyoon had grown weary of Tayoon's impassioned philosophical speeches.

"Cowards and narrow-minded people always defend themselves by attacking. The result of having no ideals and the best defense of weak men who simply get what they can for themselves out of every situation." In the end, Chongyoon's easy flexibility and realism dominated Tayoon's hot-tempered idealism.

"You're shadow boxing, brother. You can't affect the situation," Chongyoon said.

"Shadow-boxing? I have dedicated my youth to making humanity better. Why do you think concern for the human race and ideas an empty pursuit?" Tayoon spoke grandly, as if addressing a crowd.

"Human?" Chongyoon sniffed, "what's human? Life is empty and ends with emptiness," he said, goading his brother.

"You sound like a Buddha. Is that all life is about? At first you were arguing for individual responsibility and now you are rattling on about emptiness. What do you really think?"

"I think I don't want to argue with you and your expansive delusions. Give your lofty ideals to heroes. You are obsessed with the notion that you can make a difference, change something. But nothing changes. You do not improve the situation, but make it worse. What have you done? You run your big mouth, and get arrested, and did it save anybody? Is Korea any closer to independence? No, you get beaten up, cause a disaster in the family without influencing Japanese control over this country a whit." Chongyoon softened his tone and turned his attention to the end of his nails.

"Not every seed sprouts. Rarely, anyway. You don't always know; your actions could bear fruit when you aren't even there to see it."

"The seed analogy is a good one, but you'd better focus on a single exact result you want to achieve then, instead of this silly shotgun idealism."

Overwhelmed, Tayoon sprang to his feet and said, "You are just like Hongsop — no ambition, no passion."

"Hongsop? Is he still in love with Yongbin?" Chongyoon inquired dispassionately, which bugged Tayoon.

"You fancy yourself a scientist, intellectual and detached, not an excessive, hyperbolic sort like myself. Then you should know one must begin with a hypothesis to seek the truth," Tayoon restated his remark placing the word "hypothesis" for "suspicion."

"I'd rather be living in the real world than seeking some nebulous truth. I'm free to do that, aren't I?"

"Seek and you shall find. Don't and you are nowhere. No beginning, no end. Nothing."

"Okay, agreed, but not everybody can be a seeker. I told you I think it is a delusion."

"You purposely underestimate what I am doing. I am my own man; I always make my own way. A cushy life like yours is not life, but death. You leave no history."

"I don't mind a bit, little brother. History is dead documents. People live and die in the situation they find themselves."

"You're being evasive. Of course, I agree with you that people live and die in their own time, but after the end, there will be a new beginning. People die and are born again and again...."

"History repeats itself. Repeating history has no meaning."

"Not just repeats, it evolves," Tayoon insisted.

"Do you mean the order of society evolves?" Chongyoon smiled. "Sometimes we can change things, sometimes we can't. We can't control the flow of history. People live and die as individuals. They must, whether they like it or not, confront every situation alone individually. Sometimes they lose. A revolution won't help the group, only certain individuals."

"NONSENSE!" Tayoon shouted, "The group, the nation of Japan has conquered the nation of Korea. No individual did that."

"Are you trying to force me to be a patriot against my will?" Chongyoon stared at his brother coldly. "The strong always conquer the weak. That's the order of nature — and society too! Your so-called patriotism is romanticism, subconscious hypocrisy."

"People like you, Chongyoon, betray this nation. You are rationalizing Japanese imperialism!" Tayoon, losing his temper, hollered.

"I don't care what you call me because it isn't true. The power to be victorious isn't nationalism. Do you think the citizens of Carthage and Hannibal were defeated because they lacked patriotism? No. Do you think the British created an empire on which the sun never set in the name of righteousness? Ideology is the pastime of the idle. Please spare me your petty heroism and patriotism. Okay? Because I don't want to bail you out of jail again, you hear?" Chongyoon said.

Exhausted, Tayoon stopped arguing and lay back down saying, "Ah, the great cosmopolitan. . ."

Chapter Four

ॐ

Infanticide

After the boat to Yosu sailed past the piers at the mouth of the port of Pusan, the heavier seas of the Korea Strait began to pound against the portholes. When the ship approached the point where the Nakdong River emptied into the sea, the waters even became rougher, and many passengers were already lying down in the cabin. Children began crying and frail women vomiting. The weather was good, but the seas were high. There was a stiff breeze, and Yongbin, leaning against the deck rail, was watching the waves. Her pale face and the wind whipping her hair mirrored her mental state.

She returned home every summer and winter, but this was the most difficult trip. Now that she was out of college, she expected to feel free but felt more burdened than ever before. There was financial trouble at home: a boat was missing from her father's fishing fleet. He had taken a mistress, and Yongnan was still running back home every chance she got. Tayoon, having been taken into custody by the Japanese police, had just been released. On top of all these unhappy occurrences, she had her own problems with Hongsop. The previous winter he had stayed in Seoul. When she returned there after winter break, he was different. He seemed to be avoiding her as much as possible. Previously, he had occasionally seemed like a spoiled brat who had done some mischief, but now without apparent reason, he seemed afraid of her — reluctant even to get together with her. When she had asked him before she left if he would be going with her, he hesitated, and told her to go ahead alone.

"Why are you being so secretive with me?" Yongbin asked, leveling her gaze at him.

"Secretive?" Hongsop smirked, and looked away from her. She was disappointed, but didn't press him further and made the trip alone.

"His parents must have mentioned *our* marriage," she thought staring at the waves, not wanting to believe he gave in to his parents that easily. It made her miserable to think about her own family in comparison to his — always so quick to react to their own gains and losses. She looked up. To the left there was an endless expanse of ocean and to the right cliffs dotted with evergreens. She recalled the smirk on Hongsop's face.

"It must be a mistake," she said to herself, feeling distressed, but smiling. As he was the object of her affection, she accepted his every move.

The minute she had stepped into the house, a blast of cold wind hit her in the face. Nobody came to greet her. Even Yonghay looked the other way.

"Where's Mom?" Yongbin asked Yongok, who took her bag sullenly.

"In bed."

"She's sick?"

"…."

It was not that she didn't expect it, but the frigid atmosphere was worse than she could have predicted.

"Mom," Yongbin called, sitting by her mother's bedside. Punshi Kim glanced at her daughter, but turned to the wall, and did not even try to sit up. Her face was passive as a woman in a coma.

"It must be a terrible blow to her... but this bad?" Yongbin wondered, not knowing for sure how to react.

The Kim family wouldn't starve because of the loss of one boat, so she couldn't be this sick over the boat. As for Yongnan, she's been acting like this for a long time, and Mom wouldn't mention the mistress.

"What could it be?" she wondered.

Yongbin went into the study and found her father there looking thinner and slighter than the last time she'd seen him.

She bowed to him and said, "Father."

"Ah, you took the early boat?" he responded feebly.

"Yes."

Yongbin lowered her head and waited for him to speak.

"Well then, take it easy," he said, and nothing more.

"I am sure it has to do with the Chong family," she thought.

She left her father's office, washed her face and went to her room.

Punshi didn't get up for dinner. Yongbin was sure she herself was the reason for the silence in the household. However, that night Yongok told her the real story.

"They took Yongsook to the police. Her brother-in-law says she killed her baby and threw it in a pond."

"Is this true?"

"I don't know; I just hope it's a lie," Yongok sighed.

It was a strange case. A doctor from Mercy Hospital had often visited Yongsook's home since Tonghoon was frequently ill. She evidently began having an affair with him and had gotten pregnant. She was fearful that if her brother-in-law discovered the child, he would kick her out of the house and she would lose her fortune, so she had the baby, killed it and dropped the dead body into a pond. The doctor's wife went to see Yongsook's brother-in-law and they went to the police. The story was all over town; the details were being exaggerated as it passed from person to person.

"I can't believe it....I mean, a doctor? A doctor should have known better. . . should be able to handle this sort of thing better. . ." Yongbin said.

151

Yongbin could understand her sister's affair with the doctor, but she couldn't believe the allegation that she had murdered the baby. Then she heard that Hongsop returned to Tongyong three days after she did. He didn't come to see her, though. One evening at sunset, his father Cookju arrived. Mr. Chong put on a brassy smile when she greeted him, and she felt miserable.

"Is your father in his office?"

"Yes," Yongbin said and went to the door, "Father, Mr. Chong is here to see you."

"Ah, he is?" Songsu stopped smoking and got up, looking embarrassed.

"How come you are stuck at home?" asked Cookju Chong, when he followed Yongbin into the room, and said magnanimously, "Come on, let's go over to Sochong's."

As soon as Yongbin heard "Sochong" mentioned, she disappeared.

However, Songsu was not disturbed by the mention of the name. Chong sat down and picked up a fan. Unbuttoning his linen shirt, he began to fan himself impatiently. The dark auburn hair on his chest was slimy, and his thick red neck wet with perspiration.

"Songsu, don't be too upset. You can't force your children to live the way you do."

Songsu only drew a long drag on his cigarette.

"By the way, any word on the missing ship bound for Cheju?"

"I have no choice but to close the business."

"Too bad."

"I'm even having a hard time selling the remaining ship."

"Why?"

"Because that ship has gone missing before."

"Ahah, it's unlucky!? It *will* be tough to get rid of," Cookju said.

"I'll sell some land, pay you off, and manage only the fish hatchery."

Hearing this, Cookju's eyes shone and he said, "You don't have to do that, Songsu. You don't really need to sell land, do you?"

"I need to compensate the victim's families, don't I?"

"You shouldn't feel you have to do that. *You* are the one who lost the most here. Some of those guys even got advance payments."

"Well, you can't buy life with money."

"You are too soft-hearted, sir. You need a strong stomach in business."

"On top of that, I need to replace another old fishing boat and some nets."

"So you're saying you need money. Then don't sell your land; borrow the money from me. If you feel uncomfortable, you can give me the deed for your rice fields. You can always pay me back when you have a good catch, but land is land. It came from your father. Your family has owned it for generations."

It was obvious that Cookju was eager to get his hands on the deed to Songsu's land.

"All right," said Songsu without hesitation. Cookju smiled, self-satisfied.

"By the way, I saw Chungku's older son the other day," said Cookju. Songsu glanced at him, embarrassed and disgusted.

"My, he's a handsome lad. Nice build."

There was no response from Songsu, so Cookju asked, "Well, have you done any matchmaking?"

Songsu stalled. He did not want to be Chong's matchmaker and was doubly distressed because Cookju had brought the subject up at a time when he had more serious matters to ponder.

"I hear he has chosen a fiancée," Songsu said. This was true.

"Who's the girl? A Tongyong family?" Cookju raised his voice, offended at the slight — that they had found a better match than *his* daughter. Who could be better than his family?

"From Taegu. They like each other, I hear. Songsu suppressed his discomfort.

"Well, was this a decision between the two of them or did Chungku approve?" Cookju asked forcefully, as if attacking Songsu.

"He can't do a thing. Children don't behave the way their parents wish."

"Oh, they are a bunch of losers anyway. Wasn't the second son just released from prison?"

"For resisting the Japanese."

"Huh...well, I can't control my own children. My son Hongsop...." Cookju's anger turned to a cynical smile. "He's the first one to become Christian in the family, and now he's getting ready to go to America."

"America?"

"He says someone in Seoul is willing to give him financial backing...."

"And who would that be?"

"His pastor, I hear," Cookju said, smiling maliciously.

Women from Seoul

As Yongbin was getting ready for church, her father asked to see her.

"Father, did you want to talk to me?"

"Yes."

"...."

"Have you seen Hongsop?"

"Not yet ...."

"He came down from Seoul, didn't he?"

"I believe so."

"Has he mentioned going to America?"

Yongbin opened her eyes wide, "What? America?"

"I don't think it was definite. I was told a pastor in Seoul promised to help him. Hasn't he told you?"

"No, he hasn't mentioned it."

"Is that so?"

"Did his father tell you?"

"Um.... Yongbin."

"Yes, Father."

"Hongsop is not a good match for you." Yongbin and her father looked into one another's eyes. They sat silently staring at each other for a long time. In the middle of this string of hardships, they were keenly aware of the other's sadness.

Yongbin left her father's study and went to church with Yongok. The service had already started. They sat in the back row, but Yongbin was nervous and full of doubt. She wanted to reach out to a human being more than God.

When prayers were concluded and the preacher started his sermon, Yongbin noticed Hongsop in the front row. His round head looked handsome; someone was sitting next to him. Her back looked unfamiliar. She was wearing a yellow dress and wore her long hair down, a very fashionable look and quite unusual even in Seoul. Next to her sat a middle-aged woman, who looked vaguely familiar. Her hair was combed into an elegant upsweep style not often seen in Tongyong either.

"Who could they be?" she wondered. Clearly they were with Hongsop. After the service, Yongbin waited under the cherry tree outside the church. He was taking unusually long. Silently staring at the tips of her shoes, she waited. Yongok with her, they both looked down.

When most of the people had left in the church courtyard, Yongbin heard clear, high-pitched woman's laughter from inside. Looking up, she saw the elegant older woman emerging from the church with the young lady in the pale yellow dress followed by Hongsop. Just as she suspected, they were with him.

"Yongbin, who are they?" Yongok asked.

"I'm not sure."

Yongbin hid her restlessness. As soon as Hongsop saw her, he paused and smiled awkwardly. When the women came over, Yongbin met the eyes of the young woman in the yellow dress. "A pretty face," she thought. Then she recognized the older woman and mumbled amazed, "Ah, she's...." She was Minister Ahn's sister-in-law from their church in Seoul. Yongbin frequently went to services there, but had never been formally introduced.

"You've come for Sunday services," said Hongsop stopping in front of Yongbin. His eyes were full of fear. She didn't respond, but only smiled.

"Let me introduce my friends," said Hongsop, looking at the two of them.

"This is Minister Ahn's...."

"I knew who you were; I should have introduced myself," Yongbin replied, nodding. The woman returned the greeting with a gracious smile, which seemed to say, "Well, I know you, too."

Having been interrupted by Yongbin, Hongsop fidgeted awkwardly and then continued, "This is Minister Ahn's niece, Maria. She's attending the music conservatory in Tokyo." Then he turned to Maria, "Maria, this is Yongbin Kim. Your uncle cares a great deal for her. She is teaching in high school."

"Is that right? My uncle spoke highly of you."

Yongbin was not fooled. She knew the young woman was only reacting to the obligations of manners and courtesy. Minister Ahn had never mentioned his niece, but gossips said the minister's brother was terribly rich.

"Hongsop always boasts about his town as the Napoli of Korea. Ha, ha, ha...." said Maria trilling a laugh. "The sea is so beautiful. I'm glad I asked my mother to come here for a vacation."

"Where are you staying? I'm afraid it must be very inconvenient," said Yongbin, looking into Maria's eyes.

"At an inn. The facilities are rather bad. I wish we could afford to build a pretty villa by the sea." A soft sea breeze blew Maria's long hair onto Hongsop's shoulder.

"I'd like to invite you to my house. It's not big, but you'll like it better than a hotel," Yongbin said offering cordially.

"Oh thank you, but I can't. Hongsop has invited us to his house, and...." Maria said childishly. Then meeting Hongsop's eyes, she laughed and he joined her. But when Hongsop felt Yongbin staring at him, he stopped abruptly.

"At which hotel are you staying? I'll come visit you."

"I....I'll take you there, Yongbin," Hongsop said, and then interrupting her before she could reply again, "Maria, I think your mother must be getting tired. We must go."

"Okay. Please do come see me," she said, and the three of them went off.

"He doesn't talk to you the way he did before," observed Yongok, whom Yongbin had forgotten was even there.

Yongok surprised her sister back to reality. Staring straight ahead, Yongbin said, "Come on, let's go." They left the church yard and turned by the big tree walking home through the alleys.

Yongbin was quietly comparing the way Hongsop addressed her and the way he addressed Maria. He used the formal address form with Yongbin. That obviously meant something was developing between them and something was changing in her own relationship with him. She felt as if she were walking in a fog. The only thing she could see clearly was her sister's hands holding her Bible to her breast.

"She's not as pretty as you," Yongok murmured when they were almost home. Yongbin looked up at the sky and laughed bitterly.

When they stepped into the house, Yongbin asked Yomoon, "How is mother?"

"Still in bed."

Yongbin went to her mother's room. Punshi Kim was lying with the comforter pulled up over her head in spite of the warm weather. The comforter was shaking and Yongbin could see her mother was crying.

Standing by her mother's bed, Yongbin said, "Oh mother, you're crying again." The two sisters stood motionless together. Then Yongbin knelt, pulled the comforter back and lifted her mother, embracing her. She said, "Mother, please don't."

"Oh, Yongbin...." Punshi fell into her daughter's arms.

"Sh-h-h, Father can hear you crying."

"Yongbin, you poor child. All my children! Yongsook has destroyed your future."

"Mother, that's enough. Stop. What if father finds out....?"

"Yongbin," Yongok said, and Yongbin turned around, "I'm ashamed. At church, I felt everybody was looking at me. I don't ever want to go out of the house again."

"You have to overcome it," Yongbin said firmly in a low voice as if the words came from deep inside her.

"She is one of our own. How could she do such a cruel thing?"

"It's a sin. Anybody can commit a sin. We just choose not to, that's all," Yongbin said, laughing like a man. But her sister's eyes were full of fear.

Break-up

"Need to talk to you. Please be at the school gate at nine." Hongsop's message was delivered by Cookju Chong's maid to Yongbin. When she finished reading it and raised her head, the girl had already disappeared. She glanced at her watch. It was eight-thirty. A message on such short notice, true to form for Hongsop — still wavering. At the same time, she congratulated herself, having the confidence to be able to see the situation from his point of view. She combed her hair and put on her shoes, but didn't change her clothes. Just as she stepped out the back gate, she met Yomoon.

"Where have you been, Yomoon?"

"Uhm, to Taebatgol."

"Taebatgol? What for?"

"I'm coming from Yongsook's."

"Why?"

"Your mother told me to."

"So did they find the dead baby in the pond?" Yongbin asked dispassionately as if it were some other family's business.

"No, they didn't."

"Well, hurry up and tell mother," she said, walking away slowly thinking, "Poor silly mom believing her daughter would do such a thing.'

The breeze cooled Yongbin as she strolled. Now the days were hot, but as soon as the sun set, sea breezes cooled everything off quickly. It was early evening, but she saw no one as she passed through the back alleys. Her white-striped dress fluttered in the wind. She could see the flickering lights of the ships bobbing in the harbor far below. The lights from the fishing boats and the lighthouse glowed in the open waters.

Hongsop was waiting for her in front of the entrance of the elementary school, smoking. To the left of the gate, there was an ancient tree, its branches reaching out in all directions.

"When did you start smoking?" Yongbin asked, approaching him. Instead of responding, he dropped the cigarette and crushed it out with his shoe. She could see the flowers on the roof of the governor's mansion across from the school, bathed in moonlight. Looking at the flowers, she thought about all the trouble her family was having and wondered how she could stop worrying about her own. Incidents unfolded in her mind one after another.

"Let's go into the schoolyard," Hongsop said, walking toward the school in front of her. He climbed over the loose barbed wire into the school yard. She followed him. They sat side by side on the stone embankment, which was formerly the military headquarters. One end of the embankment was covered by a dark roof and next to it was the front gate of the military office — now off limits to locals — there was a row of cherry trees. The breeze had died down. Legend said a slave girl was imprisoned in the trunk of the big tree in front. People avoided the place at night because they feared her ghost would come out to haunt them.

"Is it true the police pumped the water out of the pond at your sister's house?"

"Don't ask me; I don't know," she said angrily.

"Why are you so upset?" he asked weakly.

"Well, don't you worry about it — you'll just get gray hair. If she did, she'll reap what she sowed."

"You talk like she's some stranger, not your very own sister!"

"In the end, we're all strangers, aren't we?"

He did not respond and there was a long silence.

"Yongbin," he said finally, coughing, "What do you think of me?"

"You're weak."

He pressed his teeth against his lower lip, as if trying not to laugh. "I don't mean my personality."

"Then what are you talking about?"

After a long silence, he asked again, "What do you think of me, as a spouse?"

"It takes a lot of gall to ask a question like that!" she said, trying to calm herself and postpone the moment of the ultimatum he was intent on delivering. The smell of his body so near choked her with conflicting emotions, love and hate.

"We've been friends since we were kids."

"Yeah, somebody beat you up once and I came along and picked up a stone and threw it at him," she said, almost automatically before she could recall the incident. Her eyes began to feel hot, but she squinted back the tears and smiled mischievously.

"We were like brother and sister. We still feel that way about one another."

"...."

"Married people can't have a relationship like that. I think it would be wiser for us to...."

When Yongbin laughed, "Ho...ho...ho...." Hongsop was shocked, but she kept on smiling and laughing as she spoke, "Ho...ho...ho....Hongsop, you are so naive. Do you really think you can justify what you're doing like that? It's a stupid lie and you know it."

There was a long, heavy silence. Yongbin's mocking laughter rang in his ears.

"Hongsop."

As he didn't respond, Yongbin continued. "You could be more honest with me. It's not as if we both don't know what is happening. I came here only to confirm what I already know."

"...."

"You could have told her that we were not romantically involved, and you were not obligated to marriage because a verbal agreement had never been made?"

"...."

"You intend to marry Maria, the girl I met with you today, and go to the States. Her father will support you, right?"

"Who...who told you about going to America?"

"Your father."

"...."

"I know you need my blessing to make this easier for you, and I will hate you, but not long."

Yongbin stood up, her arms looking elongated as if weighted. Hongsop felt the stripes of her dress were coming along the ground toward him. Suddenly, he knelt and put his arms around her ankles, saying "Yongbin, you're wrong."

"Wrong?" Stepping back, Yongbin broke loose and stared down at him.

"I....I made a mistake last winter."

"...."

"Maria was very fond of me. She was young...and I forced myself to...."

Hongsop lowered his head. Yongbin turned around without saying a word and walked down the stone steps holding herself high. Her face, wet with tears, shone in the bright moonlight, but she did not lower her head.

Hongsop did not go after her. As she crawled through the barbed wire opening, she disintegrated to her tears and didn't even hear her skirt rip when she caught it on the wire.

Despair

Yongbin walked toward Miss Kate's house, and when she got there, she called as she knocked on the door, "Miss Kate!" Miss Kate opened the door.

"Oh Miss Kate!" Yongbin cried, as she threw herself into Kate's arms.

Miss Kate led the girl to a chair saying, "Yongbin, sit down. What is it?"

Yongbin sobbed uncontrollably for a time, her face buried in her hands. Miss Kate put her hand on Yongbin's shoulder and waited patiently till she stopped crying. When she wiped her tears, she mumbled in a low monotone, "I don't know....I have never cried like this before."

"When you need to cry, you should."

"I remember once I cried when I was little."

"...."

"Hongsop's friends beat him up; his nose was bleeding. I cried then and again tonight."

"...."

"Miss Kate?"

"...."

"You knew about her, didn't you?" Yongbin turned around at Miss Kate, who was still standing behind her. "Maria, I mean...." Yongbin's voice wobbled.

"Forget about it."

"I'll try. I'll try."

"Poor Yongbin," Kate muttered, kissing Yongbin's head lightly. "He has deserted you, but remember God won't desert you." Now Yongbin was looking out the window across the room, her mind blank. "Yongbin, you are a healthy, intelligent young woman. You will overcome any difficulties in your path."

"I have lost confidence. I can't trust anybody or anything."

"Now, don't say that. You can't expect every day to be spring. Life is many seasons — in autumn the leaves fall and in winter the frigid winter trees stand in the cold with no leaves, but remember, spring's not far off. You mustn't lose hope."

"It's not my fault, Miss Kate. Somebody took my hope!"

"Don't despair, my dear."

"That's all that is left to me."

"You just have to wait. Think about the bright spring that will come after the winter. Trees with branches full of new leaves will make you happy again. Yongbin, don't you see, you are like a tree. Remember you have received an abundance of God's blessings. He has given you these troubles to make you stronger, to test your ability to overcome...."

"Why me? It's not fair. I'm cursed."

"Oh Yongbin, don't say that," Miss Kate reproached her. "Let's pray for your troubles and your family's," she said, patting the girl's shoulders.

Yongbin shook her head and said, "No, Miss Kate, I don't want to pray. I can't face God full of hatred and resentment."

Miss Kate knelt and prayed alone for a long time, and finally stood and looked at Yongbin with a gentle smile.

"You compared me to a young tree," she began, and Miss Kate nodded. "Well, I'm not. I can't go on." Then she said as she stood up, "I'm going."

Kate stared at her.

"I'm sorry, Miss Kate, maybe I'll come back when I have recovered my peace of mind." Miss Kate nodded understandingly and she said good night.

Yongbin pushed the gate open and saw the world bathed in pale moonlight. She ran down the hill.

'Poor child,' Miss Kate thought as she watched her go, closed the window, and sat down.

Yongbin put away her despair and ran home. Entering the house from the back gate, she saw no lights; the living room was empty. She went out onto the porch and looked up at the sky. Meeting Hongsop at the old military office and talking to Miss Kate seemed like they took place ages ago. Like scenes from a movie she had once seen, but couldn't remember when. They disappeared as quickly as they happened, deepening her sadness. Telling Hongsop they were strangers after all allowed her to leave it all behind, but left nothing but loneliness.

"Is that you?"

Yongbin turned in the direction of the voice. "Ah, Yomoon."

"Yes, Miss. Your mother wants to see you."

"All right. Tell her I'm coming."

Yongbin went to her room, turned on the light and looked in the mirror. Her eyes were red, but there were no traces of the tears she'd shed. Then she went to her mother's room. Yonghay was already asleep and Yongok was sitting across from her mother.

"Where have you been?" Punshi asked.

"To Miss Kate's."

"Did you hear about Yongsook?"

"Yomoon told me...."

"They found nothing," Punshi said, though Yongbin already knew. "I believed in her because she is my daughter. No daughter of mine would do such a thing."

"Of course. She's a rich widow. It's only natural that there are people who want to discredit her," Yongbin said automatically and her mother's face brightened.

"I just don't understand people spreading a rumor like that. They ought to be ashamed! I am sure they have no idea of what they were doing to my poor little girl."

"Well, now that they have established she's not guilty, everything will be fine. But you have to start eating and get well."

"Absolutely. I have to live long enough to see you all married and settled," Punshi said with a great effort as if it were the final flicker of energy before her own death and she was grasping desperately at this last ray of hope in the midst of all the despair.

Yongbin pushed her own sadness to the fringes of her mind, told her mother to get some sleep and went to her room with Yongok.

ॐ
Disgrace

The authorities were unable to recover a baby's body from the pond. The doctor's wife reversed herself when the incident led to public discussion and claimed she didn't know anything about the infant to save her husband. When the police found no evidence, both the doctor and Yongsook were released.

The day that Yongsook was freed, curiosity seekers surrounded the police station. Kids shimmied up the electric poles to get a better view and the old folks complained, "Hey, would ya stop shoving. We old folks want to see as much as you!"

It was market day and the vendors from Changdae Hill and the islanders from the pier had crowded into the courtyard in front of the police station.

"What's going on?" a farmer with a loaded carrying frame strapped to his back, who had heard nothing of the incident, stopped to inquire.

"This bitch killed her own kid."

"She what?!"

"You heard right. Slept with the doc, had a baby and then drowned it in a pond."

"Kill her, I say!"

"Sure she deserves to die, but mark my words; she'll march right out proud as a peacock."

"Aw, come on — she will not."

"Sly as a fox, that one. The police were enchanted by her."

"How can that be?"

A porter, listening to an old man and the farmer, laughed and said, "That's the Japs for ya. And her — that silver-tongued devil — seduced them into believing her story, she is so beautiful."

"You mean they really released her?"

"I think so. They always say a pretty face is a woman's best friend."

Suddenly, the crowd that had been only a moment before buzzing like a swarming beehive fell silent. The object of their speculation and discussion stood before them in the courtyard of the police station. The authorities dispersed the crowd, which scattered and then formed again outside the gate.

"Oh, here she comes! Here she comes!!!" shouted the children.

When she reached the door, Yongsook surveyed the crowd, then stepped forward with her head held high.

"Look, head up like a viper," someone shouted, and several people cursed her.

Yongsook paused, raised both her hands and yelled, "Look, I haven't killed anyone. Why are you abusing me?" The crowd backed away without responding.

"I'll get even with him before I die! But even if I could chew him up and swallow him I wouldn't be satisfied now."

The cursing crowd followed her, but by the time she got to Taebatgol, only the children remained. She picked up a stone and threw it at them, but they followed, giggling. The neighbors stood in front of their houses, watched and whispered.

"Listen, here! I'll get my revenge. I promise you," shouted Yongsook.

"Would you get a load of that! She'll ruin her brother-in-law for sure."

"Wicked bitch. I'd steer clear of her. You think a human being can't be more dangerous than a tiger? How can her brother-in-law sleep nights? Now that he's tried and failed to have her brought to justice."

Yongsook went inside. The old servant woman ran to her. Yongsook stared at Tonghoon angrily and shouted, "Everyone in this whole damn family stands against me. Everyone!" The boy began to cry muffled sobs. Yongsook took off her skirt, tossed it angrily into the hall and hollered, "Give me some water to wash my face."

She bathed her face, while outside the gate the children jockeyed for position at the crack by the hinges. When she finished washing, she looked out and saw their eyes peering through.

"I'll scratch your eyes out, you little bastards!" she screamed, stomped her foot and retreated to interior of the house.

"Out of here! Isn't anything for you to see here anyway," the old servant woman said as she pitched the water over gate onto them and followed Yongsook into the house.

Mrs. Kim's fond hope that all would be well with Yongsook's release was not realized. The punishments meted out by public opinion were far more severe and painful than those of the officials.

Cool winds began to blow. The millet was ripe and the people trekked up North Gate Hill to visit their ancestors' tombs. Having become infamous over summer, the Mercy Hospital doctor wound up his affairs and left town. The fact is, he didn't have any patients anyway and he couldn't endure the people's sneers any longer. Cookju Chong and his wife made a trip to Seoul — to attend their son's wedding.

Still another insult befell the already beleaguered Kim Family. Yongnan and her husband got their own house at Mende. Yongnan's in-laws could no longer support the opium-addicted Yonhak, who had begun trying to sell the family's possessions to feed his habit. They said it was time for the couple to build their own home, but actually Yonhak was being kicked out. After the move, Yongnan didn't come to her mother as frequently as in the past. Instead, Yongok saw her several times in the market. Once she was standing in the street gnawing on an ear of corn. On another occasion, eating a persimmon in front of the fruit store. She was shabbily dressed.

"Yongnan, please don't be seen eating in public like this," begged Yongok, who was so ashamed she pulled on her sister's sleeve gently.

"What am I doing wrong? You know a person has to eat, however decent he or she may be." She put the persimmons in a bundle and handed them to Yongok, saying they were for Yonghay.

"Tut, tut! Would you look at that unmanageable Kim girl! The other day her mother was in here looking weak as a spider. No wonder her daughters weary her to death. Tut, tut," the woman at the side-dish store gossiped.

"Songsu Kim is on the skids, thanks to that houseful of daughters. A robber's wife becomes a robber, and an opium addict's isn't much better. They both buy junk, so they'll be flat broke soon, I'm sure," observed the man at the grain store.

"Well, you can give a buck to a womanizer or a gambler, but not to an addict. A gambler could hit the jackpot, a skirt-chaser might find himself a decent woman, but the addicts squander everything. If a woman eats in public, she will commit adultery. If a man does, he'll be a thief."

Yongok wanted to cover her ears so she didn't hear it. Naturally, Yongnan was completely comfortable never bothering to notice anything that went on around her.

"How can she be so different from her mother?" people wondered.

Yongok ushered her sister out of the marketplace pleading, "Yongnan, please stop this."

"What? What's wrong with me?"

"Aren't you ashamed?"

"What are you talking about? Why the hell should I apologize? And why should I stay home? To take care of my baby? The husband who loves and deserves me? Oh yah!" Yongnan's vulgar response abashed her sister.

"Please sis, don't eat in the street; you know it isn't acceptable. I'll make you some food myself and send it over."

"Well, I enjoy wandering around and choosing what looks yummy and eating it."

Yongok didn't know what to say.

"So, I hear Hongsop married that girl in Seoul."

"...."

"I hope he falls down, breaks his neck and dies. What is wrong with my dear sister, Yongbin? One, she is beautiful; two, she is educated; three, she is broad-minded...." Yongnan ticked off her sister's merits on her fingers, still beautiful in spite of her shabby and generally untidy appearance. A round face and fleshy shoulders made her look voluptuous as well.

"That lousy bastard Hongsop has sabotaged his luck. Come on, nobody is as good as Yongbin. I mean, there's nobody who can compare to Yongbin." Yongnan began referring to Yongbin by name instead of as her older sister, and laughed heartily.

"She talks and acts like a streetwalker," thought Yongok, looking at her sister, guffawing loudly, but she simply couldn't hate Yongnan.

Yongnan stopped laughing and looked her sister up and down, "Yongok, are you planning to go to the convent?"

"What?"

"Girls should be concerned with how they look. We're different from boys."

"You'd do well to worry about your own appearance."

"Me? I'm married and nobody cares how I look. By the way, I hear you are going to marry Keydo."

Yongok turned her head sideways to hide her distressed, conflicted look on her face. The heartache she felt seemed to make her beautiful. That she had lost weight may have been one reason.

Those Who Leave

Yongbin was teaching at S. Girls' High School in Seoul and she brought Yonghay, who had graduated from elementary school, with her to attend high school there. Now Yongok had no sisters at home.

That fall when the Namhae was missing, Songsu Kim began to reorganize the fishing farms around Chi and Hansan Islands. He again appointed Keydo as manager, but they did not prosper. Fish had never been so scarce. Some said the tide had changed. Others said the Sea God was angry and they had to make offerings to calm him down.

In early autumn, Songsu and Punshi Kim offered an elaborate memorial service for the victims of the Namhae at Yonghwa Temple. Though the bodies were never recovered, they had concluded the ship had been wrecked.

"I have been fishing twenty years, and I never seen such a rotten year as this. The sea might as well be dry; couldn't be worse," the old fisherman Yom said. They couldn't help but be discouraged. None of them were making a decent living.

For his part, Keydo thought there should be a way to combat it, if it were not for the fishermen's constant complaining. Though he didn't believe in an offering ceremony, he himself could come up with no better remedy. Frankly, he wanted to quit. He had an ominous foreboding that Songsu's fishery would fail though he didn't have any basis for it.

One day he came into Tongyong from the island. When he entered Kim's gate, Yongok, who was dyeing some fabric, stood up startled. They looked at one another. Yongok became tense. Keydo tried to speak but couldn't, and just headed for Mr. Kim's office instead.

Keydo sat before Songsu, briefed him on the state of the fishing business and then proposed, "What do you think if we closed it for the time being?" Songsu didn't respond.

"Once a thing goes bad, it always. . ." Songsu's eyes were so intense Keydo dared not finish the sentence.

"Everything has its ups and downs. You should continue." It was obvious that he was quite determined and did not intend to continue discussing the matter. Keydo remained sitting, legs folded for a long time.

Then Keydo said abruptly, "I want to marry Yongok."

"Do you?!" The pitch of his voice suggested Songsu had not expected this offer. The senior Mr. Soh had hinted his interest in Yongok as his daughter-in-law several times and Punshi also wished to have Keydo for a son-in-law, but he never let his own wishes be known.

"Yes, sir."

Keydo rubbed his big hands together. He had a far away look in his eyes. Keydo never confronted the idea of marrying Yongok until he came to the Kim residence. He himself was shocked at what he had just proposed.

"You know we're not that well off any more."

"...."

"Her good-nature is all she has now. She was not one born to have good luck."

"I understand that. I want to marry her anyway."

Keydo repeated what he said. Songsu studied him for a long while and then brought out some pills and took them. "For indigestion..." Songsu smiled bitterly.

"He doesn't look well," thought Keydo observing Mr. Kim's weary look.

Keydo left Songsu's office and went to the women's quarter of the house. No one was about. Mrs. Kim was not home yet.

He decided to go back, but stopped and began wondering. He raised his head and surveyed the yard and garden. Beside the well, there was some leftover dye bath and the dyed silk hung over the line, but Yongok was nowhere to be seen.

Keydo stepped toward the kitchen and stopped after a few steps. Yongok sat on the kitchen terrace sobbing. She didn't even notice Keydo standing there. Her raven hair rose and fell as she cried.

"Yongok!" She stopped sobbing, but only lowered her head further. Keydo drew closer.

"May I have a sheet of paper and a pencil?" He obviously had something to say to her, but couldn't face her; he only frowned. Without speaking she went inside and returned with a sheet of paper and a pencil. She handed them to Keydo, avoiding his glance. He seemed unable to speak, and so went to the main hall, sat on the edge of the floor and began writing. The note to his father said, he couldn't stop by because he had to hurry back to the island. He also informed his father that he wanted to marry Yongok as soon as possible. After folding a five-won bill in the letter, he stood up. Then he went across the backyard and stood in front of Yongok's room.

"Yongok!"

"...."

"May I come in?"

"...."

Keydo looked down on Yongok's shoes placed neatly on the stone step.

"May I have an envelope?"

Shortly, he heard something moving in the room. The bustling continued and finally Yongok opened the door. Now she seemed to expect something from Keydo. He blew into the envelope, slipped the note in and licked it shut.

"Would you send Yomoon to my house with this letter when she comes back?"

On hearing his request, the disappointment became visible on her face.

Keydo went off, leaving the letter at the edge of the hall. It was getting dark when he reached the main road. He knew he should have said something to Yongok, but he couldn't. Not at all sure he could love Yongok as his wife, Keydo was depressed. What made him decide about this marriage so easily? He felt bound up, tied with string.

As he passed the pier, Keydo spied a slim woman walking with her head down carrying a bundle in her arms. It was Soonja. He knew her not only because she was Yongbin's closest friend and frequently around the Kim household in the old days, but because her dead husband was a distant relative of his.

He looked over his shoulder. Standing at the ticket office, Soonja glanced back at him. Their eyes met; she seemed embarrassed and turned back to the ticket seller.

"I wonder if she's going to Pusan." Though he felt there was something strange about her, he continued on his way. However, when he got to the corner of Tongchung, he met Tayoon coming toward him with a trunk.

"Where are you going?" asked Keydo.

Hesitating, Tayoon smiled.

"Are you coming from Japan?"

"No, I am going *to* Japan."

"Oh, you are not coming from your house?"

"No, I have been to a friend's."

"What are you doing here now? It's not vacation."

"Vacation or not, I have given up the goddamn studying."

"What? You quit school?"

"My parents don't know about this. I told them I was going to Japan."

"Then you are not?"

"I don't know yet. I will decide after I get aboard," he said, but didn't look like a man leaving without a destination.

"Bye. I don't know when I'll see you again," said Tayoon, offering Keydo his hand.

"Are you going to China or Manchuria?" said Keydo, lowering his voice and shaking both Tayoon's hands.

"Why there?" Tayoon said, trying to sound as natural as possible.

"To work for our independence."

"Ha, ha, ha...no. Well, not exactly." Tayoon laughed and answered evasively.

"So, well, take care of yourself."

They parted. Tayoon said he didn't know when they would see one another again. Keydo presumed that was significant. The two men saw one another once or twice a year, and Tayoon implied that it would be many years before they met again. Keydo looked back to see Tayoon carrying his trunk, just as he had seen Soonja carrying hers. The figure hurried along under the dim street lights and soon disappeared.

Refusal

Songsu Kim was heading for bankruptcy, but Yongsook, who had caused the ugliest scene in town in years, was on the road to riches. It is true that people don't remember rumors for even three months, but that didn't mean Yongsook was well-respected. Initially, people criticized her money, boldness, eloquence, but then they all seemed to forget her transgressions. For one reason nobody wanted to meddle in everybody else's business and almost everybody owed her money, so they were forced to treat her with respect no matter how they privately despised her. That way they could continue to borrow from her. She had begun to pay even more attention to her appearance and fancy home furnishings than before and demanded people who wanted loans to kowtow to her. She seemed to want retribution for every slight she'd ever received. But showing respect wasn't always enough to get a loan. She was scrupulously careful and kept exhaustive records of every detail.

"I have come to the conclusion that money is the most important thing in life," she said. This had become her motto.

Kim's gate squeaked open. It was Yongok, now married to Keydo.

"Is that you, Yongok?" Punshi Kim, idling in the main hall, shouted.

"Yes, she came back with me," answered Yomoon.

"Yongok, my baby, you are here."

"Yes, Mom, I am," she replied, following Yomoon in.

"Just when I was coming to see you, you sent Yomoon," Yongok set down the bundle she was carrying and caught her breath. She was pregnant now.

"Is Father home?"

"He is out as usual. It annoys me, too, I'll tell you." Mother and daughter sighed together.

"The fishery people complain they run out of rice. What am I supposed to do?"

"Did they send somebody again?"

"Yes, a boy was here this morning."

The conversation halted. Yomoon came in with a bowl of herbal medicine, set it on the edge of the terrace and returned to the kitchen. A lonely magpie landed on the top of the wall and cawed.

"Will we have a visitor?" People believed magpies signaled visitors.

The bird flew off after a couple minutes and Punshi picked up the herbal medicine and drank it. Her graying hair and wrinkled face reflected her deep weariness.

"Mother?" Punshi finished the potion scowling at Yongok. "Come with me to Yongsook and ask her for a loan."

"...."

"She makes loans to everybody here; there's no reason she won't make one to you."

"I have wanted to ask her a hundred times, but I just can't."

"Try. She is your own daughter. How bad can your relationship be?"

"I haven't visited her since she was released. How can I go ask her for a loan now?"

Punshi had been thinking of trying to borrow money from Yongsook for a long time. In fact, she had sent Yomoon for Yongok to accompany her to Yongsook's. But now that Yongok broached the subject, it made her hesitate. However, Yongok succeeded in persuading her mother to go. When they walked over to West Gate Hill, Yongok was out of breath, her shoulders heaving up and down trying to catch her breath.

"How is the baby? Can you feel it move?"

"Yes."

"Stop doing our sewing. I can manage it."

When Punshi could no longer afford to have a sewing woman, Yongok had begun doing it all. Though Punshi said she could manage, she was now far-sighted and had difficulty even threading a needle. Moreover, Songsu was so particular about his clothes that he was really difficult to sew for. The reversal of his fortunes hadn't changed his taste. He was particular about his food due to constant indigestion. He never allowed Sochong to sew for him even though he visited her quite frequently. Punshi couldn't complain because Songsu didn't give her money.

When they entered Yongsook's house feeling awkward as total strangers, she was dipping rice cakes in honey sitting in the main hall. She was surprised to see her sister and her mother. Ill at ease, they stopped in the courtyard before entering.

"We-ll, what do I owe this great honor to!?" said Yongsook, sarcastic from the moment she saw them. Yongok held her mother's hand and sat at the edge of the main hall.

"Come in," Yongsook handed them the plate with the rice cakes but not very enthusiastically.

"We're fine, Yongsook."

"Thanks for notifying me about your wedding. I mean I know a cast-off like me isn't welcome at a wedding, but you could have at least let me know!"

The statement itself was reasonable enough. But rather than explain how she felt, she simply wanted to parade her false generosity in front of the likes of Punshi and Yongok, who obviously had fewer options.

"You didn't miss much. There was no ceremony. We simply vowed in front of a bowl of sacred water."

"What? Why? How come a daughter of Kim, the pharmacist, has such a wedding?" Yongok and Punshi were silent as sinners. "Soonay! More rice cakes," Yongsook hollered and then turned back to her sister and mother.

"How is everything at home?" Yongsook finally inquired after the family, which she should really have done when they arrived.

"Just managing...." Punshi finally spoke to Yongsook directly.

"I hear father spends all his time at Sochong's."

"To calm his fury."

"Caused by his daughters?"

A cloud of anger distorted Punshi's drooping face. It was indeed true that Songsu resented his daughters, but it infuriated her to hear from Yongsook.

"Everybody in Tongyong knows that Songsu Kim is completely bankrupt. Don't you know?" Punshi said, managing to swallow her anger.

"And when he gets mad, he goes to Sochong, right?"

What Yongsook said didn't used to bother Punshi much, but now everything around her had changed, and she felt her eyes becoming red. The servant girl brought a small tray with more rice cakes and a bowl of kimchi. Yongsook invited them to eat, but neither of them felt like it.

"A newly-wed should pay more attention to her appearance. You don't look any better now than when you were a Christian," Yongsook said to her sister when they finished the food.

"I'm still a Christian," replied Yongok, looking down at her white bodice and navy skirt.

"Amazing. What a liberal father-in-law you have! Who is going to honor his ancestors when you, the eldest daughter-in-law, are a Christian?!"

"...."

"And why is it that a young girl like you has freckles all over her face?"

"She is not just feeding herself," replied Punshi, inferring that Yongok was pregnant.

"Oh, already!" Though Punshi and Yongok were alert to an opening in the conversation to state their business, Yongsook monopolized it, as if she were trying to keep them from bringing it up.

"Myself, I thought I was no longer a Kim daughter. When I was in trouble, not one single person from my family came around. Since that incident, not one of you has visited me. I have dreams. I made up my mind — I would never see my family again. She changed.... I don't care whether father's fishing business has failed or not. You people have never sent me so much as a single anchovy. I began to think I didn't have parents or sisters."

"It's no use complaining about the past," said Punshi, who didn't really know what to say.

"Past? It hurt me deeply. How dare you say it's the past, as if it's over and done. Wrong.

The wound I felt is so deep it will never heal till I die." She raised her voice.

"Just calm down, Yongsook. Calm down and help mother, will you?"

Yongsook fell silent, looking at them spitefully.

"In fact, I came here to...." Punshi could no longer speak, but wiped a tear from her eye. "Your father's fishing business is completely done for. A poor catch. We can't pay for nets we've had to have repaired. We have nothing but debts and nobody to ask for help. That's why I am here. Let me have just five hundred...for the same interest rate you give others." She had to pause several times as she spoke to wipe away her tears.

"I don't have enough to make you a loan. I have a son to care for. Nobody has stacks of money in the house." Yongsook said, avoiding her mother's eyes. Her golden hairpiece glittered. Yongok became pale. Punshi fumbled for her shoes and took Yongok by the arm.

"It's no surprise I am treated like this. It was a big mistake to come here. Come on, Yongok, let's go."

Outside the gate, both mother and daughter wept.

Money

"Anybody home?" the exhausted Chongim asked as she entered Kim's front gate.

"Come on in, Chongim," Punshi, glasses on, stopped sewing and greeted her sister-in-law eagerly.

"Whu-u-u, I am so out of breath, I can hardly walk," Chongim said, entering.

With fewer servants and much of their former property gone now, the atmosphere around the Kim household was dreary, but the pomegranates were in full bloom.

"Well, how have you been?" Chongim asked.

"I continue to breathe, so I continue to live."

"Signs of ruin overshadow us." They stared at one another helplessly.

"Have you heard anything from Tayoon?" Punshi asked.

"Tayoon? I wonder if he's even still alive....I have to agree, the really blessed are those with no children at all," she said. But Chongim's expression showed her deep concern for her son.

"Nothing since the letter from him in December?"

"No. He asked for some money and we got a loan and sent it. Since then, no news at all. Our letter to his address came back....Oh, my poor son! What will become of him? He quit studying! Imagine. Parents can't even control their own children. I can't stand watching my husband working day and night for that. I have no reason to live."

"But at least you have one decent son who can help support Tayoon."

"Don't mention Chongyoon. He is being totally bullheaded about his brother, saying that he won't contribute a single won for a wanderer who gives up his studies, and that Tayoon will come back when he has no money and no options. But of course, a mother can't stop worrying...." Chongim wiped her tears with her handkerchief, "I really wish Tayoon would have obeyed his brother and continued his studies. Why he manufactures trouble for himself I'll never know. Does he think that he alone can bring about the independence of Korea?"

"You're right."

"Children are only children while they are little and their parents can hold and hug them. Our efforts have all been in vain. All parents end up brokenhearted."

"You're right."

Chongim dried her eyes and asked, "How's Yongbin?"

"She's fine and sent some money yesterday."

"Did she? She deserves praise. She supports not only her sister, but her whole family."

"And you know how hard she works."

"Yongbin is really honorable and far better than many people's sons."

"But a daughter is just a daughter; she should marry into a family before it is too late. My poor husband — no money, no sons."

"Don't mention it. Son or daughter, they change after they marry. We don't expect our daughter-in-law to live with us. My husband often tells me that an old couple like us should stay out of the way, keep to ourselves as long as they are healthy, and then, when he dies, I can go to Chongyoon's."

While they discussed these grave issues, Yongok came in carrying a bundle.

"Oh hello, Yongok, how are you?"

"Fine, Aunt Chongim, how are you?"

"I can see you are working hard for everybody — both your own family and your in-laws...."

"What is this bundle?" asked Chongim.

"Father's things."

"Oh my, you did all this, though your tummy is as round as a pumpkin...." Chongim tsked, "Why doesn't Songsu have Sochong do his clothes?"

"We can't expect that. He doesn't give her money," said Punshi, "I think preparing his medicine is enough to expect of her."

"Sochong chose him, so she can't refuse to do this for him."

"But you can't criticize her. She's a *kisaeng* for money, but doesn't expect it from him."

"You should get the credit. Since you, the wife Punshi, are on her side, your family is peaceful."

All three smiled bitterly.

"What on earth will become of the fishery?" Chongim asked.

Yongok turned away her face full of blotches, and Punshi answered the question. "For three straight years we haven't made a dime. Keydo is doing his best to revive it, but it's impossible. He has tried to talk Songsu into closing, but Songsu insists on continuing. I don't understand him."

"How is that for stubborn!" Chongim said, tsking.

As the three of them sat contemplating the comment, a stranger appeared at the gate, "Hello, hello!"

"Who's there?" called Punshi, as she arranged her skirts and went out to meet him.

A short, fat man of about thirty, wearing a worn hat entered the yard, and said, "Yongsook asked me to visit you."

"Yongsook?"

"Yes."

"Well, come in and sit down, please."

He took off his hat and seated himself.

"I think she doesn't have any business with us," Punshi began.

"I know you were disappointed the other day. . ." the man said.

"Who on earth are you?"

"Me? I am sorry I didn't introduce myself to begin with. I am Yongsook's secretary. Call me Mr. Pang. I'm from Pusan." The stocky man smiled cunningly, wrinkling the crow's feet at the corner of his eyes. His hat and the worn-out bag he carried identified him as a moneylender.

"Is Yongsook so wealthy, lending so much money that she can afford to hire her own secretary?" Chongim asked, offended.

"It's a tough business for a woman alone," he said, casting a sidelong glance. "She needs me for certain errands, he, he, he...."

"Anyway, what brings you here?"

Pang reached for an envelope inside his coat pocket and handed it to Punshi, saying "As a matter of fact, this is an errand for Yongsook. She asked me to give you this."

"What is it? I can't read."

"It is not a letter. It's money."

"Money?"

"Yes, open it and see."

Punshi put her hand in and withdrew the contents of the envelope — one hundred won.

"Is this for me?"

"Yes. Yongsook sent it. Good or bad, children are the world's most precious possession, ain't that so? He, he, he...."

Clearly, the man knew the whole situation and was very glib. But Punshi put the money back in the envelope and handed it back to him. He winked an eye playfully and asked, "Why ever are you doing this?"

"Never you mind. Just give it back to Yongsook."

Punshi stopped talking to him, and turned her eyes to Chongim, but Chongim and Yongok were watching the envelope.

"Well, I don't know, I just do as I am told." The man smiled slyly, put money back in his pocket, placed the hat on his head and left.

After he was gone, they stared at the floor for a while, and Chongim broke the silence saying, "You better go after him. You know you need the money desperately. As far as that greedy Yongsook, you know she is being very generous to you...." Chongim, who didn't know that Punshi and Yongok had already begged Yongsook for money and she had refused, felt they would never see the money again.

"That much money wouldn't help a bit," Punshi said.

"Good for you, mother," whispered Yongok, moving her dry lips slightly and looking out at the mountain far in the distance.

Crows

Summer had ended and fall began; the sky was cloudless clear blue and a cool wind shook the trees. Mount Yonghwa rose over Pande into the blue void. The hillsides had begun to turn golden. The sea looked bluer and a ferryboat putted toward the land.

"Chongim, want to take the ferryboat across?" asked Punshi.

"No, let's walk through the tunnel to the temple and pray to Buddha."

The two middle-aged women went haltingly toward the temple of Mount Yonghwa to be blessed. Their starched clothes serrated as they walked.

They entered the tunnel, a short-cut to the mountain, following its deep downward slope to the left-turn bend in it. There was no light and they could only smell and feel the wet darkness.

"Do you suppose the light's burned out?" Chongim asked, her voice echoing off the walls of concrete.

"No, look, I see lights over there." Dim bulbs lit only the ceiling, so the two women fumbled in the dark, hand-in-hand. The tunnel was wet; the water had pumped out, but that particular spot always remained wet.

"Namu-ami-tabul. Namu-ami-tabul," echoed Chongim's voice. "Punshi!"

"Yes?"

"I think we will go through this kind of dark tunnel after we die."

"I think you're right."

"The road to heaven may be just like this. "Namu-ami-tabul..." Now they became accustomed to the darkness and walked without each other's support, chanting.

"Punshi."

"Yes."

"Our deaths are fast approaching. I hope we will both be prepared to make our Maker with a clean conscience, but life prevents it. Tiz, tiz....I wonder what I am to do for the rest of my life, just grow old...oh, how sad life is!"

"You have your regrets too?" asked Punshi.

"Of course," Chongim replied, "the rich have their regrets and the poor theirs."

"It's true."

"People are born and die empty-handed, but why must we live in agony?"

"We must pay the debt of our previous sins."

They resumed the chant again. The tunnel ended. They emerged into a dazzling bright field. The white road to Yonghwa appeared before them. To their left farmers tended their crops and children dug for shells. As they passed through the village, leaves fell. Autumn arrives earlier in the higher altitudes. A child collecting acorns skittered past them like a squirrel.

The two women stayed overnight at the temple and prayed from dawn till noon and then returned by way of the village. The entrance of the tunnel yawned at them like a wide-open mouth. The road forked. One led to Kangsan, the village where a group of Japanese wives lived.

"Caw-caw! Make Mom bring me lots of food! Bring me money too, please Mr. Crow!" a child cried in a voice like a baby chick. A half naked boy was sitting on make-shift privy shouting at the crows.

"Oh, that poor child...." Chongim said sympathetically. Passersby could see inside the two hovels by the roadside. In their moldy and rotting thatched roofs weeds and gourds with mottled leaves had sprouted. On the floor a woman was weaving fish nets.

"Caw-caw, come to my house, please Mr. Crow!" When the child lifted his head to the birds, he lost his balance and fell in.

"You stupid, fucking brat," the woman who was weaving screamed as she ran down to retrieve him before Chongim and Punshi could. She grabbed the child, pawing the air and struggling in a mound of human feces, by the collar, pulled him out and threw him on the ground. The boy, covered with filth, fainted. The woman continued howling as she threw a bucket of water on him. On the ground, the child began crying weakly. Punshi and Chongim could only watch helplessly.

"You stupid fucking little son-of-a-bitch, what the hell are you doing, messing around falling in privy," the angry woman went on berating the child.

"Oh, this is absolutely terrible," said Chongim, which made the woman realize Punshi and Chongim were standing there.

The woman stopped throwing water on the boy and said, "Oh God, you must be Mrs. Kim."

"Who are you?" asked Punshi.

"The wife of a diver who went down on the Namhae."

"The wife of...." Punshi stared at the woman trying to place her, becoming embarrassed that she couldn't. As she searched for the right words to address the woman, she entered the yard, but couldn't come up with anything but a stiff "Hello, how are you?" But it was obvious how she was — only subsisting in wretched poverty.

"I only live because I don't die," she said, the tears gathering in her eyes, "We're lucky to have even one meal a day." The child collapsed and began sobbing. His hunger-distended belly visible through the rag of a shirt he wore was a sharp contrast to his thin limbs, so fragile they looked as if one touch might break them.

"Is this your son?"

"No, he lives in this house."

"Then where do you live?" Punshi asked the woman.

The woman pointed next door and replied, "He was so hungry he cried all day long. His mother went to her daughter's to see if she could get some rice. It would have been terrible if I hadn't rescued him," she said, looking down at the boy.

"People think that children who have the misfortune to fall into the privy should at least get a rice cake," Chongim mumbled.

"Rice cake? Are you kidding! Even on holidays we don't have rice cake."

Hearing the words "rice cake," the boy looked eager.

"The father of this boy Tori died when the Namhae went down. His ma and me made fish nets but she hurt her leg and could no longer work, so she stopped. Now she works at the grain mill, but business has slacked off; and she doesn't get that many hours. No work, no food."

Punshi felt guilty listening to the woman as if she herself had caused their misfortune.

"Do you have children of your own?"

"Yes, they are still young and it is a struggle to feed them. They've gone to the beach to dig shellfish."

"Chongim, wait here a few minutes, will you?" Punshi said.

"Where are you going?"

"There was a peddler in front of the tunnel when we came past yesterday."

"All right."

"Oh please, we don't need...." the young woman hesitated.

Punshi hurried to the mouth of the tunnel, where she found several peddlers. They drew their customers both from another village and the nearby elementary school. She purchased some rice cakes and returned. The boy drooled when he saw them. His stomach growled and the woman watched the rice cake with an envious sidelong glance.

"Child, don't eat too many of those on an empty stomach. Have two and leave the rest for tomorrow. Okay?" Punshi handed him two.

"She's right. It's not good to eat too much at once." Chongim said, agreeing with Punshi. "These are a kind of medicine against the filth."

The boy devoured them quickly and licking his lips he looked at the rest of them longingly. So did the woman.

"You should have some, I am afraid you skipped lunch too," Punshi said.

"I-I...don't...." the woman first tried to refuse the offer, then hunger got the better of her and she grabbed one quick as a pick-pocket.

"You have become destitute, and we are bankrupt. I don't even know whose fault it is," said Punshi apologetically glancing across the road.

"It's the sins of our past lives, Mrs. Kim. No fault of yours," the woman said.

A middle-aged woman limping noticeably, balancing a bundle on her head and carrying a bottle in her hand entered the yard. Punshi concluded she was the boy's mother, just as the boy now full of energy from the rice cakes shouted, "Mom, mom!"

The woman ignored them and sighed wearily as she dropped the bundle to the floor. Her ragged cotton clothes were wet with perspiration.

"Listen! Your son had a narrow escape — he fell into the privy."

The woman only reacted by changing her facial expression. Then she removed the towel from her head and dusted off her hair. Gray powder flew in all directions.

"Did you work today?"

"Yes, I got a half-day. I didn't go to my daughter's, but I was able to buy some coarse grain, and got some brine water from preserved fish."

Then she noticed the two strangers. When she spied Punshi, she snarled. Her lips curled back in hatred. Punshi became more embarrassed.

"Tori fell in the privy just as Mrs. Kim came by and she bought some rice cakes for him," the young woman said, recounting the incident for the child's mother.

"That's right, stuff your stomach," said Tori's mother in a hateful voice, kicking her son, "You stupid little piece of shit, you'd be better off dead in the dung." The child began crying, though her anger was certainly intended for Punshi.

"Don't punish the child; he's innocent," Chongim spoke forcefully to deter the woman. However, she didn't respond, but hobbled into the kitchen.

"You know, we can't make a decent living — for ourselves or our children. Please don't be offended by her," the young woman apologized on behalf of the child's mother.

"I understand perfectly. Her husband died and she lives a miserable life because of the accident of one of my husband's ships. It is quite natural that she should hate me." Punshi took all the money out of her purse — two one-won bills and three ten-chon coins — and gave it to the woman.

"Take this money. I know it's not enough, but get some rice and share it with your neighbor." Punshi said. The young woman's face brightened. To make ten chon a day was almost impossible. It was big money for them.

Punshi and Chongim said good-bye to them and headed toward the tunnel. Unlike yesterday they did not feel like talking and just walked in silence.

"People say Mrs. Cookju Chong doesn't say anything whenever she has been to the temple to pray because she believes talking will invalidate the prayers. But I must. How could I be silent when I meet such people?" Chongim said, speaking first.

"The great Buddha knows our minds."

They walked in silence. When they emerged from the tunnel, Punshi said, "Chongim?"

"Yes?"

"I think I live a very easy life."

"Why do you say that?"

"I hear coarse rice is the worst." Punshi seemed obsessed with the poor women.

"Anyway, now they will have rice soup to live on." Chongim said.

"I bet they don't even have salt. That's why she took the bottle of salty fish water."

Chongim didn't respond.

"They say 'poverty overwhelms humanity.'"

When Punshi arrived home, she gathered up all the old clothes around the house and sent Yomoon to those women. Upon returning, Yomoon said, "Oh Mrs. Kim, one woman wept so piteously."

"Who?"

"The young woman smiled and seemed happy, but the crippled one sobbed mournfully. I felt so bad."

"Did she?"

"If I had known, I would have given her these clothes earlier."

"But there are so many poor people. Give her some soybean paste tomorrow. I am sure she doesn't have any salt either."

"Mrs. Kim, we are running out of soybean paste too. The employees at the fishery come for it every day."

"Then we may have to get some from Chongim. Our family is small now, so we don't need as much."

More Tears

"Yongok, are you in here?" said old Mr. Soh as he opened the door, giving her no notice.

"Oh, my!" the surprised Yongok stopped nursing her child and arranged her dress. He sneaked a peek at his daughter-in-law.

"Will Keydo be home for dinner?"

"Yes, he will."

"Keydo sticks with that dying fishing business while he neglects his family," he observed.

Yongok didn't respond, but only looked down at her baby. The downy-haired child contorted her face because the sunlight flooding through the open door shone in her eyes.

"Keydo is strange. Does he not want to see his own child?" There was an oddly flattering aspect to his words, but he closed the door and left. It made Yongok's flesh crawl when he opened the door of her room without warning. She became nervous and overwrought.

She laid her little daughter down and rubbed her cheek on the baby's saying, "Your daddy doesn't want to see you." Repeating what her father-in-law had said, the tears began rolling down face, "Oh, dear, dear child. We must calm down." She wiped her eyes with the ends of her bodice ties, went out to the kitchen to fix dinner. Her kitchen was so clean one could eat off the floor.

She rinsed the rice several times, put it in the kettle on the grate and started to kindle the fire. The dried pine needles ignited instantly; she spread them with the fire tongs and said, "Well, heavens, I wonder why my brother-in-law hasn't come from school yet...." as she was worrying. She hated when she was home alone all day with her father-in-law, whom she heard coughing in the yard. The rice was steaming and she stole quietly out to kitchen garden to pick some mint leaves for soy paste soup. The purple blooms of the mint perfumed the whole garden. Carefully, she pinched off the leaves, so as not to harm them.

"We still have flowers, but the frost is due soon." Her father in-law spoke from behind her.

"Yes, father," she said, bolting upright.

He approached her, stood closely and said, "Ah, they smell so good. Why don't you pick some more?" He touched her hand as if he were going to take the leaves from her. She was frightened. He blushed with shame and hurried around to the front of the house. She went silently into the kitchen, and washed the leaves. As she was working, she heard the door open and her father-in-law ask, ill at ease, "Who's there, Keydo?"

Keydo's deep voice replied, "Yes, it's me."

"Long time, no see," his father said, but Keydo sat down and said nothing.

Yongok stopped working in the kitchen and strained to hear what they were saying.

"Where is...." Keydo began, but did not finish the question.

"You mean, where is your wife?"

"Yes."

"I think she is in the kitchen fixing dinner."

The conversation ceased. Yongok took Keydo's bowl from the shelf and wiped with a towel till it shone. She overheard her brother-in-law arrive and say hello to Keydo. Wiping her hands on the apron, she went into the room, but she couldn't look at her husband's face, only asked, "Dinner?" Keydo sullenly shook his head no.

While Yongok was serving dinner, Keydo went to their room. He glanced at the baby and began smoking a cigarette.

She quickly finished washing the dishes, freshened up her face and went to their room. Keydo sat absorbed in his own thoughts, and didn't seem to notice her. She sat down and talked to him, "Please, hug your baby."

Keydo faced her coldly, but she pushed the baby softly back to him.

"What for?" he asked and pushed the child back to her. Then he stretched and said, "I am very tired."

"Would you like me to make your bed?"

"No."

"Why don't you go to bed early? You said you were very tired."

They heard Old Mr. Soh scolding Keydo's brother and drumming on the ashtray noisily with his pipe. Yongok made the bed for him. However, Keydo just stared at her. Her freckled face with its high cheekbones looked uglier than usual to him tonight. He could feel his blood becoming cold. The affection he was trying to cultivate evaporated. He loathed it all. He didn't know whether it was Yongok he loathed, or that he was supposed to feel sexual desire and didn't.

He stood up abruptly and said, "I should go."

Yongok took hold of him by the sleeve.

"What are you doing....?"

He pulled away from her and fled without saying good-bye to his father. As he walked down the street, he felt sorry for Yongok, but the sympathy he felt was not enough to carry him back to her.

"You should only marry the person you are in love with. *Only* the person you love." Keydo said over and over to himself, and then went to a bar by the shore, drank till he was numb and slept with a whore who smelled strongly of perfume and powder.

Meanwhile, after Keydo departed, Yongok tied the baby to her back, went to her father-in-law's door and said, "Father, I am going to my parents' house."

He flung the door open and remarked cynically, "What is with you two? You leave the nice room I give you in this house and go to a hotel!"

"No, Keydo went to the fishery."

"Hah! You married into this family, but instead you spend all your time taking care of your parents. If you keep it up, I won't even have a clean spoon." This was an unusual response on his part because he had never objected to her going to her parents before in order to please her. He banged the door and she left.

As she trudged up West Gate Hill, it began to rain. She asked a woman fetching water to cover the baby on her back.

"What a cute baby! — boy or girl?" the young woman she knew said, covering her.

"A girl."

Yongok crossed over the hill. She was now soaking wet, as much from the cold rain as her own hot tears. However, Yongok did not go to her family, but to the church on the edge of Kanchanggol. It was empty, with only the votive candles burning near the altar. She knelt down and sobbed for a long while, and then began praying.

"Oh Lord, forgive my sins, hear my prayers. Have mercy on me and aid me as I walk this vale of tears. Tho' the whole world forsakes me, I believe, Lord Jesus, you never will. As long as you are with me, I am loved and I will live in peace, hope and light. Lord, forgive my sins and those of my father-in-law and husband. I pray that you lead us all onto the road of righteousness."

The autumn rain pelted the tin roof of the church. Rain streamed down the windows. Lightning flashed and thunder boomed. Yongok's prayers and sobs grew more and more intense.

Chapter Five

ॐ

Blind Man's Bluff

There was a tile-roofed house with four large pillars among the humble thatched roofs at far end of Mende. Yonhak and his wife Yongnan lived there. Torogol, where Yonhak's parents lived, was at one end of Tongyong and Mende, at the far opposite end. Considering how disgusted Yonhak's parents were with their son, it was understandable they moved the couple as far away as they could. A servant from his parents' house brought them rice, firewood and money, but Yonhak's parents never set foot in the house.

Yonhak and Yongnan did not have many household goods left. In the kitchen garden there were bean and red pepper paste jars. But with their lids tipped off, the jars were full of wormy rainwater.

When Mrs. Kim stepped into Yongnan's yard, she went directly to the kitchen garden and grimaced, looking at the jars.

"Poonsoon!" Mrs. Kim called for the maid.

"Ye-eh," the girl responded indolently, taking her sweet time. "Hello, how are you, Mrs. Kim?!"

"Look at this mess! Bring me a ladle, and hurry up about it."

Punshi folded her sleeves and ladled the fetid water out. She skimmed off the top layer with the worms in it and wrapped the remaining stuff in newspaper.

"You know very well that even a wet hand can cause mildew in a bean paste jar. What do you expect when you leave the top off and it *rains* in it?"

"I was gone on an errand when it rained, ma'am."

195

"Wasn't there anybody home who could close them?" Mrs. Kim spoke angrily, washing her hands.

"My lady was home."

"God...will she ever get the hang of housekeeping? Your lady doesn't know squat about keeping a house, so you have to take care of everything — especially those jars."

"Okay."

"So, aren't they home?"

"Well, the master is out and my lady is taking a nap."

"In the middle of the day....?" Tsking, Mrs. Kim went to the porch and sat down.

"They had a fight last night," the girl said.

"Again...."

It was not surprising. They fought regularly as most people eat. Mrs. Kim looked around the house, trying to see what was missing. She saw a crumpled basin by the well, but she had bought a copper one for Yongnan's wedding. Surely, this was his doing. For her daughter's wedding, Mrs. Kim had purchased everything she could think of, including clothes, bedroom sets, accessories — enough to start the rumor that she had bought a dozen jars of spice. Now most of it was gone, bare to the four posts. There was a half empty rice bag on the living room floor. The rice chest of persimmon wood had been gone for a long time.

"Mom, is that you?"

Yongnan, just up from her nap, crawled out of her room, her hair dishevelled. Her eyes were a mass black and blue bruises, and swollen shut.

"Oh," Yongnan moaned, straightening her back.

"I'd be happier if you were dead and gone. Then you'd stop grieving me...." said Mrs. Kim.

"*He* hit me and bit my fingers because I wouldn't give him my wedding ring," Yongnan said, showing her mother the back of her hand with tooth marks and bruises on it. Only the pale trace of the ring remained on her finger. After all their battles, she didn't seem to miss the ring or think of herself as miserable.

"I should have let her marry Handol," Mrs. Kim knew regretting the decision was pointless, but she thought for a moment it would be better than this.

"He goes crazy when he needs drugs. Now, he takes things from me. I don't even have another dress to change into."

"He has rich parents. Let him take their fortune, not your things. Has he given you any gifts he can take from you?" Mrs. Kim repeated the same question every time she came to her daughter's house.

"He's not even allowed in his parents' home. The other day his brother caught him stealing. He and his father almost beat him to death."

Yongnan tried to stretch her legs and moaned in pain again. "The enemy's returning," she said.

The phrase unnerved Mrs. Kim, and suddenly Yonhak was standing there like a ghost. His face was pale, his body thin as a winter tree, and his eyes glassy as those of a drunk. When he saw his mother-in-law, he turned away.

"Come and sit here," said Mrs. Kim in an angry tone of voice.

"What do you want?" he replied rolling his tongue and ignoring her.

"I want to talk to you."

"What do you want to talk about?" He seemed ready to charge at her. Refusing to sit down, he began searching through his pockets.

"You call yourself a human being? Well, except for your skin, you are an animal."

"And what about that slut? I'm talking about your daughter, who scratched her husband's face. She's no better, is she?" He sounded very believable.

"Look, with your own two eyes, see what you have done to her. Even a butcher wouldn't beat a person like this," Punshi said.

"I am trying to break her bad habits."

"You'd better break your own before you bother with hers. She'd better off if you'd kill her."

"I don't know what bad habits I have! No one has ever accused me of anything."

"Why, you have sold everything in the house! What do *you* need money for? Don't you have enough to eat? You're young and you're healthy...." Mrs. Kim stopped. In fact, Yonhak didn't look either young or healthy.

"What are you fussing about? Did I sell the rice paddies or the house that belonged to my wife's family? What have *you* done for us?"

"When a blind man trips and falls in the river, he should blame his own eyes, not the river."

"You said it. Who else would have married that whore?"

Yongnan sat impassively listening to all this. Only the breasts protruding from her old linen bodice revealed her still-vibrant sexuality.

"I admit my daughter is a bad girl. The whole world knows it. But what about you — a drug addict and thief!" Mrs. Kim screamed furiously stomping her foot.

But without responding to the charges leveled at him, he hollered, "She flirts with every man she sees. What would you do — just sit around doing nothing and let her do as she pleases? I'll kill her."

Yonhak bent forward threatening to hit Yongnan. After arguing for some time, Mrs. Kim, ashamed to be exposed to the neighbors, fled. She could hear Yongnan's hysterical screaming as she went. "All right. Kill me! Why don't you kill me!!!"

It was dark by the time Mrs. Kim arrived home. The owls were hooting in the mountain behind the house. The branches of the zelkova tree in front of the house were swaying in the wind and scraps of white paper tucked between the twine of the rope fluttered in the dim light. Punshi Kim rushed up, grabbed the rope and tried to tear it down.

"You goddamn worthless old tree! I've prayed to you every single day, and look what's happened. Now, you get what you deserve." She pounded the tree with her fists, and then ran into the house, but shortly she came out again, knelt in front of the old tree.

"Dear Tree God, please forgive me," she said, bowing deeply as she spoke, her head almost touching the ground. "I've committed a mortal sin. A stupid, ignorant human, I did not recognize the divine power you have over me. I know you are wise and will take good care of my children. If there is payment for sin due, I am willing to be punished myself."

"What are you doing?"

Punshi jumped up, startled and frightened. Standing there in the dark was her husband Songsu. She stepped back, as if to escape the incarnation of the tree god, which she believed she saw.

"Stop that nonsense!" he said, only then she recognized her husband.

When they entered the house, it seemed filled with a kind of eerie power. But for the moths smacking into the porch light, still lit, it was dead quiet.

Songsu said by way of suggesting a solution, "Maybe we should ask Yonghay to come home."

"But she's still in school," she said, still shaking from fear. That her husband's face appeared darker was probably due to the fact that it was thinner. He wore a coat one size smaller than before, but the shoulders drooped and the sleeves were too long.

"Have you eaten dinner?"

"Yes."

"Are you feeling any better?"

Songsu burped, but said nothing. He was still nauseated.

"Why don't you stay home and take care of yourself?"

Songsu said nothing.

"Take some honey; it might be good for you...." said Punshi.

"Has Keydo been here?" Songsu asked, out of nowhere.

"Yes."

"When?"

"Day before yesterday."

Songsu clammed up again. Punshi sighed deeply, studying him closely out of the corner of her eye.

Handol Returns

"Captain Soh, what are you going to do about this? We demand you tell us now."

The fishermen surrounded Keydo, all eyes on him. With his hands in overall pockets, Keydo slowly shifted his gaze from one man to the next. His dark eyebrows rose and fell, as if trying to deflect attention from his uncomfortable situation. However, it was not an attitude of challenge. With his arms folded, pock-faced "Pits" came forward.

"We've done our share, hanging in here, this long. You know that as well as we do."

"No more, you hear?!" one of the men in the crowd shouted.

Many of the looks solidified, as if expressing agreement with the speaker.

"This island is a long way from home, we ain't seen our women. What the hell is sense of all this hard work in this bitter wind, if we don't make no money? Look, we don't think that Songsu Kim has not paid us even though he has stacks of money; we know he's fallen on hard times. That's why we hung in there this long. The smart guys left long ago, got other jobs, but because we're loyal to you guys, Capt'n Soh, we stuck around through thick and thin," said Pits in a much softer tone. It made sense.

Lighting a cigarette, tossing the match off, Keydo said, "Another company . . . hum-m-m . . . and at another company they would work you like a slave and pay you next to nothing." Typical of Keydo's usual gutsy style.

"Hey, Pits, you soft-touch. Get tough!" someone shouted. All eyes focused on Keydo again, all of them mumbling.

"Look you guys, we got to get through to him first!" said Pits, waving his hand, confidently trying to make a joke out of it. The mumbling of the men died down, but the strain of confrontation was obvious in the silence and the stares.

Stepping forward, Pits said, "Mr. Soh, okay, forget about getting other jobs; think about our families. We men eat at work, but what about our wives and kids?"

"...."

"Look, I have to tell you the truth even when it's difficult. It's true *you* did everything you possibly could for us. *You* work hard, respect tradition and really treat us like human beings. Goddamn, Keydo, we got no beef with you."

"Stop mincing words and tell me what you have in mind," said Keydo, smiling bitterly.

"We wouldn't propose this if you weren't related to Songsu Kim yourself; we would have talked to him directly. But you are his son-in-law *and* our boss. I think we can talk to you...."

However, Pits still didn't get to the heart of the matter, and knowing very well what they intended to say, Keydo camouflaged his uneasiness.

But the men were impatient, and pushed for a conclusion aggressively, "Let's sell all the equipment — all the nets and boats!"

"This isn't your business to sell. You want to go to jail?" Keydo responded in deep tones.

"Look, don't get mad; listen to me," Pits said, as if trying to appease him. In fact, Keydo was not mad. He was an excellent manager of men and his instincts were simply to control the situation.

"Whether we catch any fish or not, let's divide this fifty-fifty."

"You want fifty percent?"

"Yes, half belongs to us. We are going to sell the fish and share the profit among all of us."

"By the way, do you think you are entitled to eat? I mean, do you even catch enough fish to feed yourselves three meals a day?"

"That we can't help. That's up to the Sea God, not us. If you can't accept this, we won't even work till we get all the past due wages you owe us," Pits said as if he were throwing in his last card, rolling his eyes maliciously. His gaze looked quite menacing, perhaps from the experience of prison life. He couldn't refute Keydo on the fact that they were not catching enough to afford their own meals.

"Okay, do as you please, leave. Stay here on an empty stomach, if you want. I am sick and tired of trying to get rice on credit for you. Who's going to feed you bums then? But you had better not touch anything that belongs to this company, or you know where you will end up."

Keydo was holding the last card. There was a commotion among the men. Pits shouted and gestured for quiet and then said, "Well, let's hear your ideas. You certainly can't ask us to stay here any longer." His tone became much softer, more flattering.

Keydo puffed on his cigarette a long moment and then said, "How about cooking me up for lunch?"

"Look, this isn't a joking matter."

"This is not definite, but let me tell you what: we'll give you twenty percent of whatever you catch."

"Aw, come on, that's not fair." They became noisy again.

"Fair or not, that's the plan. And I have no idea what Mr. Kim will say to it."

"Oh, shut up!" the peeved Pits scolded, saying, "Your father-in-law is a scholar, not a fisherman. He doesn't know shit about what is going on in this business. Soh, it's up to you!"

"The fact is, the business is not mine. It's his. Got it?"

"You act like a tiger around us. How come you act like a kitty-cat around your father-in-law?"

Someone defended Keydo. However, he knew exactly how to play this scene.

"Then...."

Drawing close to Keydo, the pockmarked Pits displayed three fingers. "We take one-third of all the fish we catch."

"A fourth," screamed Keydo like an auctioneer, then made his way through the crowd and plunked definitively down on a rock. His face was the picture of resolve.

"Give it two months and see what happens," said Yom with the melodious voice, who hadn't said a word thus far, "If the cod catch is bad this year, we're done anyway. So let's accept Capt'n Soh's terms. A good catch will make Kim rich and keep us alive, but a bad one will be the end of all of us."

Some of the group agreed and some didn't, but Pits was in favor of Soh's terms — not because he was considerate as Yom, but because he knew that Keydo wouldn't give in any further and it would be tough for anybody to find another job. He was relieved to have an agreement.

The group dispersed, agreeing they had no other choice but to accept the terms. Only Keydo was still sitting on the rock listening to the waves rushing in, breaking and rolling back to sea. The moon was out, so it wasn't pitch dark.

Finally, Keydo stood up and walked toward the pier. He got into a boat and headed for town. There, he went into a tavern, where he had once gotten drunk and slept with the hostess. As he entered, he thought about Yongok and felt sorry for himself, working so hard for a wife and family for which he had no affection.

The hostess, Wolson, a woman with short hair and dark blush of rouge on her cheeks, was flirting with some of the other customers, smiling broadly showing her buck teeth.

"I'll have my usual," Keydo told her.

"A side too?"

"Yeh, anything."

"Raw octopus?"

"Anything."

Wolson poured him a drink and set the octopus with hot sauce before him, smiling and flirting with him as she did, "They say octopus has the taste of a mistress and abalone a wife."

Keydo drank without responding to her, and after several, turned to the middle-aged man sitting to his left. "Sir, let me buy you a drink."

The man, quite drunk, accepted the glass, drained it, then picked up a slice of the octopus, and said, "Heehehe...the taste of a mistress!"

Keydo emptied the glass that the man bought him in return. Then he thrust his glass at the man sitting to his right and said, "Let me buy you one as well."

The young man, silently hunched over his drink without looking left or right, startled by the gesture, raised his head and said, "Oh!"

The two men recognized one another immediately — it was Handol. Keydo threw his drink in Handol's face and said, "You son-of-a-bitch, what are you doing back in Tongyong?"

Keydo's eyes glittered angrily. Handol pulled his sleeve over his hand and wiped his face, staring at Keydo.

"Get the hell out of here or I'll break your legs."

"These are my legs, and what they do doesn't concern you. Besides, do you own Tongyong?"

"What? You bastard!"

"Hey, calm down. A two-legged beast can go anywhere he wants." A middle-aged man, who knew neither of them, muscled between and separated the two.

Handol wiped his face again, took a coin out of his vest pocket, put it on the bar, picked up his bundle and stood up.

"If I catch you in Tongyong again, I'll kill you," Keydo hollered loudly.

At the door, Handol turned and glared over his shoulder at Keydo. He hoisted his dirty bundle onto his shoulder and disappeared into the darkness.

Keydo sang and roared wild like a crazy man until he became exhausted and again fell asleep in the tavern.

ॐ

Punshi's Horoscope

The fortune teller was explaining the meaning of the picture in his book to a woman. Next to the gate, an arrow was stuck in the thatched roof of a house; a woman in a yellow skirt sat inside the house. Outside, a man was sitting on a horse in a straw hat. He said the yellow skirt meant bad luck, and the arrow stuck in the roof prevented the husband from coming home.

"You're trying to burn fresh pine needles. Naturally, they won't light, and make nothing but smoke. Furthermore, since you're sitting in an empty room crying with the lights out, nobody knows it's you."

The thirtyish woman was crying, dabbing at her tears with a handkerchief. The stuffy room reeked with the yellow skinned man's body odor, and the low ceiling had brown rain stains. Sympathizing with the young woman, Punshi Kim was also crying.

"Is your husband not living with you?" Punshi asked.

Sobbing, the woman nodded.

"Is he living with a mistress?"

Again, she nodded.

Clicking her tongue Punshi said, "He must be blind. And he has such a lovely wife...you poor girl!" She felt very sorry for the young woman and asked, "Do you have a son?"

"Yes," the woman replied, blowing her red nose in a hand-kerchief.

"You have committed a great sin in a former life. Suffering is repayment. Your husband is not good for you, so don't expect any help from him. But you're in luck with your son. In your forties you'll come to the top of this mountain and reach a plateau. Until then, your only hope is your son."

The fortune teller slapped his book closed. The woman rose up like a ghost and left.

"I have heard that you are a fine reader of futures. I've come to see what this year has in store for me," said Punshi. She inquired about her husband's luck first, then each of her five daughters in turn. They were neither terrible nor very good. Punshi was relieved and finally asked about her own future, saying, "If it's too good, that may turn out bad. Not too good; not too bad, that's fine with me."

"Your future is bad, uncommonly bad...." the fortune teller said, surveying Punshi's face. "You are like a fly that should stay home, but is out hanging around the ox tail. That can't be good. Now a door, which was once open, is now closed, and there will be some kind of commotion. You are alone in an anchorless boat on the open sea. You can't count anyone. You live in a blue-tiled house, but you are at a crossroads, wondering which way to go."

"Right. You're absolutely right," Punshi admitted, swallowing her tears and impressed by his accuracy.

"How should I say this to you? You will not live out the year. I mean you are going to die."

"What!?"

"You are standing on a cliff, awaiting the hour."

"Who me?"

"Yes. The Angel of Death is following you."

"How can you say such a terrible thing?" Punshi was dumb-founded.

"I'm only telling you what I see. Your house is haunted: haunted with the ghost of someone beaten to death, someone starved to death, someone poisoned, someone drowned and the ghost of a shaman. These ghosts will destroy your house and your family will suffer."

Punshi felt dizzy. He knew the truth, and she could not argue with him. Her mother-in-law had poisoned herself; her father-in-law, Pongnyong, having left town over fifty years ago had certainly died of starvation or illness; Wuk, who had loved her mother-in-law, was stabbed by Pongnyong. Many men had drowned on the missing Namhae.

"But I don't understand why a shaman-ghost haunts my house. There was no shaman in my family." Objecting to the part she believed false, Punshi hoped to invalidate the rest of the ominous prediction.

"That's what I see. I can only tell you what I see."

"Is there anything I can do?" Punshi asked, shuddering.

"There is."

"Does it cost much?" Money was what worried Punshi most now.

"Not much."

The seer explained how to go about it. He told her his wife was a shaman, and that he would have her take care of everything, set the date and time and what to prepare for it.

"The snowball is getting bigger!" Punshi left the fortune teller's, sighing. She staggered down the steps, finally stopped and cried in despair: "Now I know!"

She stood there recalling Handol was the son of a shaman. An autumn night twenty years before came back vividly. Sogwon Chi brought Handol wrapped in a baby blanket.

"Who's its mother?" Punshi had asked.

"What's the use of knowing?" Sogwon had said, sighing deeply, and then said, "She's dead."

Sogwon's voice echoed in her ears clearly as if it had been yesterday. She tried to console herself thinking that certainly a shaman ghost would not return the favor of raising her child with bad luck. But she was not at ease. The shaman ghost pushed her into a fearful state.

When she reached the bottom of Mount Nambang and turned to Hangbook, she saw several boats loaded with firewood lined up next to the pier. Porters were carrying it along the gangplank. At another time, Punshi might have felt bad seeing them because every autumn she used to purchase a thousand logs and even had some delivered to her daughters. However, at this moment, she could care less. She was afraid and very lonely. She felt like a patient coming home alone from the hospital where she had been diagnosed with a terminal disease, keeping the trip secret. It seemed that her husband and her loving daughters were all strangers. She had no one to share what the fortune teller had said: extremely bad luck, you have less than a year to live.

When she approached the mouth of the inlet, she noticed a crowd. After Punshi stared at them for a while, just as she was about to leave, she heard someone say, "He's a drug addict. He must have gone crazy when he needed another fix."

The mention of a drug addict brought her back to reality.

"Jump in? Didn't he know he would drown?"

Punshi pushed through the crowd and cried, "Oh, my God, is it...."

Just as she feared, it was her son-in-law, Yonhak, lying there soaking wet with his legs and arms stretched out.

"Mrs. Kim!" a familiar-looking woman called to her. "It's Yongnan's husband. He just threw himself right in. I was scared to death, but got help from somebody, and they saved him," the woman said, gasping as she spoke, but Punshi was so embarrassed she couldn't focus.

She lifted Yonhak's head and hollered, "Help me! Someone please help take him to the hospital. Help me!"

"Aw, let him die. He's only gonna be a pain in the ass. And the family's down the tubes," someone in the crowd said.

They stood, with their arms folded, finding fault with the Kim family, but no one offered to help her.

"I'll pay you. Please, someone. We need to take him to the hospital," Punshi appealed to them, shaking Yonhak as she did.

"I'll take him," said a porter who set his carrying frame in front of a nearby store and stepped forward. Then he pulled Yonhak onto his wide back. "He's heavy as a dead man," the porter said groaning in complaint as he rose with the load.

The crowd cleared him a path. Children followed them as if they were a troupe of circus acrobats.

"You kids, better watch out. You tag along with drug addicts and they'll eat your butts right off!" The adults teased, but the kids enjoying the sport, continued to follow them.

"That's the end of Songsu Kim. The daughters have destroyed the family."

"His own mother would like to see him dead, so what in the world is his mother-in-law making such a big deal for?"

"Myself, I never seen the son of a rich man grew up to be worth a hoot! They squander their parents' money. We, the poor, don't have the money to waste, we're better off. As long as we have food in our mouths and a roof over our heads, we're lucky."

"Do you think that's easy?"

Long after the rest of the crowd dispersed, the vendors were still talking.

When Yonhak came out of the coma, he realized he was in the hospital and pretended to be dying. The doctor watched him unmoved, well aware of what he was doing.

"Doc, please do me a favor, please."

Yonhak, pretending to be dying, realized it was not working and appealed, rubbing his hands ingratiatingly.

"I can't. I'll have to send you to jail."

"I'll go anywhere you want me to. Just let me have a little."

Punshi, appalled at what she was seeing, flew out of the hospital.

Sometime later, Yonhak was arrested on suspicion of robbery and sent to prison.

The police wanted to release him to his father's custody on the grounds that Sangho Choi was an influential man, and they did not want to dishonor his reputation. There had not been sufficient evidence in the robbery attempt, but they could have done him a favor and let him go. However, Mr. Choi, Sr. went to the police, frowned deeply and said, "Please keep my son here. If he's free, he'll only go back to the needle."

Choi burst into a rage because of what his son had done to his reputation.

A Fake Funeral

Punshi would have discussed it with Yongok if it was something other than her own death, and Yongok would have arranged everything for her. But she knew Yongok would call it devil worship. She also wanted to talk to Chongim about it, but she felt embarrassed about that too, as if Chongim might say, "Tsk, Punshi! An old woman like you doing this just to live a little while longer?" But this was just Punshi's lack of self-esteem. When it came to food and clothes, Punshi always put the family first.

After Punshi did what the shaman had told her to, she asked Yongnan to come. So only herself, Yongnan and the shaman were there. Punshi worried that Songsu would return from Sochong's during the spell. The setting sun became a wild shade of red. The hobbled hen squatted under the step, its eyeballs dark, round crystals. A straw mat lay next to it.

The shaman, who had been chatting as if warming up, stood up. Opening her eyes wide she said, "Now, when I cut the hen's throat, you cover your mom with this mat. Then immediately let your hair down and begin crying. Understand?"

"Yes." Yongnan and Yomoon answered like two students standing in front of their teacher. The shaman nodded, grasped the well-whetted knife in one hand and held the hen's wings with the other. The hen fluttered and rolled its crystal eyeballs. Then the shaman stepped into the house and pressed the hen to the floor. She gazed at it for several moments, raised the knife and screaming "Eck-ck-ck!" plunged it into the animal. Dark, red blood ran across the floor. The hen's pale ankles shuddered.

Yomoon ran and covered Punshi's head with the straw mat. Pulling her hair down, she began to sob. Yongnan, dazed watching the hen's blood run across the floor, loosened her hair and also began crying.

The shaman rolled the dead hen in a cloth and hurried across the courtyard, winking a signal to Yomoon, who got up abruptly, ran to the kitchen and brought the food she'd prepared. Together, she and the shaman went out the gate. Punshi took the mat off her head.

"Tee-hee-hee-oh-h-h," Yongnan laughed at the fake funeral, "it was really funny."

"Oh, stop laughing, Yongnan!" Punshi said, but Yongnan kept on giggling, hands over her mouth. Punshi washed up with water from the well and changed her clothes.

"Well, I need to live a long time. Children need their mothers."

"Will this save your life, Mom?"

"We're only trying to keep my life from being taken away," said Punshi uneasily.

"Well, if shamans' spells work, then everybody could live a hundred years."

"You can't avoid your fate. Lots of people meet sudden deaths...."

Punshi went to the kitchen. Yongnan followed her. Punshi arranged three kinds of nuts — walnuts, pine nuts and gingko nuts — on one plate and three kinds of fruits — apples, pears and persimmons — on another. Then white rice cake, fried cookies, preserved fruits and various vegetables in wooden bowls ornamented with shiny nickel designs.

"If I had a daughter-in-law, I wouldn't have to do all this work myself," Punshi fretted to herself.

Yongnan sampled the food and commented on the taste of each.

"You are so silly," said Punshi.

"Why?" replied Yongnan, her mouth full of cookies.

"Your mother is going to die and you're not even concerned; your husband is in prison and that doesn't concern you either. Since you never worry, I guess you'll never grow old."

"Worrying doesn't help, Mom. Besides, I wish that opium addict was dead or in jail for good."

"What a terrible thing to say! You'd better watch your mouth, young lady."

"When he gets out of jail, he'll just beat up on me again. He's always accusing me of having an affair and going crazy."

Punshi Kim swallowed as her daughter spoke. "It's your fate to have him for a husband, mine to have you for a daughter. We must live the life given us."

"Do I have to live this way till I die?" the girl asked sadly, her eyes sparkling with tears as if the lights of her soul had returned. Punshi watched her daughter out of the corner of her eye and felt that Yonhak's impotence made her unhappier than his being a drug addict.

The shaman returned. She had buried the dead hen on the mountain behind the house. This completed the funeral service for it, which she had killed in place of Punshi. After the shaman washed her hands, she looked toward the kitchen and asked, "Ready to go?"

"Yes, everything's ready."

212

They headed out, Yomoon carrying the food. When Yongnan tagged along, Punshi said, "Stay home."

"I don't want to. I'm scared."

Stubbornly, Yongnan insisted. They left the empty house and went up to Chilbang well. It was pitch-dark. They could hear only their own footsteps in the darkness. They passed another well, and went deep into Mount Andwi. Next to a rock in front of thick bushes whose leaves had now turned to autumn tones, the shaman placed her accouterments, lit four candles, each on a corner of the rock. Yomoon and Yongnan watched her every move. The shaman's face glowed as she lit a piece of offering paper and drew circles around it in the air. Owls hooted. Breaking the stillness of the night, the shaman prayed in the darkness. Punshi bowed her head reverently.

Yongnan yawned and thumped down on the grass. The shaman widened her eyes and stared at the girl. The ritual was over. After they sprinkled the offerings of food, Yomoon packed the empty dishes.

"Do NOT turn around going back down," the shaman ordered. Holding her skirt up, Punshi walked down the hill without looking. A dog barked in the distance.

When Punshi opened the gate, she froze. Songsu, in his gray overcoat, stood in the lighted courtyard. Elbowing the shaman back out, Punshi whispered, "Stay here," and hurried in.

"When did you get home?" she asked him.

He didn't respond, but stood mute as a statue. Punshi cowered as if afraid she would be struck by lightning. Then she went to the kitchen.

Handing the money she had hidden on a shelf for the shaman's service and the leftover food to Yomoon, she said, "Tell her that my husband is home. I can't come out."

Yomoon left and returned immediately.

"Is she gone?"

"Yes."

"Has Mr. Kim gone to his study?"

"No, he's sitting in the living room."

Punshi hurried to the living room. Yongnan was nowhere to be seen; she must have disappeared to the room at the back of the house. Songsu was sitting, one hand on top of the other on his cane.

"Where have you been? There was nobody in the house when I came home." It was not an angry tone, but Punshi was at a loss for words. She couldn't make up a lie in so little time.

"Where have you been?"

"...."

"Can't you answer me?" Songsu screamed.

"This year's fortune was so bad, and...." Punshi tried to hide what she had done, but she could not.

"I am going to die?" Songsu raised his head and stared at Punshi. She could not escape her husband's eyes by stepping back. She had never seen his eyes this fierce.

"No, no. I am the one destined to die."

"Ha, ha...." Songsu's laughter echoed around the quiet courtyard of the spacious house.

"Nonsense! Don't you worry. Most certainly, I will die before you," he said in a soft trembling tone. His eyes were sunken, his cheekbones raised, and his pale face now looked dark. Songsu stood up and went to his study. "Poor souls...." he whispered to himself as he went. He took off his overcoat and sat down, drawing the chessboard.

"You are an old man!" he recalled Sochong's complaint as he played chess against himself.

Songsu had slapped her cheeks and left. Her passionate love frightened him. He was not young at heart or physically vigorous enough to respond to her. When he was young and healthy, he often felt empty but never lonely. He didn't mind living alone without a woman. He never felt strong physical desire. He could have lived a quiet life if he had never met Sochong. Now, however, he felt his body deteriorating every day. Alone, he sat enjoying the quiet moments of the good old days.

Sochong recognized that Songsu was over the hill. She stared at him hatefully, angrily, eyes full of derision.

Songsu put the chessboard aside, lit a cigarette and took a long puff off it. He saw himself heading for her house; she was not the woman he fell in love with. He was visiting her not because he loves her but only to calm his continued restlessness.

Insects chirruped in the forest, as if they, too, were restless. There was no sound in the house.

Some Shocking News

The early-morning market takes place on the seashore where they filled the sea in, between two points of land, and is always throbbing with vitality — full of life as a flipping potful of fish just dumped from the net. Morning-fresh people move about enthusiastically, shouting through the mist. Women coming to the market from Choongnim, Chunwha Island and Changdae under bright morning stars carry loads of zucchinis, sweet potatoes and vegetables on their heads or backs and enter the city through the North Gate. Clam sellers from the inlets around Mount Andwi pass Chungnyolsa on their way. Fishermen with their catches come from Pande. Nearby, workmen on small steamboats haul seaweed and fish ashore. From Tongyong come the dealers of silk, cosmetics, thread and fruits. This vast stream of humanity all wends its way toward the market on the reclaimed bridge of land. Finally, at sunrise, villagers with their carrying baskets strike out for the market.

There was a time only fish were sold there. Boats gathered mornings, and the fish sellers from Tongyong, Pusan and Chinju came to buy at auction. But over time it was transformed into a general market for commerce between the islanders and people from the main land. The fish market moved on shore to a spot in front of the Fishermen's building, but occasionally there were a few auctions still.

By the time everyone has finished breakfast, the market has become quiet; everybody has returned to where they came from — vendors to Tongyong, islanders to the islands, farmers to their farms, and the housewives to their homes. Only the garbage remains on the deserted plaza.

That morning, the market was unusually crowded; Chusok was just around the corner. Chungku Lee's wife, Chongim, saw fresh squash just inside the entrance. It's one of the traditional foods, essential for the Chusok celebration. She leaned forward to choose one.

"You can't buy these, I have bought all of them!" said a woman with curly hair wearing a lead hairpiece in it, opening her arms trying to hide the squash in the basket. Her big cotton money sack dangled from her waist; she was a vender from Tongyong Market.

"No, no. I didn't sell them all to you. Please, choose one," the countrywoman said to Chongim, desperately pulling the basket to herself.

"What are you talking about? What's wrong with my money? I said, I am going to buy them all, and that's what I'm going to do. Don't you interfere with my deal."

She was obviously trying to intimidate Chongim into moving on.

"Oh, that poor woman," Chongim mumbled as she left the vendor's stand. It's quite common for naive country bumpkins to be strong-armed into selling their produce for less than it is worth.

Chongim was swept along in the thick crowd. Tongyong wholesalers seemed set on buying everything the farmers brought with an eye toward making a big profit before the Chusok holiday. In fact, many farmers were already sold out and were buying fabric from the yard goods vendor who had set up shop on a big mat. These shrewd wholesalers turned around and sold the produce they'd just bought from the farmers at inflated prices or hurried to Tongyong Market.

Chongim was selecting fruit at the fruit stand.

"Mrs. Lee, I'm all out of good fruit. You should go to Tongyong Market; you'll get better quality," said Keysoon, who had been in the same elementary school class as Yongbin.

"Fruit is so very expensive before Chusok."

"I'll only charge you the wholesale price, Mrs. Lee."

"But that's not fair to you."

"Will I become a millionaire selling fruit to you at a big profit!?" Keesoon was being kind to Chongim because she had been friends with Yongbin.

Yongsook, also at the market with a servant to carry her purchases, spied her aunt's back and hurried off in the opposite direction to avoid meeting her.

Chongim considered the abalones for sale in a big pot. Her elder son, Chongyoon liked them. He and his wife were at home to spend Chusok with their parents.

"How much are these?" she asked, taking a large one out of the pot.

"Ten chon!"

Chongim was shocked — that was twice the usual price.

"This is Chusok week," said the vendor sitting next to the pot. Everybody in the market looked familiar to her because they were from Tongyong Market. Chongim bought five abalones and put them in her basket.

"Fine clams, ma'am," said the clam seller, continuing to shuck without even looking down. The next clam seller gave her an ingratiating smile.

"Well, it's you Mrs. Lee. Doing the Chusok shopping?" Chongim turned toward the voice and found herself face-to-face with Mrs. Cookju Chong, standing there arrogantly with many gold rings prominently displayed on her bodice tie. Typically, the two women never spoke in the street, when they met. They were not on good terms thanks to the two failed marriage proposals between their families: Yongbin and Hongsop; Chongyoon and Mrs. Chong's daughter. Chongim was curious why Mrs. Chong addressed her.

"Do you hear from your son?"

"Yes," Chongim wasn't sure which son she was referring to, so she gave her an ambiguous answer.

"Then you must know." There was something mysteriously serious in her voice.

"What are you talking about?"

"My son told me he saw your son in Seoul."

"He what? Tayoon!?" Chongim could not hide her surprise.

"Yes, your younger son...."

"Wh-where is he?"

"I don't know where. But you know — old Mr. Song's widowed daughter. The one they say eloped with her boyfriend — was with him."

"And?" Chongim was dying to hear what she had to say.

"He's living with her."

"Wh-what!?"

Mrs. Chong stared at Chongim, who nearly collapsed with the shock of the news, then turned around and escaped into the fish store with the servant woman.

"Chungku! Chungku! Where are you?" Chongim hurried home and ran in the house looking for her husband.

She stopped shouting. Her husband was nailing some furniture in his workshop. Her daughter-in-law, who was brushing her teeth by the well, looked at her strangely. Chungku simply kept on working ignoring her shouting.

These days Chungku was always in a sour mood. He had become even more remote since his daughter-in-law came to visit. Chongim decided she would keep quiet and went to the kitchen.

"Is Chongyoon still sleeping?" she asked her niece, who had come to help for a few days.

"He said he was going to Mount Nambang."

However, Chongim couldn't concentrate, only pacing around the kitchen in a daze.

"Is the mother-in-law fixing the meal while the daughter-in-law is resting?" Chungku demanded sharply, and the young niece, who planned to stay while Chongyoon and his wife were with them, began preparing breakfast.

At breakfast, Chongim couldn't eat. Her face flushed, then she turned white.

"Mother, you don't look well. Are you sick?" asked Chongyoon.

"No, no," answered Chongim.

Chungku also eyed his wife quietly, as he continued eating without a word. He returned to his workshop just as soon as he had finished eating and drinking his rice tea.

"Why does he work day and night?" Chongyoon said, critical of his father. His wife, Yoonhee, sat unperturbed.

"Don't let it bother you," said Chongim. "He enjoys his work."

"Does he have to do it when we are visiting? It makes us uncomfortable...." he complained bitterly.

"If that's what he likes, you shouldn't pay that much attention to...." said Yoonhee.

She was quite indifferent to Chungku's attitude. Her quaint benign smile, which seemed to suggest some infirmity, was not mischievous. She was not beautiful, and though she was not stylishly dressed, there was a refined quality about her.

Chongyoon and Yoonhee had met and fallen in love in the hospital in Taegu, where she was being treated for tuberculosis. Chongyoon, neat and discreet both of word and deed, was attracted by her quaint alluring smile. Yoonhee was neither sweet nor kind, but had an indefinable relaxed ease and sense of resignation about her. They married after she recovered sufficiently, but she was not a good housewife either. Nor was she especially interested in her appearance or clothes.

Sometimes Chongyoon stared at Yoonhee's resigned features, which were so eerie that they made him comfortable. He had seen many patients who cried and struggled to hold onto life. He realized he was becoming more and more cold-hearted, living in the middle of this uncertainty. He administered treatment coldly, without emotion. Yoonhee, however, did not struggle for life. It was not a question of intelligence. If she were highly intelligent, he would not have loved her. The very reason he didn't think highly of Yongbin the way Tayoon or Chungku did, was her intelligence and the superior way she looked due to it.

Chongyoon feared the misery he would feel if Yoonhee cried, distorting her smiling face. This thought always aroused his sympathetic love for her. Not to worry, Yoonhee never cried. However, Chongyoon was deeply saddened whenever he imagined she might. This thought constantly replenished his love for his wife.

By the same token, her resigned face and morbid smile were the reasons Chungku wasn't overfond of his daughter-in-law. Of course, the fact that she was a tubercular didn't add to his affection for her.

That afternoon, Yoonhee announced she was going for a walk on the seashore. Chongim hastily summoned Chongyoon and Chungku and told them what he had heard from Mrs. Cookju Chong. Both men were surprised, but they did not say a word.

Chongim, however, couldn't restrain herself, "He must be crazy to take up with a widow! Oh, my God! And the wife of a friend on top of that! Oh God, no!!!"

"Calm down. He's not our son any longer, no need to make a fuss about it."

Chungku stood up abruptly and went out of the room.

I Missed You

Rays of sunlight filtered into the room through a hole in the torn paper-paneled window. Yongnan was lying on her back eating an apple. Scattered about her head were empty cracker bags. There was a fly swimming in the water bowl she hadn't finished the previous night.

"Punsoon!"

"Ye-s, ma'am," Punsoon answered in a slow drawl from the kitchen.

"Is dinner ready?"

"No, not yet."

"I'm absolutely starving."

Yongnan rose up on one elbow and spat out some apple skin. After she finished it, she wiped her lips, studied the ceiling and began singing, "Night has reached around the old wall...." She was not a very good singer.

An open jar of face cream was sitting in front of the cracked mirror on the wall. Yonhak hadn't tried to sell it because it wasn't worth much with cracks.

"How much longer before dinner, Punsoon?"

"It's almost ready."

Punsoon was busy running back and forth between the kitchen and the terrace.

"What will I do after dinner? I can't stand this boring life." Yongnan mumbled and after some fumbling under her mattress fished out a one-won bill and fifty-chon coin.

"How about a motion picture?" Yongnan was hatching a plan.

"Ma'am! Ma'am!" Punsoon shouted.

"What?"

"Somebody's here."

"Who?"

Yongnan looked out the door, sweeping her mussed up hair back, her bodice ties undone.

"Who's there?"

"It was a guy," Punsoon whispered in a low voice.

"A man?"

"Right. He told me to give this to you. He is standing at the gate." Punsoon handed her the note, glancing back in the direction of the gate.

"What on earth could it be?" Yongnan asked unfolding the note.

"Dear Yongnan," it read, "I'm here in Tongyong. Please come to shooting range on Mount Nambang tonight. I'll be waiting for you. Love, Handol."

The writing was childlike and awkward, and she didn't read very well herself, but she could make out the name, Handol, very clearly, and her face became red.

"Oh, my God. Is—is he outside?"

"Yes," Punsoon responded and leaned back to look at the gate, then said, "No, now he's gone." She ran to the gate to make sure. "Yes, he's gone."

Holding the note in her hand, Yongnan paced back and forth between her room and the main hall, then hollered, "Punsoon, did you wash my slip?"

"Yes."

"What about my cotton socks? Where are my socks?"

"I washed them but I didn't starch them."

Yongnan ran out to the well. She dropped the bucket in, drew it up again hurriedly, and dumped the water into the basin. Splashing water in all directions, she washed her face.

"Ma'am, dinner is ready."

"I'm not going to eat."

"But you said you were hungry...."

"Well, I'm not."

She went into her room, wiped the dust off the face cream jar, dipped her fingers in the unstained portion and spread it on her face.

"Are you going out?"

"Yes...."

"Where are you going?"

"Um...."

"I asked you. Where are you going?"

"I....I am going to a movie."

She rose, searched the wardrobe, and put on her best clothes.

"Punsoon, my socks. Where are my socks?"

"They're not ready yet."

"That's okay. Bring them here."

Punsoon brought the wrinkled cotton socks. Without comment, Yongnan turned them inside out and pulled them on. As she was about to go out, she realized the sun had not set; it was still bright. She sat down in the front hall and stared out to the open sky, glowing red with the sunset. The darkness beyond the red ball of sun was about to descend.

"You're not going?" Punsoon asked.

"I'm going. Yes, I'm going."

"You look so very beautiful."

"Do I?"

"Yes, you're really beautiful."

"Oh, please don't make fun of me." Yongnan was flattered and went back into the room. She looked in the mirror and tried to smile, but tears ran down her face.

"Oh Handol, have come really come back for me?"

When it was completely dark, she went up to the shooting range on Mount Nambang. The sound of the waves breaking on the shore echoed in the dark deserted woods where there were no houses.

Handol stood watching the hill leading to the shooting range, leaning against an old tree. He stepped forward when he spied the fluttering white skirt in the darkness.

"Yongnan!" whispered Handol, standing there as if he were glued to the ground.

"Is it really you, Handol? Is it true I'm looking at you, Handol?" murmured Yongnan, her white face glowing in the darkness.

"Yongnan!" He embraced her and her face was soon wet with his tears. "It's me, poor ole Handol."

He sobbed for a long time. So did Yongnan. Arms about one another, they went into the woods. Handol, who had just come from the barber, smelled of hair oil and Yongnan of cheap face cream. The two of them sat under a tree smelling one another like a mother dog and puppy.

"I missed you so much, Yongnan. I wanted to see you — even in my dreams."

"Oh, I missed you too, Handol," she said and they began to hug again.

Though there were the sounds of the waves, the wind in the pines and the distant whistle of a ship, they heard nothing. They hugged and wriggled together in breathless crazy ecstasy, caressing and inhaling and breathing in one another's scents.

"I wanted to make some money and come back here and get you. Go away with you. But it's not easy to make money."

"Where were you?"

"Yosu, Pusan. I even worked as a porter in Kunsan."

"You must have had a hard time."

"I did. And most of all, I cried a lot because I missed you."

"I didn't cry," Yongnan said, "but I missed you. No tears though."

"You don't love me, that's why!" Handol shuddered with his old fear. "I hear your husband is in prison."

"Yes, how did you know?"

"I spied, listened. He's an opium addict, right?"

"Yes, and a stupid blockhead."

"Are you going to stick with him, though?"

"I despise living with him."

"Then how come you have stayed with him so long?" he said, sounding very jealous.

"I had no other choice."

"Now are you going to stay with him?"

"I don't know. I just want him dead!"

"How dare you say such a thing! He is your husband and the man you slept with...."

"Wrong. You don't know anything about him," Yongnan said.

"What are you talking about?"

"I mean you don't know anything about him." Yongnan laughed trying to block her laughter with her hand.

"What do you mean?"

"My husband is...ha, ha, ha."

"Why are you laughing? It makes me nervous."

"He is impotent. Ha, ha, ha. Isn't that funny?" She laughed openly this time.

"He's what?"

"He is sexually handicapped. He has never slept with me. You are the only man I know, and that's no lie." Yongnan's words were suddenly filled with sexual desire.

"Is it really true?" he said, embracing her violently.

They became breathless looking at one another and smelling one another's scent increased their excitement. "Oh, oh." They fell down on the grass. They were rolling tangled together intoxicated with the love that seemed to fill the vast, shining sea. He helped Yongnan up, tidying her hair.

"I feel like crying, Yongnan," he said, tying her bodice ties.

"Me, too. I missed you terribly," she said, cuddling in Handol's arms.

"Shall we drown ourselves? Die together?"

"That scares me."

"Why does it scare you? You will be with me."

"Why should we die? You can make money and we can live together." Handol took out a cigarette and lit up. His thick eyebrows met in the middle of his forehead over his nose.

"Um. I did everything I could to make money, except stealing. It was so difficult. I'm just unlucky. I tried gambling, selling door to door, worked as a servant, but I couldn't save any money. I starved when I was out of work because of wet weather. I tried to hang myself, but I wanted to see you once more before I died. That's why I came here to Tongyong."

"Well, there's nothing to steal in my house. We're all broke...." It was the most thoughtful statement Yongnan could think of.

"Don't blame yourself, Yongnan. I was born with bad luck, but now I can die without spite or anger," he said, feeling her hand.

Again, he started to sob. Though Yongnan didn't feel such strong emotion, his sobbing made her cry, too.

ॐ

The Man Who Seduced Yongnan

"Mrs. Kim, we have big trouble!" Early morning a few days later, Punsoon knocked on Punshi's gate. Punshi didn't have time to pin her hairpiece in, so she hurried to the gate.

"What's the matter?" Her eyes were trembling with fear.

"My mistress...."

"Now what's happened to Yongnan?"

"She's left home."

Punshi, who assumed that Yonhak got out of prison and beat her to death, breathed a deep sigh of relief. "Where did she go? Is Yonhak home?"

"No, he's not. Last night my mistress packed and went to a room she had rented."

"She rented a room?"

"Yes. Outside the North Gate. I carried the bundle to that place. She told me not to tell anybody, but I know I have to tell you."

"Why would she be doing this?" Punshi couldn't fathom the reason.

"Mrs. Kim," Punsoon lowered her voice and continued, "A few days ago, a man came to see her. She went out every night and then finally...."

"What?!" She was appalled, and glanced toward Songsu's office. "Punsoon, come into my room." She pulled Punsoon into her room, this time glancing toward the kitchen where Yomoon was.

"Who was he, this man?" Punshi whispered standing close to Punsoon.

"I don't think I've ever seen him before."

"Oh, my god! What am I going to do?" Punshi never suspected that Handol had returned. She simply assumed that Yongnan started having an affair since Yonhak was gone.

"Punsoon, don't say anything about this to anybody. If somebody visits her, just say she is probably at her mother's. You understand?" Punshi said nervously.

"Okay. Yes."

When Punsoon left, Punshi sat thinking, but she couldn't come up with anything that might address this situation. Anything that was appropriate.

After lunch she sent Yomoon for Yongok. Sometime after she left, Songsu went out without having lunch or saying anything. Punshi watched his stoop-shouldered figure as he went, but she just sat and watched him go.

"It's too sad," she mumbled, mulling over her endless misfortunes, "beyond tears."

Yomoon returned after some time.

"Is Yongok coming?" Punshi asked.

"She wasn't home. She had to take the baby to the doctor."

"Oh," Punshi said, remaining fixed where she sat without doing anything. She was so distracted that she didn't notice Yongok when she came in carrying the baby tied to her back.

"Why are you sitting there like that, Mother?" Yongok asked, soothing the baby.

"Um, um. You're here."

"Is something wrong?"

"Have you been to the doctor with the baby?" Punshi asked, ignoring Yongok's question.

"How did you know?"

"I sent Yomoon to ask you to come."

"Then it's a good thing I decided to drop by. Her diarrhea has gone on endlessly...."

Punshi used to cuddle her grandchild, cooing, "Oh, my dear little puppy," to her, but now she didn't even look at the baby when Yongok laid her on the floor. When Yongok sat down on the hall floor, Punshi related what she had heard from Punsoon. Punshi talking and Yongok listening, both sat emotionless, as if exhausted.

"I know I have to bring that wanton child of mine home here...."

"...."

"I must get her before Yonhak is released."

"...."

"He will kill her when he gets here."

Dry-skinned Yongok looked sad and said, "I feel so sorry for Yongnan, Mom."

Punshi raised her head abruptly as if she had been outwitted. Her eyes reflected the sadness of her soul. "So do I."

"...."

"I should have given her some money and let her go with Handol...." She said, admitting what she had always thought. "But we can't change the past. This is her fate. She is destined to live with Yonhak."

"She's out with a man; will her husband take her back? She's already...."

Yongok was about to say Yongnan was spoiled and not chaste any more. But she had been with Handol before she was married, and that deterred Yongok. While the mother and daughter sat together worrying, Keydo walked in unexpectedly. Yongok flushed a bit. Keydo hesitated, seeing her there.

"Come in, please," said Punshi, standing up, as if he had come to rescue them.

"Have you been home?" Yongok asked discreetly. Keydo shook his head and avoided looking at his wife.

"Come over and sit down."

Punshi, who was seated next to Yongok, made room for Keydo to sit next to his wife, but he chose a spot opposite her, sat down and hastily lit a cigarette. Though she didn't look at him directly, Yongok pondered Keydo's coldness to her.

"The baby had diarrhea....I have been to the doctor with her," said Yongok. She looked at her child, then her husband, but he only smoked silently, his eyelids drooping.

Punshi, however, was not cognizant of the distance between the young couple because she herself had never been close to her husband during the thirty years of her own marriage. Songsu was as remote as Keydo. They say a loving husband takes care of things at his wife's home too. It never occurred to her that Keydo might not be a loving husband because he had aided the Kims so reliably in all their business difficulties. Without reservation, Punshi told Keydo about Yongnan.

"I can't tell your father-in-law, and I don't have a son to talk to. You are the only one I can count on. Yongok and I were sitting here confounded. How nice you stopped by! I suppose we'd better bring that bad girl home as soon as it gets dark or the neighbors will get wind of it."

Keydo remained impassive.

"Now, I regret I did not let her go away with Handol. It would be better, at least if she were out of sight. Who could be seducing my poor married daughter?! The way rumors fly around here soon the whole town will know. And that madman Yonhak will try to kill her when he gets out of jail."

As she had no one to talk to, she grumbled to Keydo. Suddenly, he stubbed the cigarette out and stared at his mother-in-law. "You really don't know whom Yongnan is with?"

"How would I know? Punsoon said he was a total stranger. I think you should break his legs. Seducing a married woman! My poor Yongnan! There are plenty of single women out there!"

Keydo sighed deeply, "It's Handol!"

"Wh-what?"

"I'm sure it's him."

"But how do you know?"

"I ran into him in a bar on the pier a few days ago."

Yongok looked up. "Handol?"

"Yes, I ran into him." There was a subtle self-mocking smile on his lips.

"You were in Tongyong last week?" asked Yongok.

"Yes...." he admitted reluctantly without looking at her. Her tears welled as she held the drowsy baby and breast-fed her. She tried to keep remorse from overtaking her, but holding the baby, her hands were trembling. The three of them sat silently, each at the mercy of his or her own emotions: Punshi at a loss for words, Yongok looking down at the baby, and Keydo his well-formed shoulders rigid as if carved from stone.

"No, no. I should not leave them alone." Punshi said, shaking her head. "It was one thing when they were young, but now she has a husband...." She kept mumbling and shaking her head as though no one were listening to her.

It was almost dinnertime. Keydo, sitting silent and still as a boulder, said to Yongok, "It's time for you to go home."

She gathered the baby's things without responding and tied the baby on her back. She said good-bye to her mother and started through the yard, but after a few paces, stopped. She paused for a long moment and then asked, "Are you coming home tonight?"

"I don't know yet," he responded bluntly.

Yongok's thick lips twitched like a paralytic's as she turned and propelled herself through the gate.

A Crazy Son of a Bitch

Punsoon in front, Punshi and Keydo plodded along a dark road. His breath smelled of wine. When Yongok left, Keydo told Punshi he would return shortly, but he came back late reeking of wine. They passed through the military office and went into the alley between the court and a temple and through the North Gate. Up over North Gate Hill, they climbed the mountain slope. There stood a cluster of thatched houses with grimy windows.

"I'm all out of breath. Let's take a break," said Punshi, slumping down on the ground. She was dizzy and realized she hadn't had anything to eat. She wondered why she wasn't eating since she was worrying less than before and hadn't been crying. Keydo stood beside her and stared vacantly into space. A willow near the twig gate of the house swayed rhythmically in the darkness. Because he was still hung-over, he felt a chill.

"Are we there yet?" Punshi asked.

"No, it's a way up the hill yet," Punsoon answered.

Punshi got to her feet with a deep sigh and said, "All right. Let's go."

They walked on in silence. A dog barked; a child cried as if being slapped.

"Shut up, you damn brat. Eat me! There's no food. Why do you keep begging for food? Go out and die! Why were you born?" A woman's angry voice echoed out into the alley. It reminded Punshi of the crippled woman who lived near Mount Yonghwa. Together the two voices pierced her being.

"I live far better than most women, far better," she murmured to herself, as if dreaming.

"Well, here we are. I'm going back now," said Punsoon.

"Yes, do," Punshi said.

Punshi tried to compose herself. Keydo frowned at the twig gate, then turned his head and said to her, "After you, please."

The house was unusually quiet. Punshi pushed the gate with all her might, but it did not come open. She looked back at Keydo, pleading. He kicked it open with a thwack. The house was a dilapidated shanty. There were two rooms with no lights and no sign of people. Their dim shadows moved along the ground. Punshi looked at her son-in-law imploringly again. Breathing heavily, Keydo did not budge.

"Yongnan! Are you here, Yongnan?" Punshi hollered, but there was no answer.

"YONGNAN!" she yelled again, louder.

"Who is it?" came Yongnan's groggy reply.

"It's your mother," said Punshi in a low voice.

"Oh, my God!"

Noises from the room sounded like people frantically searching for clothes. A match was struck and two figures were reflected on the paper-covered door. Silhouetted like artists' cutouts, naked Yongnan and a man's body, also naked, faded back and forth before their eyes. The two hurried into their clothes. Keydo watched the scene on the door with savage eyes, breathing deeply, and groaned. Full of shame, Punshi turned her head away, when the door was opened.

"Well, Mother?" Yongnan said sullenly.

"Oh, Yongnan, you tramp!" Punshi said as she stepped in.

Handol sat in the corner hanging his head.

"Keydo, come here, please," Punshi said. As she waved him into the room, Yongnan and Handol looked up, surprised, but when they saw him, both looked down again. In the dim lamplight both trembled. Keydo, too tall for the low ceiling, bent to enter. The dirty old wallpaper was grimy and stained with the blood of insects.

Punshi sat down and said, "What are you thinking of anyway?"

Handol had no answer.

"You bastard! What are you doing back here again?" Punshi said.

"I'm so sorry," Handol murmured.

"If you can't be grateful to me, you are an animal. When your father came to me with you in a quilt....I gave you my breast, treated you like my own child. What are you doing to me?"

Punshi wiped her tears with a handkerchief.

"If you hadn't been around, Yongnan would have married a decent man. Look at her — she's a beauty, but miserable. Why? I'm wasting my breath talking about the past...but she has a husband whether he's a thief or betrayer. How could you seduce her again? You are a wolf in human skin!"

Punshi, who had begun calmly, became overwhelmed with anger, but restrained herself and said, "Leave Tongyong immediately before anyone finds out about you and Yongnan. You are handsome enough to marry a woman and have a nice family. Forget Yongnan. If her husband Yonhak knew, it would be a big disaster."

When she finished berating Handol, she took Yongnan's arm and said, "Let's go." But Yongnan pulled loose and said, "I'm not going."

"You must," said Punshi.

"I don't want to live with an impotent guy. Why should I? I am a healthy woman, and why should I spend my life with him?" Yongnan retreated to the corner and sat sullenly.

"Are you crazy? Do you want to see me die here?" Punshi fell to her knees and pulled her daughter to her.

"No! I won't go with you." Yongnan resisted and Punshi fell over on her back. At that moment Keydo's rough hand flew at Yongnan's cheek, slapping her twice.

"Why are you hitting me?" Yongnan shouted and began crying. Punshi was panic-stricken and Handol stood up. The burning eyes of the two men met. Keydo snorted like a beast and Handol gave him a look that was a curse of hatred. When Keydo stopped growling, his lips quivered in a short, self-deprecating smile. He turned to the door, kicked it open, and went out. His uneven footsteps echoed into the night.

"You slut, you ought to drown yourself. Aren't you ashamed to be slapped around by your younger sister's husband?" Punshi hit Yongnan on the face, who was crying angrily.

"Let's get out of here before I die in front of you." Punshi, now in a state of fury, shoved Yongnan out the door. Yongnan, crying, didn't resist.

Handol put his hands over his face and prostrated himself.

Punshi drove Yongnan before her across North Gate Hill like a goat. When they had almost reached the house, Punshi recovered her composure. "Does the owner of that house know who you are?" she demanded.

Yongnan looked up into the zelkova tree vacantly, "No, she doesn't."

"What does she do for a living?"

"She is a peddler."

"Was she there tonight?"

"No."

Punshi was much relieved.

Meanwhile, Keydo walked on the beach. Jealousy burned him like a strong thirst, but he didn't feel like drinking. He walked from Dongchung beach to Sohchung.

The night fish market had already finished. The fishery building stood grotesquely quiet in the dark. A lone streetlight lit the road. Ships anchored, others loaded with fish steamed off toward Pusan. A few lay silently at anchor.

"A crazy son of a bitch!"

Keydo lit a cigarette under the streetlight, and railed at himself, "I'm a crazy son of a bitch."

Disaster on a Stormy Night

"Eck! Eck!"

Punshi opened her eyes, but saw only darkness. She was soaked with perspiration. She flung the door open and went out to the well. She drew a bucket of water and drank deeply, feeling the icy water run all the way to her stomach.

"Huooh...."

She stepped into the front hall and sat down. The full moon had just passed, but she could not tell as the moon and stars were obscured by clouds.

"Perhaps I am obsessed with Yongnan," she thought, shivering.

She had dreamed that her family was in the midst of the spell. A shaman in a long costume was dancing with two swords. Many people were watching. Yongnan was laughing and Yongok crying. The shaman lifted a hen that had been squatting on the ground. She danced with it for a long time.

"Oh, hear me, ghosts. Oh, ghost of one who has taken arsenic. Oh, ghost of one who succumbed to a sword. Oh, ghost of one who died of hunger. Oh, ghost of one who died so young. Oh, many ghosts of those who drowned." She stamped her feet and rolled her eyes as she called the ghosts. Then, she put the hen on the doorsill, raised the sword high in the air and abruptly turned her head to Punshi. The shaman had the face of Yonhak and he was giggling.

"When did he get out of jail?" she asked out loud.

Yonhak brought the sword down and hen's head rolled to the floor. The sound of the rolling head became laughing — Yongnan's laughter. Standing on her tiptoes behind the crowd, Punshi saw it was not a hen's head, but Yongnan's.

"Eck, Eck."

The scream had awakened her. Soaked with perspiration, she hugged herself in the darkness thinking, "Ominous, something is going to happen."

Yongnan had left with Handol the night before Chusok. When Punshi went to her house in Mende, Punsoon the servant said she was gone with her clothes.

"Where did she say she was going?"

"Out to the North Gate, but she told me to keep it a secret, though."

Punshi was not brave enough to go looking for Yongnan at the North Gate again. Then she heard that Yonhak was out of prison.

"Oh, they are in big trouble if he finds them. Nobody can stop him."

Punshi had been pondering Yongnan's future. She had made up her mind to help her daughter and Handol escape together, but then she had hesitated. Now, she went to her room and rummaged in her closet. She saved some jewelry for Yongbin's marriage. Though Punshi had sold every bit of her own — even her twenty-year-old wedding ring — she still had Yongbin's.

Wrapping it in a cloth folded over many times, she put it inside her jacket. Then she tiptoed to the kitchen so as not to wake Yomoon and found a lamp. A gust of wind banged the kitchen door. She lit the lamp and let herself out the back door. As she walked, the lamp swung and threw eerie shadows onto the dark and empty road before her. Recalling her hen nightmare, she grew increasingly anxious it made her legs shake. In spite of the lamp, her sense of foreboding made the road before her seem darker. She could not dispel the conviction that Yongnan's bloody body would be waiting for her....

"Oh, my God!" Punshi tripped and fell in the dark. Groping around, she found the lamp that had rolled away from her. But she didn't have a match or any other way to light it. So she stumbled through the dark. When she reached the temple wall, it began to rain; by the time she got to the North Gate, it was pouring. She tossed the lamp aside, pulled her skirt up to protect her head and ran. A fish truck splashed by. Raindrops were dark spots on its headlights. She could see the trees and roofs of houses along the roadside dimly through the haze of headlights and streaks of rain.

In the downpour, Punshi felt as if she were back in her nightmare. She turned into the alley and went up the hill. When she reached the house, there was a clap of thunder and the rain pelted down, but there were neither lights nor sound in the house. She collected herself, relaxed and wiping the water from her face, shook the gate. There was no answer.

"YONGNAN! Yongnan!" she shouted, but her voice dissipated into the rain.

"YONGNAN! It's me. Open the door!"

"Who is it?" A deep, thick voice off a rolling tongue that could only be Yonhak said.

"Oh, my God!" Punshi sighed.

"Who is it?"

"It's me. Please open the gate."

Punshi shoved the gate with all her might. Suddenly, it flew open and a dark shadow appeared there laughing, "Hhuy, heh, huy."

Punshi felt a painful pounding on her head, "Oh, oh...." She reached up and an ax blow hit her hand.

"Oh...help! Help me!" she screamed and fell to the ground.

The noise woke Yongnan and Handol, who had been sleeping soundly. They saw Yonhak as he approached them flourishing the ax. Handol watched him raise the ax and wave it in the air. Yongnan stood up and ran. Yonhak followed her. She hopped over Punshi, who lay on the ground, and escaped out the gate. Yonhak, however, stumbled over her and fell. Realizing he missed Yongnan, he jumped up and ran to Handol, now trying to scale the wall. Yonhak caught him with a blow to the shoulder, hopping up and down dancing as he chopped at him.

A church bell tolled, spreading chimes over the land in concentric circles.

Daybreak. Punshi lay by the front gate and Handol by the wall. A puddle of rain water standing in the yard was red with blood. That was the end of two poor souls and their sad lives. Yonhak slept soundly on the floor of the front hall. To the east, a small section of jade-blue skies was lit with the morning glow. The sky was crystal clear as if it had no recollection of the night and the tumultuous storm.

Meanwhile, Yongnan, her skirt torn, was walking in the marketplace diligently asking every one, "Have you seen my Handol?"

"Oh, this beauty is out of her mind," the people whispered.

"My God, that's one of Kim's daughters." People paused and gathered around her.

"Who has taken my Handol? Hi! Tell me, have you seen my Handol? He has a big mole under this eye. Have you seen where he went?" Yongnan asked passers-by over and over again.

"Poor thing! Totally insane. Pity ole Sangho Che, he's ended up drug-addict of a son and a lunatic of a daughter-in-law. How sad!" a man in the market said.

Busily asking people about Handol, she worked her way to the auctioneer's platform.

"Oh, there he is! Here's my Handol. Handol, why did you go away and leave me alone?"

she asked, taking the auctioneer's hand.

"Good God, you crazy bitch!" the surprised man said stepping back, but Yongnan followed him. Panic-stricken, he escaped into the crowd. She began to sob and sat down in a heap on the ground in the middle of the market. Keydo appeared. He had come to sell some fish, and saw her there. He picked her up in his arms and muscled his way through the crowd to her parents' house in Kanchanggol. Sobbing like a small child, she didn't resist him. When they got there, he sat her down in the hallway and took out a cigarette.

"Huoo," he blew smoke in her face. When Yomoon came from outside and saw Yongnan, she turned pale.

"Where is Mrs. Kim?" he asked her.

"Oh-h, I...." she couldn't finish.

"Where is she? Go lock the gate." Keydo cast a sidelong glance at the crowd that was now gathering outside and blew some more smoke in Yongnan's face. Yomoon locked the gate, returned running and he asked her again, "Where is Mrs. Kim?"

"I-I don't know. When I woke up, she was already gone."

"You haven't seen her?" said Keydo, turning white.

Strangers

As Songsu was on his way to Sochong's, he spied Chongim coming along in opposite direction. Embarrassed, he had no choice but to walk on looking down at his stick.

"Hi there, Songsu! Where are you off to?" she asked, though she knew very well.

"Hello, Chongim, how are you?" he said, lifting his head to greet her.

She was surprised to see his haggard face, "OH-h my, you don't look well." Though they lived in the same town and were relatives, she hadn't seen him for six months. Songsu simply smiled and stared at her shocked features.

"How's Chungku?"

"He's fine, but really, you don't look well. You should pay more attention to your health. Money is here today, gone tomorrow, but health, once it's gone....Chongyoon was very worried when he visited on Chusok, and advised us to take you into the Chinju General Hospital. At the time I thought since you once ran a pharmacy, you yourself would know...."

"Has Chongyoon left?"

"Yes, yesterday with his wife."

Songsu rolled the walking stick in his hand as if he were eager to move on.

"Do me a favor, Songsu — go see the doctors in Chinju as Chongyoon suggested."

"Oh, I'll be fine soon."

"By the way, is Punshi home?"

"I think she is."

"I'm on my way to get her advice on a difficult matter."

"Well, so long...." Songsu continued on.

"Please — do take care of yourself," she reminded him, glancing back several times.

When Songsu arrived at Sochong's, her maid greeted him.

"Where is Sochong?"

"Madame went out to see a movie."

"By herself?"

"I'm sorry, sir, I don't know."

He went into her room, took off his hat and coat, hung them on a hanger and sat down on a cushion. He didn't really care if she were there or not. He went to her now only out of habit — he had nowhere else to go. Bent forward, he studied the floor, breaking the ends off some matches. Her cat meowed in the background.

"Should I go to see the doctor in Chinju?"

The thought unnerved him. He pondered the idea not because he had any hope of recovering, but because he was humiliated. It was, however, not the humiliation of an Oriental doctor who has never been to a Western hospital and who can not treat himself, but the pain that pierced every thought and made him weak. He was irritated, nevertheless attached to his life. The more he realized his days were numbered, the more he wanted to conceal this heartbreaking fact. He wanted to keep the pain a secret so no one else knew. Songsu's distinctive personal obstinacy made him not only unable to sympathize with others' agony, but also accept sympathy.

He had felt that his wife, his daughters, son-in-law and even his lover Sochong were all strangers.

An ordinary libertine, leading a life of dissipation would be reduced to guilty frustration, but an egoist like Songsu, self-sufficient and independent, feels desperate, more frustrated and lonelier than an ordinary lush. Now, Songsu feared the solitude he had cultivated so diligently and even enjoyed formerly.

He wasn't ready to die. He often wondered how his mother found the courage to end her own life. He had been tempted to commit suicide a few times, when he had found himself restless and repulsively attached to life.

"Poor things...." Recently he had begun to feel sympathy for his wife and daughters. He repented for the years he had vainly spent engrossed in his own thoughts, locked in his own prison. He calculated his property. Nothing would be left for them. The property he owned was equivalent to his debts. The land had already been taken by Cookju Chong. The thought that his family's memory of him would be a cold and remote figure sitting in his study saddened him immensely.

The maid brought his dinner on a low table.

"It is becoming dark already...." he said.

"Yes sir, it is," she agreed, and went out.

He only had a spoonful of seaweed soup and had the table removed. He would have liked to have had something to drink, but for health's sake did not.

Sochong returned drunk around midnight. Late, to avoid Songsu.

"Hello, my darling, did you come to see me because you love me?" The brims of her eyes were red. She continued. "Well, luv, what have you done for me lately? I'm only sick and tired and bored to tears with you. At first I was fascinated by your coldness. Love is a two-way street, but you never loved me. What are you doing here, always sitting on the floor, rooted like a trumpet shell? You have never given me any affection. I'm a person, made of flesh and blood."

"...."

"I find myself in an awkward situation. If you were as rich as you once were...but now you're broke and I can't stop because I'm tied to you with affection and morality...you know, I'm a *kisaeng*, but I loved you from the very beginning, but not because of your money." She smoked as she talked. She was outspokenly pretending to be more intoxicated than she was.

"I understand. I won't come again," he said, quietly cutting matches in half.

"You got me wrong. I don't mean you shouldn't come here. I mean you should love me. You have never loved me, have you? Tell me if you have ever loved me!"

Sochong actually wanted to put an end to the relationship, but being softhearted, she wasn't able to because Songsu had been reduced to poverty. Moreover, she was young; he couldn't satisfy her and she wasn't really happy with his love. Instead, she needled him, saying he didn't love her.

He said he would never visit again. Though Sochong was eager to part with him, she was in tears recalling the past and her love for him. She was sentimental and compassionate.

"Why, oh why, don't you tell me you love me? Tell me whether you love me or not."

"I used to see you because I once felt affection for you, but nowadays," he said, smiling bitterly, "I'm sorry I don't have anything to give you for our days together."

Feeling that she was being excessively harsh with him, she cried. She knew he would never come to see her again because he kept his word. It bothered her conscience turning Songsu out broke.

When Songsu awoke the next morning, she was nowhere to be found. The maid brought him a water basin for morning wash and said Sochong had gone to the market.

But then she returned panic-stricken.

"What's happened?" asked Songsu.

Sochong stared at him for a long moment, then covered her face with her hands and sobbed, "Oh my God ... poor Mrs. Kim...she was so kind and...."

Chapter Six

Encounter on the Train

The click-clack-click-clack of iron wheels against the rails seemed as if the sound itself or the vibrations it made were the actual power that drove the train forward. The relentlessness of it gave new meaning to the word "monotonous."

Yongbin, her eyes closed and leaning motionless against the seat back of a third-class compartment, felt as if she had become suspended there, part of the metallic sound and vibration. She did not want to open her eyes to look at her watch or see how far she had traveled.

The chatting of the other passengers drifted around her. "The Chinese are so dirty they bake bread in a stove, roll it in dust and eat it. Some Chinese are so rich they...."

"Koreans are mean. Some won't even pay for their ricksha rides. Just slap the driver in the face. I hate to see them behave that way because they are backed by the Japs...."

"Not all Koreans are mean. A few, not all...."

Autumn scenes ran through her mind with fall-colored leaves — yellow, red and orange; peppers, pumpkins and squash lying on the thatched roofs, and children eating roasted ears of corn. Yongbin imagined these scenes with her eyes closed, detached from them.

Scene after scene unfolded like so many one-act plays. Some of them connected, some ran forward into other scenes, but she couldn't comment. She observed them uncritically like a spectator amused by the newest experimentation with theatrical surrealism. Dark colors. Inky blackness. The drowsy morning sun, waves on the beach, faces. The most recent scene she had seen in front of Puminkwan.

"Are you here for the performance?"

"Ah, yes," said Hongsop, in a navy blue suit. Over his shoulder, Yongbin could see his wife, Maria, glaring hatefully at her, trying to camouflage the look with one of simple derision.

"To a concert, with my wife...." he said feebly, fidgeting restlessly.

"I see you haven't left for America yet," said Yongbin, beaming as if a smile could smack Maria in the face. However, when Yongbin had bumped into Hongsop in Chongno five or six months ago, he was alone and she didn't mention studying in the U.S.

"You worry about a lot of things," Maria said, frowning, as if to challenge Yongbin.

"Oh, I just wanted to say hello," Yongbin replied blithely, then said goodbye and started off down the pavement. After walking a calculated distance, she turned around and saw Maria going into the theater alone; Hongsop, his head bowed, followed at a distance.

"He's thinking about me," Yongbin laughed — but it was not a bright laugh.

The train slowed and stopped with a jolt. Yongbin opened her eyes. Passengers were getting up, hefting their luggage out. It was dark and there were only dim red lights inside the train. Taegu station. The train disgorged a crowd of people and there were empty seats here and there. Outside vendors shouted, selling Taegu apples; inside the train, saturated with dark red color, the people looked lonely.

Two men, carrying duffel bags and with their collars up, entered. One of them was tall; the other medium height, wearing glasses. Securing their bags on the empty seat opposite her, one of them said, "They suck like spiders."

Hearing a familiar voice, Yongbin looked up. "Oh my!"

"Oh! Oh-h Yongbin!!!" It was Tayoon, understandably very surprised. "Going home for Chusok?" he asked, trying to hide his bewilderment and embarrassment.

"No, for mom's memorial ceremony."

"What?"

"Mom died this time last year...." Yongbin looked away.

"Oh, I didn't know."

"Of course, we haven't heard from you in years."

"Now, I realize!" He bowed his head. "She made so many sacrifices, never enjoyed her life...and now she's dead."

At last Yongbin's face registered her emotion. It was pain that seemed to tear her flesh.

The man who was with Tayoon watched it calmly.

"How is Soonja?"

"What? Aah...." Tayoon sighed deeply.

"Your mother knows about her."

"...."

After a brief silence, Tayoon turned to the man next to him and said, "Introductions are in order. You know this lady." Indeed, the man did seem to know her and was studying her.

"This is my cousin, Yongbin. Yongbin, this is my friend Kug Kang."

Expressionless, she lowered her eyes.

"I've heard a lot about you," he said. His voice was soft and low. Hearing it, Yongbin studied his face. He did not avoid her gaze, but looked straight into her with his cold and clear eyes. When she saw agony hidden in the coldness, Yongbin turned her eyes away, shocked.

"Are you going to Tongyong?" Yongbin asked.

"No, I'm not."

"Where then?"

"Pusan."

"Pusan? On the way you can stop by your house."

"...."

"Where have you been all this time?"

"Wandering from place to place."

"Your mother is worried about you."

"...."

"Why don't you go see her?"

"I, ah I don't have time," said Tayoon, frowning.

"Nobody is *that* busy! Doing worthwhile things is good but...." Yongbin began in a cautious but reproachful tone. Tayoon blushed. He would like to have explained what he was doing, but this was not the place to talk. He suppressed the desire and fell silent.

Mr. Kang removed a cigarette from the pack in his pocket and seemingly without moving a muscle in his face, placed it between his lips. Yongbin, responding to Tayoon's questions, began to feel a strange sort of pressure from Kug. He didn't look bored or embarrassed, but rather sat expressionless. However, he had an air of nobility about him and could not be ignored. Compared to Tayoon, Kug was generous and warmhearted.

When they arrived at Pusan Station, it was quite late. "Are you catching the boat now?" Tayoon asked, as he was almost swallowed by the crowd.

"Well, I...have lots to tell you. I know it is going to be difficult to tell you all of it." Yongbin cast a brief glance at Mr. Kang, who had pulled his hat low over his brow.

"Yes, we need to talk. Why don't we all stay at the same inn? You can take the morning boat."

"Let me see...." Yongbin debated whether she should and finally said, "All right. Where are you staying?"

"We don't have a place; we have to look for one."

"Let's go to Haeundae," Mr. Kang volunteered.

Tayoon readily agreed, and at Haeundae, they took two rooms. After a light dinner Tayoon stood up and asked, "How about a walk on the beach?" However, he directed the question to his friend, not to Yongbin.

"Fine," Kug said, rising quietly, as Yongbin sat wondering because she had thought she was the one Tayoon wanted to talk to.

"Come on, let's go," he said, nodding at Yongbin this time. She rose and followed them.

When they got to the beach, Kug said, "Why don't you two talk?" He nodded lightly to Yongbin and went off in the opposite direction. Yongbin and Tayoon sat down in the sand. The waves sounded threatening.

"He's strange."

"Not strange, a mystery," Tayoon said.

"Can a person be a mystery?" Yongbin laughed.

"Yes. I'd say he is a mysterious man."

"Then he's not a revolutionary. Is he an artist?" Yongbin asked, laughing again.

"Politics *is* an art; the highest art."

"Oh, is that so?"

"That's enough about him. Tell me about Tongyong."

"Tongyong...ah yes. There is so much to tell, I'm afraid I'll leave something out...."

Yongbin's eyes glistened with tears. Each story she told surprised and shocked Tayoon as if it were some other family's. And she managed to control herself and continue speaking till the end of her tale.

"Um...."

"Well, I've told you everything." Yongbin said, picking up a handful of sand and squeezing it. She felt her palm sweat.

"You've suffered so much, Yongbin. Where is Yongnan now?"

"At home. Yonghay is taking care of her. She had to drop out of school."

"How could things have turned out so bad?" They sat in silence for a long time
contemplating the question.

"After father dies, I want to go as far away as possible."

"Away?"

"Yes, as far as possible. I hate this country — this land of Choson."

"It's a shame. Your father's very particular on top of everything else."

"He won't live long. I got a letter from Chongyoon, and while I'm home I'm going to take him to the hospital where he works."

"I don't know what to say. I'm so glad you are taking care of these things."

"Now, it's your turn; tell me what is happening with you?"

"Soonja is doing fine."

"And...is that all?"

"I am anxious because of course I never know what is going to happen next, but I am strong....I have courage."

"Aren't you even going to ask about your family?"

"I think I know."

"Did you know Chongyoon is married?"

"I figured, considering the time that's passed."

Insane with Grief

"Father," Yongbin said, after she completed her bow to Songsu. "You've lost weight." Songsu looked as if he were having trouble focusing. He blinked.

"I'll be out," Yongbin said, retreating from Songsu's study.

The following day was Chusok, Korean Thanksgiving, and the day after that was the anniversary of Punshi's death, but there were no signs anyone had made any preparations for either. Yonghay stood leaning against a column, looking sad as an evening primrose. Yomoon, Kim's long-time live-in maid, had returned to her parents' home and married, so the big house was now home to only three people: Songsu, Yonghay and Yongnan.

Yongbin went to the backyard without a word. Yonghay followed her. The courtyard was overgrown with bushes and weeds. Mice scampered away without much fear of people. Yonghay unlocked the latch and deferred to her older sister. When Yongbin stepped in, a pale white face turned toward the door and smiled. Yongbin stared at the face and said nothing.

"Is that you, Handol?"

"Yes."

"Did you have any trouble getting past Yongbin?"

"I snuck out."

"I've been waiting for you. We're going to run away. I stole this from Mom. Where is it? It was just here," said Yongnan looking around.

Yongbin came forward to Yongnan, and rubbing her back, she said, "We don't need that."

"Can we live without it?" Yongnan asked.

Yonghay brought in lunch.

"Who is it? Is that you, Handol?"

"Yes," Yonghay answered. Just as Yongbin had done, she also answered as Handol.

"How come you're late?"

"Sorry, I couldn't help it."

Yonghay set bowls of rice and kimchi in front of Yongnan, who looked at her sisters in turn suspiciously and smiled. Then, she grabbed the bowl of rice and stuffed it into her mouth as if she were starving.

"Great fish! Is it broiled red snapper? Did they bring it in from the fishery?" asked Yongnan, chewing the kimchi and calling it fish, which brought tears to Yongbin's eyes.

"Yonghay, this is an awful lot of work for you," said Yongbin calmly, looking at Yonghay.

"Yongok does all the work. All I do is cook...." Yonghay said, resigned and mature beyond her years.

"Does Yongok come by often?"

"She came by yesterday and washed this crazy woman's hair and changed her clothes, then went home," Yonghay told her sister. Yonghay called her sister "crazy" setting her jaw as she said it because she believed Yongnan was responsible for her mother's death.

"She seems quieter than before."

"When she gets wild, I can't restrain her. Last time she took off all her clothes and went to the market place, asking everybody if they had seen Handol. Keydo managed to get her home. It's strange, but she would only listen to him."

"Is she eating all right?"

"Sometimes she doesn't eat a thing for three or four days."

"I hear Keydo's gone to Pusan."

"Yes, he's got a job with the Fishermen's Union."

On Chusok, the following day, Songsu was not seen in his study. In the evening Chungku and Chongim came with special delicacies for the holiday.

"Is your father out?" Chungku asked after Yongbin greeted him with a bow.

"Yes, he's out, I think," Yongbin answered, looking to Yonghay for help.

"He's probably gone for a walk on the hill behind the house," Yonghay said, sounding depressed.

"On the hill? Then let's go bring him home." Yongbin hurried restlessly.

"Father gets angry. The other day he screamed at me to go back," Yonghay said, lifting her head to keep the tears from rolling down her face.

"Let him go. He can no longer control his anger," Chungku said.

"Did you make offerings to your mother and trim the grass around her grave?" Chongim asked.

"Yes, we got groceries last night and made offerings with Yongok, but we haven't visited the grave yet."

"Tsk, poor Punshi. There's no one to make an offering at her grave! It is so sad. Yongbin, I'm glad at least you are here. What an awful fate! And Punshi was such a grand and generous person too. God has certainly made a mistake."

"Nonsense," said Chungku, to his complaining wife, but that did not deter her.

"And have you ever seen a bitch like this big sister? The family's in trouble, and she never shows up, acts like a poisonous snake. What? Did she drop from heaven or sprout from the ground? A child has parents and some obligation to them. Doesn't she care that her father is starving? No, apparently not; she walks around town in foxy silk dresses. She's supposed to be mourning her mother, and there she goes in a gold hairpin and colored dress, no less. Can you imagine? Doesn't care what anybody thinks, the dirty little bitch!" Chongim's anger caught fire and finally exploded.

"Stop ranting, Chongim," her husband said.

"Honey, what good is a mouth if you don't speak the truth? Am I lying?"

Chungku paused filling his pipe and stared at her uneasily. "What is wrong with you? They know it. So, all you've done is hurt their feelings unnecessarily."

"I just said it because she's so mean and makes me so sick," Chongim looked down.

"Aunt Chongim, you shouldn't be too upset with her. Yongsook sent us money for Chusok, though father doesn't know. She tries to help; I do think blood is thicker than water."

Neither of the old people responded. After a long pause, Chungku asked, "By the way, Yongbin, what are you going to do?"

"...."

"Your future looks bleak. Will you be a teacher all your life?"

"I don't really want to get married yet."

"Well, I don't blame you. You have seen many bad things."

"As long as father is healthy enough to manage, I'd like to take him to Seoul, but...." Yongbin had a troubled look on her face.

Chungku insisted, "Songsu won't go to Seoul, you know."

"That's why I didn't bring it up. First, I'm going to try to get him to go to Chinju and get an examination."

"I, myself, have asked him to go many times because of what Chongyoon told me, but your father doesn't listen."

"I got a letter from him too."

"Who could have imagined this? Money comes and goes, but wealth is not all you have lost. You've lost family, health and wealth. Who could really keep their sanity in this situation?" said Chungku, who normally didn't say much.

"Oh-h, how can you say something so hurtful?"

Chungku only smiled at his wife's reproachful tone.

She began, "Yongok is a sweetheart. It's hard enough to live with her in-laws, but she is taking good care of her sister, not to mention her father. Now, she's a good daughter." She continued to rhapsodize about Keydo and Yonghay. Meanwhile, Yongbin was hesitating — wondering whether she should tell them that she had seen Tayoon in Pusan.

"Well, Tayoon...." Yongbin found she couldn't continue, so she left the sentence hanging midair.

"Dead or alive, I don't want to know. He's given me such heartache," Chongim said, wiping the tears at the corners of her eyes. Thinking of him only the night before, she had cried.

"He takes up with a widow trying to be faithful to her dead husband, so I know he will not return home while we are alive."

Yongbin squinted when she heard Soonja mentioned.

"Don't mention his name in my presence!" Hot-tempered Chungku got angry whenever Tayoon was mentioned.

"I saw him in Seoul."

"What?" Chungku, who had just tried to end last discussion, was the first to respond. Only Yongbin didn't have the heart to tell them she saw him in Pusan.

"I ran into him in Seoul on the street, going about his business...he looked quite well." "He's alive, and all this time he doesn't care enough even to write one letter home," Chungku, who always spoke as if he had already given up on his son, revealed his true feelings.

"What did he say he was doing?" Chongim asked, observing her husband's genuine desire to know, and leaned close to Yongbin.

"I think Soonja is not to blame. He didn't say what he was doing, but I am sure it is something he considers important." Yongbin couldn't say any more though she was certain her aunt and uncle found the news stressful.

"He'll waste his whole life on it."

"Our government is in China...."

"Then he's going to China?"

"Probably...but don't worry."

It was dark already and a full moon was shining on the bank above. Songsu pushed the gate open and let himself in. His eyes shone like a ghost's.

Ripe Persimmons

On the first anniversary of her mother's death Yongsook showed up in mourning clothes. She had already sent food and money. Before, when there was work to be done, she tried to avoid it, but not now. As the eldest sister, she had the right to have her say. She changed some as she became older, but still talked constantly. However, she had only one listener — old Mr. Soh, Keydo's father; everyone else kept silent.

The rest of the family came, but Keydo, Punshi's one and only son-in-law, did not. Though he worked out of town, Chungku and Yongbin believed that he would certainly make it to Punshi's first mourning ceremony, so they were very disappointed. Old Soh made all kinds of excuses for his son's absence, but Yongok, with the baby tied to her back, only worked silently.

The following day Yongbin and Songsu set out for Chinju to the province hospital. On Chusok evening, in response to pressure from Chungku and Yongbin, Songsu had finally consented to go with his daughter for medical tests.

Swaying back and forth on the bus, Songsu stared out the window at the farmhouses. The persimmon trees were turning orange. He recalled the figure of the country girl disappearing into the backyard with the wild sesame stalks many years ago. The vague memories came alive and began to glow vividly. He thought of the donkey ride through the fields in the fall with Pongjay, the face of the old farmer, the face of the girl as she brought the rice drinks. It had happened nearly forty years ago, but it seemed like yesterday.

Songsu looked away, sighed deeply without even realizing he'd made a sound. Yongbin, who had been watching her father, heard the sigh and turned to him, "Father?"

"...."

"A penny for your thoughts."

"Um...the persimmon trees. Such beautiful fruit."

"...."

"After you have the tests, would you consider going to Seoul? Yonghay should continue studying. Seoul is a big city...you can forget everything...you are too lonely here."

"I would be even lonelier there."

Being lonely and regarding Seoul as no place for lonely people didn't seem to go together, but Yongbin understood her father. "You can feel loneliest in a crowd of people," she thought, but said nothing.

They got off the bus in Chinju. Since her father looked exhausted, they checked into an inn. Yongbin told him to rest and went down to the hospital. When she saw the red brick building, she felt overwhelmed. On the lawn across the street, a nurse and a male assistant were playing table tennis, smiling brightly. Before she got to the reception desk, a nurse passed.

"Excuse me," Yongbin said. The nurse stopped. She had a black mole under one of her eyes and a face that gave the impression of loneliness. "I am looking for Dr. Chongyoon Lee. Does he work here?"

"Yes, he does," she answered after a long pause, surveying Yongbin.

"Would you please tell him he has a visitor from Tongyong?"

"Certainly." The nurse turned around and walked back. She wore a tight belt and her waistline was small and beautiful.

In a short while, Chongyoon appeared, his hair tousled. Yongbin waited for him, standing next to a magnolia tree. He looked handsome to her with his broad white forehead and wide framed glasses.

"Where's your father?" he asked.

"At an inn."

"An inn?"

"Yes. He was pretty tired."

"You should have brought him to my house."

"Well, I don't have the address, and anyway, father would prefer to stay at an inn."

Chongyoon looked at his watch. Then, without a word, he led her off to a not-so-crowded area of the hospital lawn and took out a cigarette.

"I am so sorry I couldn't make it to your mother's first memorial; I was so very busy," he blurted out unexpectedly, looking dead ahead.

"You didn't miss anything. She's already gone." said Yongbin, as if she didn't like the topic.

"Is Yongnan still out of touch with reality?"

"No change."

"I wonder what made your father decide to come here."

"I begged him."

"Is he any better?"

"I believe he's weaker."

Chongyoon continued smoking. Yongbin noticed the bluish trace of a razor scrape on his neck, found it attractive, and as she felt herself a longing for a man, she blushed.

"The nurse who gave you the message was very pretty," she said.

"What?" Looking at her, he felt embarrassed.

"The nurse I met a few minutes ago. She looked lonesome. Especially her eyes."

"The patients say her eyes are like lanterns."

"How romantic!"

"That's the kind of talk poets love."

"How's your wife?"

"...."

"Is she doing all right?"

"So-so, I guess."

"Do you have any children yet?"

"Not yet."

"You must be lonely."

"You must be too, Yongbin. By the way, you haven't met her, have you?"

"When could I have met her? It's been years since I saw you."

"Yes, of course."

"Is she pretty?"

"You can't escape being a woman, that's why you're interested."

"Hee...hee, why would you think I am not? You looked at me very coldly, so I had to ask."

"Yongbin, you are covering up your own pain."

"Do you think so?"

Chongyoon turned to Yongbin and stared into her eyes. He saw much sadness there.

"Did you hear about Tayoon?"

"...."

"I saw him the other day." She told him everything but he didn't respond.

"Do you hate your brother?"

"I simply try not to think about him." Chongyoon stubbed his cigarette out. "I need to talk to you about your father's illness."

The words yanked Yongbin back to reality.

"Of course, we haven't done the tests yet, so I can't say for sure, but from what I observed while I was in Tongyong and from his symptoms, I'm afraid he has cancer."

"Cancer." Yongbin's face became pale.

"I can't be totally sure, but that's my guess. We'll know for sure when we see the X-rays. If they show otherwise, good. I thought you should be aware of the possibility."

"If the tests prove he does, that will be the end," she mumbled.

Rising abruptly, Chongyoon said, "My wife and I will come to your inn tonight. Where is it?"

"It's called Mongwol."

Yongbin emerged from the hospital feeling as if the air smelled of blood and it was suffocating her. "He's not going to live long, anyhow," she thought. She walked in slow, wide steps.

Thinking about her father sitting alone at the inn, she swallowed something that felt thicker and stronger than tears. She wandered around the unfamiliar streets for a long time before returning to the inn.

Her father was sitting, waiting for her, "Did you see Chongyoon?"

"Yes, Father, he's coming here after dinner with his wife. He said you could stay with them, but I told him you preferred an inn."

"Right. I am more comfortable here."

"Is tomorrow okay for the tests?"

"Whenever it is convenient for you."

"Did you take a nap?"

"No, I couldn't."

After they ate lunch served by the innkeeper, they sat opposite from one another, idling. Outside, they heard cheerful women clerks greeting and laughing with their customers.

"Would you like to see downtown Chinju, Father?"

"All these towns look the same."

"How about a movie then?"

"No, thanks. Are you bored?"

"No."

They were killing time when Chongyoon and his wife came into the inn before dinner. Yoonhee, Chongyoon's wife, bowed to Songsu and with a smile extended her hand to Yongbin. Yongbin shook her hand, studying her face, which was graced with a mysterious smile. Yongbin's elegant and controlled attitude of intelligence and experience gave the impression she was older than Yoonhee.

"Living so far from one another, we have never met," Yoonhee said, using the polite formal address form for someone older, though Yongbin was younger.

Yongbin invited her to sit down and asked, "Do you like living here in Chinju?"

Yoonhee smiled like a patient in a hospital. Chongyoon was talking to Songsu. The two women looked at one another though neither felt awkward. Yongbin was too educated for small talk and Yoonhee was indifferent.

When Yongbin saw Yoonhee's pathetic smile, she felt her cousins' wives reflected their husbands well. She could feel their pain, the agony behind heavy glasses both wore.

Chongyoon certainly loved Yoonhee with her pathetic T.B.-patient smile, and Tayoon loved Soonja, a widow who had not had the opportunity to receive much education. Perhaps they both reflected a kind of need for dominance, through loving these rather abnormal women. Both were too intelligent to fall in love blindly, Yongbin decided.

"Do you ever come to Seoul?" Yongbin asked Yoonhee.

"Seoul?"

"Yes, you should come visit me in Seoul."

"I have been there before and it was very tiring."

"You are smiling, but you look a little tired now."

At this point, Chongyoon turned around and looked at his wife's face lovingly.

"Not a bit," Yoonhee said, combing her hair back from her face with her fingers. Yongbin didn't mean it that way, but she didn't correct herself. Yoonhee looked out the window for a while and then said, "Please come to our house."

Yongbin said, "I'll come and visit you tomorrow."

"You should stay with us."

"My father feels more comfortable at an inn."

"Really?"

The two men continued talking in low voices and the two women just listened.

"Father and I almost went to the movies. Good thing we didn't; we would have missed you. We really didn't expect you this early." Yongbin said, resuming their conversation.

"Do you like movies?"

"I go often," Yongbin answered.

"The other day we saw *The Blue Veil,* a French film."

"Yes, I saw it in Seoul. I like Gaby Morlay, she's a good actress." They continued to talk about film. After nine, Chongyoon reminded them of their appointment the following day, and rose to leave.

Yongbin walked them to the gate of the inn and watched them disappear down the street.

"Cancer. Could it be cancer?" she wondered, turning around and looking down at the ground, white with the light of the street lamps.

Diagnosis

The day after her father had the tests and X-rays done, Yongbin asked him if he wanted to go downtown again, but he still didn't feel up to it.

"You go on, child. I'll be fine here."

"Going alone is no fun."

"Ask Yoonhee."

In fact, Yongbin didn't feel like going herself. Waiting for the results of the tests made her anxious and ill at ease. Sitting by the window, Yongbin gazed down upon the garden of the inn. There were sculptured trees and moss-covered stones arranged in meticulously geometrical patterns. She hated the artificiality of it. Likewise, she hated the restlessness forming in herself! "Everything is decided for us. Prearranged, especially death," she thought.

Yongbin realized that she had begun to accept the idea of fate, but she did not like being a fatalist. "I must face reality! I have been trained to overcome obstacles, destined or not."

She was interrupted by footsteps in the hall. "There's a phone call for you," a maid said without opening the door.

Yongbin got up and said to her father, "Certainly from Chongyoon."

She tried not to reveal her emotion, but felt the muscles of her face had become rigid. Songsu gazed at his daughter in despair. Yongbin ran to pick up the receiver. Her heart beat fast, and her hands became numb. "Chongyoon."

"Yongbin?"

"Yes." There was a long pause. It seemed very long to Yongbin.

"I have the X-rays, and it is as I suspected...."

"As you suspected...."

"It's stomach cancer. There is nothing we can do. It has spread."

"...."

"Yongbin?"

"Yes."

"He only has three or four months to live. Do you understand me?"

"Yes."

"You should probably tell him it's an ulcer."

"I understand."

"You have been through so much, so take it easy yourself."

"...."

"Yongbin, you're not crying, are you?"

"No, I'm not."

"Well, I have to go, but I need to get together with you again."

"Come to the inn."

"No, I'd rather not. Meet me at the shrine by the Nam River."

He hung up. She stood stock-still, holding the receiver for a while. Then she walked back to the room and smiled brightly.

"Father, it was Chongyoon; he said you have an ulcer. If you rest and take the right medicine, you'll be all right. He told me he was relieved."

"Really?" Songsu, staring transfixed at the white wall, didn't even blink.

"What are you doing, Father?"

"Am I acting strangely?"

"Forget everything. When you're better, you and I and Yonghay will go to Seoul."

Songsu Kim smiled a lonely smile.

"God knows, we deserve some good news. Things will get better. Don't you think, Dad?"

"Good things. Well, am I going to see you married before I die?"

"Why are you asking that?" Yongbin's eyes stung hotly. "My wedding, Yonghay's wedding, you should see them both. Cheer up." Yongbin smiled, and her eyes filled with tears.

In the evening, Yongbin made the bed for her father and left the inn saying she was going to get some air. She asked directions to the shrine. Walking up the stone steps to it, she felt she had been on an endless journey. In the wide courtyard, cherry leaves were turning red and the whole city spread before her. She could see the cars crossing the Nam River bridge, which reminded her of a ladder. Mist obscured the riverbank. A swaying sound came from the nearby bamboo grove.

"You're early!" Chongyoon, in a navy suit, was standing there with one hand in his pants pocket. Yongbin looked at her watch. Five on the dot. "You're punctual as an alarm clock."

"I checked to make sure I got here on time."

"That's tiresome. Are you always conscious of the time?" she asked, looking at the city.

"Time is better than space. Being a prisoner of time is less tiring than freedom."

"I thought you were strong, but you react to the emptiness more strongly than Tayoon."

"I don't know."

"Why does a person die?"

"You must ask yourself that question."

Yongbin was still gazing at the city. "Can we sit down somewhere?"

"Let's go to Choksongnu."

Chongyoon strolled with his hands in his pockets. They passed old Choksongnu and walked up the road lined with trees. When they reached the pavilion at the top, they had a wider view of the landscape now, and the river was a tiny line below the cliff. Yongbin sat down on the edge. Chongyoon leaned against a column and took out a cigarette.

"Do you think it is possible for a woman like me to get married?" she asked.

Chongyoon stopped lighting the cigarette and looked at his cousin, raising one eyebrow. "When I saw you and your wife, I felt very lonesome. I wished I had someone to share my burdens with, even if he doesn't love me."

After Chongyoon tossed off the match and took a long drag, he said smiling, "I didn't think you had such a feminine side."

"I'm disappointed," she said, her face clearly displaying the sadness she felt.

"Yongbin, you are being selfish if you don't want to share love, only your burdens."

Yongbin's laughter sounded empty. "You're right. I was being selfish."

"It's quite all right. I'm like a brother; I understand."

"It doesn't matter. Right now I'm tired and hungry for sympathy."

However, Chongyoon showed her no sympathy, and if the truth be known, she didn't really want any; she was cool and collected.

"Yongbin, do you think that each of us has his or her own fate?"

"Yes, of course."

"But saying that essentially means it's *not* fate. What I mean is, as a doctor I see so much death. Death is human destiny. Early or late, one way or another, each one of us will die. And death looks the same to everyone. Let's not think about it."

"Is fate altered by an individual's abilities? Does my situation reflect me and my abilities?"

"Every situation is different. And we see many deaths before we ourselves die. Your mom's death put you in this situation."

"Is that all there is to it?"

"If we blame everything on fate, we won't have much of a life, will we?" Chongyoon laughed.

"It's a beautiful view from here. I like the river better than the ocean — less threatening." Leaning over the guardrail, Yongbin gazed down on the riverbanks. Chongyoon sat down next to her with no trace of emotion on his face.

"Did you intend to sympathize with me?" Yongbin became talkative around Chongyoon, who didn't usually say much, unlike Tayoon. She was trying hard to forget the diagnosis, her father's death sentence.

"I wanted to be of some comfort to you, but I know I can't. Anyway, there is something else I must discuss with you."

"And what might that be?"

After a long pause, he began again, "I hear Yonghay dropped out of school. True? "

"Yes."

"She must finish school, don't you think? I am ready to offer to help her."

"I don't think so."

"And why not?"

"I can afford to support her myself. She said she wouldn't leave father here to go to Seoul."

"Not now, maybe, but after he dies."

"You are cruel. I don't want to plan for father's death."

"Well, you had better. You had better be practical and prepared."

"Thanks for the offer, but I'll take care of her."

"Yongbin, you need to be out from under all these obligations and free to find your own life. It may sound world-wise to you, but I feel obligated to pay for Yonghay's education."

"You mean because my father paid for yours?"

"Exactly."

"You aren't under any obligation."

"Do you think I am the kind of person to ignore that obligation?"

"Did you talk to your wife about this?"

"No, not yet, but she won't mind. She's not especially sympathetic or cold. It won't matter to her if she's living with Yonghay or not. She'll adjust."

"Bring your father, then."

"Father would never come here. He is set in his ways, his little routines."

"Let's not talk about it any more. It makes me feel terrible. Even though he's sick, I wish he would live for Yonghay's sake. Poor kid."

Chongyoon said nothing more. When they came down from the pavilion, it was dark.

The next morning Chongyoon and Yoonhee came to see Songsu and Yongbin off. The day after they arrived in Tongyong, Yongbin left for Seoul.

The Old Beast

"He should have at least come for appearances' sake. Kims don't have a son — they don't have another son-in-law!" Old Mr. Soh complained vigorously, but it was clear he was only trying to flatter Yongok by berating his son.

"It's Chusok and he doesn't show up to see his parents, his wife or his child! Disgraceful! Is this any way to live?" He paced and mumbled, and though he tried to ingratiate himself to Yongok, she was all the more revolted. She tried to busy herself with washing and sewing, with the baby on her back. By concentrating on her work, she was able to forget her pain.

After she set the dinner table, she filled a small jar with some of her delicious radish kimchi. She wrapped Songsu's newly sewn silk top and pants in a cloth and went out with the bundle, saying, "Father, I'm going to Kanchanggol."

He hated her going to church, but normally he didn't mind her going to her parents' house. Today, however, he scowled.

"You'd better wait until tomorrow; Keysoo is not home yet." His second son, Keysoo, soon to graduate from elementary school, was on the class trip to Kyongju.

"I would rather go now," she said stubbornly.

"Then come back early," he said, knowing he could not stop her.

Yongok was worried how things were going after Yongbin went back to Seoul. But she couldn't walk as fast as she would have liked with the baby on her back and kimchi in one hand, clothes in the other.

"How come you are sleeping out here, Yonghay? I'm afraid you are going to catch cold." When she arrived, she found Yonghay, sleeping on the porch. Yonghay didn't move, but when Yongok removed the book, she saw the tears. Yonghay was crying.

"Yonghay!"

"Yongok, when did you get here?" Yonghay stood up slowly.

"Why are you crying?"

"It would be better if we lived in a smaller house. I don't like this big old house," Yonghay said, evading the question.

Yongok untied the baby from her back and nursed her, saying, "I think it's time for you to go to Seoul."

"Then who would be here to take care of father?"

"We could hire a servant."

"Hardly. And who would come in here and take care of a crazy girl?"

"I will," Yongok said, but she herself doubted that she could and wondered why she said it.

"Why do you say that kind of nonsense?" Yonghay asked.

Yongok had a response on the tip of her tongue, but couldn't say it. "Here are father's clothes and some radish kimchi as well. Give me your dirty clothes. I have to go back now."

"I was so bored that I did all the laundry myself." Yonghay told her, "But please don't hurry off, stay with me a little longer."

"Oh no, I must go. Keysoo is on a school trip and my father-in-law insisted that I come back early. Is Yongnan eating okay these days?"

"Not since yesterday."

"Take good care of her, and don't get short-tempered with her. Poor thing!"

Yongok tied the baby, who had fallen asleep while suckling, on her back and peeked into Songsu's room. "Bye-bye, father," she called out as she left. He coughed a couple of times, which meant he had heard her.

The return walk was easier. With both hands free, she boosted the baby rhythmically on the bottom as she went over West Gate Hill. The stars flickered and the road was deserted.

"Dear God," she prayed as she walked, "forgive my weak faith. Please grant me the grace to live forever in your abundant love."

She trudged up and over the hill. When she got to the gate, it was unlocked; she latched it and tiptoed to her room. The room was dark; there was no sign of husband. She always hoped he would return, but she always ended up disappointed and sad. Nevertheless, she opened the door quietly as if her husband were sleeping there.

"Are you back?" she heard Old Soh's voice from his room.

"Yes."

Yongok went in and lit a lamp. The room seemed large and deserted. She laid the baby on the sleeping mat and sat in front of the mirror. In it, she saw a dark dry-skinned face with freckles and the sturdily built body of a handyman. She touched her cheekbones with thick, heavy hands.

"Um...."

She recalled that a neighbor said she had seen Keydo come out of a bar one morning, as if he had spent the night there. The baby was now fast asleep, and she patted her face, and then took out the cosmetics she had bought when she was married. She smoothed some cream on her face and then powdered it to conceal the freckles. She rouged her cheeks, darkened her eyebrows and applied lipstick. Combing her thick stiff hair, she brought a coarse lock down across her forehead. She studied the stranger in the mirror, then covered her face with her hands, and sobbed bitterly. Tears ran between her thick-boned fingers. Recovering herself after a while, she knelt to pray.

Then she wiped her tear-stained face with a towel and opened the door. Winter was coming on and she had a great deal of sewing to do for both her father-in-law and the baby. She stirred the fire she'd lit before she'd left to visit her father's house, sat down and began to sew a jacket for her father-in-law from silk she had washed and ironed, becoming absorbed in the task. Yongok was a fine nimble-fingered seamstress, and handling the hot iron, she forgot her fatigue.

The old clock on the wall struck one. The sound alarmed her and she stopped sewing. She stowed her needle, thread and thimble in the sewing basket, spread the sleeping mat and locked the door. Turning off the light and lying down, she fell asleep immediately. Sometime later a rustling sound awakened her. Thinking it was morning, she threw back the covers. But when she saw a shadow reflected on the paper-screen door, she realized it was not morning and an intruder had entered the house! She lay stock-still. A hand reached through the hole in the door. The hairs stood up on the back of her neck. The hand unlocked the door; fear chocked her voice. Silently, the door swung open allowing a gust of cold night air and dim light into the room.

"Wh-who is it?" she whispered fearfully.

The shadow paused. Yongok jumped to her feet and ran to the corner of the room, as if to hide herself.

"Who are you-u?" she said in a voice that was almost a cry. The shadow stepped into the room. It ran to her and covered her mouth so she wouldn't scream.

"Fa—...." she tried to shout for her father-in-law, but the hand stopped the sound and pressed her mouth so tightly that she couldn't even breathe. She struggled to free herself from the thief's grasp.

"Take everything...." she tried to say as she continued to struggle. He threw her down on the floor, still covering her mouth and began fumbling for her breasts with his other hand.

"Ah, ah!"

Shock made her blood stop, as if it would reverse direction. Struggling with the man, she had grabbed a cigar pouch. Doubling her fists, she fought him with all her might. However, though he had released her and she was able to, she didn't shout because by then she knew her attacker was her father-in-law, old Mr. Soh. She bit his arm hard as she could.

"Stop! There's nobody watching us! Nobody," he mumbled.

They were like fox and wolf battling in the night. Yongok managed to toss the ash from the fire pot at Soh, but then he knocked her down and the ash got into her eyes.

"Uh!" she groaned, jumping up and running out of the room.

He followed her and when she got to the front gate, old Soh seized her by the back of the neck. She reached down, grabbed a large wooden spoon she had left sitting on the mortar near the gate, and whacked him across the face. He fell down; she opened the gate and ran for all she was worth.

She collapsed in a heap on the wet ground under the camellia tree at Chungnyolsa. She could hear a dog barking in the distance. The Chungnyolsa shrine could be seen in the light of the half moon. A dreamlike solitude pervaded everything, not even a leaf trembled. The chirping of the crickets only deepened the solitude.

Footsteps broke the silence as the moonlight faded and morning began to break in the eastern sky. People were coming to fetch water from the Myongjonggol wells.

Yongok was so embarrassed she stepped behind the tree to avoid being seen. Her swollen breasts hurt when she tied her loose bodice ties. Then she thought of the baby. She flew back to the house like a crazy woman. Pausing to listen cautiously before the gate, she heard nothing. She feared the baby may have died in the fight, but when she opened the door of the room, she found her sleeping soundly. She tied the sleeping baby to her back and packed diapers and other clothes with her hands trembling, not really thinking of what she was packing. She stuck some money between her breasts, and left.

"Where are you going?" Her youngest brother-in-law demanded, regarding her suspiciously as he was on his way from the toilet to his room.

She didn't respond.

"Where are you going? Who's going to cook breakfast for me if you are going away? Father! Father!" he hollered.

Yongok hurried out the gate. By the time she reached Taebatgol, the vendors coming from Mount Ahn were already beginning to set up shop. She slowed down. She neither knew what time it was nor when boats left for Pusan. Vendors with bundles of produce on their heads or backs passed her and disappeared into the misty morning fog.

Suddenly, somebody grabbed her by the back of the neck. She dropped the bundle in her hand.

"Where do you think you are going?" Old Soh asked.

Yongok was frozen with horror.

"I'll spread the rumor that you came into my room in the middle of the night."

Yongok's shoulders shook like fish out of water. She turned around. She saw his eyes fiery red as the devil's or someone who committed a murder.

"Look, if you don't tell anybody, it'll stay a secret between us. I am sure nobody saw us."

Her father-in-law's terrible eyes now only begged her to be quiet. On her face there were still streaked traces of the make-up she had put on before she went to bed.

"Look, you will be in as much trouble as me. Keydo will not forgive me, but he will certainly take the opportunity to divorce you. Just remember: nobody saw us."

She picked up the bundle from the ground and began to walk.

"Do you understand? Everything is up to you." She heard his voice trembling with despair behind her.

On the Boat to Pusan

With her smeared make-up, Yongok sat on the hard wooden bench in the waiting room of the ferry terminal. She was going to buy a ticket for the morning ship, but somebody told her that it was going to Masan. She sat and stared at the small, dilapidated boat from the window of the waiting room. She remained seated, mistakenly believing its final destination was Masan. Only after the boat left she found it was bound for Pusan with a stop in Masan. The boat stopped at every good-sized city on the Changsungpo peninsula, sailed slowly and took a long time.

"That boat is filthy. You'd be better off to wait and take the day ship. It gets to Pusan at about the same time," said a man who was waiting for the boat to Namhae. Nevertheless, Yongok was disappointed to have missed it. He looked like a vendor and smelled heavily of tobacco. While he was kind to her, he eyed her oddly on account of her smeared make-up.

"What a fine day! Perfect for traveling. Are you meeting someone in Pusan?"

"My husband," she replied, looking at him stupidly and turning away.

"Oh-h, you're going to see your dear husband!" he said smiling meanly.

"Candy bars, sir?"

The man tossed a vendor two coins and picked up two dusty candy bars. Handing one to Yongok, he said, "Try this."

She refused, shaking violently. He put it in the baby's hand and broke his own in half. He stuck one half in his mouth and chewed it. The baby licked the candy and dribbled it down her chin, so Yongok took it from her and then hesitated — at a loss what to do with it. She took her handkerchief out, wrapped the candy in it and rubbed the baby's sticky face with a corner of it. The child, wanting the candy, began to cry. The crying distorted her face and she looked like old Soh, sending a chill down Yongok's spine. Reflexively, she slapped the baby's face, which made her cry louder.

"Don't hit the baby, lady," said the man who had been harassing her. As the departure time approached, he said goodbye and went to the gate to board the boat.

"Oh, I must be living in hell," she thought, feeling crazy and nauseous. She tried to relax, but it was impossible. "What am I going to do when I get to Pusan?" she wondered. 'Will he even see me?' She felt herself descending into a pit of despair, the depth of which she had no idea. "If he ignores me," she thought, "I will die. Truly, I will die."

After it seemed she had been sitting, waiting for hours, she heard the noon siren. Other passengers began to gather to buy tickets. She bought one.

"Hurry back, Mother."

"I'll try, but you know how it is once you're there."

At the sound of a familiar voice, Yongok raised her head. It was Mrs. Cookju Chong. The skinny Mrs. Chong, who was surrounded by a bevy of relatives to see her off, looked arrogant and righteous as a saint with a halo. The employees of the ship line bowed to her every time she came near one of them. All the passengers greeted her as if they were grateful for even the slightest nodding acquaintance with her. Yongok dropped her head in shame. Her father's financial capitulation to Cookju Chong, Hongsop's rejection of Yongbin and the resulting antagonism and hostility made her feel inferior and want to escape notice of the whole group.

The ferry whistled as it steamed into port, docked and while passengers disembarked and those in the waiting room got up with their luggage preparing to move. Mrs. Chong led the large family group out to the pier, even before the gate was opened and the signal given. The rest of the passengers looked at the privileged Chong clan, resigned. An elderly woman with many gourds tied to the bundle she was carrying tried to attach herself to the group, but the ship company employees stopped her, with a severe scolding.

Yongok, looking weary with the baby on her back, stood patiently in line. From the gate on the left, disembarking passengers streamed out endlessly. It seemed to be an exhibition of the largest variety of human types imaginable, all carrying bundles. When everyone was out, the gate was opened for the embarking passengers. Yongok passed through the gate and stepped up on the narrow gangway, talking softly to the fussy baby. Under the gangplank, she could see the dark water, shiny with spilled oil. She hopped off the end of the plank onto the deck and went to the cabin. Mrs. Chong was on deck talking with her relatives.

Yongok had never been out of Tongyong, and this was her first time on a ship. Even before it set sail, she began to feel seasick from the smell of the oil. Likely too, the fact that she hadn't eaten anything the previous evening made her nauseous. Along with some passengers from Yosu, she lay down on the floor of the cabin. The ship weighed anchor and began to move with a noisy shudder of the engine, which shook the whole boat. Surprised vendors jumped back to the dock as the ship moved away.

"I don't understand why it is so crowded today," Mrs. Chong said, seeing the passengers coming into the cabin.

"Well, hello there, are you on your way to Pusan?"

"Oh hello. You're Okja's mother, aren't you?"

From where she was lying, Yongok could overhear the conversation around her. Okja's mother was Tackjin's sister-in-law — the younger sister of the woman Tackjin married after Yonsoon died. Therefore, she was effectively Yongok's aunt, though of course not a blood relative. The Kims and Tackjin never got on. However, Yongok recognized her because Punshi used to greet her when they met in the street.

"It's very nice to see you. I was afraid this would be a very boring trip with no company."

"I'm alone too," Okja's mother made room for Mrs. Chong and said, "Do sit down."

"On your way to Pusan, visiting?"

"Me? Oh no, as a matter of fact, I'm going to Seoul to my son's home."

"Lucky you. There are so many famous places to see."

"It is not my first visit; I've already seen anything worth seeing," she said proudly.

"I hear your daughter-in-law is a lovely girl."

"She certainly is: from a wealthy family, educated and beautiful. You can travel the whole country and not meet such a girl very often." The truth was she had many complaints about her daughter-in-law, but nevertheless, bragged about her anyway.

"Not surprising you have such a daughter-in-law when you have such a wonderful son."

"Well, I don't like to brag, but he is good-natured, good-looking, uh, an arrow that will go far from the bow. Ha, ha, ha."

"You're too modest; you and your husband are the most accomplished couple in the town of Tongyong."

"Well, that may be, but of this I am certain: our son will go far."

Her bragging was endless.

"You are very lucky. Everybody knows an only son can be easily spoiled. What a disaster it would have been if he had married the daughter of Songsu Kim."

Still lying, Yongok switched sides.

"Well, I have to say you are absolutely right. Fortunately, the marriage between Hongsop and Yongbin Kim never came off. My son is a lucky boy. He was born under a good star. We became prosperous right after he was born. He himself decided to stop seeing Yongbin. We were about to force him to change his mind, when the Kim family began to decline, and he decided to marry a girl he met in Seoul. He has never given us a moment of trouble."

They chatted for a long time. Then they called the waiter and ordered lunch. They gossiped about the Kims right through lunch. "Now how could a family go to wrack and ruin so fast like that? And they don't have the slightest hope of recovering either."

"Well, you know that house is badly located. When we were kids, everybody was afraid to go near the place. Songsu Kim's mother committed suicide by taking arsenic. His father died somewhere — who knows? After he killed another guy. So, how many ghosts inhabit that house? I felt ill at ease myself when my husband talked about marriage with that family. I see now why I had such a sense of foreboding."

"Yes, indeed, it's really a good thing your son did not marry the Kim girl," Okja's mother said.

"Absolutely," said Mrs. Chong with a shudder. "It would have been terrible if the marriage had come off. Then there would be a child with that bad blood."

"Of course, it is well known descendants of someone who dies of arsenic never prosper. Would you look at those Kim girls — five of 'em and every single one, a mess. The oldest is a widow; the second, she's still single; the third, crazy as a hoot owl — folks say she caused her mother's death. The fourth, married to some poor guy, and having such a hard time of it."

"That Songsu Kim is awfully arrogant. Everything changes. Nothing can be good or bad forever," said Mrs. Chong, licking her fingers as they finished lunch.

"Is that a diamond?" asked Okja's mother, eyeing Mrs. Chong's ring.

"Why yes it is."

"Oh, it's very big. You better be careful in Seoul. They say there are many pickpockets up there."

"Don't you worry."

Yongok was sick of listening to them. She hadn't slept a wink during the night under the tree and she'd missed breakfast. When she began feeding the baby, she was exhausted, and though the engine-noise disturbed her, she soon fell asleep.

Suddenly, someone shook her. "Hey, wake up, Lady." She sat up surprised.

"Tickets, please."

The conductor looked down at her with his punch in hand. She took out the purse she had hidden between her breasts and handed him the ticket.

"This is a third-class ticket, Lady. You're in second class."

Yongok's face became red with embarrassment.

"Get out of here." he said, staring at Yongok disgustedly. She wasted no time leaving.

"Well, how about that? Songsu Kim's daughter!"

"Yes, I believe the fourth one."

"Did you get a good look at her? I wonder what happened to her."

Yongok was embarrassed to hear them talk about her. She staggered with the baby in one arm and the bundle in the other. She felt the waves break and rock the ship. It seemed to her that the ship was standing still and only the sea was moving. She had the sudden impulse to dive into the sea. She felt extremely tired. Everything about her was reeling, but she managed to get down to third-class, where the stench was terrible. She found a seat and almost fell into it.

When the boat sailed into Pusan harbor, the sun was sinking behind Mount Chunma. There were many fishing vessels anchored in the port. The walkway along the pier was damp and dirty, and people had thrown banana peels and pear skins about. Stacks of cargo stood waiting to be carted into warehouses and black smoke obscured the sun. Yongok could see automobiles and streetcars passing noisily on the broad avenue where crowds of people walked.

"Excuse me, could you please tell me where the Fishermen's Union is?" she asked a passer-by. With a blank expression, the man explained how to get there. It was not very far from the pier.

Yongok stood in front of the building hesitating. She looked down at her dress. Now, she couldn't believe that she would leave the house in such disarray. Only then did she realize that she didn't even wash her face that morning. Pulling the handkerchief from her pocket, she found that it was gooey and matted with melted candy. She glanced both ways, saw no one, and wiped her face with the inside hem of her skirt. Then she entered the building. There was nobody in the front office but a boy cleaning.

"May I ask you something?"

The boy looked at her with large eyes.

"Ah, um, I want to see Mr. Keydo Soh; he's from Tongyong."

"Oh, yes. There is a man named Keydo Soh here."

"I came from Tongyong to see him. Do you know where I can find him?"

"I don't think he come in today."

"Oh, no! He's not here?" Yongok was almost in tears. Seeing her so greatly disappointed, the boy thought for a moment and tilted his head.

"You say you're from Tongyong?"

"Yes."

"Wait just a minute. Mr. Kim on night duty is also from there. I'll ask him if he knows about Mr. Soh."

Unable to focus, she stood there not caring that the baby on her back had begun to cry. Her arms, both the one with the bundle and the other without, hung tiredly at her sides.

"Oh my, Mrs. Soh! What on earth are you doing here?"

She turned around and found herself face-to-face with one of Keydo's friends, Mr. Kim. She knew that Keydo had gotten the job at the Fishery through his connection with Mr. Kim. She was speechless, overwhelmed with both relief and discomfort.

"Have you come all the way from Tongyong?"

"Yes, on the ferry."

"Oh, I am sorry to say....Keydo left for there on a ship this afternoon."

"What? He went to Tongyong?"

"Yes, he said he hadn't gone home for Chusok...."

She could no longer stand straight. Her shoulders slumped and she wanted to lean on someone and sob. "Then, I must go back to Tongyong."

"You should rest and go back tomorrow," he said. "It will be very difficult to go back on the night boat with a baby."

"But it leaves yet today, doesn't it?"

"Yes, but it is a small boat and stops at every little port, it takes forever. You'd be better off to spend the night and catch the morning one."

"Oh no, I must go back now."

Yongok hurried out hastily without saying good-bye. However, Kim ran after her, "Wait, wait!" he said. "You still have time before the evening boat. I'll buy you a ticket and something to eat before you board."

"Oh, no thank you, I'm fine," she said slowing, on hearing that there was time before departure.

"Did you have lunch?"

"Yes, on the boat coming over," she lied.

"You'll have dinner and then get on board."

"No, I'm okay."

Mr. Kim did not insist as he thought it might be uncomfortable to eat with the wife of a friend. When they reached the pier, he went in to buy her the ticket. She waited outside.

He handed it to her and said, "It's second-class."

"Let me pay you," she said, reaching for her purse.

"No, no. I'm going back to the office," he said waving as he walked off.

She did want to pay him, but he rushed off and would not take the money from her. In the midst of her pain and disappointment, she felt the warmth of human concern.

Sitting in the waiting room, Yongok realized that she couldn't endure another night without eating. The baby fussed when her breasts were dry. There were vendors selling rice cakes, porridge and noodles all along the pier. She left the waiting room carrying her bundle and bought a bowl of noodles and ate it crouching on the ground. A teardrop fell into her soup. She felt miserable. A pier worker glanced at her as he drank his soup.

The entrance gate opened and she got on. Passengers boarded quickly, but departure was delayed as loading continued. It was the filthy little boat that had left Tongyong in the morning, and though she was in second-class it was far shabbier than third class in which Yongok had traveled to Pusan originally. In fact, the boat was actually a cargo transport and most of the passengers were men accompanying shipments.

"How come they keep loading? It's time to leave."

"It's windy, and they expect heavy seas tonight."

A few men sat down and began playing cards as if they were in their own living rooms. The women chatted and compared prices in Pusan and Tongyong. Some of them said there was no difference between the two cities. Others said you couldn't make a profit in Pusan, no way. The boat itself was noisy as a marketplace.

The lights from a huge ship big as an island were reflected on the sea. When the streetlights along the pier came on, the boat finally started its engines.

Shipwreck

Keydo, who left Pusan with a little money in his pocket, headed for Kanchanggol. Whenever he came back to Tongyong, he went either to the bar on the pier or to his in-law's house at Kanchanggol. In the days when he worked for Songsu, it was obvious that he had to see him for business. But now he had no business with Songsu Kim, and he didn't know why he was going there himself, when he had a family at home. He walked to Kanchanggol, in wrinkled ready-made clothes, not knowing exactly what he intended to do there.

"I couldn't make it for Chusok," Keydo said, bowing to Songsu, who looked ill. Then he sat down on the floor with his legs folded under him.

"You must have been very busy."

"Yes."

That is really all they had to say to one another. Keydo sat silently for a long while and then left.

"Keydo, crazy Yongnan has had another fit. She tears the paper screens in the door and won't eat a thing. Please go and see her," said Yonghay, who was waiting for him to come out of her father's room. A flicker of delight flashed across his face. His thick hand trembled as he unlocked the door. Yongnan was crouching there and raised her white face. In the darkness of the room, her face seemed even whiter.

"What's the matter, Yongnan?" he asked tenderly and she smiled brightly.

"Oh good, you're here at last. Where have you been? You know, I have been waiting for you so long. Did you get the boat tickets?"

"Yes, I did."

"Then it is time for us to escape. Be careful and nobody will notice."

She held his hand tightly. He imagined himself to be Handol.

"Oh, poor thing...."

Keydo came out of her room after telling her he would be back with the tickets. It was of no consequence to Yongnan whether he had already bought the tickets or was going to buy them. She could no longer distinguish reality anyway. He smoked in the hallway for a long time.

Yonghay informed him, "Yongok was here last night."

"...."

"Why didn't you come for Chusok?"

"...."

"Yongbin and Aunt Chongim were very upset that you didn't come."

"Did Yongbin go back to Seoul?"

"Yes. Right after she returned from Chinju."

"She went to Chinju?" he asked, "Why?"

"She took father to have some tests at the provincial hospital there."

"What did they say?"

"He has a stomach ulcer. The doctors said it's not serious."

"Yet, he doesn't look well."

"Sick with worry, no doubt."

Keydo went home to Taebatgol. As soon as he entered the gate, old Mr. Soh, who was smoking on the stone step, bolted up in surprise. He looked quite pale, though it was difficult to tell in the dim light.

"What are you doing, sitting here in the dark?"

Soh was relieved to hear his son was not upset. He stepped in the front hall and turned the light on, closely observing his son's reactions.

"Is she out?" he said, asking where Yongok was.

"I don't know," Old Soh said, without turning to his son.

"She packed and left early this morning," Keydo's little brother stuck his head out of his room and reported.

"This morning? Packed?" Keydo repeated, savoring every word.

"Now, do your homework," Old Soh said, banging the door of his youngest son's room, staring at him furious.

"Damn," the boy swore, "What have I done? I don't understand you, father," the boy complained loudly.

"She went out this morning and hasn't come back yet?"

"...."

"I heard she was at Kanchanggol last night....Was there something wrong with her?"

"No, no. I haven't done anything to upset her. I never complain though she goes to church and to Kanchanggol all the time."

Old Soh couldn't look directly at his son, but glanced about restlessly. Keydo secretly believed that he himself caused his wife to leave home.

"Where could she be if she didn't say where she was going. Probably...." Keydo thought.

"I think she is probably meeting another man. It must be hard for a young woman to be alone all the time like that," Old Soh said trying to sound plausible.

"Oh, shut up!" Keydo screamed angrily. Old Soh was intimidated.

"She is the last woman who would ever have an affair. No, she wouldn't." He spit the words at his father and stood up. Then he threw a few wadded-up bills on the floor and went out.

A paralyzing fear appeared in his father's eyes.

Keydo wandered along the pier like a lost soul and finally went into a bar. He always had compassion on Yongok, but he did not love her and could not dispel the disaffection that sprang up in him whenever he saw her. He now believed it was his destiny to wander like a hobo in search of a home for the rest of his life.

He began drinking silently, but the drunker he got, the more he swore at the barmaid and slapped her face. He spent the night there, abusing the girl and behaving meanly.

When morning came, he wasn't sure if he'd slept or not. He reached for his cigarettes and lit up. The bitter taste in his mouth reminded him of green unripe persimmon.

"Where could she be?" he wondered. "She must be home by now."

Lying with the pillow under his chest, he stared at the smoke wafting upward. He figured the girl he had slept with had already gone to prepare breakfast.

"She might have gone to Pusan to see me." This thought had also occurred to him the night before when he first heard she was gone.

"Hey, you. Wake up! Get going. I have to open this bar."

Suddenly, an ominous sense crept over him, but it was not what the barmaid had said. He dressed and went to the dining room.

"You must have a horrible hangover, drunk as you were last night. How come you drink so much?" the woman asked, smiling affectionately, as she placed a hot bowl of soup and some rice wine before him. Then she opened the front door, combing her hair with her fingers, and said, "Got a late start."

The morning sun shone on the table. Vendors hurried past the door. Keydo intended to rush home as soon as he woke, but while he was eating, his worry about Yongok was transformed to disgust. He didn't want to go home. A few workmen came in for breakfast. They chatted pleasantly and drank wine.

"A horrible disaster!" a man with a beard shouted as he came in. "We have to recover bodies before we can go fishing."

"What happened?" asked the barmaid setting chopsticks and a spoon before him.

"The Sankang sank near Kaduck Island last night."

"What?!" shouted a big man eating soup, "Oh, no. No!" he said, and shot out of the place like an arrow.

"Poor devil; his wife is a grain dealer; she was on that boat." The man with the beard craned his neck to watch him go.

A horrified woman asked, "Is that really true?"

"And why would I concoct such a story?" he asked, and the others just stared at the mouth of the bearded man.

"Shit!" said one of the men, "There's more damn accidents around that island. And nobody could have made it to shore in the pitch dark."

"I don't understand it," another said, "there was no wind last night...."

"Aw, hell, they always overload that crate; it's old and rusted to begin with. Ummm...turns my stomach. Give me something to drink."

The woman placed wine before him. "Where's my soup?" he demanded, and the woman ladled it out in dismay.

"Oh, those poor people."

"Well, the sea cucumbers and octopuses have hit the jackpot!"

"Divers will be busy too...."

"Damn, there was an accident in the very same spot two years ago. The bodies were a mess. Looked as if a whole school of fish had a feast. Not a single one had eyes."

"Hair-tails like human eyes."

"The octopuses and sea cucumbers like human flesh. Sea cucumbers eat assholes and octopuses eat eyes. Hair-tails eat flesh. Octopuses eat live people too, if they can get them."

"Stop! You're making me sick before I even have my breakfast."

"Fish that have eaten people taste great."

"Oh, imagine how they struggled. Drowning has to be the worst way to go. I want to die instantly. The poor things!"

"When you hear about something like this, it makes you grateful just to be alive. Of course, doesn't take long to forget that!"

Though the men made cavalier comments, they all felt horrible when they left the bar. Keydo said nothing, however. Only sat smoking with one hand on the table and asked for another drink when the workmen left.

"Another drink!" the barmaid said, "From early in the morning till...."

"It's none of your business if I drink all day and all night. Just pour."

"You got drunk and harassed me all night long. Now you start again?" she stared at him.

"Are you my wife or what? It's no concern of yours whether I drink or not. The more I drink, the more money you make anyway."

Keydo went home drunk and red-faced. "Is she home yet?" he asked his father, staring at him with bloodshot eyes.

"No, no. Not yet."

"Is she dead somewhere?"

He went to his empty room, lay down and fell asleep. It was late afternoon when he woke up and someone was knocking on the front gate, hollering, "Telegram!"

Old Soh walked to the gate dragging his feet, "Keydo, it's a telegram from Pusan."

He got up and opened the envelope, and read, "Yongok and Yonhee on Sankang. Stop. Deepest Sympathies. Stop. Kim." Keydo became white.

"What does it say?"

"She...she is dead."

Now Old Soh also became ghostly pale.

Keydo collapsed where he was standing. Hitting the floor, he began to cry. Old Soh, after reading the telegram himself, seemed composed and relieved. Yongok's death buried his disgrace forever. But shortly, all the veins stood out on his forehead as he could not avoid the punishment of his conscience.

A few days later, the Sankang was lifted from the sea off Kaduck. Yongok's body was found undisturbed. The rescue crew thought it strange that it was so perfectly preserved, having been under the sea that long. She was holding on so tightly to the baby that the rescue workers had trouble trying to pry them apart. And when they finally did, a cross fell out on the sand.

ॐ

Another Encounter

"Miss Kim, you have a visitor," an errand boy told Yongbin, who had just finished teaching her class and was walking down a long hall illuminated by the light from the setting sun.

"A visitor?"

"Yes, ma'am. It's a man."

"A man? Where?"

"Out front. On the steps of the school."

She assumed it was Hongsop, but when she got there, she was surprised to find her cousin, "Oh, Tayoon, it's you!"

He greeted her with a sweet smile. "Done with classes for today?"

"Yes. What are you doing here?"

"Visiting you, surprised?"

"Yes, of course. You didn't let me know you were coming."

"You certainly have the air of a teacher about you."

Yongbin smiled in her typical black teacher's suit.

"Let's go for a walk," he said.

"OK, but please wait a minute." She went to the teachers' room, got her purse and returned shortly.

When they got to the Tonwha gate, Yongbin asked, "Well, what brings you here so suddenly without notice?"

"Well. It really is sudden. In fact, I hadn't the slightest notion of visiting you this morning, but the idea of seeing you struck me, so — here I am."

"Then you have an appointment with someone else, I suppose?"

"Yes."

"I'd rather not tag along, the uninvited guest."

"But it is someone you know," he said.

"Soonja?"

"No, it's Mr. Kang." ·

"Oh, Mr. Kang!"

"Wouldn't you like to see him?"

"Why, yes, of course, but why? Why are you doing this?"

"Ha, ha. My intention, dear Cousin, ha, ha, heh," Tayoon laughed loudly, "is that I hope two of you will become close friends."

"Don't you have anything better to do?"

"I always have time for you. We are not machines."

"Does he want to see me?"

"Well, he is waiting for me at Changkyong Palace."

"And I'll be an uninvited tag-along," she said, but smiling, followed him anyway.

Kug Kang stood in front of the zoo in the palace smoking, and appeared quite surprised when he saw her with Tayoon. Nevertheless, he lifted his hat and greeted her.

"Have you waited long?" Tayoon asked him.

"Yes."

Then he addressed Yongbin, "Why don't you go have a look at the monkeys? We must have a word together. We'll be right back." They retreated to a quiet spot at a distance, talked in low voices and returned with tense looks on their faces.

"I'm sorry to keep you waiting," Kang said, dissolving the tension with a smile.

"Oh," thought Yongbin, observing him out of the corner of her eye, "he is relaxed, calm."

"How about some dinner?" Kang asked, directing the question to neither of them in particular. He seemed to be leading the trio, unlike in Pusan.

Yongbin felt vaguely uncomfortable, but followed them anyway. Kang led the way through the back alleys to a Chinese restaurant. He clearly knew the area and the restaurant. They were seated, but none of them talked. Normally Tayoon discoursed loud and long, but he was strangely mum. A nerve under his eye twitched as if reflecting the seriousness of what they talked about.

The food arrived. Kang put out his cigarette and took a hot towel from the waitress. Then he turned to Yongbin and asked, "Well, what do you think about the revolution?" A frank question, which brought a mysterious light to Yongbin's eyes; she smiled to conceal her delight.

"The revolution is a dream, a hope people will never realize."

"Yes, it is. Even more, it is a mystery," Kang replied.

"I didn't expect you to admit it. Why do you think so?" Yongbin asked, feeling the intimacy growing between them.

"Only romantics make revolutions. Realists make hay while the sun shines and call the romantic a loser, but he simply gets up again and again. He often leads a whole new generation to a turning point in history."

"You understand perfectly, so I don't understand why you continue," she said.

"Why not, as long as I am not corrupted?" Silently they picked the meat from the chicken bones.

"If the revolutionaries heard you calling them romantics, they'd be quite angry."

"I don't think so," Kang countered. "Romanticism is the energy, the force behind a revolution. Say, I heard you were arrested during the students' revolt. Is that true?"

"Along with many others."

"What did you and the others feel? Patriotism. Romantically buoyant and transported by the idea of heroism. If they had not been stimulated by this mysterious notion, they would never have bothered with the idea at all. So in the end it has a sort of tragic beauty."

Oddly, Tayoon had said nothing, but seemed to be brooding quietly.

Yongbin was fascinated by Kang's analysis of revolutionary motivation. She recalled what Tayoon once said: Kang didn't have a hint of that idealistic and righteous indignation one often associates with revolutionary types.

"Well, Miss Kim, would you like to join us romantics?" he asked suddenly in a businesslike tone of voice.

"Under whose control?"

"Your own. You can interfere with another's control simply with the strength of your own will."

"What makes you say that?"

"Because you and I think alike." His words seemed to be an indirect admission of his affection for Yongbin. She blushed in spite of herself, which made her embarrassed.

Then she asked, "How can you judge a person you have met only once or twice?"

Kang smiled, called the waiter and ordered another beer. Then he said, "At first, I thought Tayoon overestimated you, but...." Tayoon looked up at hearing the mention of his name.

"You're right!" Yongbin laughed, "You should only believe half Tayoon says about me."

"Are you two making fun of me?" Tayoon said, smiling for the first time.

"Unbridled romanticism can cause no-end of difficulties. I earnestly want him to stop that," Kang said, tongue in cheek.

"Hey, stop trying to make me the butt, you two bums!"

Yongbin smiled and said, "My, I didn't realize you were so eloquent, Mr. Kang."

"Ha, ha." Kang addressed her, "I made a bad impression on you in Pusan, didn't I?"

"I figured you were insensitive. Tayoon praised you to the high heavens, so I tried to dislike you."

"Am I to blame again?" Tayoon asked.

"I'm sorry," Yongbin said.

"Yongbin, you don't know this reprobate," said Tayoon. "He is the consummate actor. If you take him for what he seems to be, you'll be in real trouble. He's got you under his spell."

"I'll take that as a compliment and we'll end up swapping praises," Kang said, refilling Yongbin's beer glass. "Yongbin, what do you think of going to China?"

"China!?" Yongbin's eyes became wide and Tayoon's expression became tense as before.

"Well, I would consider it after everything's settled."

"When might that be?"

"In a few months, five I'd say...." Her face, bright and happy since they arrived, suddenly became grim.

They discussed many more topics and finally left the restaurant.

Outside, the alleyway was dark. "Give me your arm," Kang reached for her arm, but embarrassed, Yongbin pulled back saying, "No thanks."

Kang however skillfully and naturally slipped his arm through hers. Tayoon had said he was a good actor, and so he was. The Kang she had met that day in Pusan was totally changed.

"Do you live in a boarding house?"

"Yes, I moved from the school dorm."

"May I have the address?"

"Hayhwa Dong."

"And the number?" Kang stopped under a streetlight and pulled out an address book and a fountain pen. She was at a loss.

"In case I have to write you about Tayoon." he said.

"Two-seventy-five Hayhwa Dong."

Kang wrote the address, slapped Tayoon on the shoulder and said, "Good luck in your travels, Tayoon, my good fellow. I am going that way. Miss Kim, I'll see you again." He disappeared like a gust of wind around the corner and down the dark street.

Goodnight

One morning just as she was leaving for school, Yongbin received the news that ten days earlier Yongok had died in the wreck of the Sankang and was already buried. She returned to her room, sat down and burst into tears.

Unable to focus, she walked around restlessly, standing up, sitting down nervously all day long. The letter informing her of Yongok's death intensified the agony of waiting for news of her father's. Yongok never mentioned the relationship, her marriage. But Yongbin knew she had become much more fanatical about attending church after her wedding because of her personal unhappiness. Her sad face and listless eyes sometimes made Yongbin worry secretly, but she always seemed to forget her sister's presence in the whirlwind of mishaps their lives had become. She despaired thinking she should have paid more attention to her sister. It felt as if a battalion of soldiers were marching across her heart.

"Hello, Miss Kim, somebody is here to see you," the landlady called to her.

"Oh please, leave me alone. I'm sick in bed." She didn't want to see anybody. The woman left, but shortly she heard footsteps.

"Hello there, Miss Kim."

"Oh, my!" Yongbin was shocked to hear Kang's voice.

"May I come in?"

Yongbin hurriedly stood up from her bed and began to tidy up the room.

"I'd like to see you for a moment," he said.

After a while, she said, "Come in, please." She stood stiff-backed and opened the door. On entering the room, he saw that her eyes were red and bloodshot.

"Are you sick? Do you have a fever?" he asked, taking off his coat and sitting down.

"No."

"Your eyes are red and bloodshot," he said, frowning.

"I've been crying."

"Why?"

"My sister has drowned," she said, feeling herself falling to pieces, "she was sweet and meek as an angel...." Covering her eyes with her hands, Yongbin began to weep. She looked very young to him and he regarded her with more curiosity than sympathy. Though he had seen her grim face agonize before, he never imagined she could cry.

"Has Tayoon told you about my family?" she asked, drying her eyes.

"No...."

"I am actually awaiting another death," she said looking into his eyes, "my father's. Last month he was given five months to live. Tests determined he has stomach cancer. Neither he nor the rest of the family know about it." She continued, "My father was an orphan. His father killed a man and never returned to Tongyong. His mother committed suicide by taking arsenic. He has five daughters. The first one is a widow, who has been to prison on suspicion of killing her child. The second, me, is an old maid. The third is a raving lunatic, out of her mind because she loved a servant in our house. Nobody in the family, including myself, accepted the fact that she loved him. Instead, because she wasn't a virgin, she was married to a drug addict from a rich family. Her husband murdered my mother and the servant with an ax. The fourth, I just told you, drowned; I received the letter this morning."

Yongbin stared at the wall and sighed throughout her monologue. He watched her wretched face and finally said, "Come, let's go out, shall we?"

"Out?"

"A walk will do you good; you'll sleep well."

"Should I try to escape my suffering?" she asked. "No, I should share my dead sister's pain. I never tried to relieve her anguish."

"But you didn't cause your sister's misfortunes," he argued coldly.

"You are thoughtless."

He looked deep into her eyes and asked, "Am I?"

"Don't stare at me so intensely; you're scaring me."

"Come on, let's go. You need a drink. I'll wait outside. Change and come out when you're ready." He took his coat and left.

"You need a drink....Oh ...." she repeated his words, and then thought, "Okay, don't think it over. Just go." She stood up, and in no time got dressed.

They walked along through the fallen leaves, passing Kyongsong Imperial College.

"Where is Tayoon now?" asked Yongbin, who had become calm thanks to the cool air.   "Are you feeling better? You see, you needed the fresh air," Kang said, changing the subject.

"You didn't answer my question," she said. Breaking the silence, she asked, "Did anything bad happen to him?"

"Don't worry about him. He's safe."

They continued walking to Changkyong Palace. In the dim light the trees threw long shadows and the wind blew cold.

"Miss Kim, may I tell you a story?"

Yongbin glanced at his face in the darkness, but couldn't see his eyes because his cap shadowed his face.

"It happened some time ago. I have a dim recollection of my father's death, but I have heard about it several times. No, hundreds. He was neither a revolutionary nor a patriot. A man of means, killed by the Japanese. Our servant brought his body home on a horse. I only remember it vaguely. My sister married a Japanese man. So you see, Yongbin, you are not the only one who lives with a terrible burden." Kang used her first name instead of last.

"Is this the reason you are fighting Japan?"

"No, it's not, I hate the Japanese rule. I did when I was young, but of course that was from immaturity. Sometimes national consciousness sounds ridiculous to me."

"You're not really a romantic, are you?" Yongbin said with a sad smile.

"Right. Tayoon is excessive. I'm spare," he chuckled and added, "If you were a man, we'd get drunk." He then changed the subject again. They followed the stone wall of Changkyong Palace, passed Ancook-dong and ended up in Samchong Park.

"I'm tired," said Yongbin, collapsing on the lawn. Kang studied her idly. She raised her chin, looked up at him and asked, "Are you married?"

"No, but I loved a woman like this."

"Like what?" she asked.

"The way I feel when you and I stand face-to-face," he said.

"That's funny," she laughed nervously, but it reminded her of Yongok.

"I left her. I couldn't share her spirit. Anyway you look tired. Let's go back."

Yongbin closed her eyes trying to avoid the image of her sister's dispirited face. Kang hailed a taxi and took her back to her lodging. When she got out and saw the house, she shuddered at the thought of pain she had suffered in that room.

"Good night," he said, as the flying ends of his coat disappeared in the darkness.

ॐ

Departure

Songsu awaited death, lucid with clear eyes. He saw his daughter Yonghay weeping. He studied her brown hair for a long time. Then he moved his eyes to Yongbin, whose fleshy wide forehead caught his attention when she bowed her head. Feeling his gaze upon her, which had the feel of trembling sobs, Yongbin looked up.

"Oh, father!" she said, but Songsu turned his eyes away and fixed them on the ceiling.

"He's dead," the doctor informed Yongbin. Yonghay threw herself on his body. Yongbin put her hands to her mouth in horror. Yongsook pulled out her handkerchief. Chungku stood like a wooden statue.

"Oh, no! Hhhhhhhh...." Chongim disintegrated to sobs.

Songsu died staring at the ceiling, his eyes open. Chungku stood up and went to Songsu, his voice shaking, "Close your eyes, cousin," and closed them for him.

Both Sochong and Cookju Chong came to the funeral, but Cookju was clearly uncomfortable, pacing back and forth restlessly saying, "Yes sir, Songsu Kim was an unlucky man. What a shame! Died of anger over his misfortunes. Anger did him in, anger...." It sounded true. Old Soh, who came in wearing a dirty cotton coat and a ragged brown hat, echoed Cookju eagerly, "Yes, absolutely. His death is lamentable. Mr. Kim never did anybody any harm. Never. He lived an honest life. How relentless God is." He found it difficult to focus, a problem that became worse after Yongok died. He mourned Songsu extravagantly as he hoped to atone for his guilty secret. He found it difficult to look at his son Keydo directly.

They buried him in the public cemetery, and Yongbin began to sort out the household goods. The old house and some furnishings were the only property left. The real estate and fishery paid the debts and he had no creditors. Consoling herself with sorting through things, Yongbin found a leather-covered Bible. A gift from Miss Kate, left for her when she returned to England. There was a one-line message on the inside cover: "Yongbin, don't lose your faith."

She sighed, set the Bible on the desk and continued her task.

With dark eyes, Keydo smoked and paced around the house.

Yongsook was talking to Yomoon, who came to help organize things, "Look at this bronze pot! These old cooking utensils are the best. They just don't make things the way they used to." Yongsook had already had her servant move some things to her house, but that didn't stop her from finding more valuable items in her parents' home. Yongbin wasn't concerned about Yongsook's taking them. She had the right to go after those things and it was just her nature. Though she objected at first, she had taken care of Yongnan for two years.

The sound of ships' horns filled the dark sky. Gas lamps from the vendors' shops emitted a light like mist. Chongim and Keydo came to the quay to see Yongbin and Yonghay off. Chongim bought some cookies, gave them to Yonghay, cried and blew her nose several times.

"Keydo, please give this to Yongnan, though I'm sure she won't have any idea what...." Yongbin gave Keydo the package, carefully wrapped.

"What is it?" he asked.

"A Bible. Please help her. Be kind to her. Visit her, talk to her." Yongbin pleaded.

"Don't worry. I will," Keydo answered in a low voice, studying the pier. The crew tossed the anchor rope onto the ship.

"Yongbin, Yonghay, you'd better go." Vendors were hopping off the sides.

"Good bye, Aunt Chongim, Good bye." Yongbin and Yonghay waved as the ship slid away from the dock. The propellers turned white water and the horn sounded....BU-uoong.

The gas lamps, porters shouting, Chongim and Keydo were left behind on the pier, as if a curtain were slowly drawn over the port of Tongyong.

On the narrow deck of the ship, Yonghay's white face could be seen shining like sunlight, as Yongbin sobbed silently in the moist air.

Spring wasn't far, but yet the piercing wind seemed cold.

The End

 *More Titles from Homa & Sekey Books*

Modern Fiction from Korea Series

Father and Son: A Novel by Han Sung-won
Translated by Yu Young-nan & Julie Pickering
ISBN: 1-931907-04-8, Paperback, $17.95
A Kiriyama Pacific Rim Notable Book winner
An age-old struggle between the generations of modern industrialization and the battle for democratic freedoms in Korea. The author explores the role of the intellectual in modern Korean society and the changing face of the Korean family.

Reflections on a Mask: Two Novellas by Ch'oe In-hun
Translated by Stephen Moore & Shi C. P. Moore
ISBN: 1-931907-05-6, Paperback, $16.95

Reflections on a Mask explores the disillusionment and search for identity of a young man in the post-Korean War era. *Christmas Carol* uses the themes of hope and salvation to examine relationships within a patriarchal Korean family.

Unspoken Voices: Selected Short Stories by Korean Women Writers
Compiled and Translated by Jin-Young Choi, Ph.D.
ISBN: 1-931907-06-4, Paperback, $16.95

Stories by twelve Korean women writers whose writings penetrate into the lives of Korean women from the early part of the 20th century to the present. Writers included are: Choi Junghee, Han Musook, Kang Shinjae, Park Kyongni, Lee Sukbong, Lee Jungho, Song Wonhee, Park Wansuh, Yoon Jungsun, Un Heekyong, Kong Jeeyoung and Han Kang.

The General's Beard: Two Novellas by Lee Oyoung
Translated by Brother Anthony
ISBN: 1-931907-07-2, Paperback, $14.95

In *The General's Beard*, a journalist tries to solve the mystery of a young photographer's death. In *Phantom Legs*, a young girl studying French literature meets a student wounded during demonstrations and begins an ambiguous relationship with him.

More Titles from Homa & Sekey Books

Farmers: A Novel by Lee Mu-young
Translated by Yu Young-nan
ISBN: 1-931907-08-0, Paperback, $15.95

The novel is about Korea's Tonghak Uprising in 1894. A farmer-turned Tonghak leader who left the village several years ago in the wake of a severe flogging returns to his village to take revenge of his exploiters.

The Curse of Kim's Daughters: A Novel
By Park Kyong-ni. Translated by Choonwon Kang, et al.
ISBN: 1-931907-10-2, Paperback, $18.95

An engaging and heart-wrenching novel about the five daughters of a fishing fleet owner who are cursed by their fate. A fascinating story of Korean women masterfully told by one of the most important Korean women writers.

Korea-American Literature

Surfacing Sadness:
A Centennial of Korean-American Literature 1903-2003
Edited by Yearn Hong Choi, Ph.D & Haeng Ja Kim
ISBN: 1-931907-09-9, Hardcover, $25.00

An anthology of poems, essays and short stories by thirty-seven Korean-American writers, it is the first serious effort to bring together the Korean-American experiences to join mainstream American literature.

"A literary celebration of Korean immigration to America."
-- Korea Times

Forthcoming Titles on Korean Literature

A Floating City on the Water: A Novel
By Jang-Soon Sohn. Trans. by Jin-Young Choi

Korean Drama Under Japanese Occupation:
Plays by Ch'i-jin Yu and Man-sik Ch'ae
Trans. by Jinhee Kim

More Titles from Homa & Sekey Books

Modern Poetry from Korea Series

Flowers in the Toilet Bowl: Selected Poems of Choi Seungho
Translated by Won-Chung Kim & James Han
ISBN: 1-931907-11-0, Paperback, $12.95

Selected poems by Choi Seungho, a poet with an unusual ability to observe things around him and a critic of man's false desire in modern society. In many of his poems, Choi portrays the rampant desires of the "hypnotized" man and the gray landscape of the late consumer society.

Drawing Lines: Selected Poems of Moon Dok-su
Translated by Chang Soo Ko & Julie Pickering
ISBN: 1-931907-12-9, Paperback, $11.95

Selected poems by Moon Dok-su, a poet whose poetry is characterized by a spirit of experiment and exploration both in content and expression. These poems cover a variety of subjects and show Moon's perception of the world as well as his modernistic approach to poetic inspiration

I Want to Hijack an Airplane: Selected Poems of Kim Seung-Hee
Translated by Kyung-nyun Kim Richards & Steffen F. Richards
ISBN: 1-931907-13-7, Paperback, $15.95

Selected poems by Kim Seung-Hee, a conceptually-oriented poet whose work is a blend of rigorous intellectualism and lyricism that borders on the sentimental. Her works also deal with the cold and dehumanizing aspects of modern urban life, and the longing for freedom as an absolute ideal.

What the Spider Said: Poems of Chang Soo Ko
Translated by Chang Soo Ko
ISBN: 1-931907-14-5, Paperback, $10.95

A collection of short "epigrammatic" poems by Chang Soo Ko originally written in Korean. The narrator of the poems is conceived to be a "spider," which to the poet's mind represents a mystic observer with "spiderly" sense of humor. The poems were written with substantial attention to poetic vision and metaphor.

 *More Titles from Homa & Sekey Books*

Books on China

Flower Terror: Suffocating Stories of China by Pu Ning
ISBN 0-9665421-0-X, Fiction, Paperback, $13.95

"The stories in this work are well written." – Library Journal

Acclaimed Chinese writer eloquently describes the oppression of intellectuals in his country between 1950s and 1970s in these twelve autobiographical novellas and short stories. Many of the stories are so shocking and heart-wrenching that one cannot but feel suffocated.

The Peony Pavilion: A Novel by Xiaoping Yen, Ph.D.
ISBN 0-9665421-2-6, Fiction, Paperback, $16.95

"A window into the Chinese literary imagination." – Publishers Weekly

A sixteen-year-old girl visits a forbidden garden and falls in love with a young man she meets in a dream. She has an affair with her dream-lover and dies longing for him. After her death, her unflagging spirit continues to wait for her dream-lover. Does her lover really exist? Can a youthful love born of a garden dream ever blossom? The novel is based on a sixteenth-century Chinese opera written by Tang Xianzu, "the Shakespeare of China."

Butterfly Lovers: A Tale of the Chinese Romeo and Juliet
By Fan Dai, Ph.D., ISBN 0-9665421-4-2, Fiction, Paperback, $16.95

"An engaging, compelling, deeply moving, highly recommended and rewarding novel." – Midwest Books Review

A beautiful girl disguises herself as a man and lives under one roof with a young male scholar for three years without revealing her true identity. They become sworn brothers, soul mates and lovers. In a world in which marriage is determined by social status and arranged by parents, what is their inescapable fate?

 *More Titles from Homa & Sekey Books*

The Dream of the Red Chamber: An Allegory of Love
By Jeannie Jinsheng Yi, Ph.D., ISBN: 0-9665421-7-7, Hardcover
Asian Studies/Literary Criticism, $49.95

Although dreams have been studied in great depth about this most influential classic Chinese fiction, the study of all the dreams as a sequence and in relation to their structural functions in the allegory is undertaken here for the first time.

Always Bright: Paintings by American Chinese Artists 1970-1999
Edited by Xue Jian Xin et al.
ISBN 0-9665421-3-4, Art, Hardcover, $49.95

"An important, groundbreaking, seminal work." – Midwest Book Review

A selection of paintings by eighty acclaimed American Chinese artists in the late 20th century, *Always Bright* is the first of its kind in English publication. The album falls into three categories: oil painting, Chinese painting and other media painting. It also offers profiles of the artists and information on their professional accomplishment.

Always Bright, Vol. II: Paintings by Chinese American Artists
Edited by Eugene Wang, Ph.D., et al.
ISBN: 0-9665421-6-9, Art, Hardcover, $50.00

A sequel to the above, the book includes artworks of ninety-two artists in oil painting, Chinese painting, watercolor painting, and other media such as mixed media, acrylic, pastel, pen and pencil, etc. The book also provides information on the artists and their professional accomplishment. Artists included come from different backgrounds, use different media and belong to different schools. Some of them enjoy international fame while others are enterprising young men and women who are more impressionable to novelty and singularity.

 *More Titles from Homa & Sekey Books*

Ink Paintings by Gao Xingjian, the Nobel Prize Winner
ISBN: 1-931907-03-X, Hardcover, Art, $34.95

An extraordinary art book by the Nobel Prize Winner for Literature in 2000, this volume brings together over sixty ink paintings by Gao Xingjian that are characteristic of his philosophy and painting style. Gao believes that the world cannot be explained, and the images in his paintings reveal the black-and-white inner world that underlies the complexity of human existence. People admire his meditative images and evocative atmosphere by which Gao intends his viewers to visualize the human conditions in extremity.

Splendor of Tibet: The Potala Palace, Jewel of the Himalayas
By Phuntsok Namgyal
ISBN: 1-931907-02-1, Hardcover, Art/Architecture, $39.95

A magnificent and spectacular photographic book about the Potala Palace, the palace of the Dalai Lamas and the world's highest and largest castle palace. Over 150 rare and extraordinary color photographs of the Potala Palace are showcased in the book, including murals, thang-ka paintings, stupa-tombs of the Dalai Lamas, Buddhist statues and scriptures, porcelain vessels, enamel work, jade ware, brocade, Dalai Lamas' seals, and palace exteriors.

The Haier Way: The Making of a Chinese Business Leader and a Global Brand by Jeannie J. Yi, Ph.D., & Shawn X. Ye, MBA
ISBN: 1-931907-01-3, Hardcover, Business, $24.95

Haier is the largest consumer appliance maker in China. The book traces the appliance giant's path to success, from its early bleak years to its glamorous achievement when Haier was placed the 6th on *Forbes Global*'s worldwide household appliance manufacturer list in 2001. The book explains how Haier excelled in quality, service, technology innovation, a global vision and a management style that is a blend of Jack Welch of "GE" and Confucius of ancient China.

"The book throws light on a number of important issues about China's development path...comprehensive and up-to-date...highly readable."
— Dr. N.T. Wang, Director of China-International Business Project, Columbia University

 *More Titles from Homa & Sekey Books*

Breaking Grounds:
The Journal of a Top Chinese Woman Manager in Retail
by Bingxin Hu, translated from the Chinese by Chengchi Wang, Prefaced
by Professor Louis B. Barnes of Harvard Business School
ISBN: 1-931907-15-3, 256 pp, Hardcover, Business, $24.95

The book records the experience of a Chinese business woman Bingxin
Hu, who pioneered and succeeded in modernizing the aging Chinese
retail business. Based on her years of business experience, the author
recounts the turmoil, clashes of concepts and behind-the-scene decisions in the Chinese retail business, as well as psychological shocks,
emotional perplexes, and intellectual apprehension she had gone through.

Musical Qigong:
Ancient Chinese Healing Art from a Modern Master
By Shen Wu, ISBN: 0-9665421-5-0, Health, Paperback, $14.95

Musical Qigong is a special healing energy therapy that combines two
ancient Chinese traditions-healing music and Qigong. This guide
contains two complete sets of exercises with photo illustrations and
discusses how musical Qigong is related to the five elements in the
ancient Chinese concept of the universe - metal, wood, water, fire, and
earth.

www.homabooks.com

ORDER INFORMATION: U.S.: $5.00 for the first item, $1.50 for
each additional item. **Outside U.S.:** $10.00 for the first item, $5.00 for
each additional item. All major credit cards accepted. You may also
send a check or money order in U.S. fund (payable to Homa & Sekey
Books) to: Orders Department, Homa & Sekey Books, P. O. Box 103,
Dumont, NJ 07628 U.S.A. Tel: 800-870-HOMA; 201-261-8810. Fax:
201-384-6055; 201-261-8890. Email: info@homabooks.com